Lavish Praise for Jane Feather and

Violet

"Great fun. . . . Feather's well-paced plot generates lots of laughs, steamy sex and high adventure, as well as some wryly perceptive commentary on the gender stereotypes her heroine so flagrantly defies."—*Publishers Weekly*

Valentine

"Delicious . . . ★★★★ out of 4 stars . . . Comes much closer to the Austen spirit than any of the pseudo-sequels."
—*Detroit Free Press*

"More than just a few cuts above the average. Each novel she pens is another challenge to her fellow writers because she has raised the quality of the historical once again."
—*Affaire de Coeur*

Velvet

"An exceptional reading experience on all levels."
—*Rendezvous*

Vixen

"*Vixen* is worth taking to bed. . . . Feather's last book, *Virtue*, was good, but this one is even better."
—*USA Today*

Virtue

"Jane Feather is an accomplished storyteller. . . . The result—a rare and wonderful battle-of-the-sexes story that will delight both historical and Regency readers."
—*Daily News*, Los Angeles

Also by Jane Feather

VIOLET
VALENTINE
VELVET
VIXEN
VIRTUE

And coming soon:
VICE

Vanity

Jane Feather

BANTAM BOOKS
New York Toronto London
Sydney Auckland

VANITY

A Bantam Book / January 1996

ISBN 0-553-57248-2

Published simultaneously in the United States and Canada

Bantam Books are published by Bantam Books, a division of Bantam Doubleday Dell Publishing Group, Inc. Its trademark, consisting of the words "Bantam Books" and the portrayal of a rooster, is Registered in U.S. Patent and Trademark Office and in other countries. Marca Registrada. Bantam Books, 1540 Broadway, New York, New York 10036.

PRINTED IN THE UNITED STATES OF AMERICA

OPM   0 9 8 7 6 5 4 3 2 1

Vanity

Prologue

SUSSEX, ENGLAND: 1762

The three boys scrambled up the steep grassy incline to the clifftop above Beachy Head. A gust of wind grabbed at the kite flying high against the brilliant blue sky. Philip Wyndham took another turn of the string around his hand as he increased his speed.

Gervase, the eldest of the three, paused, doubling over to catch his breath with the painful wheezing of the asthmatic. Cullum held out a hand and hauled his brother up with him to the clifftop. Cullum's sturdy young body had no difficulty taking Gervase's slight weight despite the two-year age difference, and they were both laughing as they reached Philip.

The three stood for a minute, gazing down at the funnel carved into the cliff, falling away beneath them to the jagged rocks and pounding surf far below.

Gervase's thin shoulders hunched as he shuddered. He always found the funnel mesmerizing. It seemed to invite him to jump, to follow its inexorable narrowing tunnel in a violent swirl of rushing wind to the foam-tipped teeth at the bottom.

He took a step backward. "My turn with the kite."

"No, it's not. I'm supposed to have it for half an hour."
Philip snatched his arm away as Gervase reached for it.

"You've had it for half an hour." Cullum spoke with
his habitual authority as he too reached for the kite string.

A seagull swooped low over the cliff, its mournful cry
picked up by a second and then a third. The three boys
swayed together, grabbing for the disputed kite string while
the seagulls circled above them, shadowed against the puffy
white clouds.

Cullum tripped over a loose tussock and fell to one
knee. As he scrambled to his feet, Gervase lunged for the
string held by a now laughing, taunting Philip. The
younger boy's slate-gray eyes narrowed abruptly. As Gervase leaped upward to catch Philip's wrist, Philip side-
stepped. His booted foot shot out, catching his brother on
the calf.

Gervase's scream went on forever, vying with the
skirling calls of the seagulls. And then it stopped.

The two boys on the clifftop stared down the funnel at
the inert bundle lying on a flat rock far beneath. The waves
sucked at Gervase's nankeen trousers.

"You did it," Philip said. "You tripped him."

Cullum gazed at his brother, shock and horror on his
face. They were fraternal twins, but the only features they
shared were the distinctive gray eyes of the Wyndhams.
Philip was an angelic-looking child with a mass of golden
curls framing his rounded face; his frame was slender,
though without the thinness of ill health that had character-
ized Gervase. Cullum had a wavy thatch of dark-brown hair
above a strong-featured face, and his body was broad and
strong, his legs planted foursquare on the turf.

"What do you mean?" he whispered, and there was
dread in his voice and a ghastly vulnerability in his eyes.

"I saw you," Philip said in a low voice, his eyes still
narrowed. "You tripped him, I saw you."

"No," Cullum whispered again. "No, I didn't. I was
trying to get up myself . . . you were . . ."

"It was you!" his brother interrupted. "I'll tell them
what I saw and they'll believe me. You *know* they will." He

gazed at his brother, and Cullum felt the old helpless frustration wash through him as he read the triumph and the malice on the cherubic face. They would believe Philip. They always did. Everyone always believed Philip.

Suddenly, he turned aside and ran wildly along the cliff, looking for a way down to his brother's lifeless body. Philip stood and watched him until he'd disappeared over the clifftop a few yards away, his fingers for a second grubbing at the springy turf before he committed himself to the treacherously sheer climb to the rocks beneath.

Then Philip ran back down the incline toward the narrow lane that led to Wyndham Manor, the seat of the Earl of Wyndham, the story of the accident to the earl's eldest son bubbling from his lips, ready tears filling his eyes.

The kite he still held flew high and jaunty behind him.

Chapter 1

The crowds had been filling the streets since before dawn, jostling for the best places along the route to Tyburn, the luckiest finding spots around the gibbet itself. Despite the light snow and the raw wind, there was a holiday atmosphere: farmers and their wives, come in from the country for the entertainment, sharing the contents of their hampers with their neighbors; children dodging in and out of the throng, chasing each other, collapsing in squabbling heaps to the cobbles; sharp-eyed townsfolk, lucky enough to have houses along the route the cart would take from Newgate, shouting their prices for a seat in the window or on the roof.

It promised to be a spectacle worth paying for, the execution of Gerald Abercorn and Derek Greenthorne, two of the most notorious gentlemen of the road who'd terrorized travelers across Putney Heath for the better part of a decade.

"You'd think if they could catch them two, t'other wouldn't be 'ard to get," a rosy-cheeked woman mumbled through a mouthful of pigeon pie.

Her husband took a bottle of rum from the capacious pocket of his great coat. "They'll not nab Lord Nick, woman, you mark my words." He took a hearty swig and wiped his mouth with the back of his hand.

"You seem very confident, sir," an amused voice said behind him. "What makes this so-called Lord Nick harder to catch than his unfortunate friends?"

The other man tapped the side of his nose and winked significantly. "He's clever, see. Cleverer than a barrel of monkeys. Give the Runners the slip anytime. They says 'e can disappear in a puff of smoke, he an' that white 'orse of 'is, jest like Old Nick, the devil 'isself."

His interlocutor's smile was slightly mocking as he took a pinch of snuff. He made no response, however. He was close to the front of the crowd and, standing head and shoulders above the majority of the spectators, could easily see the gibbet over the surrounding heads. All trace of a smile was wiped clean from his face as he heard the low rumble of excitement from Tyburn Road that indicated the approach of the cart with the condemned men. Using his elbows, he pushed through the crowd, ignoring the curses and complaints, until he'd reached Tyburn Tree.

John Dennis, the hangman, was already positioned on the broad cart stationed beneath the gibbet. He brushed snow from his black sleeve and peered through the now fast-falling flakes, watching for the arrival of his customers.

"A word with you, sir."

Dennis jumped and looked down from his perch. A man, unremarkably dressed in a plain brown coat and britches, fixed him with a gray-eyed penetrating stare. "How much for the bodies?" he asked, drawing out a leather purse. It chinked richly as he rested it against the palm of his other hand, and Dennis's eyes sharpened. He examined the man closely and saw that although his clothes were plain, they were well cut and of excellent cloth. His linen was spotless, although without frills, and his hat was liberally adorned with silver lace. His sharply assessing gaze encompassed the fine soft leather boots with buckles that he immediately recognized as real silver. Highwaymen—or at least Mr. Abercorn and Mr. Greenthorne—clearly had well-to-do friends.

"Five guinea apiece," he said without a moment's consideration. "And three for their clothes."

The stranger's lip curled, and an expression of acute distaste flickered over his countenance, but he opened his purse without another word.

Dennis leaned down, extending his hand, and the man in brown counted the gold coins into his palm. Then he turned and beckoned four burly carriers, leaning on their carts on the outskirts of the crowd. "Convey the bodies to the Royal Oak at Putney," he said without expression, handing them a guinea each.

"Like as not, we'll 'ave to fight the surgeons' messengers for 'em, guv," one of the four said with a leering wink.

"When they're safely at the Royal Oak, there'll be another guinea each," the man in brown said coldly. Turning on his heel, he made to push his way back through the crowd. He'd done what he'd come to do, ensured that his friends' bodies would not end up on the dissecting table under the surgeons' knives, but he had no stomach to see their deaths.

He made fair progress until he reached the middle of the crowd; then the noise swelled from the Tyburn Road, heralding the imminent arrival of the prisoners from Newgate, and he found he couldn't take another step as the excitement rose to fever pitch around him and the throng pressed ever closer to the gallows. Resigned, he stood still, bracing himself against the buffeting as the crowd jumped on tiptoe, pushed and pulled, cursed and shouted, jostling for a better view.

"Take yer 'at off, woman!" The raucous yell was accompanied by a none too gentle shove at the monstrous confection of straw and scarlet-dyed feathers.

The irate owner, a florid-faced carter's wife reeking of gin, swung round and launched a stream of Billingsgate obscenity that was answered in like form. The man in brown sighed and tried to close his nostrils to the stench of alcohol and unwashed humanity as the atmosphere heated up despite the still-falling snow and the vicious wind. Something brushed against him; he felt a fluttering against his waistcoat, and he was instantly alert. He clapped his hand to his waistcoat, knowing what he would find. His watch was gone.

Furious, he stared round at the sea of eager, panting faces, eyes glowing with excitement, mouths ajar. His livid gaze fell on an upturned face beside him, standing so close to him a wisp of cinnamon-colored hair brushed against his shoulder. It was the face of a madonna. A perfect, pale oval, with tawny gold eyes set wide apart beneath a smooth, broad brow; luxuriant dark-brown eyelashes fluttered, and her beautiful mouth quivered in distress.

Suddenly a loud voice bellowed, "Take care of your pockets! There's a bleedin' pickpocket around!" and a chorus of indignation rose in the close air as people patted their clothing, felt through pockets, and discovered that they too were missing sundry items.

Almost instantaneously, the girl standing beside him swayed, moaned, and sank downward. Instinctively, he caught her up before she could be lost in the sea of legs and heavily booted feet stamping on the cobbles. She hung limply against him, her face even paler than before, perspiration pearling her forehead.

Her eyelashes fluttered and she murmured, "Your pardon, sir," before she collapsed again and began to slip through his hold.

He hauled her upright, maneuvering her into his arms, and turned to push his way out of the crowd. "Let me pass. The lady is swooning," he declared repeatedly, the harshness of his voice having some effect so that at last he managed to make his way to the rear of the throng, who were now taken up with the spectacle at the scaffold. He'd reached a relatively empty space when the great roar from the crowd told him that the cart had been driven from beneath Gerald and Derek, leaving them swinging from the gibbet. His expression grew grimmer, and his eyelids dropped for a second over eyes that were gray and cold as arctic ice.

"My thanks, sir," the bundle in his arms murmured in a faint voice as the girl stirred. "I have lost my friends in the crush, and I was so afraid I would be trampled. But I'll manage very well now."

Her voice was surprisingly deep and rich. Her velvet cloak had fallen open as he'd pushed through the throng, revealing a simple gown of fine muslin, a discreet white fichu at the neck as befitted a modest young lady of good family. Her hands were buried in a velvet muff. She gazed up at him and offered a tremulous smile when he seemed disinclined to set her down.

"How do you intend finding your friends?" he asked, looking around pointedly at the seething press of humanity. "They could be anywhere. This is no place for a gently bred young woman to wander alone."

"Pray don't let me trouble you further, sir," she said. "I'm certain I shall find them . . . they'll be looking for me." She moved in his hold, and he detected more than a touch of determination in her efforts to free herself.

Suspicion flickered in his brain as he thought of the sequence of events. It had all been very convenient . . . but surely he was wrong. This sweet-faced, honey-voiced innocent couldn't possibly have been light-fingering her way through the crowd.

Philip's face sprang unbidden to memory. Philip as he had been as a child. Angelic, gentle, coaxing, innocent little Philip. Neither of his parents would hear a word against their darling—not his parents, or his nurse, or his tutor, or any member of the household where young Philip ruled supreme.

"Put me down, sir!" The girl's now indignant demand brought him back to the present with a jolt.

"In a minute," he said thoughtfully. "But let us first devote some attention to finding your friends. Where exactly did you lose them?"

"If I knew that exactly, sir, I would have little difficulty finding them again," she responded tartly. "You have been very kind, and I know my uncle will be very grateful to you for rescuing me. If you give me your name and direction, I'll ensure that a reward is sent on to you." She wriggled again with serious purpose.

He tightened his hold, hitching her higher up against his chest. His voice was suave as he protested, "My dear ma'am, you insult me. It would be the act of a dastard to leave such an innocent girl to fend for herself in these circumstances." He looked around him with an air of anxious interest. "No, I really must restore you personally to your family."

He glanced down at her again. The hood of her cloak had fallen back, and snow was gathering on the glowing brown hair coiled smoothly around her head. Her expression was one of acute exasperation, banishing all trace of the helpless swooning maiden in distress. "Perhaps if you told me your name, we might make some inquiries," he suggested gently.

"Octavia," she said through gritted teeth, praying that he'd be satisfied and set her on her feet. Once on the ground, she'd be free and clear in a second. "Octavia Morgan. And I do assure you, there is not the slightest need for you to remain with me any longer."

He smiled, convinced now that he was right. "Oh, but I believe there is, Miss Morgan. Octavia . . . what an unusual name."

"My father is a classical scholar," she responded automatically, her mind now working swiftly as she finally understood that he was playing with her. But why? Was he intending to take advantage of her present vulnerability? On the whole, he didn't strike her as a man likely to ravish a young lady in distress. He looked and spoke like a gentleman, although his plain garments and unpowdered hair indicated someone who didn't inhabit the Fashionable World.

But if not that, why wouldn't he let her go? The fruits of her morning's work were concealed in a pouch tied around her waist and lying snugly against her thigh beneath her top petticoat. She could reach for it through the slit in her dress that enabled her to adjust the position of her whalebone panniers when moving through a narrow doorway. He couldn't possibly feel the pouch, even holding her as he was, but it was time to bring this dismayingly intimate encounter to a close.

Her hand came out of her muff, and she drove the heel of her palm into his chin, jolting his head back. At the same time, she twisted her head and bit his upper arm hard.

He dropped her like a hot brick, and she was up and running, weaving through the crowd with a desperate agility; but she knew he was on her heels, a silent, deadly pursuit. She ducked into an alley, gasping for breath, hoping she'd given him the slip, but then she saw him advancing on the mouth of the alley, a look of set purpose on his face.

She plunged out of the alley and back into the rowdy crowd that was beginning to disperse. The mood was now quarrelsome and voices were raised in streams of abuse, fights erupting as knots of people struggled to get out of the square. A rank of chairmen touted for custom as the throng eddied past them and Octavia headed for the line. She glanced over her shoulder, praying that her pursuer had followed her into the alley, but he was still behind her, keeping pace with her, pushing through the crowd, seeming not to hurry and yet somehow gaining. There was a relentlessness to this dogged pursuit, and her heart began to thump, the first tremors of panic fluttering over her skin. She had his watch. If he'd guessed and was intending to capture her and bring her before the magistrates with the evidence still about her, then she'd be facing the hangman as surely as the two unfortunates whose deaths had just provided the crowd with such an amusing morning.

Her hand slipped through the slit in her skirt, feeling the laden pouch. The tapes beneath her petticoat fastened at her back and were impossible to reach one-handedly through the slit, so she couldn't untie the pouch and throw it from her at this point even if she wished. And she didn't wish. It would be a cowardly waste of a morning's work. There was enough to pay the rent, redeem Papa's precious books and buy his medicine, and put good food on the table for a month to come. And if she gave it up, those heart-stopping, nauseating moments of terror that had ac-

companied every artful brush of her fingertips would have
been for nothing.

Resolutely, she withdrew her hand and slithered sideways through a noisy family group bewailing the disappear-
ance of a child. They closed up behind her, arguing
violently. The rank of chairmen was almost ahead of her
now . . . three more steps . . .

"Shoreditch!" she gasped to the leading chair, and
moved to step inside as one of the two chairmen held open
the door.

"No, I don't think so, Miss Morgan." A hand closed
over her shoulder as the quiet voice spoke, gently mocking,
behind her. "You see, I really do feel I have a duty to see
you safely restored to the bosom of your family."

She was caught. But he couldn't know for sure that she
had his watch. She was hardly dressed like a common thief,
and the only evidence he had was that she'd been standing
beside him when the cry of "pickpocket" had gone up. She
turned to him with a haughty toss of her head. "Sir, I find
your attentions unwelcome. I trust you won't oblige me to
summon the constable."

Amusement glittered in the gray eyes bent with such
mocking solicitude upon her. "On the contrary, ma'am.
Perhaps I should summon him for you."

"You goin' to Shoreditch, lady, or not?" the chairman
demanded truculently before she could gather her wits to
deal with this very deliberate calling of her bluff.

"Most certainly I am." With relief she turned again to
enter the sedan chair.

"No," her infuriating companion said in the same affable tone as before. "No, I really don't think so." Taking her
arm now in a grip that meant business, he drew her away
from the line of chairs. "You and I are going to have a little
talk, Miss Morgan."

"About what, sir?" she snapped.

"Oh, I think you know," he said equably. "A little
matter of private property and public assaults. But let us get
out of this crush."

She seemed to have no choice, but at least there was no

more talk of constables. Maybe he'd be satisfied with the return of his property and that would be an end to it. She said nothing, offering no further resistance as he swept her along before him through the gradually decreasing crowd.

Suddenly the atmosphere changed. The mob began to push and shove with greater force, and a panicked murmur ran through their ranks. Voices were raised in warning, and the murmur of panic became a full-throated roar.

"Odd's blood," Octavia's companion swore as he identified the roar. He tightened his grip on her arm. "Trust the press gang to know where to find good pickings. We have to get out of here before they run amok."

Octavia lost all desire to free herself from her companion, who was suddenly her only anchor. Her feet were swept from beneath her, and if he hadn't dragged her against his body, she would have gone down to the cobbles. The whole mass of humanity surged forward, men, women, and children screaming as they fought to get out of the square and into the surrounding streets where they could run freely. An army of cudgel-wielding sailors headed by a group of naval lieutenants poured into the square from the Edgeware Road, rounding up men and boys indiscriminately as they swept down upon them, inexorable as a tidal wave. Women's sobs and cries of protest as their husbands and sons were torn from their sides rose above the angry, frightened roar of the frantic crowd.

The press gang wouldn't take up a gentleman, and Octavia's captor was undoubtedly a gentleman, but their danger lay in being swamped by the crowd. The screams of the trampled rose high-pitched with anguish, then faded into long drawn-out groans of pain and despair as the heedless feet kept coming, kicking and stamping on fallen bodies.

Octavia lost all sense of direction; she was aware only of the strong comforting grip on her arm as they were tumbled along on the tide. She could see nothing except chests and arms until something flashed across her sideways vision.

"Over there!" she yelled, trying to make herself heard above the tumult. She darted sideways, lowering her head and pushing like an enraged bullock toward the deep doorway that had caught her eye. Her companion added his own bulk to the process, carving a path sideways through the throng until they were huddled in the doorway and the tide was sweeping past them.

"Thank God!" Octavia leaned against the door at her back trying to catch her breath. Her hair had come loose from its pins, and her fichu was torn, exposing the creamy swell of her bosom. Her companion's gaze slowly drifted over her disordered appearance, and abruptly she pulled her cloak tighter around her, covering her dishevelment, aware of the weight of the pouch lying heavily against her thigh.

"You have sharp eyes, Miss Morgan," her companion observed calmly, leaning beside her, watching the passing stampede. "We'll stay here until it's over."

"I presume you too have a name, sir," she said in an attempt to recapture her earlier assurance.

"Oh, most certainly," he agreed, taking a japanned snuffbox from the deep pocket of his coat. He flicked the lid and delicately took a pinch.

Nothing else was forthcoming. Octavia tapped her foot on the stone lintel. "Am I to be told it, sir?"

He looked at her, one eyebrow quizzically raised. "I confess I hadn't given the question any thought. However . . . " He bowed, managing an elegant flourish in the confined space. "At this moment Lord Nick is at your service, Miss Morgan."

She stared at him, trying to remember where she'd heard the name before. And what did he mean by *at this moment*? "Oh?" she said, her jaw dropping. "Lord Nick, the highwayman?"

He smiled and shrugged. "Such calumny. I don't know where people get these stories from."

Octavia shook her head as if trying to clear her thoughts. No gentleman, after all, but Lord Nick, the highwayman given the devil's colloquial name for his uncanny ability to evade the law. If he was who he said he was—not that he looked in the least as she'd imagined a highwayman would look—then it seemed unlikely he was intending to lay a charge against her. But it seemed only reasonable and friendly in the circumstances to return his property without further delay. She slipped her hand inside her cloak, sliding her fingers into the slit in her gown, intending to extract the watch from the pouch. Then she realized that he was watching her every movement, a sardonic spark in his eyes.

She let her hand fall to her side and smiled nonchalantly. She didn't like the look in those slate-gray eyes, and this was far too public a spot for an unsolicited admission of guilt, even to a fellow pirate.

The rushing mob was diminishing now, the cries and screams fading into the distance.

"Come," Lord Nick said. "I think it's safe to leave now."

"You go your way and I'll go mine, sir," she said, stepping out of the doorway. There was no sign now of a sedan chair; the chairmen would have made off to safety as soon as the cry of "press gang" had gone up—they were strong, well-muscled men, perfect candidates for His Majesty's Navy.

"You seem remarkably obtuse for someone who I'm convinced has a sharp head on her shoulders," her companion remarked in a tone of mild exasperation. "We have yet to have our little discussion, if you recall." He looked round, getting his bearings. "My horse is at the Rose and Crown . . . this way, I believe."

Their "little discussion" was obviously unavoidable. But at least there would be relative privacy at an inn. Resigned, Octavia allowed herself to be guided through the littered but now quiet streets to the Rose and Crown.

However, instead of entering the inn, they went round to the stableyard. "Do you prefer to ride pillion or before me?" Lord Nick asked with casual courtesy as he gestured to an ostler.

"Neither," Octavia said. "What are you talking about?" Every time she thought she understood what was happening, this man shuffled the pieces on the board.

He sighed. "I'm not usually considered inarticulate. . . . Bring my horse, lad. . . . We have about five miles to ride, Miss Morgan. So . . ." He turned his hands palm up as if the rest were self-explanatory.

A hot tide of anger chased guilt, resignation, and apprehension into the mists. She'd allowed him to call the tune thus far because of the guilty weight of the pouch beneath her skirts, but he'd taken sufficient advantage of her disadvantage.

"I'm not coming with you," Octavia said quietly, her anger visible only in her snapping eyes and her increased pallor. "I don't know what you have in mind, but if you attempt to abduct me, I'll scream so loudly it'll bring every constable in the area."

He appeared not to have heard her, his attention directed toward the lad bringing his horse, a big-shouldered roan who looked easily capable of carrying two riders.

"Now, Miss Morgan . . . pillion or in front of me?" He turned back to her. "Either will be perfectly comfortable, I assure you. Peter is as steady as a rock."

"Are you perhaps hard of hearing?" Octavia asked, her voice low and fierce. "I bid you good day." She spun on her heel and stalked out of the yard, her back prickling as she waited for the arresting hand on her shoulder. But nothing happened. She walked unmolested out of the yard of the Rose and Crown and into the narrow cobbled lane.

The cobbles were slippery with wet snow, and she shivered, but with the dull fatigue of anticlimax as much as with the cold. A church clock chimed nine. It seemed extraordinary that it should still be so early after all the excitements and the dramas of the morning. Her father would be deep in his texts by now, unaware of the time or the weather, probably unaware of her absence. If she didn't answer his call, Mistress Forster would.

Mistress Forster was owed two weeks' rent.

Octavia's step lengthened at the thought. She could look after that now.

The pounding of hooves behind her at first didn't intrude on her reverie. When they did, they were almost upon her. She was hurrying down the center of the lane, avoiding the filthy water and refuse in the kennel at the side.

Now she had no choice but to jump sideways, splashing through the kennel, if she wasn't to be run down. It was a common enough hazard in the side streets of the city.

"A pox on your knavish soul!" she swore in most unladylike accents as the kennel filth caked her boots and soiled the hem of her cloak and gown that she hadn't had time to lift clear. "May you rot in . . ."

The rest of the curse was lost as the rider drew abreast of her, swooped low in the saddle, and caught her up with all the dexterity of a performer at Philip Astley's Amphitheatre.

Octavia found herself in the saddle of the roan, the hard body of Lord Nick at her back, his encircling arm holding her steady on her perch.

She opened her mouth and screamed, a shrill, piercing clamor. Casements were flung open along the lane, curious faces hanging out, peering down through the thickening veil of snow.

"You wish to visit the local magistrate?" Lord Nick murmured against her ear, making no attempt to still her screams. "I'm sure he'll be interested in what you're concealing beneath your skirt."

Her scream faded into the pale cold air. "And I'm sure he'll be interested to know who's laying the charge," she hissed. "They hanged two of your kind this morning, I'm sure they'll be delighted to lay hands on the third."

"And just who is going to identify me, my dear Miss Morgan?"

She had no evidence but his own words. And she carried on her own person the most damning evidence of her own thievery. Once again she acknowledged defeat in bitter silence.

They turned out of the alley. The snow was falling heavily now, and Octavia had no sense of where they were or in what direction they were proceeding.

"Where are you taking me?" Not that it would make much difference to know, she reflected dourly, trying to control her apprehension.

"Into the country. Somewhere quiet where we can have our little discussion."

"I have nothing to say to you." It was a feeble defiance, but she felt it was necessary to make, anyway.

"But I have something to say to you."

"Let me down and I'll give you back your goddamned watch!" Octavia exclaimed.

"Oh, yes, you will give it back to me," he agreed equably. "All in good time, though, Miss Morgan. All in good time."

Chapter 2

They rode through a maze of streets becoming ever narrower and poorer until they reached the river. Octavia felt she was inhabiting some dreamscape rapidly becoming nightmare as her own familiar London was left behind. For one wild moment she contemplated leaping from the back of the roan, but she was a long way from the slippery ground, and her companion's encircling arm was holding her far more tightly than mere safety required. Women were frequently abducted from the streets, sometimes even from their own homes, but they were usually wealthy widows or young heiresses to be coerced into marriage. She didn't qualify on either count. Did the highwayman simply have rape on his mind?

"What do you want with me?" she demanded. "Why would you be interested in a common pickpocket?"

"A most *uncommon* pickpocket," her companion corrected in the amused, equable tones he'd used throughout. "A beautiful, well-spoken, well-dressed, and most artful pickpocket. That little fainting ploy was very clever. You rob me of my watch, then use me to effect your escape from the scene of the crime." He laughed. "What a gull you must have thought me."

"So it's revenge you want," she said slowly, although he didn't sound in the least vengeful. "What are you going to do? Ravish me? Rob me? Kill me?"

"What a vivid imagination you have, Miss Morgan. Ravishment has never appealed to me." He chuckled. "At the risk of sounding a coxcomb, I've never found it necessary, to be perfectly honest with you."

Octavia could think of nothing to say to this, since it struck her as probably perfectly true. Despite her anger and apprehension, she had to acknowledge that there was something dismayingly attractive about the highwayman.

"However," he continued thoughtfully, "if the idea appeals to you, I'm sure we could find a way to enjoy it."

The cool effrontery of this, tuning so neatly into her thoughts, brought her swinging round in the saddle, palm raised to wipe the mocking little smile from his lips.

But he was ready for her, catching her wrist in his whip hand and forcing it down to her lap. "You're a little too quick with your hands, Miss Morgan. I haven't forgotten your earlier attack, for which I'm afraid I do intend to take reprisals." There was no laughter on his face now, and his eyes were cold gray pools. "I don't take kindly to being assaulted. Best you remember that."

"It was provoked," she said, pale with fury. "You wouldn't release me. And now you insult me!"

"Your pardon, but I didn't realize it was an insult," he responded with a careless shrug, but still maintaining his hold on her wrist. "We're two of a kind, my dear. I could imagine we might enjoy each other a great deal in the right circumstances."

"Arrogant, insufferable cur!" she hissed, aware of how helpless she was to do more than use her tongue to express her outrage.

"So I've been told on occasion," the highwayman said indifferently. "But this discussion is becoming irksome, and if I'm not mistaken, we're heading for a blizzard, so I suggest you hold your tongue until we find ourselves warm and dry again."

The weather was growing increasingly miserable, and

her words would only be snatched away on the wind, so Octavia lapsed into fulminating silence. They crossed over Westminster Bridge, and the wind sweeping off the river came at them in vicious gusts, blowing stinging snow into their faces. The few travelers they encountered scurried along with their heads down, cloaks pulled tight around them.

They cantered through the village of Battersea, where doors were shut tight. They passed an inn, and Octavia looked longingly at the smoke curling from its chimneys. But the highwayman clearly had a destination in mind and wasn't going to stop until they reached it. The houses were farther and farther apart now, little hamlets shrouded in snow, only a mangy mongrel or two cowering in the narrow village streets. Octavia wondered what her father was thinking, huddled in their lodgings on Weaver Street. If he thought about it at all, he'd assume she'd taken shelter from the storm. . . .

But perhaps she'd never see him again.

As they rode deeper into the countryside, that possibility seemed ever more a probability. Since her arrival in London three years earlier, she'd never been this far outside the city, and she couldn't imagine how she would ever get back, even supposing the highwayman released her after he'd done whatever he intended to do with her. . . . What did he mean by taking reprisals because she'd forced him to drop her at Tyburn?

To her annoyance tears filled her eyes. Tears of fright and cold and helplessness, they trickled warmly down her icy cheeks, mingling with the snow. Then she bit her lip hard, concentrating on the pain until the moment of weakness passed. She would not give her insufferable abductor the satisfaction of seeing her weep.

"There's no need to be afeared," he said suddenly, and again she wondered how he could read her mind. "I don't intend to hurt you."

"I'm not afeared," she denied. "I'm angry and I want to go home. My father will be worrying about me. You can't just sweep an innocent person off the street as if they have no family, no responsibilities."

"But strictly speaking, Miss Morgan, you're not an innocent person," he pointed out gently. They were cantering now through Putney village, the inhospitable expanse of the snow-covered heath crowning the hill ahead of them. "When someone earns their bread in the dubious fashion you've chosen, they must expect the unexpected."

"And what of *you,* sir? What of the way you choose to earn *your* bread?" she fired back, trying not to think about disappearing into the desolate heath in a blizzard. He could as well be taking her to the craters of the moon.

"Oh, I always expect the unexpected," he returned serenely, swinging the horse down a side street just before they would have begun the ascent to the heath. "And what more unexpected than having one's watch stolen by an intriguing pickpocket?"

Whatever response Octavia might have made died on her lips as she saw the lights of an inn glowing up ahead, throwing a welcoming shaft through the gray-white veil of driving snow. The sign of the Royal Oak swung violently in the gusting wind, and as they drew rein, Peter blowing and snorting with the effort of cantering five miles against the wind and the snow, the front door flew open and a burly man in a baize apron emerged, accompanied by a gangly lad.

"Eh, Nick, such filthy weather! We've been waitin' on ye," the man said as the lad grabbed Peter's reins. "Is it done?"

"Aye, it's done. They'll bring the bodies here." The highwayman swung down and took the man's hand in a tight grip. Then they both nodded as if they'd put some issue to rest, and Lord Nick turned back to Octavia, still on her perch. "Journey's end, Miss Morgan." He reached up to lift her down. "In with you now." A hand in the small of her back propelled her into the inn, to the left of a stone-flagged passageway and into a room where the heat from two massive fireplaces nearly knocked her sideways.

The taproom was brightly lit, tallow candles augmenting the firelight, and seemed full of faces, all turned toward her. Mouth-watering aromas came from the kitchen Octavia could glimpse through an open door behind the bar, and she realized how hungry she was. It must be past noon now and she'd eaten nothing since before dawn, when she'd had a piece of bread and butter before going out to work the crowd at Tyburn.

"Well, what's this ye've brought back with ye, Nick?" a jovial voice demanded from the inglenook, where the owner sat placidly puffing on a long churchwarden pipe.

"This, my friends, is Miss Octavia Morgan," Nick said, shrugging out of his snow-covered cloak and tossing it onto a settle, together with his hat, whip, and gloves.

"Is that so?" A woman stood in the doorway to the kitchen, her angular body swathed in a floury apron. Her arms were folded across a meager bosom, and she held a wooden ladle in one hand. Her eyes were sharp and unfriendly as they rested on Octavia, who stood in the entrance to the taproom, melting snow from her cloak dripping to the flagstones to form a puddle around her sodden boots. "And jest who's Miss Morgan, Nick?"

"A most artful young lady, Bessie," the highwayman responded. He regarded Octavia with a quizzical smile that merely increased her unease. "Do take off your cloak, Miss Morgan."

When she didn't immediately obey, he deftly unfastened the clasp at her neck and removed the sodden garment, handing it to a wide-eyed serving wench. "Dry it, Tabitha. . . . Now, your muff and gloves, Miss Morgan."

They were removed in short order, and Octavia felt uncomfortably exposed in her demure gown of cream muslin. Her fingers twitched at the torn lace fichu. She was totally out of place in this room full of rough countrymen, the only other women the hard-eyed Bessie in the doorway and the little serving girl.

"Now, to the first order of business," Lord Nick said cheerfully. "Time to pay your dues, Miss Morgan." Catching her round the waist, he swept her up and onto the long deal table in the center of the room.

Octavia was for the moment too stunned to say anything. She stared down at the sea of faces, amused and anticipatory now, as if waiting for some entertainment to begin.

"Somewhere on her person, Miss Morgan has concealed the fruits of her morning's work at Tyburn," Lord Nick solemnly informed the room. "And not incidentally, my watch. One of my most valued possessions," he added judiciously.

"Not the one ye nabbed from old Denbigh, Nick?"

"The very same, Thomas," he concurred with a grave nod. "Now, Miss Morgan, I think it's time for you to reveal your hiding place and show us your proceeds."

She stared at him, her cheeks crimson as she understood what he was saying. In the doorway, waiting for the mob to pass, he'd seen her hand move stealthily when she'd been about to restore his watch. He knew precisely where she kept the pouch. He would know it was fastened around her waist, and to untie it, she would have to raise her skirts.

"You pox-ridden bastard," she said softly.

"Retribution, Miss Morgan, remember?" One eyebrow lifted. Casually, he reached up to the rack of clay pipes above the bar and took one down. She stood unmoving on the table as he filled the pipe, struck flint on tinder, and lit the tobacco. A plume of smoke rose to mingle with the wood smoke, and the already heavy cloud of pipe smoke, in the low-beamed room.

"Of course, Bessie could assist you if you find yourself in difficulties," he observed, gesturing to where the aproned woman still stood in the kitchen doorway. He held Octavia's livid gaze, his eyes cool and penetrating and not in the least amused. This was not a man to cross, Octavia recognized with dull foreboding as Bessie readily stepped forward, wiping her hands on her apron.

She had no choice but to comply—not if she was to prevent the woman from stripping the gown from her back in the middle of the room.

Closing her mind to the grinning circle of faces as they pressed closer to the table, she hitched up her skirt and her top petticoat. In her haste and embarrassment, her fingers were all thumbs. During an eternity of mortification she fumbled desperately with the ribbon that secured the lamb-skin pouch to her waist. But at last it fell free.

The highwayman was standing at the table, one hand extended for his prize, the other cradling the bowl of his pipe. His face was expressionless. Octavia hurled the heavy pouch at his head with all her force; then she jumped from the table and ran for the door, shoving her way through the audience. She grabbed her soaked cloak from the girl who still held it in the doorway and raced into the passage and out into the blinding blizzard, not knowing where she was going or what she was going to do, just running down the street, her feet sinking in the drifting snow.

The wind cut through the flimsy material of her gown as she struggled to wrap herself in her cloak while she was running. She'd left her gloves and muff behind, and her fingers were quickly numbed, but she continued to run, head down into the storm, sobbing with rage.

The pounding footsteps behind her were deadened by the snow and she heard nothing until a hand descended on her shoulder and the highwayman declared in tones of con-siderable exasperation, "Odd's bones, woman, are you mad?"

"Let me go!" She twisted away from him, glaring at him through the thick curtain of snow. "Scum! You got what you wanted, now leave me alone."

"I do not want your death on my conscience," he declared.

"What conscience? You don't know the meaning of the word, you filthy piece of kennel slime!"

Disconcertingly, the highwayman laughed, and it was a rich, merry sound this time, worlds apart from the mockery of before. "You're entitled to that, I grant you. But I owed you something for a bite on the arm and a fist to the chin. You weren't hurt, and you showed no more than a petti-coat, so cry truce now and come back in the warm before you catch your death."

"I'd rather die!" She swung back into the storm, plowing her way up the narrow street, blinded now by snow-flakes clinging to her eyelashes.

"You are given to extravagant language and dis-tempered freaks, Miss Morgan." So saying, he swept her off her feet. She yelled with the full force of her lungs, but the sound was snatched away on the wind, and she could do nothing to save herself from being carted unceremoniously back to the Royal Oak.

He kicked the door closed behind him and headed for a flight of wooden stairs, calling, "Bessie, send Tabitha up with mulled sack and towels. And we'll have dinner in half an hour, if you please."

Bessie appeared in the doorway, watching as Lord Nick ascended the stairs two at a time, seemingly unhampered by his still struggling and cursing burden. She pursed her lips disapprovingly and returned to her kitchen. "Tab, you heard Lord Nick. Mulled sack in his parlor."

"Aye, mistress." Tabitha curtsied and hastened to the range, where a copper pot of mulled sack steamed fra-grantly.

Above stairs, a door banged resoundingly.

"Lord of hell, woman, for such a slip of a thing, you're no lightweight," the highwayman declared, setting his cap-tive on her feet with a sigh of relief. "Now, just stop cursing me and settle down. You can't go anywhere at the moment, so you might as well accept my hospitality with a good grace."

There was an inexorable logic to this that even Octavia in her fury couldn't deny. And at least they were private, away from the sea of grinning faces that had witnessed her embarrassment.

She fell silent and looked around the chamber. It was warm and well lit with wax candles, a checkered carpet on the oak floor, a round table in the window, two upholstered chairs set on either side of the hearth, where a log fire blazed. The scent of lavender and beeswax mingled with the wood smoke; the andirons gleamed with polish, the pewter candlesticks shone, the wooden furniture had the rich pa-tina of good housekeeping.

Suddenly, she was very tired, and her hunger rose anew with the aromas wafting up the stairs. With a little shrug she tossed aside her sodden cloak and stepped over to the fire, bending to warm her frozen hands, wincing when her fingertips tingled with returning sensation. Her eyelashes and hair were white with snow, her feet numb in her wet boots. The hems of her skirt and petticoats were drenched, and an uncontrollable shiver ripped through her.

The highwayman stood watching her, a speculative frown in his eyes. Her body was a graceful curve as she bent toward the flame, and now that she'd ceased her vilification and her struggles, he absorbed again the madonnalike beauty of her oval face, the innocent radiance of her tawny eyes.

One couldn't judge a package by its wrapping. His lips tautened at the bitter reminder, and he waited for the angelic image of his twin to fade with the violent surge of icy rage that always accompanied it. It was a familiar cycle, one he'd lived with for eighteen years. But one day very soon he'd be able to put the evil to rest, and he'd be free of the malignant chains of deceit and injustice. And Philip would know his twin again. . . .

A knock at the door cut into his reverie. He bade the knocker enter, and Tabitha came in, a tray with a jug and two tankards in her hands, a pile of towels under one arm.

" 'Ere y'are, sir. Will I set the table for dinner?"

"In ten minutes, Tab." He waved her away. She put her burdens on the table, curtsied, and left.

Octavia turned from the fire. The highwayman tossed her a towel. "Dry your hair, Miss Morgan."

She caught it automatically and began to unpin her hair while he poured two pewter tankards of mulled sack. Bending once again to the fire, she rubbed her loosened hair vigorously, but she was still shivering in the thin, damp gown and her feet were still numb.

"Drink this." He handed her a mug. She cradled it between her hands, inhaling the heady, spicy fragrance. She could think of nothing to say to him and no reason for the moment to quibble with his curt commands.

Abruptly, he left the room. Octavia drank deeply of the sack before sitting in an armchair to pull off her boots and stockings. With a sigh of relief she wriggled her frozen toes in the fire's warmth. It hurt dreadfully as they came back to life, but the pain was almost welcome.

"Take off that gown and put this on. Tab will dry your clothes."

In the bliss of warming herself, she'd almost forgotten her abductor and hadn't heard him return. She looked up, startled. He was holding out a velvet robe, his expression impassive.

"My gown will dry quite well on my person," Octavia declared icily.

"Don't be a fool, you'll have an ague by morning if you stay in those clothes." He dropped the robe into her lap. She continued to stare at him, that delicate, innocent beauty a picture of outraged modesty, and for a moment he was almost persuaded by it.

But one should never judge a package by the wrapping. She'd fooled him once today already, and he knew her for a consummate actress. She was a grown woman, a thief who worked the streets. And she would have used her body as currency whenever necessary.

"Don't pretend it would be the first time you've removed your dress in front of a man," he said with dismissive scorn. "However, I don't object to the play. Games can add a little spice, I agree." He smiled but it was not a nice smile. "Shall I turn my back?" He suited action to words.

Octavia looked for a knife . . . for anything. She found the poker.

He caught the chink of iron as it touched the fender and spun round just as she raised the weapon, her little white teeth bared, murder in her eyes.

"Lord of hell!" He jumped sideways as she brought the poker down with a force that would have cracked his skull. She came after him again and he caught her arm. They swayed in a deadly ballet, and he was surprised at how strong she was—or maybe it was her fury that gave her strength. Grimly, he twisted her wrist until her fingers opened and the poker clattered to the floor.

"What on earth was all that about?" he demanded, taking her shoulders and shaking her vigorously. "You would have killed me."

"That was my intention," she said with soft venom. "You dare talk to me like that . . ."

"Now, wait a minute!" He held up a hand imperatively. "You're not going to tell me you're still a maid."

"What gives you the right to assume that I am not!" Golden fires burned in her eyes, and her face was deathly pale. And he knew absolutely that this was no act.

"Hell and the devil!" He released her and ran a hand over his chin, his mouth twisting ruefully. "How was I to assume otherwise, knowing what I do about you?"

"You know nothing about me!"

"No," he conceded. "Clearly not. Well, for what it's worth, pray accept my apologies for the uncalled-for assumption, Miss Morgan. And now I suggest you get out of that gown while I turn my face to the wall and contemplate my sin." He stalked over to the window and stared fixedly out into the driving snow and the darkening afternoon.

In silence Octavia picked up the robe that she'd tossed to the floor in her fury and turned back to the fire. The wind rattled the windowpanes, and an icy draft needled its way into the room. She knew she couldn't stay in her soaked clothes. Hastily, she threw off the muslin gown and unfastened the tapes of her whalebone pannier, dropping it to the floor. Shivering in her chemise and starched cambric petticoat, she reached behind her for the laces of her corset.

"Death and damnation!" Her fingernail broke as she struggled with a knot that had unaccountably developed. Her arms and shoulders began to ache with the twisted position behind her back.

"Problem with the laces?" The highwayman spoke from the window without turning round. "Perhaps I can help."

How could he possibly know! She set her teeth. "Go to the devil!"

"I'm not unfamiliar with the garment," he observed, and there was a touch of that rich, merry laughter in his voice now.

"You do surprise me!" Octavia renewed her battle, biting her lip in frustration.

"It will take me but a moment if you'd come over here. I'll keep my eyes closed if you wish."

"And just how do you intend unlacing me with your eyes closed?" she demanded.

"By touch." The amusement in his voice was now full-fledged.

Octavia struggled with herself for a second, then stalked over to him. "Close your eyes."

He turned from the window, eyes obediently closed, and she gave him her back. His fingers moved deftly over the laces, feeling for the knot.

She looked suspiciously over her shoulder, but his eyes were still closed. He was, however, grinning broadly. The recalcitrant knot flew undone, and in a second she was holding the unfastened corset against her body.

"My thanks, sir," she said formally.

"The pleasure is all mine, ma'am," he responded. "I find I'm quite an efficient lady's maid. Is there any other little service I can perform?"

"Turn your back!" she commanded, wondering why she found his mischievous grin so infectious. It struck her as an insane reaction after the insults he'd heaped upon her since she'd been fool enough to pick him for her gull.

She slipped out of her petticoats and pulled the velvet robe over her thin chemise. The robe was warm and thick and voluminous. "You may turn around now." She bent to gather up her discarded garments.

"The view was getting a little monotonous," he commented, turning back to the room and coming over to the fire. He took up his tankard of sack and drank, regarding her thoughtfully over the rim. "We really do seem to have got off on the wrong foot."

"Abduction is hardly a recipe for friendship," Octavia snapped, folding her clothes neatly, conscious of her near nakedness beneath the velvet robe and a faint fragrance coming from the garment. It was a lingering mélange of lavender, soap, and pomade with an underlying tang of warmed male skin—the highwayman's own smell, she realized, one she'd been inhaling most of the day.

"Will I set the table now, sir?" Tab popped her head around the door. "The mistress says dinner's aspoiling."

"Then you'd best bring it up without delay," Lord Nick responded. "I don't fancy the rough edge of Bessie's tongue."

"No, sir," Tab said feelingly, hastening to the round table with a tray of linen, cutlery, and glasses. Task completed, she glanced at Octavia, still huddled over the fire. "Will I take miss's clothes to be dried?"

"If you please, Tabitha." Octavia answered her before the highwayman could reply. "As soon as they're dry, bring them back."

"Yes, miss." Tab gathered up the clothes and hurried out.

"You'll not need them again today," Lord Nick observed, going back to the window. "It's almost full dark, and the storm shows no sign of abating."

"I'm not remaining here," Octavia said flatly.

The highwayman merely shrugged. There was no point arguing the toss; the facts spoke for themselves, and she'd have to accept the realities soon enough.

Bessie, Tabitha, and the landlord arrived in a solemn procession, bearing laden trays and, in the latter's case, two bottles of burgundy that he placed on the table before reverently drawing the corks.

Octavia sniffed hungrily as Bessie lifted the lid of the tureen of oyster soup and began to ladle the contents into two deep pewter bowls.

"Will ye carve the mutton yourself, Nick, or shall Ben come back to do it for ye?"

"I'll carve, thank you, Bessie." Lord Nick came to the table. He took a sip of the burgundy that Ben had poured into a glass and nodded his appreciation. "Where've you been keeping this one, Ben?"

The landlord's ruddy color deepened. "I've a few bottles left, Nick. It's by way of thankin' ye."

"No need, Ben, no need. They were my friends too."

The two men looked at each other with the same quiet intensity Octavia had noticed before, then nodded in unison, and Ben backed out of the chamber. Bessie cast a final glance over the table and the steaming leg of mutton on the sideboard; then she waved Tabitha from the room, turning to follow her.

At the door she paused. "She'll be lyin' with ye, then?" She inclined her head in Octavia's direction, the gesture contemptuous and hostile.

"Aye," the highwayman said shortly. Bessie left, closing the door with a sharp click.

Octavia stood immobile, stunned by her own powerlessness. She was trapped in this place, at the mercy of this man and his friends.

"Before you start heaping abuse upon my head again, Miss Morgan . . ." Lord Nick held up an arresting hand. "This is no place for a woman to lie alone."

"Before you robbed me, sir, I had sufficient funds to pay my own way," Octavia declared, finding her voice and relieved to hear that she sounded much stronger than she felt.

"We have an interesting morality here," he observed. "Come to the table before the soup cools. . . . To what extent can it be said that a robber can ethically be guilty of robbing a robber?"

Octavia followed her nose to the table, too hungry to fight enticement. "Clearly you've never heard of honor among thieves, Lord Nick."

"On the contrary . . ." He held out a chair for her, then reached into his pocket and dropped the lambskin pouch onto the table beside her. "You will find that I've simply retrieved my own property, Miss Morgan."

Octavia had not yet had the opportunity to examine the proceeds of her morning's work. She weighed the pouch in her hand, for the moment forgetting both her hunger and the dark, swirling currents of frustration and apprehension. If she had money, she could leave this place. She could hire a carriage to take her back to London. She could hire a bedchamber until the storm died. She would not be dependent on the mercy and whim of the highwayman.

She could even pay for her own dinner. She laid the pouch beside her place again and calmly picked up her spoon.

"The Royal Oak," the highwayman said, picking up his own spoon, once again reading her mind with uncanny accuracy, "does not cater to stray travelers. There are no bedchambers available for hire."

She looked up sharply. "How could that be?"

"Other trades are plied here." He cut into a loaf of barley bread and passed her a slice on the end of the knife, that little mocking smile playing over his lips. "The business we conduct at the Royal Oak is best kept to ourselves, Miss Morgan."

"A den of thieves," she said bitterly. "Why?" She dropped her spoon in her sudden vehemence. "Why did you bring me here?"

"A whim," he responded, dipping bread into his soup. "You intrigued me . . . I'm not usually taken advantage of . . . and besides . . ." He smiled lazily. "I had thought, once we'd settled our business, we might come to some arrangement for a pleasant evening."

Octavia's fingers closed around the stem of her wineglass. "I trust you've now had second thoughts, sir."

He shrugged. "I confess I hadn't expected that you'd still be in possession of your maidenhead."

"And now that you know differently?" she asked tautly.

"Oh, I daresay I can live with the disappointment," he responded carelessly, pushing back his chair. "May I carve you some mutton?"

"But why, then, did you tell Bessie I would lie with you?"

"Because you will not keep your maidenhead for more than five minutes, Miss Morgan, if you do not," he said with a touch of impatience. "I thought I had explained that."

"So I'm to trust *you*?"

"I don't see that you have much choice, my dear." He placed a laden platter before her. "Eat your dinner, Miss Morgan. You'll sleep all the better for a full stomach."

Chapter 3

ᛒᛦ Miss Morgan's appetite was undiminished by her present circumstances, the highwayman reflected in some amusement, carving another slice of mutton for her as she heaped roast potatoes onto her platter and reached for the bowl of onion sauce.

Her countenance was now delicately tinged with pink from the warmth and the food and wine. While she offered no conversational sallies, she seemed relaxed for the first time since she'd crossed his path that morning, as if she'd come to some acceptance of her situation.

Such a woman would not be picking pockets at Tyburn for the fun of it. He sipped his wine, regarding her closely through half-closed eyes. Presumably she was no stranger to hunger and cold, despite the elegant gown and the smooth white hands that didn't look as if they'd ever performed a menial task.

He'd first taken her for an occupant of one of the exclusive nunneries around Covent Garden. Mrs. Goadsby's for instance, where clients were ruthlessly vetted by the abbess, and the young ladies educated and cared for like the most precious daughters of any noble house. In such establishments one could find many a young woman of elegant appearance waiting for a rich protector, or even a husband, and many an aristocratic rake had been lost to the artful wiles of such a genteel seductress.

It was by no means unheard of for such a lady to take her place at court without causing so much as a raised eyebrow. He thought of Elizabeth Armistead, who had recently graduated from Mrs. Goadsby's into the arms of the Prince of Wales, her past very much a thing of the past.

For his own part, though, he'd be chary of marrying such a one. A man would be imagining a pair of cuckold's horns at every turn, the highwayman reflected. His gaze rested on the serenely beautiful countenance opposite him —such innocent beauty concealing the talents of a successful thief and the devil only knew what else. He'd already seen evidence of a murderous temper. She and Philip . . . what a pair they would make.

His long fingers idly stroking around the rim of his glass suddenly stilled as the idea rose fully formed in his mind. He sat quietly, allowing it to grow and spread its wings. His most brilliant inspirations came to him in this way and had done so since childhood. He knew to leave his mind free rein to examine potential problems, discard certain possibilities until lighting upon the perfectly plotted arrangement.

A slow smile spread over his face, but his eyes were terrifying in their icy detachment. It would work. But how to sell such a scheme to a woman who didn't seem to fit any recognizable mold? What motives would capture her? She was to some extent an adventuress and maybe, therefore, open to a profitable venture. But was she a free agent?

"Tell me . . ." He broke the silence so suddenly that she jumped, spilling ruby drops from the wineglass she was carrying to her lips. "Tell me why you happen to be working the crowd at Tyburn."

Octavia frowned, dabbing at the stain on the pristine-white cloth with her napkin. She'd been rather surprised he hadn't posed the question earlier. "I haven't been educated to earn my living in the conventional ways." She forked another potato from the dish.

"But why would it be necessary for you to do so?" Obligingly he pushed the bowl of cabbage toward her. She nodded her thanks and took a large spoonful onto her plate.

"For the same reason I imagine you ride the highways," she responded. "One must eat. One must put a roof over one's head. And in my case I have a father to care for."

Lord Nick leaned back in his chair, crossing his legs at the ankle. "Forgive me, but why is the father not providing for the daughter?"

"I don't consider that your business, sir," she replied icily.

"No, it's not." He leaned forward to refill their glasses. "Nevertheless, I should like to know." His smile was suddenly coaxing, inviting, his voice quiet, his eyes no longer arctic but the gray of a soft dawn.

Since the disaster Octavia had had no one to talk to, no one to share her desperate struggles or to listen to the fierce bubbling rage of helplessness. She'd fought alone to keep herself and her father out of the workhouse, biting her tongue when the urge to heap angry recriminations on his head had become almost overpowering. She could say nothing to him because he didn't understand their situation. He had no idea they were penniless, no idea of the means she was forced to adopt to keep them from starvation. The invitation to speak of the unspeakable suddenly became irresistible. The highwayman would understand her life because, as he'd said earlier, in some ways they were two of a kind.

She pushed her plate away.

"My father is a very clever scholar but a fool in the ways of the world," she stated. "And since his . . . his misfortune he has withdrawn even further into his books. He sees and hears nothing outside his texts. Three years ago he had a sizable fortune, enough to keep him in comfort and to provide me with a respectable dowry, only—only he fell among thieves."

She looked bleakly across the table. "If I'd been there, it wouldn't have happened, but I was away visiting an aunt, and while I was gone, two men wormed their way into his confidence and persuaded him to invest heavily in a silver mine in Peru. Needless to say, the mine does not exist."

"I see," he said neutrally. There were thieves and rogues at every level of society, even at court, ready to prey on the unwary under the guise of friendship. "So your father lost everything."

"Yes, but his *friends* appear to be doing very well," she said bitterly. "They live high at court, and now inhabit my family home. They lent him money with the house as security to meet the original cost of his investment. Needless to say, they were very sorry when they were obliged to foreclose."

Her mouth was tight, and he read murder again in her eyes. "The whoresons allowed him to take his books. But I daresay they had no use for them."

"What of your mother?"

"She died when I was born. There's only ever been the two of us."

Silence fell, broken only by the spurt of flame as a piece of green wood caught in the hearth. A log shifted, and the highwayman rose from the table to mend the fire. "But why choose a life of crime? You're presumably well educated— you could go for a governess."

"Or a lady's maid," she said sardonically. "Yes, I suppose I could go into service . . . it would be the respectable way of dealing with our difficulties. But as I said before, I haven't been educated to consider myself a servant. I'd rather die."

Exultation surged in his veins. Octavia Morgan was made to be the perfect accomplice. But he merely said coolly, "Pride, Miss Morgan?"

"Do you not understand it?" she fired back.

"Oh, yes," he said, straightening from the fire and turning back to the room. "Oh, yes, *I* understand it. But many would consider thievery more humbling than honest toil."

She met his eye as he scrutinized her pale, set face. "Perhaps."

He knew what she was thinking: that servants were

almost universally exploited and demeaned, the gap between them and their employers as vast as between a slave and his master in ancient Rome. If one were bred to the life, then perhaps one could live it with some self-esteem, but if one were not, then it would indeed be a living death.

"You don't dream of revenge?" He raised an eyebrow.

"I might dream about it," she said. "But I live too close to reality to indulge in fantasy, sir. I make shift as I can, and when things become impossible . . ." She shrugged and sipped her wine. "Why, then I turn to thievery. I do less harm than those who robbed my father. I take a little from many people . . . not everything from one. No one is ruined by my activities."

"Nor by mine, I believe," he remarked, returning to the table. "Do you care for some Stilton with Bessie's apple pie?"

The change of subject was a relief, breaking the intensity of the last ten minutes. It had been a strange sensation to speak aloud the seething fury and to express the hatred she felt for the men who had ruined her own life as ruthlessly and indifferently as they'd ruined her father. But she felt oddly comforted by this near stranger's attention, by the knowledge that he understood and the certainty that he didn't judge.

"What of you?" she said suddenly. "What brought you to the road, Lord Nick?"

He cut into the latticed pastry of the apple pie without replying for a minute. Then he said offhandedly, "A piece of the past . . . a misunderstanding, if you will."

"A misunderstanding?" Octavia looked at him in astonishment. "How could a misunderstanding turn you into a highwayman?"

"In much the same way that your father's lack of understanding turned you into a pickpocket." He slid a slice of pie onto a plate and passed it over to her.

Octavia hesitated, unsatisfied with this reply but sensing that it was all she was going to get. The confidences seemed to be flowing only one way. She shrugged and dug a spoon into the round of Stilton, placing a creamy blue-streaked mound on her plate beside the pie. There was no point neglecting a good dinner just because her confidences weren't reciprocated.

"Will your father be worried about you?" Her companion took a forkful of his own pie.

"What do you think?" she demanded. "When people are abducted, they usually leave worried people behind."

"How worried will he be?" the highwayman asked steadily.

Octavia sighed. There seemed little point in exaggerating the situation; the highwayman wasn't going to suffer any guilty pangs, anyway. "He's not always aware of the time," she explained. "His grasp of the past . . . well, of classical times . . . is very acute, but he doesn't really live in the present. Mistress Forster will look after him, and she'll no doubt assume I've taken shelter from the storm somewhere."

He nodded. "I will return you home in the morning, if the storm's blown itself out."

"You are too kind," she said, not expecting the irony to make much of a dent, but she had been forcibly reminded that her virtue this night was totally dependent on the good faith and moral principles of a notorious highwayman.

As she'd expected, her companion was unmoved by her tone; indeed, he barely noticed it in his own exultant absorption. His long, slender fingers traced the diamond cuts in his wineglass, the firelight catching his amethyst signet ring, the red and blue colors refracted by the glass. Octavia Morgan could be the perfect accomplice for his long-awaited vengeance, and she had laid out for him the perfect motive to persuade her to join with him. He guessed that the promise of her own revenge would be more potent than an end to her financial difficulties, but the latter would be added incentive.

However, he was convinced she wasn't ready for the proposal yet. She was an adventuress of a kind, but he sensed that her commitment to the dark realms beyond the law was not yet wholehearted. For all her hardships, she hadn't touched the desperation that pushed a man inexorably over the edge. . . .

Octavia suddenly felt cold, as if a draft had touched her back. The highwayman was looking at her across the table, but he wasn't seeing her. His eyes were as blank and flat as polished slate, and there was no expression on his face. She wanted to speak, to say or do something to break the dreadful masklike intensity as he sat gazing upon some grim internal landscape, but words wouldn't come to her lips. Then his features came to life again, and his gaze became once more alert, once more recognizing her as his eyes rested shrewd and assessing on her countenance. And the silent assessment was almost as unnerving as the blank stare of before.

The highwayman was thinking that before Octavia Morgan would embrace their joint vengeance, she would need something to bind her to him, to make her see herself differently, to see herself as a woman who could perpetrate a deadly confidence trick on the vanity and twisted complacence of those who'd injured them both. He could see one obvious way to move her across the border into his dark world, to break the fragile chains of maidenly gentility.

"Excuse me for a moment, Miss Morgan." He rose from his chair, offering a courtly bow before leaving the room.

Unnerved, Octavia abandoned her pie and propped her elbow on the table, resting her chin on her palm. She gazed out of the window. It was pitch-dark and the pane was crusted with snow. From the taproom below drunken voices rose in a raucous chorus of some ribald song, and there was a clatter as a chair went over. There was an edge of menace to the noise, a sense that whatever order was maintained could at any moment be plunged into anarchy. This highwayman's haunt was definitely not a good place for a woman alone.

There was a scratching at the door, and Tabitha popped her head around. "Should I clear away now, miss?"

"By all means." Octavia rose from the table and went

to warm herself at the hearth. There was a renewed chorus of shouts and crashes from below. "What's going on?"

"A fight or summat," Tab said, piling crockery onto a tray.

"Are there no women here except yourself and Bessie?"

"No, miss . . . leastways, not unless they brings 'em in." She carried the laden tray to the door, adding matter-of-factly, "They does that oftentimes."

"But what of you? Where do you sleep?"

"Me, miss?" Tab looked surprised at the question. "I sleeps with Bessie over the wash'ouse . . . 'ceptin' when Ben wants 'er of a night. Then I sleeps by the kitchen fire."

No room in those sleeping arrangements for an extra female, however benighted.

"The fire's been kindled in Lord Nick's bedchamber for ye, miss, when y'are ready to retire," Tab said cheerfully, following the thrust of the discussion, balancing the tray on her raised knee as she opened the door. "An' there's an 'ot brick in the bed, and I've passed the warmin' pan 'tween the sheets, so it's all snug." She beamed as Octavia murmured a faint thank-you, then left, banging the door behind her.

"Do you prefer rum or brandy punch?" The highwayman returned in a few minutes, rubbing his hands together with an air of anticipation. "Bessie's bringing the makings to the bedchamber so we may have a nightcap."

"It's too early to retire," Octavia said hastily.

Lord Nick's mobile eyebrows lifted. "It's past eight o'clock, and I for one was up at three this morning to reach Tyburn by dawn."

"As was I. But I am not in the least tired. You go if you wish. I'll stay by the fire in here."

"No, I don't think so," he said in the tone she'd been hearing all day. "I have assumed responsibility for you, my dear Miss Morgan, and you'll spend the night behind a locked door in my company." As if in orchestrated punctuation, renewed shouts and crashes came from downstairs, interspersed with the sound of breaking glass.

Octavia shivered. There seemed no way out of the situation.

"Come," he said, holding open the door.

She brushed past him, conscious again of her bare legs beneath his robe, of her flimsy shift. She felt small and vulnerable in the voluminous robe, totally without the means to defend herself.

His hand was in the small of her back, urging her down the passage and around a corner, away from the sounds of the taproom. "It's much quieter at the back of the house," he said casually, reaching over her shoulder to unlatch a door. "Oh, good, Bessie's left both brandy and rum for the punch. You must have a preference." He pushed her gently ahead of him into the room and closed the door.

"Brandy," Octavia said numbly, watching as he dropped a heavy bar across the door and turned an iron key. Impassively, he removed the key from the lock and slipped it into his pocket. He could not be expecting anyone in this house, where he was clearly a friend and honored guest, to break into his room in the night—so the lock was presumably to keep his unwilling guest within.

"You'll find a commode and hot water behind the screen." He indicated a worked screen in the corner of the room. "While you refresh yourself, I'll prepare the punch."

The room was large and well appointed, warmed by a fire and lit, like the parlor, with expensive wax tapers. There was a deep armchair with elbow pieces beside the hearth, and Octavia decided she would sit up there until dawn.

The highwayman was busy with his punch, considerately removing his attention from her, and she hastened behind the screen, grateful for the amenities it concealed. A freezing visit to an outhouse in the yard was an unappealing prospect at the best of times, let alone in a blizzard.

When she emerged, her companion was grating nutmeg onto the contents of a silver punch bowl. The air was sweet with the scent of warmed brandy, oranges and lemons, cinnamon and nutmeg. Involuntarily, Octavia yawned, realizing how bone tired she was. Her eyes darted longingly

to the deep feather mattress on the bed. Perhaps the highwayman would be chivalrous enough to allow her the bed
and take the chair for himself.

"Come to the fire." His smile was inviting as he ladled
punch into a goblet. "Taste this and see if it needs any
adjustment. There may be a want of nutmeg."

It seemed pointless to resist the comforts offered in this
cozy prison. Octavia sat in the big chair, curling her toes
onto the gleaming brass fender, and took the goblet.
"Plenty of nutmeg," she pronounced after a judicious sip.
"But perhaps just a touch of cloves."

"Ah, I forgot the cloves." He unscrewed a twist of wax
paper and dropped a pinch of dark ground spice into her
goblet. "Better?"

She sipped and nodded. "It doesn't taste quite like
cloves, though."

"Oh, they're a very rare variety, from the Indies," he
said, drinking deep of his own goblet before taking off his
coat and sitting down to remove his boots and stockings.

When he pulled loose his neck cloth and began to
unbutton his shirt, Octavia realized he was undressing for
bed . . . right there in the middle of the chamber . . .
right in front of her eyes. He was unfastening his britches.
She stared, mesmerized as he pushed them off his hips.
Candlelight flickered on his broad bare chest, and her eye
moved inexorably downward, following the trail of dark
hair snaking over his belly, down from his navel and into the
waist of his woolen drawers that molded his hips and legs
and clung tightly to a bulging shape. . . . She choked on
her punch, turning her head away, eyes streaming.

The highwayman appeared not to notice. He crossed
the room to a deep cherrywood armoire. Octavia wiped
her eyes with her fingertips, but she couldn't stop herself
from peeping through them, gazing at the hard-muscled
shape of his buttocks clearly outlined in the drawers as he
stood with his back to her at the armoire. He took out a
fur-trimmed dressing gown and slipped it over his bare
torso before disappearing behind the commode screen.

Hell and the devil! Octavia pressed a palm to one

flushed cheek. He hadn't seemed to give her a thought. He'd undressed as casually if he were in a brothel with a whore. But at least he hadn't removed his drawers in front of her. It was small comfort. She took another gulp of her punch, and to her astonishment a little giggle developed in her throat. If she was totally honest, she'd enjoyed the spectacle. As fascinated as a rabbit in the eye of the cobra. What on earth was happening to her?

Another wave of tiredness washed over her, but there was a tingling sensation in her belly, and her toes were curling of their own accord around the fender. She felt both tired and strangely expectant.

Her companion emerged from the screen, still in his dressing gown. He moved around the room extinguishing the candles until only one remained by the bed; then he turned back the patchwork coverlet and glanced expectantly at her. "Miss Morgan?"

"I'd prefer to sleep in the chair," she said, aware of her flaming cheeks.

"That's your privilege, of course," he said. "But you'll be cold once the fire dies down. I don't believe there are sufficient logs to keep it in all night."

"I'll be warm enough, thank you," she replied stiffly. "If you don't mind letting me have a pillow and the coverlet, I shall be perfectly comfortable."

He shrugged, pulled off the coverlet, and tossed it over to her. A pillow followed. Then, without another word, he tossed off his dressing gown. He must have removed his drawers behind the screen. For a breathtaking second his body glimmered, naked and powerful in the dim light, and then he'd climbed into bed. He leaned over and blew out the bedside candle, and Octavia was left in the firelight.

She dragged the coverlet over her, thumped the pillow behind her head, and tried to settle to sleep. But it was impossible. That curious unfocused excitement grew, together with the tingling in her belly that soon spread to her fingers and toes. But perhaps it wasn't unfocused. Perhaps it had everything to do with the last few minutes, with what she'd seen, with the knowledge of that naked male body a few feet from her. She gazed into the fire, trying to calm herself with the ruddy glow and the deep-blue undertones.

But as the fire died, the room grew colder and darker, and still she was wide awake. Wide awake and freezing. So cold that deep shudders racked her body and all she could hear was the wind whistling around the now silent inn, rattling the ill-fitting panes.

She looked toward the bed. The highwayman was a humped shape at one edge, sleeping tidily and deeply, judging by the steady, rhythmic breathing. If she put the pillow down the middle of the bed, separating them, surely she could creep in without disturbing him and sleep on the farthest edge. She had to get warm. Even if she didn't sleep, she had to get warm if she wasn't to be frozen solid by morning.

Softly, she got up, dragging the coverlet around her shoulders, her feet like blocks of ice on the hard wooden floor. She approached the bed. Barely breathing she lifted the feather quilt and pushed her pillow into the middle. The sleeper made no movement. Still holding her breath, she climbed up onto the high mattress and slid beneath the quilt, where she lay shivering, trying desperately to keep still but unable to control the violent tremors of her body, which seemed to rock the bed.

Gradually, however, she began to warm up. She was acutely conscious of the form in the bed beside her, weighing down the mattress so she had to concentrate on not rolling down into the valley that separated them. But now she was hot, the heavy velvet robe twisted around and beneath her in cumbersome folds that took on the consistency of hardwood pressing into her flesh. Perspiration gathered between her breasts, trickled down from her armpits. And now those strange currents of restless excitement swirled more vigorously in her veins, so that she could hardly keep her feet still, and strange half-formed thoughts kept drifting into her mind, then sliding out again before she could grasp them.

The robe had become an instrument of torture, enclosing her so she could barely breathe, setting her skin on fire.

She wriggled out of it, forgetting in her desperate urgency to move only discreetly. The robe fell to the floor beside the bed, and she heaved a sigh of relief, conscious now of her body beneath the thin shift.

The strange drifting thoughts increased, twining like thick lazy serpents in her head, more sensations than thoughts, and her body was suffused in a deep, dreamy languor that overlaid the urgent restlessness without banishing it. She was conscious of her body in a way she'd never known before. Her hands moved over the shape of herself, startled to discover that her nipples were hard, lifting to her touch. Her skin was warm and tingling as she passed her hands over her belly, feeling the sharp points of her hipbones. Her thighs parted as her hand slipped between them, feeling the moistness of her core, a strange sensitivity; and the aching restlessness rushed upon her anew.

She stroked herself, slipping slowly into a rich and sensual dreamland as the warmth crept over her and her body sank deeper into the feather bed. The twisting images in her head lost definition, and her eyes looked upon a soft, pulsating landscape without form or substance that drew her onward into the enticing glow.

She dreamed of a mouth on hers, of a kiss so light and delicate, it barely stirred the air. She dreamed that her hands were moving over a warm, powerful male body and she was inhaling the scent of skin, a scent that she knew but that was nonetheless unfamiliar and didn't belong to herself. She dreamed that her own skin now touched the skin of the body beside her, that fingers caressed the small of her back, touched her breasts, swept down her form in long strokes that soothed the urgent restlessness but replaced it with a clearer sense of need. She dreamed her lips were parted for a different kiss, one that took driving possession of her mouth; she heard little feline cries in the humid sensual darkness of the deep enclosing feather mattress, and she dreamed they were her own. She dreamed a joyous fulfillment that seeped into every cell of her body, that made her soul sing in wonder. She dreamed that every part of her body was lost in this other shape, that her limbs were joined with his, that as she dipped into the darkness of oblivion and surfaced again into the warm glowing light of her dreamworld, she was entwined with this other body, that her eyes were in her fingers and in her skin where it touched his. She dreamed the moments of joy again, the long slow sleepy slide into infinite pleasure, before she slipped again into the dim green glowing light of the sleep-filled trance.

The dream was with her all night, her body moving through the strange landscape, ever new and more glorious waves of pleasure breaking over her as she adapted herself with such wonderful ease to the large, powerful frame that both took from her in possession and gifted her with itself.

And when she awoke, her eyes opened onto washed-out sunshine, and she was alone.

But the dream was still with her. Its threads still twined beneath her skin, its images, blurred now, still inhabited her mind. She lay burrowed in the feather mattress, bewildered and disoriented, conscious of a sense of loss as she tried to recapture the defined images of the night.

Her hands moved over her body. She was naked. But she had not gone naked to bed. The disorientation faded, but her confusion increased as the room took shape in the early-morning light and memory returned.

She was naked and her skin felt different: used, marked, in some strange and frightening way. There was a soreness between her legs—not a bad soreness, more a kind of warm and satisfied ache. Tentatively, she touched herself. There was a stickiness, and when she drew her hand away, she saw the smear of blood on her fingers.

Octavia kicked aside the covers and sat up. There was blood on the sheet and on the inside of her thighs . . . not much blood and it wasn't flowing anymore.

It was three weeks before her next monthly terms. She lay down again, pulling the cover to her chin, and stared up at the chintz tester. The highwayman had raped her.

But he hadn't. Nothing had happened that hadn't brought her the most exquisite pleasure. She had believed herself to be dreaming, but the evidence was overwhelmingly in favor of reality.

And reality meant consequences. She might have conceived a child. *How had it happened? How could such a thing have happened? What had happened to her that had allowed such a thing to happen?*

Slowly, Octavia sat up again and took stock. She was alone in the room. The fire now burned brightly, and someone had scraped the snow from the outside of the window so that a feeble ray of sunlight fell across the wooden floor.

Where was the highwayman? Her dream lover? If she hadn't been so devastated, Octavia could almost have laughed at herself for such whimsical folly. *What had happened to her? What had taken her into that fantastic world?*

Her eyes fell on her clothes, neatly arranged over the chair by the fire. Her boots had been polished. At the end of the bed were draped her shift and the velvet robe.

"Lord of hell!" she muttered. There was nothing dreamlike about this morning.

The door opened. A booted foot stepped into the room. The door closed. Each sound unnaturally loud. Dreams and fantasy trances vanished into the woodwork.

Octavia turned her head warily. The highwayman walked over to the bed. Except that it wasn't the highwayman. Oh, it was the man of her night, but she no longer looked upon the plainly dressed gentleman of the previous day.

"Who are you?" Her voice came out as a whisper. The highwayman was dressed in a suit of turquoise velvet, rich Mechlin lace edging his shirtsleeves, his hair concealed beneath a high-dressed powdered wig, a black solitaire at his neck, tied in a bow around his starched white stock. He wore a sword and jeweled buckles on his red-heeled shoes, but his smile was straight out of the night.

"At this moment, Miss Morgan, Lord Rupert Warwick is at your service." He bowed with a deep flourish, and as his hand moved through the ray of sunlight, the amethyst on his finger sparked fire.

Octavia's voice shook with angry confusion, banishing the lingering memories of joy. "So yesterday you were Lord Nick, the highwayman, and today you're Lord Rupert Warwick, the courtier. Do you have other identities, sir? Or have I met all of you?"

The slate-gray eyes glittered and his voice was lightly humorous. "Not quite, my dear. But all those you need to know . . . at least for now."

"You gave me your word you would not ravish me."

"I did not ravish you." His eyes met hers steadily.

"But I may now be with child," she said in a low voice, accepting his flat denial by default.

"No, Octavia, you need have no fear of that." He sat on the bed beside her, reaching for her hand, his expression gentle, his eyes reassuring. "I don't know what you know of such things, but there is a device that a man may use. It's known as a condom."

"You used such a thing?" She stared at him in disbelief, unable to imagine how in that entwined dream such a practical, wide-awake consideration could have come to him.

He nodded. "I would not hurt you, my dear. You must believe that."

"But how did it happen? I don't understand how it happened."

"You invited me," he said simply.

Had she? It seemed impossible . . . and yet she had been willing. More than willing.

"I don't understand anything," she said helplessly.

"There's nothing to understand. We enjoyed each other last night as men and women do. And now you will get up, dress, break your fast, and I will take you home to your father."

And it would be over. She would forget all about it. All about that tangling of limbs in limbo.

Perhaps.

Chapter 4

🦋 Someone had mended the torn lace of her fichu—
Tabitha, Octavia presumed. It was difficult to imagine the
hard-eyed, unfriendly Bessie performing such a service.

She dressed before the fire in the deserted bedchamber.
The highwayman had said that he would await her in the
parlor where breakfast was ready and had left her to herself.
She was grateful for this unusual consideration from a man
who hitherto had shown little or no recognition of a need
for personal privacy. Indeed, after such a night of intimacy,
she'd expected him to offer to lace her corset at the very
least.

Octavia felt very peculiar as she retied the leather
pouch around her waist, its weight a comforting reality. She
was confused, dismayed, and yet curiously excited, as if
she'd crossed some boundary and entered uncharted territory. Her body was thrumming and her skin felt acutely
sensitive. Surely she must look different after such a night.
She gazed at her image in the spotted cheval glass on the
dresser, but only her familiar face stared back at her. There
was a deeper glow to her skin, perhaps; maybe her eyes
seemed larger; and her hair was springing out around her

face in a dark unruly halo as if it had been vigorously combed with a thousand fingers.

She took up the comb on the dresser and dragged it through the tangling waves. Her hairpins were still in the parlor where she'd taken them out to dry her hair yesterday afternoon. Just yesterday!

Octavia sat down abruptly, staring into the fire, trying to connect herself with the person she'd been yesterday . . . before she'd stolen the highwayman's watch. She *was* different this morning, but time would distance the memories of that fantastic dream. She would return to Shoreditch, to the drear poky lodgings above the chandler's, to her father's self-obsessed world of the mind, to the daily struggle to maintain some sense of pride as she negotiated with the pawnbroker and the grocer, the butcher and the baker, and darned her stockings and mended her gowns, and went out on the streets to risk her neck whenever there was nothing left to pawn.

She jumped as the door suddenly banged open to admit Bessie, who stood with arms folded, leaning against the doorjamb. "There's some of us as 'as work to do," she announced. "Can't lie abed all day like some bleedin' lady muck. You goin' to get yer breakfast, or shall it be cleared away?"

Octavia stood up and fixed Bessie with a cold stare. "If you'd tell me what my shot is, I'll pay it directly, my good woman."

Bessie raised an eyebrow. "Hoity-toity! I don't want yer money. Nick takes care of us. And you'd best make 'aste. He's got work of 'is own to do this day."

"If he has something to say to me, he can come and say it himself," Octavia declared. "I'll join him in five minutes. Perhaps you'd like to pass that on."

The air stilled as she stared fixedly at the woman with all the hauteur of Miss Morgan of Hartridge Folly. Bessie stared back and then sniffed, spun on her heel, and marched out, banging the door behind her.

With a little smile Octavia returned to her dressing, arranging the repaired fichu at the neck of her gown. She felt much better after that little show of assertion. Gathering up her cloak, gloves, and muff, and leaving her hair loose around her shoulders, she made her way to the parlor.

The passage was chilly, and there was a reek of stale beer and pipe smoke wafting up the stairs from the tap-room. She could hear the thumping and dragging of furniture, a splash and slop of water as a bucket was emptied over the dirty flagstones, the thunder of a full barrel being rolled over the cobbles in the yard outside. The Royal Oak was preparing for the new day.

At the door to the parlor, she unconsciously squared her shoulders before raising the latch. The highwayman was sitting at the same round table addressing a platter of sirloin. Again she had a shock as she took in his costume, the strong lines of his face, the broadness of his brow, accentuated by the high-piled powdered wig, his eyes somehow more piercing, their gray deeper and darker.

He rose with a courteous bow as she entered. "My dear Miss Morgan, I trust you passed a pleasant night."

The mischievous undercurrent to the formal pleasantry took her breath away, and she was momentarily speechless. Then she saw the laughter in his eyes, the twitch of his firm mouth, the air of complicit enjoyment.

"Phantasmagoric, I believe, sir."

Something—a touch of discomfort—flickered across his eyes and then was gone. "Pray come to the table, ma'am." He moved to draw out the chair for her. As she sat down, he swept the loose mass of cinnamon hair from her neck and bent to kiss her nape.

Octavia shivered; her skin prickled beneath the warm pressure of his lips and the cool rustle of his breath. No, she thought, she was not at all the same person who'd entered this room yesterday. Her head dropped beneath the pressure of his mouth and she yielded to the delicious sensation, her body responding as if to a familiar stimulus . . . only her mind didn't recognize it in the same way. Her mind had not been in her body during the long, joyous hours of the night, and only her flesh knew this for what it was.

How had it happened? How could she have been both waking and sleeping through such a pivotal experience?

But she could find no answer. It had happened, and her body now was telling her it wanted it to happen again, only this time with the participation of her mind.

As he straightened, she jerked her head up abruptly, shaking her hair loosely over her shoulders again. "What turns Lord Nick into Lord Rupert Warwick?" she asked with an assumption of carelessness, wondering if he was aware of her reaction to that caress. One glance at his smiling expression told her the answer.

"Business," he said, returning to his own seat. "I have different kinds of business to deal with and so different roles." He passed her a slice of ovenwarm bread, as white and fragrant as any to be found in the most exclusive establishments. "Coffee?"

"Thank you." She took the slice and watched as he poured coffee from a pewter pot into a deep china mug. "And what business is it that requires the role and costume of a courtier?"

"Court business, I should imagine," he said dryly, lifting the lid on a chafing dish. "Bacon, Miss Morgan?"

"I beg your pardon, I didn't mean to pry." Octavia's mouth thinned at this implicit reproof. "No, I don't care for bacon."

"Mushrooms, then?" he inquired with a solicitous air, gesturing to another dish. "Or perhaps a slice of ham? I'm sure Bessie would prepare you eggs if you would prefer."

"I doubt very much that Bessie would give me the parings of her nails," Octavia declared with vigorous vulgarity, digging the spoon into the platter of mushrooms.

Lord Rupert—for so she decided she must call him in his present guise—merely laughed and sat back, one hand curled around a tankard of ale. "She's not one for the niceties of polite discourse, I grant you."

"Her impertinence is insufferable," Octavia snapped, buttering her bread. "And I would prefer to pay my own shot, Lord Rupert."

Her companion frowned and said in the tone she'd

heard so often since the previous day, "No, I don't think so."

"What do you mean, you don't think so?" she demanded in irritation. "That is what I wish to do and I intend to do it. So perhaps you would inform Bessie of that fact, since she wouldn't hear it from me." She speared a forkful of mushrooms and carried it to her mouth.

"No, she wouldn't hear it from you," he agreed. "You see, she is not accustomed to taking orders from anyone but me. And she's well aware that you're my guest. I trust you have no fault to find with my hospitality," he added gently. "I should be very sorry to think so after we've had such a pleasant time together."

Octavia's cheeks warmed. Was he saying that he was paying for her favors? That, after all, he did see her as a whore?

And dear God, why shouldn't he? She'd behaved like one.

Abruptly, she pushed back her chair and stood up. "I bid you good day, sir. I trust Lord Rupert Warwick's business will prosper." She stalked to the door, flung it wide, and allowed it to bang shut on her departure.

Her feet flew down the stairs, and she burst out into the bitterly cold sunshine, breathing deeply, drawing the icy air into her lungs, enjoying the sharp, cleansing pain. Everything was white and pristine under its fresh carpet of snow, the usual filth and squalor of the narrow streets buried a foot deep. The sky was a brilliant blue, and her boots crunched across the snow as she turned to the side of the inn in search of the stableyard. They would presumably have some kind of vehicle for hire that would carry her back to London.

The only vehicle in the yard, however, was a carter's dray drawn by two massive shire horses. Ben and the gangly lad were unloading barrels. Ben glanced up at Octavia and then carried on with his work as if she weren't there. She stood awkwardly, looking around. The stable buildings were all closed up, and she knew that one horse, at least—the highwayman's roan—was stabled within. Maybe, if they didn't have a carriage or gig she could hire, they would have a riding horse. She wasn't dressed for riding, but that was the least of her worries.

She walked up to the dray. "Your pardon, innkeeper, but I wish to hire a carriage of some kind . . . or a horse, if that's all you have available."

"Not a livery stable, miss," Ben said shortly. "Don't 'ave nuthin' like that." He was less rude than Bessie, but no more helpful.

Octavia slipped her hand into the slit in her skirt, feeling for the pouch. Maybe a little gold could persuade Ben to change his mind. She shivered, realizing for the first time that in her dudgeon she'd abandoned her cloak, gloves, and muff, in the highwayman's parlor. It was a damnable nuisance. Apart from the fact that she'd freeze to death between there and Shoreditch without them, they were her only decent outer garments, essential to her appearance as a respectable young woman of good family, and she couldn't afford to replace them. But the prospect of trailing foolishly back to the parlor after such an exit was insupportable.

"Death and damnation!" she exclaimed, stamping her foot in the snow in frustration.

"Forgot something, Miss Morgan?"

Lord Rupert's suave tones came from the back door of the inn. He stood in the doorway, a dark velvet cloak lined in turquoise silk hanging from his shoulders, a black tricorn tucked beneath his arm. Over his other arm he carried Octavia's cloak, her muff and gloves in his hand.

"I'm afraid you really will catch your death of cold if you persist in running around in just that flimsy gown," he said, coming toward her, shaking his head in reproof. "It's really not at all sensible, you know."

Octavia ground her teeth as he carefully placed her cloak around her shoulders and fastened the clasp at the neck.

"Gloves," he said, taking her hand and manipulating her fingers into the right holes as if she were a toddler who couldn't manage to do it for herself.

"For heaven's sake, I can do it!" Octavia jerked her hand away and pulled the glove on before snatching the other from his hold. "I wish to hire a carriage to take me home, but the innkeeper says they don't have such a thing. I suppose they might find one on *your* authority," she added bitterly, drawing the hood of her cloak over her hair. "Well, I daresay I can walk."

Lord Rupert sighed. "You are a most obstinate and perverse girl. I said I would convey you home this morning, and I will do so."

"I have no wish to be beholden to you any further, sir. *I am not for sale!*" To her fury she could hear tears in her voice, and even the knowledge that they were tears of anger rather than hurt didn't make such weakness easier to bear. She turned from him with a rough gesture as if she would push him away.

"You are not beholden to me, Octavia. If anything, the shoe is on the other foot." He laid an arresting hand on her arm. "I told you yesterday that you were given to extravagant language and distempered freaks, and I must confess I begin to find them irritating, not to mention insulting in the present instance. Whoever said anything about buying you?"

"You want the phaeton, Nick?" Ben called before Octavia could reply to Lord Rupert's exasperated question. "Freddy'll 'ave it ready in a trice."

"My thanks, Ben."

"So they *do* have a carriage," Octavia exclaimed. "I knew it."

"As it happens, it's not for hire," his lordship said. "It belongs to me, you see."

"You own your own carriage?" Incredulous, she forgot her earlier distress. "A common highwayman owning a carriage!"

"Ah, but you see, Miss Morgan, I am no more a common highwayman than you are a common pickpocket. I thought we'd established that."

He drew an enameled snuffbox from his waistcoat pocket and flicked the lid. Taking her hand, he turned her wrist upward and delicately dropped a pinch of snuff onto the blue-veined skin. Raising her wrist, he took the snuff, his eyes smiling at her as he did so. "The scent of a lady's skin enhances the delicacy most powerfully."

Octavia was again at a loss. She had the conviction that no lady would permit a gentleman such a liberty, and yet she wanted to meet his smile with her own.

She was saved from having to respond by Freddy, who appeared from one of the stable buildings leading a pair of chestnut geldings harnessed tandem between the shafts of an elegant phaeton.

" 'Ere y'are, Lord Nick. Shiny in't they? I groomed 'em for an hour last even." The lad beamed proudly as the horses clopped over the cobbles. "Fresh they are, too," he added.

"They haven't been out for several days," Lord Rupert agreed, running a flat palm down the nose of the leader before going to the side of the carriage. "Miss Morgan, permit me to hand you up." He held out his hand.

Octavia could see no sensible alternative, although pride was a hard nut to swallow. She climbed into the phaeton, disdaining the proffered assistance.

Lord Rupert followed her with an agile leap. "Let go their heads, Freddy." The lad obeyed, and the chestnuts leaped forward toward the entrance to the stable.

Octavia huddled into her cloak, covertly watching her companion's profile as he steadied the horses and took them neatly through the narrow gates. She was disinclined for conversation, and, fortunately, Lord Rupert seemed content with his own thoughts until they'd crossed London Bridge and were once more in the town streets familiar to her.

Her companion spoke as they drove up Gracechurch Street. "You must help me now, Miss Morgan. We came over London Bridge because I remembered Shoreditch, but I'm at a loss to know which direction to take from here."

"If you would take me to the Aldgate, sir, I can find my own way from there," Octavia said. Regardless of the intimacies they'd shared in her strange trance, regardless of the knowledge that he too pursued a crooked course in the world, she didn't want him to see the poverty of her dwelling. The highwayman's life seemed far removed from the grim realities of her own daily struggles; indeed, he appeared to lead a life of luxury and authority in whatever guise he chose to present himself, and the contrast with her own circumstances was too mortifying.

"No, I don't think so," he said. "I believe I will take you to your door."

"And if I choose not to direct you, sir?"

He cut her a sidelong look that to her chagrin was brimful of amusement. "Then I should be obliged to take such steps as to ensure your compliance, my dear."

Octavia wondered vaguely what such steps would entail. Whatever it was, she didn't think she would enjoy it. She told herself firmly that she had no reason to be ashamed of her circumstances; the man was a highwayman, a common felon. She sat up with an air of determination. "Very well. But you won't object to stopping first at the pawnshop on Quaker Street, I trust. I have some things to redeem."

"Not at all," he said politely. "And anywhere else you please. I am quite at your disposal, ma'am."

She directed him through the maze of East End streets, admiring his skill and the way he appeared oblivious of the stares and catcalls that greeted such a magnificent equipage in such an area. Ragged children huddled on street corners, beggars paraded their mutilations, coming dangerously close to the phaeton when Lord Rupert was obliged to draw rein for some obstacle in his path. A young woman darted out in front of the horses, clutching a baby to her breast. She raised her haggard eyes in pitiful appeal and thrust out her hand, clawlike, over the side of the carriage as they slowed and swerved to avoid a tribe of mangy, starving dogs in pursuit of a squalling cat.

Lord Rupert barely looked at her, but he reached into his pocket and tossed her a coin. She fell back, scrabbling as it tumbled to the cobbles. "She'll only spend it on gin," he said with a cold indifference that made Octavia wince, although she understood the helplessness that lay behind it.

"Perhaps," she said. "But it might make her more patient with the babe."

"And when she's killed herself with gin, what will become of the child?" The same detachment was in his voice, but Octavia had the feeling that it was a mask for his true feelings. She'd learned her own ways of dealing with the horrors that lived and breathed on these streets, and she knew that if one didn't cultivate a certain detachment, one would be driven mad with the knowledge of one's own powerlessness.

She made no answer to the rhetorical question, merely directed him to Quaker Street. He drew up outside the sign of the three golden balls and beckoned an urchin who was standing in the frozen gutter, his bare feet wrapped in a piece of sacking.

"Can you hold the horses, lad?"

"I'll go in on my own," Octavia protested. "I'm quite accustomed to doing so."

Lord Rupert ignored this, merely jumped from the carriage and held up a hand to assist her to alight. The urchin had hold of the leader's bridle, a grin splitting his filthy face as he contemplated his amazing good fortune.

Octavia shrugged and stepped down, aware of the curious eyes at windows, their less inhibited neighbors staring openly out of their doors at the extraordinary sight of Mistress Forster's lodger riding in an elegant carriage in company with an exquisitely dressed gentleman. Her companion opened the door, the bell tinkling merrily. He held it for her, and she stepped into the crowded, dark, and frowsty interior, where the smell of old clothes and dust and mold dominated.

"Come fer yer pa's books, then?" An elderly man, so short his head barely topped the counter, blinked into the dimness. "Thought you wasn't comin' to pay yer installment this week. Due yesterday, ye were. Lucky I didn't sell 'em on ye."

"Oh, come on, Jebediah. Who around here would buy Plato's *Republic* and two volumes of Tacitus?" Octavia said dismissively, reaching into her skirt for the pouch. She extracted several coins and dropped them onto the counter.

"And two shillin' interest," Jebediah said, scooping the coins off the counter. "Due yesterday."

"There's no interest if I redeem them," Octavia declared. "So don't try your sharp tricks on me."

Jebediah gave her a toothless grin and stared over her shoulder at the tall, elegant figure of her companion. "I see ye've got yerself a gennelman friend, then. Quite the gent 'e looks."

Octavia flushed angrily. "Fetch me the books, Jebediah."

"All right, all right." He shuffled off in his carpet slippers into the dark recesses of the noisome shop, returning after a minute with three leather-bound, gilt-edged volumes. "Doin' ye a favor, I am, takin' these fer good money," he asserted. "Much good they'd do me if'n ye didn't come fer 'em."

"Exactly what I said," Octavia agreed serenely, opening the volumes and clapping them together. A cloud of dust filled the dank air. "But don't think I'm not grateful, you old rogue." She dropped another shilling on the counter. "That's just to show my appreciation."

"Come into a fortune 'ave ye?" He picked up the coin and bit it to test the metal, his shrewd eyes returning to the silent figure of Lord Rupert. "A fortune, eh? Well, who can blame ye when yer face is all the fortune ye've got."

Octavia swung on her heel and made for the door, clutching her father's books. There was no hope of explaining the true situation to Jebediah, who saw what he saw. And what he saw was what everyone would see, she knew. Yet another reason for not wishing to be taken to her door by her present companion. Lord Nick would have been one thing, but Lord Rupert Warwick was quite another.

"How often do you have to go through that?" Lord Rupert inquired, handing her up into the phaeton. "He seemed a most encroaching gentleman."

"Too often, and he is," she responded, examining the books carefully. "He's a rogue, and I'm always afraid he might decide he has a use for the pages and tear them out.

Papa frets so whenever a book is missing from his library, I dread to think how he'd react if they came back damaged."

"Does that rogue hold anything else of yours?" Rupert handed the urchin a sixpence before taking the reins again.

"Some jewelry . . . a few pieces that belonged to my mother," Octavia said with a shrug. "So long as I pay the weekly installments, he'll keep them. Although I can't imagine when I might ever wear them again."

It was said without self-pity, Rupert noticed, but he also heard the underlying bitterness. "One day you might get your revenge."

Octavia laughed without humor. "And it snows in hell, I suppose."

"One can dream," he returned neutrally.

"One can dream," she agreed. "Turn right at the end."

They drew up at a narrow, crooked house in a narrow, crooked lane, the overhanging eaves on either side almost touching to form a roof across the street below. A grimy window on the ground floor exhibited the wares of the chandler. Above, a bow window jutted into the alley.

"My thanks for your escort," Octavia said formally, jumping down before he could come to her assistance. "I trust you'll be able to find your own way back."

"Yesterday I said I felt obliged to restore you to the bosom of your family," Rupert said with a bland smile, alighting beside her. "I haven't changed my opinion. I look forward to meeting your father."

"Your horses?" Octavia pointed out without much hope. Why on earth would he want to pursue this?

"I'm sure someone will be glad to walk them for me." As he spoke, Mistress Forster's eldest appeared in the doorway of the chandler's, staring with wide-eyed astonishment at his mother's lodger in such company.

"Walter, take his lordship's horses," Octavia directed with a resigned sigh. "Pray come within, sir." She went ahead of him into the shop, wondering what frame of mind her father would be in. Sometimes he could be charming, at others so irascible, it was impossible to stay in the same room with him.

"Well, I never did. Just where've ye been, Miss Morgan? Out of my mind with worry, I've been." A short, round lady bustled out from the back of the shop. "Your pa's been creatin' something chronic. He would 'ave it somethin' 'ad 'appened to ye, although I told 'im ye'd taken shelter from the storm, like as not, and . . ." Her voice died as she took in Octavia's companion. "Well, I never did." She dropped an awkward curtsy. "Well, I never did."

"This is Lord Rupert Warwick, Mistress Forster," Octavia said hastily. "He's come to visit Papa. This way, sir." Without waiting for a further word from the astounded landlady, she swept up a narrow flight of stairs at the rear of the shop, his lordship on her heels.

Rupert inclined his head in a slight bow as he passed Mistress Forster. The woman seemed relatively well disposed toward her lodger, he thought, and the chandler's shop, while hardly affluent, had a prosperous air at odds with the grimness of the surrounding streets.

It wasn't the depths of poverty, but Octavia was as out of place as a diamond in a coal mine.

He followed her lithe figure up the creaking rickety wooden stairs, her hair glowing a burnished reddish brown in the light thrown by a candle in a wall sconce illuminating the tight spiral curve halfway up. At the head of the stairs she paused before a closed door, turning toward him as he came up to join her on the narrow landing. The golden eyes were lambent in the dimness, her full lips slightly parted as if she were about to say something. A warm pink tinged the high cheekbones, highlighting the creamy translucence of her complexion.

A veritable diamond—and if she would listen to him, then she would have a setting worthy of her.

Smiling, he cupped her chin in his gloved hand, but she pulled away sharply.

"You would ruin what reputation is left to me!" she hissed in whispered outrage. "It's bad enough that I've been absent all night and then appear with you in this compromising fashion. The gossip will be all over the neighborhood, but there's no need to spell it out for them."

He drew back, offering an apologetic bow, although his tone was ironical rather than conciliatory. "Forgive me, Miss Morgan, I didn't mean to presume. Now, may I pay my respects to your father?"

Octavia opened the door and stepped swiftly into the room. "Papa, I have brought you a visitor."

Rupert came in and closed the door behind him. The room was small and ill furnished, lit with smelly tallow candles and an oil lamp, a small coal fire spluttering in the hearth. A narrow cot with a patchwork quilt stood against one wall. The bow window looked out on the street, and sitting at a desk set in the window was a thin man with a mane of white hair and the same tawny gold eyes as his daughter. He wore an old-fashioned, full-skirted coat of faded gray velvet, his shirt was collarless, and a coarse horse blanket was draped over his shoulders. His features were well-defined beneath a bony, prominent brow, but he bore an air of distraction as he turned toward the door, frowning at the new arrivals.

"Octavia, child, where have you been? I do believe you weren't here all night."

"No, Papa, I was caught in the storm," Octavia said, hurrying across the room, bending to kiss him. "Lord Rupert Warwick was so kind as to bring me home." She gestured to her escort, who stepped forward and bowed.

"An honor, sir."

Oliver Morgan's eyes suddenly and disconcertingly sharpened. "And what have you to do with my daughter, sir? I've no time for courtiers."

"No, a trivial breed, I agree," Rupert said with a disarming smile. "Your daughter found herself in some difficulties in the storm, and I charged myself with the duty to return her to you. She has come to no hurt." His eyes flickered toward Octavia, standing still and silent beside her father.

"Lord Rupert was all kindness, sir," she said quietly. "And as you see, I am returned safe and sound. I've redeemed your Plato and Tacitus." She placed the books on the table.

"Ah," her father said, instantly distracted from whatever paternal anxieties had momentarily pierced his absorption. "I have been at my wit's end without Tacitus. There's a reference I've been trying to chase up for this article. . . ."

His voice faded to a murmur as he began to leaf through the volume. "I believe it's in the sixth book. . . . Ah, yes, here we are. . . . Forgive me, sir . . . but this is most pressing. My publishers await this article most urgently. Octavia will dispense the hospitality of our poor quarters." He gestured vaguely with a thin but elegant hand before picking up his quill from the inkstand.

Rupert accepted this dismissal and stepped back. He looked around the room again. The smell of boiling pudding wafted from below, and he saw the cracks in the wainscot, the broken leg of one of the two straight-backed chairs at the square table in the center of the room, the cushionless settle beside the fireplace, the cracked and grimy windowpanes. And he realized that the warmth of the fire was superficial, doing little to combat the bone-deep chill in the cheerless room.

Octavia had no illusions about her present lodging and met his returning gaze with a challenging defiance. He'd insisted on coming up, but she'd tolerate no pity from him.

Rupert made no comment, however, and walked to the door. "I'll bid you farewell, Miss Morgan. I have an engagement at noon."

So simple, so casual, so final. But what else had she expected? What else had she wanted?

"I'll accompany you to your carriage," Octavia said formally.

"No, please, there's no need," he returned. "I can find my own way out."

"I'm sure you can, sir. Nevertheless, I am not inclined to be deficient in the obligations of a hostess despite the meanness of my lodging."

Rupert made no answer to this challenging statement, merely walked ahead of her down the narrow staircase, through the shop and out into the street.

"Farewell, sir." Octavia curtsied and gave him her hand. "I should thank you, I imagine, but I'm at a loss to know what for, since you would have had no need to escort me home if you hadn't carried me off to Putney in the first place."

"I ask no thanks," he said solemnly, raising her hand to his lips as he bowed. "On the contrary, I extend my own." A raised eyebrow and a half smile left her in no doubt as to his meaning, but she wouldn't respond in kind, merely stepping back out of the road, waiting like a patient and polite hostess for him to depart.

The phaeton bowled away down the narrow lane, and Octavia turned to go back indoors. Life had been dreary before; now its bleakness made her want to weep. For a few glorious hours she'd participated in a shared dream, but it was over now. She had the memories, but in her present misery she knew they would torment rather than soothe.

Chapter 5

℘ The Earl of Wyndham advanced through the crowded antechamber at St. James's Palace, pausing to greet acquaintances, bowing low to the influential, a word of greeting and compliment always ready to his lips as he drew closer to the salon where the king was holding his levee.

He approached the circle of intimates gathered around the king. The Prince of Wales was standing to one side, glowering and tapping one foot in obvious boredom. He loathed the court ceremonies that his father conducted with rigorous and punctilious order, and his expression brightened when he saw the earl.

"Ah, Philip, come to pay your respects, eh?" He offered his snuffbox. "Damnable waste of a morning this, don't ye think?"

Philip Wyndham accepted a pinch from the royal snuffbox. "Thank you, sir." He smiled at the corpulent young man whose face shone red beneath his elaborately powdered coiffure. "When Your Highness attains your majority, you will no doubt have your own establishment," he said in soothing accents.

"Yes, and you may be damned sure that'll see the end of my attendance at these damnable levees," the prince declared morosely, raising his quizzing glass to examine the assembled company.

Accepting this withdrawal of attention as dismissal, the Earl of Wyndham bowed low, took his leave of the prince, and approached the circle around the king, hoping to catch His Majesty's eye.

George was listening to the Duke of Gosford. The king's head was courteously inclined to one side to catch the elderly duke's wheezing tones. "Quite so, my dear sir," the king murmured every now and again. "Quite so, Gosford."

Philip drew closer until he was standing just behind his father-in-law. When the king raised his head, he would be bound to see him.

The duke's discourse died in a fit of coughing. He buried his face in a handkerchief, and the king considerately looked away and caught the slate-gray eyes of the duke's son-in-law. "Wyndham, beautiful morning, what . . . what?"

"Indeed, sir." Philip bowed low. "We must be grateful yesterday's blizzard was no worse."

"Oh, the princesses are quite delighted with the snow," the king said genially. "They're all for skating on the lake . . . plaguing their mother for permission." A fond parent, he chuckled indulgently. "And how's Lady Wyndham, recovered I trust from her lying-in, what . . . what?"

"She's waiting on the queen this morning, I believe, sir." Philip bowed low again.

"And the child . . . thriving, I trust?"

"Yes, sir. You are too kind."

The king smiled a dismissal and the earl stepped backward. He offered his father-in-law a brief bow and a curt good morning. The man warranted no further attention. He was an old dodderer and had served his purpose. Once the marriage with Gosford's daughter was celebrated, the Earl of Wyndham was assured of a place in inner court circles and had no further use for the duke's connections.

He melted into the throng, aware of the eyes, some

speculative, some envious, that had watched his audience with the king, gauging its length and intimacy. It had been a very personal conversation, one that marked the Earl of Wyndham as one of the king's favored courtiers.

Philip moved into a window embrasure and discreetly dabbed his forehead. It was hot in the room and his scalp itched beneath his wig. He adjusted the frills of his lace cravat and regarded the Prince of Wales still holding his place across the room. It was no secret that the prince caused his parents endless heartache with his intransigence and debauchery, but at least the king had a male heir. Unsatisfactory in his character, perhaps, but a strong male heir nevertheless. An unsatisfactory male heir was better than some mewling female brat.

An unconscious frown drew his thin eyebrows together, and one hand moved involuntarily to the small pocket in his waistcoat. His fingers brushed the silk pouch, feeling the shape of the tiny ring it contained. One of the three Wyndham rings. It had been slipped on his finger at birth—his to keep in trust for his own son.

Letitia would have to do better next time . . . if he could bring himself to cover her pallid, doughy body again. The woman revolted him. And even more so since the birth. She whimpered and sniveled whenever he came near her. He knew from the doctors that she hadn't healed properly from the birth and was plagued with intermittent bleeding, but of course she was far too nice in her sensibilities to mention such a thing to her husband, who was presumably expected to divine from the air whether she was in a fit state to receive his advances.

He took snuff and debated whom he should approach next. The Duke of Merriweather would probably warrant cultivation. He had the king's ear when it came to patronage.

As he moved away from the window, his eye caught that of a tall, elegant man in a turquoise velvet suit, standing in the doorway to the salon.

There was something about the man that raised Philip's hackles. Something about the way he stood so negligently surveying the room as if no one in it could have the power to engage his interest. Philip had seen Lord Rupert Warwick around in the last few months, an ever-present face but one who strangely never attempted to attract the attention of the king. He had his own friends among the most reckless and extravagant sets and was known to drink deep and play high at the gambling tables and to have an eye for the ladies that was generally reciprocated. But he was something of an enigma. It was generally held that he'd lived on the Continent until his arrival in London some months ago, but no one seemed to know much else about him. But he was personable, well-bred, and apparently wealthy enough to live as high as he pleased, and that was all that counted.

Lord Rupert continued to hold his eye, and Philip inclined his head in a small bow of acknowledgment that was immediately returned with a flickering smile. Philip turned away, frowning. There was a quality to that smile that disturbed him. It had a complicity to it, as if the man held some secret that he believed Philip shared. Which was patently absurd, since, apart from a brief introduction, he didn't know the man from Adam.

Suddenly wearied of his attendance in the hot salon, the Earl of Wyndham made his way to the double doors leading into the antechamber. To his annoyance he found Lord Rupert Warwick ahead of him, standing in the doorway almost barring his exit.

"I give you good day, Lord Wyndham."

"And I you, Warwick." Impatiently, Philip moved to step around his accoster, but somehow Lord Rupert seemed still to be in his way.

"I trust Lady Wyndham is in good health," Lord Rupert inquired, taking a delicate pinch of snuff. "And your daughter, of course."

That smile flickered again over the well-shaped mouth, but the slate-gray eyes remained impassive, resting on the earl's countenance. "Even daughters ensure the continuation of one's line . . . and it's to be assumed that where daughters lead, sons will follow."

His smile broadened and he bowed again before Philip

could find a suitable response. "Excuse me, I see Alex Winterton trying to attract my attention." And he strolled off, leaving the earl frowning in annoyance, wondering why he felt as if the man had been making mock of him and why he'd been left without a word to say for himself.

His exit now clear, the earl returned to the antechamber. Margaret, Lady Drayton stood by the window in a circle of eagerly attentive gentlemen. She plied her fan vigorously, and her high, trilling laugh could be heard clearly above the chatter that sounded like a rookery of starlings. The air, overheated from the fires and myriad candles, was heavy with perfume and pomade, overlaying the ripe odor of stale bodies, less than immaculate linen, and the richness of brocade, velvet, and silks stiffened with use.

Philip crossed the antechamber and joined the circle around Lady Drayton. She smiled at him over her fan, her heavily rouged cheeks startling against the white of her high-piled powdered coiffure, her china-blue eyes round beneath the thin arch of her plucked eyebrows. He noticed that she was wearing the emerald eardrops he'd given her after their last assignation. He didn't recognize the silver fillet she wore in her hair and wondered sourly which of the incomparable beauty's other admirers had been responsible for that. Maybe even the half-senile Viscount Drayton.

That ancient and unsavory nobleman, a footman in attendance, was sitting in a bath chair by the fire, nodding to himself and muttering, his wig askew, his linen spotted. It was common knowledge that he turned a blind eye to his wife's lovers and opened his purse strings wide for her so long as she accommodated his own particular, and it was rumored somewhat deviant, needs. But Margaret had been educated in a King's Place nunnery, and there was little she wouldn't do in the realms of fleshly intercourse if the price was right.

She was still damnably desirable, though, Philip thought, his loins stirring as his gaze rested on her ripe bosom, two powdered white globes swelling from her décolletage. Her nipples would be rouged, he knew, and it would take but a fingertip to expose them above the lace edging . . .

"La, my lord, but you're drooling like a starving wolf," trilled Viscountess Drayton, tapping his wrist playfully with her fan. "I do believe his lordship would like a bite." She brushed the back of her hand carelessly over her breasts and laughed around the circle all of whom joined in, eager to participate in the mockery.

Philip flushed but hid his discomfort. "Indeed, my lady, when such lush fruit is on offer, a man must be but half a man to refuse the invitation to dine."

"Bravo, my lord." Laughing, the lady linked her arm through his. "Lud, but it's monstrous hot in here. You may escort me to my carriage before I melt."

"Before the paint runs," murmured a gentleman sotto voce as the two moved off, the lady's flowing silk saque billowing around her.

"Wicked, Carson!" The comment was accompanied with a rich, merry laugh.

Peter Carson turned, grinning. "But irresistible, Rupert."

"Oh, I grant you that." Rupert watched Lady Drayton and Philip Wyndham disappear into the farther chamber. "She is a veritable Toast."

"Oh, most certainly," his friend agreed. "But I'd be careful about dabbling in that pond, myself. It's said she had to have a course of mercury not so long ago."

"Calumny!" Rupert chided mockingly. "One of the High Impures with a dose of clap? Surely not."

"I'll lay odds Drayton gave it to her," Peter said with his lazy grin. "The old goat's been riddled with it for years."

"A stiff price to pay for a title and fortune, even for such a one as Margaret," Rupert observed, raising his glass to examine the doting viscount, still nodding beside the fire, apparently unaware of his wife's departure.

"Life's short, my friend, best to make it as sweet as possible," Peter said easily. "On which subject, do you play at Lady Buckinghamshire's tonight? It's said the stakes are to be a hundred guineas at the faro table."

"Worth the visit, then," Lord Rupert observed. "Yes, you may look for me there, Peter." He bowed and moved off in the wake of the Earl of Wyndham and Lady Drayton.

Philip still physically resembled the twelve-year-old boy of eighteen years ago, although the angelic golden curls were concealed beneath his wig. But his physique was still willowy, his countenance smooth, his eyes clear, with that ingenuous glow that had deceived so many. Only his twin could see the cold flicker of calculation beneath the openness of his expression, the occasional cruel twist to the wide, full mouth. He could see them because he knew them. He knew his brother almost as well as he knew himself; it was a knowledge that ran with the blood in his veins. They were like two sides of a playing card, only the reverse image was strangely distorted.

Rupert moved aside into an alcove from where he could watch his brother relatively unobserved. He often found himself doing this even when it would serve no useful purpose. It was a form of obsession, watching his brother's lips move, watching the way he walked, smiled, exerted his charm. Occasionally, Rupert could see a resemblance to Gervase in the way Philip tilted his head, the upward sweep of his lashes, and always in the slate-gray eyes that were his own. But whenever he saw that resemblance, he would be swept with a crimson tide of rage so powerful, it made his hands shake and brought black spots dancing before his eyes.

In the dark reaches of the night he still heard Gervase's scream on that long-ago cloudless summer day. And he heard Philip's taunting voice. *"You tripped him. I saw you."* He felt again his own desperate helplessness as his twin said, *"They'll believe me. They always believe me."*

And they had, of course. As they had always been ready to believe the worst of young Cullum, who was always in trouble, sometimes of his own making and sometimes not. He'd become accustomed to it and accepted the earl's brutal beatings with a philosophical stoicism. But this had been different. The accusations had not at first been open. How could one accuse a boy of deliberately murdering his brother? Philip said he was sure it had been an accident, that Cullum had been playing a game when he'd tripped up Gervase. Of course Cullum couldn't have known that Gervase would go over the cliff when he lost his balance. Cullum would never had done such a stupid thing if he'd thought.

But the whispers had grown and the stares had become more accusing. He couldn't walk into the village without feeling the eyes on his back, hearing the forest fire of whispers as he passed. And in his own house it was worse. Everyone looked at him askance. His father had beaten him with such savagery that even now he carried the memory in his nerve endings, but worse than the physical pain had been the contemptuous rejection that had banished him to dark corners of the house, where he lurked, ignored, while Philip basked in the golden warmth of approval. Philip, who had tripped Gervase. Only no one would believe that truth; to speak it would bring worse punishment.

But Philip was the younger twin by two minutes, and Gervase's death had left Cullum heir to the earldom. His father had raged at this, had screamed at lawyers when they'd told him nothing could be done to change the laws of primogeniture. Philip could not be his heir while his elder brother lived. So his elder brother, in a black despair, had removed himself.

Twelve-year-old Cullum Wyndham, no longer able to endure the taunts and the cruelties, seeing himself through his father's eyes—the unworthy and unwanted son—almost believing himself now that his twin's version of the accident was the truth, had disappeared one day. His clothes had been found on the beach. It was said in the village that the guilt had been too much for him. And the Earl of Wyndham had rejoiced in the heir he wanted.

And now Lord Rupert Warwick stood in St. James's Palace and observed his twin. It had been eighteen years since he'd called himself Cullum Wyndham, and he felt no regrets for the loss of the tormented lad who'd staged his own death. But the desire for vengeance burned like hot coals in his vitals. He had come to claim his birthright, and Octavia Morgan would help him to that end.

Deciding abruptly that he'd indulged his obsession sufficiently for one day, Rupert left the palace. He would play a waiting game for a few days, give Miss Morgan time to reflect on the pleasures of his company—and, he hoped, to miss those pleasures—give her time to see herself as someone who could indulge in them again and turn such indulgence to their mutual advantage.

The Earl of Wyndham dallied pleasantly with his mistress, who seemed disposed to single him out this morning for special attention. "Will you drink tea with me this evening, my dear sir?" she inquired prettily as he escorted her to her carriage at the end of the levee.

"Do you expect a large party, ma'am?"

The viscountess seemed to consider this as she stepped aside to avoid a dog's bone left carelessly by some royal pug in the middle of the corridor. "One or two, perhaps."

The earl smiled, responding smoothly, "I'm not sure I've the time to share your favors, my dear ma'am."

Lady Drayton was so unused to objections to the way she played her courtiers that she looked at him in surprise and, in even greater surprise, realized that there was something chilling behind the sweet smile, that the clear gray eyes held a shadow of menace. It was a look that the Countess of Wyndham would have recognized immediately, setting her knees atremble, but Lady Drayton had no reason to fear the Earl of Wyndham. And yet she found herself saying, "Well, if you would prefer a tête-à-tête, Philip, I'm sure it could be arranged."

"Such indulgence, my dear. I protest you do me too much honor." His smile broadened and he took her hand, raising it to his lips. "Shall we say at five-thirty?"

The viscountess inclined her head in agreement, displeased with the arrangement merely because it had been pressed upon her. Yet she couldn't decide how she had come to agree so tamely. The earl had become a trifle possessive in recent weeks, and she'd intended to tease him a little, to show him that she was not to be taken for granted. But, instead, she'd agreed to cancel her previous arrangements and accede to a private assignation that would inevitably end in her bedchamber.

*P*hilip handed her into her coach with the Drayton arms emblazoned on the panels and set off to walk home down Pall Mall. Wyndham-House stood on the south side of St. James's Square, a handsome mansion that never failed to give the earl a surge of pride in his heritage. He preferred it to Wyndham Manor, a house he privately considered an unimposing and inconvenient country seat with all the disadvantages of early Elizabethan architecture. However, he had plans to add a Palladian facade and a new wing, which would give the house more consequence.

His brothers had both loved the manor, he remembered. They'd probably turn in their respective graves if they could see the architect's plans for improvements. The idea made him smile as he ascended the steps to his own front door.

His wife was hastening down the stairs as he entered the hall. "Oh, my lord, I trust you haven't forgotten that we expect my father and the Westons for dinner," she said, offering him a timid smile.

"No, I haven't forgotten," he replied. "But did I not also desire you to invite Lord and Lady Alworthy?"

Letitia's color ebbed. "Yes, yes, indeed, sir. But I thought it was perhaps unwise—"

"Let us conduct this discussion in the salon," her husband interrupted icily as a footman crossed the hall to the dining room.

Letitia followed him into the salon, her eyes frightened in her pale face. She was a plain woman, five years her husband's senior. Her predilection for sweetmeats showed in her ample waistline and the folds beneath her chin.

"Now, let me understand this, my dear," Philip said

softly as she closed the doors behind them. "I directed you to invite the Alworthys, and you took it upon yourself to ignore my order. Is that correct?"

"Oh, no . . . no . . . not precisely, sir. It was not precisely like that," Letitia stammered.

"Then, pray, how precisely was it?" There was no sweetness on his face now, no curve to the full lips, no light in the slate-gray eyes.

"My father . . . my father and Lord Alworthy have an old quarrel," Letitia explained, her color fluttering in her cheeks like the wings of a wounded bird. "I felt it might offend both of them if they were invited to dine at the same table."

"So you took it upon yourself to go against my express commands," he repeated softly. *"Come here!"*

The shocking contrast of the shouted command with his previous softness drained all color from her face, and she flinched, cowering against the door.

"Did you hear me?" His voice was once again soft and silky.

In terror Letitia took a step toward him, one hand raised to ward off the blow she knew was coming.

"Put your hand down," he commanded in the same tone, and his eyes were alight with a vicious pleasure as he saw her terror and her helplessness.

Whimpering, she lowered her arm, ducking her head, hunching her shoulders.

His hand lifted and he watched her shake, but he had no intention of marking her face, not when they had dinner guests arriving within the hour. Her father was an ineffectual fool, but even he might remonstrate at his daughter's bruises.

Philip lowered his hand slowly and instead caught her wrist, twisting it, watching the pain blossom in her tear-filled eyes. When she cried out, he released her.

"In future, when I give you an instruction, you will carry it out to the letter," he said coldly. "Won't you, my dear?"

Letitia was sobbing, massaging her wrist that hung limp and useless, the strength wrenched from it.

"Won't you my dear?" he repeated.

"Yes, my lord," she whispered through her tears.

He stood looking at her as she shrank back against the wall, tears tracking down her plump cheeks, her gown of purple taffeta increasing the sallowness of her complexion. Her lank, mousy hair was mercifully concealed beneath an enormous curled and powdered wig, but some ill-fated instinct had led her to decorate the coiffure with purple ostrich feathers that waved ludicrously above her dumpy figure. "Oh, get out of here," he said in disgust. "And paint your face. You're as sallow as a jaundiced frog."

Letitia turned and fled the room, sobbing as she ran across the hall, no longer able, after two years of this marriage to summon the pride to conceal her shame from the servants. She stumbled up the stairs and along the corridor to the nursery wing, where her only comfort lay sleeping peacefully in her cradle.

The nurse glanced once at her mistress's tear-streaked countenance and tactfully lowered her eyes, busying herself with her sewing.

"Has she been good, nurse?" Lady Wyndham asked finally, in an attempt to sound collected and in control.

"Oh, she's an angel, my lady," the nurse said, smiling fondly at the sleeping Lady Susannah. "Good as gold."

Letitia gently stroked the smooth, round cheek. The earl had no time for the child because she wasn't a son. He resented her, and Letitia knew what happened to those who displeased her husband whether through their own fault or not. She shuddered, swearing to herself that somehow she would protect this little mite from the viciousness of her father.

Chapter 6

"Papa, I have brought your medicine." Octavia hurried into the room, throwing off the hood of her cloak. Her father, convulsed with a fit of coughing, appeared not to have heard her.

"Much good it does," Oliver Morgan declared when his racking coughs had died. "Waste of good money. I've a greater need for parchment for my article, but I'm cursed with an undutiful daughter who . . ." Another fit took him, and he hunched over in the narrow cot, his white head quivering with the spasms.

Octavia was too used to the reproaches to be upset by them. "You know the doctor said you must have the medicine," she said calmly, shaking the small bottle that had cost three of their precious shillings. "The apothecary made it up stronger this time." She uncorked the bottle and carefully measured a dose into a small tin cup.

"Here, Papa." She came over to the bed, holding out the cup.

Oliver glowered at her, his eyes sunken in his hectic cheeks. "It's this damnable coal smoke," he grumbled. "If we had a decent wood fire, I wouldn't have this cough."

"There are no logs in London," Octavia said patiently.

"At least not for the kind of money we have." She bent to support his shoulders, holding the cup to his lips.

For a minute it looked as if he was going to refuse the medicine; then, with a muttered "Odd's bones, I'm not on my deathbed, child," he straightened abruptly, snatched the cup from her, and drained it.

Octavia hid her relief, since it would only exacerbate his ill temper. The medicine contained a hefty dose of opium and it would bring him much-needed sleep as well as quiet the cough. In fact, it would bring them both peace and quiet for as long as he slept.

She set the cup on the table with the medicine bottle and bent to plump up the thin pillows and smooth the coverlet. "Can I bring you anything else?"

"Parchment," he said, lying down again with a little moan of weakness that he couldn't conceal.

"If I buy parchment, I must pawn the Virgil," she pointed out. "And you can't work without that. I must find some work tomorrow, anyway, as we're down to our last five shillings. I'll buy some vellum then."

A look of distress crossed her father's eyes, and his air of petulance faded, replaced for a moment with an expression of dismayed bewilderment. Then his eyes closed.

Octavia moved softly away from the bed to the hearth, still huddling in her cloak. A small fire burned, and she added a few more coals. It was extravagant, but the day was bitter and ice crusted the inside of the windows. Most of the time her father didn't really comprehend his own part in bringing them to this wretched pass. But there were moments, like just then, when he would deliberately turn away from the understanding and from the mental distress it caused him. He had so few inner resources for dealing with poverty and deprivation. It was true he'd never had to go without anything in his life before—but, then, neither had she.

She blew on her hands and held them over the meager orange flame, the noxious fumes of the sea coal thick in her lungs. But at least they had a fire, unlike the majority of their neighbors, shivering in icy garrets and cellars. By those standards Oliver Morgan and his daughter were rich beyond the dreams of avarice.

The sound of his breathing, rasping but deep, came from the bed, and Octavia relaxed, wondering how to spend the few hours of blissful solitude. At Hartridge Folly she would have curled up with a book, or played the harpsichord in the music room, or walked in the shrubbery.

Vigorously she scolded herself for bootless repining. It only made the situation worse, and since this was now her life and it was unlikely to change, she'd do well to make the best of it. But it had become much harder to do since her adventure with the highwayman. Adventure—was that the word for it?

She gazed into the fire wishing she had more concrete memories of that night. She'd lost her virginity, and yet she had the sense only of a magical dream. The waves of pleasure that nibbled at her memory had no shape or reality. She couldn't reproduce them because they had no reference to anything she understood. She knew only that a pair of slate-gray eyes and a rich, merry laugh accompanied her through the long night hours, and she awoke every morning to a sense of loss and acute disappointment, her body feeling alone and somehow wasted. The uselessness, the waste of her self in her present existence, overwhelmed her when she looked down the long, dark tunnel of the future.

Tea and toast, she thought with sudden inspiration. Not a terribly extravagant indulgence—a nursery indulgence. Mistress Forster would let her have some butter, and she could make tea and toast bread and slather on the butter so it melted and soaked into the crisp toast.

Her mouth watering, she leaped up and took the kettle downstairs to fill it at the water butt in the yard behind the shop. Mistress Forster was kneading suet pastry on the kitchen table, her muscular forearms bare, her hands caked with flour. She looked up and offered her lodger a nod of greeting.

" 'Ow's yer pa, then, dearie? Coughin' somethin' terrible 'e was in the night."

"He's sleeping now," Octavia said. "The apothecary

made up some more medicine for him. Do you think you could let me have twopence worth of butter?"

The landlady shook flour off her hands and took a wooden paddle to the thick golden pat on a dish in the middle of the table, slicing off a generous wedge. "This do ye?"

"Thank you." Octavia put her two coins on the table. "I've a fancy for tea and toast."

"Don't go spoilin' yer appetite, now. There'll be a nice steak-and-kidney puddin' for dinner." Mistress Forster returned to her suet. "Ye'll need to break the ice in the water butt, dearie."

Octavia went out into the yard, shivering despite her cloak. She took a stone and cracked the ice on the surface of the water, making a hole big enough to dip the kettle, trying not to get her gloves wet as she filled it. Then she hurried back into the warmth of the kitchen and up the narrow stairs to her own chilly apartments.

Her father was still asleep. She put the kettle on the hob to boil and then threw off her coat, fetching a fur-lined wool dressing gown from the massive armoire that contained both their scanty wardrobes. She slipped the garment on over her thin gown and returned to the fire, where she speared a slice of bread on the toasting fork and then knelt to hold the fork to the spurting flames. Soon the delicious smell of toasting bread filled the room, and she allowed her mind to drift back into the past, to the warmth of nursery fires and the sweet taste of honey on her tongue . . . to the blazing fire in the Royal Oak at Putney and the rich aromas of roasting mutton and oyster soup . . .

There was a sharp rap at the door, and Octavia jumped, startled from her reverie. Mistress Forster, presumably. She bade the knocker enter, taking the half-toasted slice of bread off the fork, burning her fingers as she turned it over to brown the other side.

"Something smells appetizing."

Octavia dropped the toasting fork. The voice was so unexpected, and yet as she heard it, she realized how it had been echoing, an ever-present memory, in her mind since she'd last seen him. It was a voice that belonged to the dream, and she had thought never to hear it again.

"You?" She stared at her visitor. He wore his own hair, unpowdered and tied at the nape of his neck with a black ribbon. A high-collared caped cloak of dark broadcloth hung from his shoulders, opened to reveal a striped-green silk waistcoat and dark-green coat over britches of the softest beige kidskin. Simple enough garb, and yet in this drear room he looked as exotic as a tropical butterfly in an English meadow.

Rupert bowed with a touch of mockery. "Yes, Miss Morgan. At your service." He glanced toward the bed and closed the door softly. "Your father's sleeping?"

"He's unwell," she replied, still on her knees before the fire, still too astounded to absorb this visitation. "But he won't wake for several hours."

The lid of the kettle rattled vigorously as the water boiled, and she reached automatically to lift it off the hob. "Will you have some toast and tea?"

It struck her as a ridiculous offer even as she made it, but she could think of nothing else to say. She was over-poweringly conscious of the threadbare wool of her dressing gown, of the tattiness of the fur edging the deep cuffs. Five years ago it had been the most elegant garment of dishabille, and it was one piece of luxurious clothing she hadn't sold after the catastrophe because it was warm and practical. But it was now no longer luxurious or even particularly warm as the fur lining grew thinner and flatter with continual wear.

"If you have a second fork, I could toast my own," Rupert said, throwing off his cloak and taking a seat on the settle. "I trust this isn't your dinner. It seems very insubstantial." He had taken in the threadbare condition of the clothes she wore when not out about her street business, but he was more aware of the pale oval beauty of her face, the lambent tawny eyes, the thick burnished rope of hair hanging over her shoulder.

Octavia passed him a second fork. "We board with Mistress Forster," she said with a touch of hauteur, carefully measuring tea into the pot and pouring on the boiling water. She didn't add that they shared the landlady's table only when they could afford the one and sixpence a day. Today they had it, but tomorrow she would have to venture into London's West End to raid the pockets of the rich. Just the thought made her sick with apprehension, so she chose not to anticipate the terror.

"I see," Rupert said neutrally, spearing a slice of bread and holding it to the fire. "Do you skate?"

"Skate?" It was such a non sequitur that she almost laughed aloud. "On ice?"

"Is there another kind of surface suitable for skating?" He turned his bread on the fork, raising his eyes to her flushed, startled face.

"I used to skate on the horse pond every winter as a child," she said, passing him a thick china cup of tea. "Why?" It was quite ridiculous to be kneeling before the fire sharing nursery tea and discussing winter memories of her childhood. And yet, paradoxically, it felt natural.

"Well, I thought we might amuse ourselves thusly this afternoon," he answered, blowing on his tea in a most inelegant fashion. "The Serpentine is frozen, and everyone who can beg or borrow a pair of skates is out there."

"Unfortunately, I can do neither," she said with constraint. "Skates didn't seem a particularly useful item when it came to packing up to leave Hartridge Folly."

"Your family home?"

"In Northumberland."

"You must have been used to the winter cold."

"It was a different kind of cold from London's. This is damp and bites to the marrow," she said. "I'm accustomed to a dry, bright cold."

He buttered his piece of toast. "I have two pairs of skates in the phaeton. One will certainly fit your boots." He took a bite, licking butter from his lips with an appreciative nod.

Octavia nibbled her own toast, forcing herself to recapture reality. An invitation to go skating on the Serpentine belonged in some other world; it had nothing to do with this dank, freezing room and her father's stertorous sleep and the prospect of Mistress Forster's steak-and-kidney pudding for dinner, followed by her own chill garret bed as soon as the light faded. Candles and fires after dark were a luxury they couldn't afford.

Rupert leaned over, caught her chin, and wiped away a smear of butter with his handkerchief. "Well, what do you say?"

"I can't leave my father."

"Nonsense. You've done so before, and you'll do so again. The estimable Mistress Forster will attend to his needs. Besides, I have a proposal to make to you . . . one that I trust will be to our mutual advantage."

"A proposal?" In the light of their past dealings, Octavia could think of only one kind of proposal he might term mutually advantageous. Her eyes narrowed, their golden glow fading to be replaced by a cold glitter. "And just what might that be, pray?"

"I'll explain later."

"Oh, please don't stand on ceremony, sir." Her voice was dangerously low, her eyes icy slits. "I'm sure I can hear it here as well as anywhere."

Rupert stood up. "No, I don't think so," he said in habitual fashion. "It's rather complicated."

Octavia jumped to her feet, two bright flags of color flying in her cheeks. "I told you once, my lord, that I am not for sale. Perhaps you think I should be flattered, grateful even . . ." She gestured with expressive contempt at the room. "But I must beg to disillusion you. *I want nothing of your proposals.*"

"Even if you *were* for sale, my dear, I would not be buying," he returned coolly. "I can assure you I've never had the need to pay for a woman's favors."

"Get out!" Octavia commanded with low-voiced ferocity. "You may think that whatever happened the other night gives you the right to insult me, but I tell you straight, sir, that you are a slubberdegullion whoreson and a pox-accursed cur!"

There was a moment of stunned silence; then Lord Rupert began to chuckle, his rich, merry laugh sending the dark shadows scurrying into the corners like bats escaping the light. "Well, that's telling me!" he declared. "What an impressive vocabulary of insults you have, Miss Morgan."

"Get out!" she repeated, folding her arms and glaring at him with an intensity of loathing.

"No, I don't think so." He glanced around the room, and his eye fell on the armoire. "You will need your cloak and muff—and boots . . . the ones you were wearing at Tyburn will do, I believe."

He strode over to the wardrobe. Octavia bounced across the room in his wake, grabbing his arm as he moved to open the door. "Will you listen to me?"

"With the greatest of pleasure, when you start to say something sensible," he responded equably, freeing his arm and opening the door. "But so far you've prated little but arrant nonsense. Now, let me repeat . . . and listen carefully." He drew out her cloak. "I have a proposal to make to you, one that involves no buying or selling. . . . Put this on. . . . One that I trust will work to our mutual advantage." He bent and lifted out her boots. "Put these on, the skates will strap to them easily. Now, where's your muff? Ah, here it is."

With an air of great satisfaction, as if he'd just found a treasure trove, he reached up to the shelf for her fur muff and gloves. "There you are. Now hurry and dress, while I go and explain to the good Mistress Forster that you will not be back until after dinner."

"No . . . wait . . ."

He paused at the doorway and turned with an air of exaggerated patience. "Now what?"

Octavia stared at him, at a loss. She was rarely at a loss and didn't care for the sensation in the least. "You cannot take over in this way," she said finally, aware of how lame it sounded.

"If I don't, my dear ma'am, it's clear that nothing will be accomplished," he responded. "Join me below stairs, please. I trust it won't take you more than a couple of minutes."

He was gone, pointedly leaving the door slightly ajar.

Octavia chewed her lip, glancing at the still-sleeping figure in the cot. The opium had done its work well, and she knew that when he awoke, her father would be groggy and disoriented. Mistress Forster could attend to him perfectly well until she returned, and she would be able to pay her from the proceeds of tomorrow's expedition.

If Lord Rupert wasn't going to propose that she become his mistress, then what could he possibly have in mind?

A weak ray of sunshine crept through the grimy window, falling across her face as she stood in indecision and confusion. And suddenly she knew that it didn't matter what he had in mind. Whatever it was, it was going to alter her present circumstances in some way.

And the sun was shining and the Serpentine was frozen and there was a long afternoon to be spent outside this drear prison.

She threw off the shabby dressing gown. Flinging the cloak around her shoulders, she slipped quietly from the room, closing the door gently behind her, then ran down the stairs, unable to control a surge of exuberance that seemed to belong to some long-ago and half-forgotten person.

Rupert was talking with Mistress Forster at the foot of the stairs as she jumped down. The landlady was looking gratified, and Octavia caught the glint of silver in her palm.

"You go an' enjoy yerself, dearie," Mistress Forster said, winking. "Yer pa'll be fine wi' me, never you fear. I'll leave the back door unlocked fer ye, jest in case you comes back late, like." Another broad wink.

Octavia winced, but an attempt to deny the construction the woman was putting on the circumstances would be pointless. She wouldn't be believed, and, indeed, how should she be? What more natural than for a young woman down on her luck to accept the protection of a well-to-do gentleman? No one would think less of her around there—in fact, quite the opposite.

She followed Lord Rupert out into the street, where his phaeton stood, drawn by the same pair of chestnuts. He handed her up, springing up behind her, and within ten minutes they'd left the mean streets behind and were driving through the City toward the Strand.

"Of course, I'll repay you whatever you paid Mistress Forster," Octavia said.

"Of course," he agreed affably. "I merely thought you might be easier in your mind if you felt you were not under an obligation to the good woman."

"I expect to be in funds again tomorrow," she said a little stiffly.

"Going apicking again, Miss Morgan?" He raised an eyebrow, turning his horses onto Piccadilly.

"I do what I have to," she retorted. "You of all people should understand that."

"Who said I didn't? I do wish you wouldn't keep jumping to conclusions," he complained.

Octavia was silent for a minute, then said, "I can't help jumping to conclusions when everything's shrouded in mystery. What is this proposal, my lord?"

"All in good time," he said, turning through the Stanhope Gate into Hyde Park. The park was alive with carriages, riders, and pedestrians strolling through the crisp air engaged in the vital society business of seeing and being seen.

If things had been different, she would have been part of this elegant throng, Octavia thought bitterly. She would have had her season, made a good, convenient marriage, and this would have been her world for life.

"I imagine your father lost his money before you had a season?" her companion observed, again evincing that uncanny ability to tune into her thoughts.

Octavia shrugged. "I don't suppose I would have enjoyed it anyway."

"Fibber," he accused gently. "How old are you, Octavia? Twenty-one, two?"

"Twenty-two," she answered. "On the shelf." She laughed, but without humor.

"I doubt you'd have been happy with some fribble for a husband," Rupert remarked, raising his hat and bowing to a lady curtsying to him from the path beside the road. "You're too fond of asserting yourself, Miss Morgan, to make a compliant wife for a conventional husband."

Octavia wondered if this was a compliment or a criticism, but it had the ring of truth. "You seem to have a great many acquaintances," she observed, adding tartly, "An extraordinary number for a highwayman, if I might be so bold."

He chuckled. "But here, Miss Morgan, I am no more a highwayman than you are a pickpocket."

He drew rein on the bank of the Serpentine beside a small wooden hut where a man was dispensing mugs of chocolate and chestnuts roasted over a brazier. A group of lads stood ready to walk the horses of the skaters, swooping and dancing over the ice to the strains of "Greensleeves" played by a troupe of gypsy musicians.

Rupert sprang down from the phaeton, a pair of wooden blades in his hands. "Allow me, Miss Morgan." Standing beside the carriage, he deftly strapped the pair of blades onto the soles of her boots, then reached up and lifted her out. He carried her easily to the ice and set her down at the edge, his hands still at her waist until she got her balance. "Tell me when you're steady."

Octavia stood for a minute, getting the feel of the blades; then by way of answer she gave an exultant little chuckle. Turning out of his hands, she swooped away on a one-foot glide that carried her almost into the middle of the lake.

Spinning, she waved at him as he sat on the edge to strap on his own blades.

She reminded him of a canary released from a cage as she swooped over the ice, and he could hear her joyous laughter as he skated over to her. "Isn't it wonderful!" Her eyes shone, her cheeks pinkened with the cold, her lips parted in a flashing smile.

A current of desire shocked him, jolting his belly. He wanted her with an incontinent urgency he didn't remember ever feeling for a woman before. But he wanted her like this, awake and laughing, glorying in the purity of physical sensation, not responding involuntarily to the dictates of a sensual trance.

She caught his expression and the laughter died abruptly, but her face remained open and alive, her lips still parted, her eyes still shining, but with a different light now, a light that matched his own. She glanced around the thronged lake with an almost desperate air, as if she too were in the grip of an urgent hunger that required instant gratification.

"Come, let's skate farther along, away from the crowd," he said, his voice a husky rasp, cutting the invisible line of tension between them. "I want you to listen to what I have to say without interruption." He took her hand, drawing her around the lake to a less densely populated spot.

Octavia knew now that she was going to agree to anything he suggested. She was riding a tide of reckless inspiration like a piece of tumbling flotsam, and she would come ashore wherever the tide tossed her. She no longer knew how to define herself, knew only that the ghastly present and the equally grim future it would spawn must be avoided. She must seize the lifeline offered her or drown in the mire of hopelessness.

"So?" she invited, doing a neat three-turn that brought her round to face him. "What is your proposal, Lord Rupert?"

"A marriage," he said simply. "A social deception that will enable you to be revenged upon the men who ruined your father and will enable me to be revenged upon my own enemy."

Octavia's jaw dropped. Whatever she'd been expecting, it hadn't been this. "What do you mean, a social deception?"

"Well, of course I'm not suggesting we really go through a marriage ceremony," he said, as if it were axiomatic. "Only that we present ourselves to society as a newly married couple. I have sufficient funds to set up the enterprise, a good house, servants, carriages . . . And then we will exchange vengeances."

The light and laughter had faded from his face now, and his eyes were that arctic gray she'd seen before, his expression almost masklike. "Who . . . who deserves your vengeance?" she asked tentatively.

"A man . . . the man responsible for the misunderstanding that drove me to the road," he said, his voice curt. "You need know no more. Your task will be to pick his pocket. The item you will steal lies very close to his person, so you will have to become intimately acquainted with him. If necessary, you will have to seduce him. . . . I don't believe you will find it difficult. He's a man who can be relied upon to covet what belongs to someone else . . . a man whose vanity is such that the attentions of a beautiful and desirable woman will sweep away his guard."

Octavia heard the venom in his voice, and its chill slowed the blood in her veins.

"I must seduce him?" she said slowly, struggling to grasp the implications of such a suggestion. "You would have me lie with this man?"

"Yes, if it should prove necessary in order for you to remove from his person the object I require to achieve my own ends," he said with cold detachment. "Somewhere on his body he carries at all times a certain very small ring, a ring to fit a baby's finger. You will steal that ring."

"But how can you be certain he always carries it?" She looked at him in confusion.

He knew because he carried his own. Philip would obey the same Wyndham tradition—superstition some might call it—that the ring must never leave its owner's possession until either he placed it on the finger of his own son or it was buried with him.

"I am certain of it," he said evenly.

And then, when he had the ring that fitted with his own, Lord Rupert Warwick would step forward and present himself as Cullum Wyndham, the legitimate Earl of Wyndham. Philip would be destroyed, his pride in the dust, his influence ashes in the wind.

"You would have me lie with this man?" Octavia repeated slowly, seizing on this one aspect as at least vaguely comprehensible in this extraordinary conversation.

He looked at her, his eyes snapping into focus. "In exchange for which I will engage to ruin the men who ruined your father, and I will return your fortune to you."

"But how will you do that?"

"I'll explain how later, when we have set the stage. But you may be assured that I *will* do it, and when our little play is over, you and your father will have your fortune and property returned to you."

It was too much to absorb. Whatever scheme he might have for fulfilling his side of such a preposterous bargain, the whole idea was impossible to take in. How could she deliberately set out to seduce and lie with a stranger?

"And this . . . this marriage?" She grasped feebly at another loose end waving just beyond her comprehension.

"When we have no further use for it, then we will part company," he said easily. "You will have what you sought, and I will have what I sought. We will create some fiction to ensure that you can live the life you choose."

"You would have me play the whore," she stated flatly. It was suddenly the only simple fact. The highwayman *was* attempting to buy her as he would buy a whore. But not for his own enjoyment—as a tool to accomplish his own purpose.

"My dear, in this world liaisons are common practice, and women who practice them are not called whore," he returned. "I would ask you to do what countless other women are doing, have done before you, and will do after you. Your mind and emotions will not be engaged."

And what of her father? Where did he come into all this scheming? But, presumably, the highwayman hadn't given Oliver Morgan a thought. And at this moment, even to Octavia, her father's role in all this seemed irrelevant.

Octavia turned away to hide from Lord Rupert the confused responses chasing across her countenance. Her voice sounded stifled to her ears as she said, "And what of us? Of this counterfeit marriage? Is that also to incur no involvement of the mind and emotions?"

He was silent for a moment, then said dryly, "I doubt that."

When she said nothing, but remained half-turned from him, he continued in a quiet, matter-of-fact tone, "But if you would prefer to play the part of my wife only in name, then I would respect that."

"Is that what you would prefer?" Still she wouldn't look at him.

"No," he said readily. "No, I would not wish that."

He put a hand on her shoulder and gently turned her toward him. His eyes were soft now, his mouth smiling. He cupped the curve of her cheek in his gloved hand. "If you enjoyed the other night, Octavia, I swear to you, sweeting, that it was as nothing compared to what could be."

Octavia swallowed, felt herself melting under the buttery warmth of his voice, the heat of his eyes, the lascivious intent of his words.

"We would have all that together, and we would be revenged upon our enemies. And we would make fools of every one of the vain, posturing idiots who see nothing of the world that exists beyond the sugary confection of their own making."

Suddenly he laughed and the intensity was broken. "Will you teach them such a lesson, Miss Morgan?"

She looked behind her at the brightly clad crowd of skaters in their furs and velvets, secure in the knowledge that food and warmth and pleasure were theirs for the taking. She saw the children, barefoot in the frozen gutters, eyes sunken in their starved faces. The women sprawled in the mud, clutching an empty gin bottle to their breasts, the neglected babies wailing thinly on the ground beside them.

She and the highwayman knew that other face of London. Dirk Rigby and Hector Lacross had ensured that she and her father would know that face intimately for the rest of their lives.

What the highwayman was proposing was preposterous. It was madness. But if it could work . . . ? Oh, if it could work, it would be an adventure to challenge fantasy.

But if it was necessary, could she cold-bloodedly seduce some unknown man?

For such a purpose and such an adventure? Yes, of course she could. The Octavia Morgan who would have reacted to such a prospect with revulsion had long lost her delicate sensibilities. They were a luxury she hadn't been able to afford for three years. Besides, it wasn't as if she were still a maid. And for a woman who regularly risked her neck picking pockets for a living, simple seduction was nothing. It wouldn't put her neck in a noose . . . unless, of course, she was caught stealing the ring.

An icy shiver ran down her spine. In this scenario there'd be no crowd in which to lose herself.

But she wouldn't be caught. She was too good at it for that. Too deft and quick. She would *not* be caught. And when it was done . . . oh, when it was done, there was the promise of restitution and once again a future worth having.

Rupert watched as her thoughts flew across her expressive countenance, and he read them as clearly as if they were written on the pages of a book. He didn't need to hear her speak her agreement and said after a minute, "Do you know the names of the men who robbed your father?"

"Men?" she said scornfully. "Swine."

He inclined his head in grave acceptance of this correction. "Do you know the names of these swine?"

"Dirk Rigby and Hector Lacross. Do you know them?"

"They're intimates of the Prince of Wales, I believe," he said. "I know them to bow to across a room. But it shouldn't be difficult to deepen that acquaintance. Do they know you?"

Octavia shook her head. "I was away when they approached my father. He was taking the waters at Harrowgate, and they made themselves agreeable to him. . . ." She shrugged.

"Good. Much better that they don't know you," Rupert said briskly. "Come, you're getting cold. Let's skate back to the crowd. I would show you your prey."

Octavia remained where she was for a moment. "But what are we to do with my father while we're putting the world to rights?"

"Tuck him up safe and warm with his books," the highwayman said airily. "Whatever you wish to tell him, I'll back you up to the hilt."

Octavia knew perfectly well that her father wouldn't ask awkward questions in case he didn't like the answers. He'd accept a change of circumstances with his usual insouciance, at least on the surface.

So there it was. A wild, fantastic contract lay between them. Her life was about to change out of all recognition. And yet there was nothing to mark such a momentous bargain. Not even solemn words of acceptance.

He had taken her hand and was drawing her along beside him as they skated back to the wider area where the fashionable skaters congregated. She glanced sideways up at his face and saw no change. She'd half expected to see some demonic twist of satisfaction to his mouth or in his eyes, but he wore his usual expression of cool serenity with the little half smile of mockery playing over his lips.

"Over there," he said quietly. "Do you see the tall, slender gentleman in the burgundy velvet cloak with the fair curly hair? That is the man who calls himself the Earl of Wyndham."

"Calls himself?" Octavia looked sharply at her companion. "You mean he is not?"

"No, he is not," said the Earl of Wyndham quietly. "But for the purposes of our little play, you will acknowledge his title."

What mystery was this? Octavia looked across the ice toward the man she was to seduce and rob. He was skating with marked grace, his willowy figure moving elegantly around his partner. He wore no hat, and his unpowdered hair was a luxuriant tumble of golden curls, restrained at the nape of his neck with a scarlet ribbon. He was too far away for her to form any impression other than of fair grace and assured elegance.

"What is he to you?" she asked, unconsciously whispering.

"My enemy."

Such a flat, bald declaration left no room for further questioning, but she tried. "And you won't tell me how he has injured you."

"It's not necessary for you to know that."

Octavia was silent, continuing to gaze across the ice at the man who called himself the Earl of Wyndham. The hairs on the nape of her neck prickled, and a shudder rippled down her spine, but it was not the cold.

Excitement or apprehension, she didn't know. But, then, the two were for the moment inextricable.

Chapter 7

⏤ "Come, let us go and seal our contract."

Lord Rupert's calm voice sounded like a pair of cymbals crashing into the tight circle of her own thoughts.

"I promised you dinner," he said, smiling now, no mocking twist to his mouth, and a gleam in his eye that turned her knees to water.

"Where?" The question came out muffled, and she cleared her throat. "Where should we have dinner?"

"Well, now, that rather depends on you, Miss Morgan." The gleam in his eye intensified. "I'm sure we could dine well enough in the Piazza, if you'd care to. And I'll drive you back to Shoreditch afterward.

"Then, again," he continued in a musing tone, "your gown is hardly in the first style of elegance, and the Piazza is popular with society. There's nothing more uncomfortable than feeling underdressed in such circumstances. You could always keep your cloak on, though . . . but that might make eating dinner rather awkward, don't you think?"

"It might," Octavia murmured equably, waiting with interest for this tortuous reasoning to reach its conclusion. It seemed Lord Rupert had his own plans for the evening, and this apparent desire to solicit her opinion was little more than a game.

"Of course, we do have a great deal to discuss," he went on. "Details and suchlike. It might be easier to do that in a more secluded place than a crowded eating house on the Piazza."

"I'm sure you're right," Octavia assented demurely. "What do you suggest, my lord?"

He stroked his chin, frowning reflectively as if seriously considering a variety of options. "Well, I would suggest the Royal Oak," he said finally. "We would be perfectly private there, and I can vouch for the dinner."

"But it might be difficult for me to return home afterward," Octavia pointed out consideringly. "It would be very late to drive from Putney to Shoreditch, and then, of course, you would have to drive back again."

"There is that," he said, nodding. "Yes, certainly, one must take that into account."

"Of course, Papa will probably sleep through until morning, and Mistress Forster will take care of him if he wakes . . . so I could always lie overnight at the Royal Oak," Octavia mused with the same due consideration. "That might be a solution, don't you think?"

"It might," he agreed. "Should you wish to do that, ma'am?"

"If such a solution would perhaps advance my education in some way, it might be said that we could kill two birds with one stone," Octavia murmured, her eyes lowered as she idly traced a pattern on the ice with the toe of her skate.

"Oh, I could guarantee it," Lord Rupert declared. "It would be a most efficient use of time."

"And efficiency is vital when planning such a grand enterprise, sir."

"Just so."

Octavia raised her eyes and met his gaze. Laughter danced across the cool gray surface of his eyes, but beneath that surface the color deepened as if she were looking into the depths of a bottomless well.

"Then I believe, sir, that the Royal Oak will be the best solution."

He bowed with a flourish. "A happy decision, my dear ma'am."

"And one I came to all by myself, of course," Octavia murmured, following as he skated to the edge of the ice.

He glanced over his shoulder, observing airily, "Rest assured, ma'am, that I shall always strive for consensus when it comes to making important decisions."

"My mind is quite at rest, sir." She sat at the edge of the ice to unstrap her skates, aware that her flushed cheeks belied the statement. The pointed banter had aroused and excited her in a way she'd never felt before. She could think only of the promised lesson, of recapturing the joy of her dream, only this time with her mind as essential to the pleasure as her body.

When he reached down to take her hand and pull her to her feet, the simple strength in his gloved fingers turned her knees to water, and for an instant she swayed toward him as if her legs wouldn't bear her weight.

He slipped an arm around her waist, holding her against him for a second, and his scent filled her nostrils, making her giddy. With a muttered exclamation she pushed herself free and walked over to the phaeton, mortified by this absurd weakness, by the extraordinary excitation of her nerves. Anyone would think she was some feeble swooning maiden in need of burned feathers and hartshorn.

She climbed up into the phaeton before Lord Rupert could offer assistance and sat primly on the seat, drawing her cloak tightly around her before clasping her hands in her lap and gazing with apparent fixed interest at the scene on the lake.

Rupert said nothing but cast her a sideways glance, his eyes hooded so she couldn't read their expression. But she had the feeling that he both knew what had happened and was amused by it. It didn't help her sense of embarrassment, which grew as these strange, tormenting desires showed no sign of abating, until she was beginning to wonder if she would fall upon him as soon as they were alone, tearing his clothes from his body with hungry cries of primitive passion.

Absurd! She huddled into her cloak, drawing as far to the edge of the seat as she could. It would be less mortifying, of course, if her companion was subject to the same urgencies, but somehow she doubted it. They rose, she was convinced, from her own inexperience, and Lord Rupert Warwick was too cool and collected, too experienced in these realms, to be ruled by tidal waves of unbidden and unruly emotion.

"If you inch any farther sideways, you'll fall out," Lord Rupert observed. "Am I taking up too much room?"

"No . . . no, of course not," Octavia disclaimed hastily. "I didn't want to get in the way of your arm . . . make it difficult for you to control your horses . . . or . . . or something." She stumbled to a halt, her face on fire.

"How very considerate of you," he murmured. "But I assure you there's not the slightest danger of that." Transferring the reins solely to his right hand, he slipped his left around her waist and yanked her along the bench until she was sitting so close to him his shoulder brushed her cheek. "That's a little more friendly, I believe."

"But hardly decorous," she said, trying to hold herself rigidly upright despite the encircling arm.

Rupert chuckled. "Perhaps not, but decorum is not on the day's agenda."

Octavia pursed her lips and kept silent until she'd recovered some measure of equanimity; then she changed the subject, hoping that a new topic would focus her attention on something other than erotic fantasy. "Have you thought where we should set up house for this charade?"

"I've taken a lease on a comfortable furnished house on Dover Street."

The change of topic worked like a charm. Octavia was so startled, all thoughts of the indecorous hours lying ahead vanished. She jerked herself sideways, away from his encircling arm, and nearly toppled off the bench. "Already? But . . . but how could you know I would agree?"

Rupert withdrew his arm and devoted both hands to his horses. "I was optimistic."

"You take too much upon yourself, sir," she declared icily.

"Do I?" He glanced at her with open amusement. "Come off your high horse, Octavia. I've always said we were two of a kind. I could guess how you would react as easily as I could guess my own response to such a proposal."

"Of all the arrogant, impertinent . . ." She fell into a fulminating silence.

"Words fail you?" he inquired, raising an incredulous eyebrow. "I never thought to see the day."

"This is madness!" Octavia exploded. "I detest you! What am I doing here?"

"Oh, I think you know the answer to that perfectly well," he responded, whipping up his horses as they turned off Westminster Bridge and entered the quieter realms south of the river. "You're as eager for a certain course of lessons as I am to teach them, sweeting. And you're as eager for your own vengeance as I am for mine. So let's be done with pretense . . . at least between ourselves."

"For a supposed aristocrat you show a most remarkable lack of finesse," Octavia retorted.

"I'm a believer in plain speaking," he said. "A plain, blunt man, my dear. If my bluntness offends you, then I can only beg pardon, but I fear I can't change the habits of a lifetime."

"What kind of a lifetime?"

"Maybe I'll tell you one day."

"You know my story, why am I not to know yours?"

"Because I choose not to tell you."

"We're to live under the same roof, perpetrate this fraud, and you expect me to follow your lead without knowing anything about you . . . about what brought you to this?" she said with indignant frustration. "I don't even know your real name. Lord Nick . . . Lord Rupert Warwick? They're just fabrications, aren't they?"

"Yes."

The simple agreement rendered her speechless. She sat

beside him, unable to think of anything to say that would puncture her companion's infuriating self-possession. His air of world-weary cynicism sat easily on his broad brow, and he exuded an indefinable aura of mastery that she knew she couldn't withstand. He'd swept her up into his life, made her a part of his schemes, but where she saw herself as a self-determining, decision-making individual, in his eyes she was merely an adjunct, a useful tool to be bent to the correct shape.

The winter afternoon was drawing in, lights appearing in the cottages they passed. Her companion showed no inclination to break the silence, although her mute anger buzzed around the phaeton like a nest of invisible hornets. Octavia thought about telling him that for once he'd misjudged the situation. That she didn't want to participate in his schemes on these terms. That he should turn the phaeton and take her back to town.

She thought about saying these things, but she didn't say them.

The lights of the Royal Oak shone brightly in the gathering dusk, and again Ben and the gangly lad emerged to greet them as Rupert drew up beneath the creaking sign.

"Eh, we wasn't expectin' ye this early, Nick," Ben said as the highwayman jumped to the ground. "I see ye've brought miss again."

"So I have, Ben," Rupert agreed cheerfully, turning to lift Octavia out of the phaeton. "We have some important matters to discuss, and this seemed the quietest place for it."

"Oh, aye," Ben said with a snort of laughter. "We knows all about such 'portant matters in the Royal Oak."

Octavia stood still in the yellow lamplight from the open door. Folding her arms, she glared at the innkeeper, who was grinning from ear to ear. "I doubt you know anything at all, Ben. What I'm doing here is no concern of yours, and I'll thank you to keep your observations to yourself." Then she spun on her heel and entered the inn. If she couldn't do battle with the highwayman, she could at least show the people in this den of thieves that she was more than one of their precious Lord Nick's toys.

"Eh, that's a sharp tongue an' no mistake," Ben said, still grinning, apparently quite unperturbed by Octavia's rebuke. Rupert shrugged acceptingly and followed Octavia into the inn.

Bessie came out of the kitchen, her face flushed from the fire where she'd been turning a haunch of venison on a spit. She ignored Octavia and greeted Nick with a nod. "Ye'd best go to the fire in the taproom, Nick, until yer parlor's warmed up. Tab's only jest lit yer fire. We wasn't expectin' ye until after dark."

"No matter," Nick said easily. "I'll have a tankard of ale, and Miss Morgan will take a glass of madeira." He swept Octavia into the busy taproom under Bessie's baleful stare.

Octavia wondered how many of the occupants of the taproom had been there on her last visit, and her eyes darted involuntarily to the long deal table in the middle of the room, two spots of color burning on her cheeks.

Voices were raised in greeting and Rupert answered them cheerfully, escorting Octavia to a seat on a settle beside the fire. If he was aware of her embarrassment, he gave no sign, except that he treated her with a deferential formality quite at odds with his usual manner.

"Allow me to take your cloak, ma'am." He unclasped it without waiting for her to do it for herself and slipped it from her shoulders. "Pray take a seat and warm yourself. Tab will bring you a glass of madeira directly."

An interested silence had fallen. Octavia felt herself the focus of every gaze. She turned her face to the fire and pretended to be warming her hands. After a minute the conversation picked up again, and her skin ceased to prickle with the sense of a hundred eyes upon her.

Rupert handed her a glass of madeira, then stood beside her, his back to the fire, his body offering a partial shield from the rest of the room. This unlooked-for consideration went some way toward soothing her ruffled temper. She relaxed, leaning against the hard oak back of the settle, sipping her wine, stretching her feet to the fire.

"Eh . . . is Nick 'ere?" A harsh voice broke urgently

through the pleasant hum of voices. Octavia looked up sharply and saw that Rupert had suddenly tensed.

"Aye, Morris," he said. "I'm here. Do you have something for me?"

"Like as not."

Octavia glanced toward the door, where stood a villainous-looking individual huddled in a rusty black cloak over a laborer's smock, a frayed straw hat on his head, a corncob pipe cradled in the palm of one hand.

"A pint of yer best, Bessie," the new arrival shouted, stepping into the room. "Charge it to Lord Nick."

Rupert crossed the room toward Morris. He jerked his head toward the door. "Step outside, Morris."

"Eh, but it's cold as charity out there," the newcomer grumbled, taking the tankard of ale Bessie pushed across the counter to him. He buried his nose in the tankard and drank noisily, emerging with a mustache of froth that he wiped off with the back of a ragged sleeve. "You want to know what I 'eard at the Bell and Book."

"Outside!" Rupert's voice was a whip crack. He glanced toward Octavia, who was watching this scene with unabashed interest; then he stalked out of the taproom. Morris drained his tankard, slammed it down on the counter, and shambled after him.

"Beats me where that Morris gets 'is information from," Ben observed to the room at large. "But he's always comin' wi' summat or other. Nick says he's 'is best informer . . . doesn't waste no time on anythin' but fat pickin's."

What on earth were they talking about? Octavia curled into the corner of the settle, happy to be forgotten as the discussion buzzed around her. What information would Rupert find valuable?

Her reverie was interrupted by the return of its subject. He was looking somewhat preoccupied, a frown creasing his forehead.

"Tab assures me the parlor is now as warm as toast," he said. "Shall we go up?"

Octavia rose, forgetting the mysterious Morris in her eagerness to get away from the public taproom.

"I'll send dinner up to ye in 'alf an hour, Nick," Bessie announced from the other side of the counter, still ignoring the highwayman's companion. "I've a nice haunch of venison with red currant jelly, a neat's tongue, an' a dish of lampreys. Which d'ye fancy?"

"Oh, all three, if you please," Rupert said carelessly. "We're both sharp set." He ushered Octavia up the stairs ahead of him into his parlor.

"Is Bessie always unpleasant to your visitors?" Octavia inquired.

"Believe it or not, my dear, you're the only visitor I've had," he said, pouring madeira into two glasses.

"Goodness me, I am honored." Octavia took the glass he handed her. "I was sure you must have had a stream of panting females eager for the attentions of such a notorious highwayman. A veritable Macheath."

Rupert regarded her thoughtfully over the lip of his glass. "We seem to be on the wrong foot again. A short time ago I was congratulating us on having achieved a state of harmony that could only be increased as the evening continued, and now we're at daggers drawn . . . or, at least, you are. I'm at a loss to know how it came about."

"Don't be disingenuous, my lord. You know perfectly well how it came about." Octavia sat down in the armchair beside the fire. "You expect me to follow your direction without giving me so much as a scrap of information in exchange or involving me in the most elementary aspects of this crazy scheme. Perhaps I won't like this house on Dover Street, but that won't matter to you, will it?"

Rupert raked a hand through his hair, looking for once somewhat nonplussed. "Why would it matter what the house is like? It's only a temporary accommodation. The situation is good, it has decent-sized rooms, the furniture is unobjectionable. There's a suite of rooms that I imagine will suit your father very well," he added. "Compared with where he finds himself at present, almost anything would be an improvement."

Octavia couldn't argue with this. She took another tack. "Don't you imagine he would expect to witness his only child's wedding?"

"That is a difficulty," he conceded. "But I'm certain we can overcome it."

He regarded her closely. "Don't make difficulties just for the sake of it, Octavia. Either you agree to accept my direction with this play, or we bring it to a close now. It won't work if you pull against me."

Octavia stared into the fire, reluctantly acknowledging that the scheme was his and it was only reasonable he should have the direction of it. It was his manner of doing so that offended.

"Look at it this way," he said, coming over to her, catching her chin in his palm and lifting her face. "If this marriage were not a counterfeit, you would be obliged by law and the Church to accept the direction and authority of your husband. This situation is the same, only the reasons for it are a little different."

There was a teasing note in his voice, but dark currents swirled beneath the calm surface of his eyes as he held her gaze. She could see herself reflected in the dark irises and could imagine herself slipping beneath the surface into the vortex of those currents, losing herself in the tide of passion that they promised.

"You are most beautiful, Octavia Morgan." He ran his thumb over her mouth, his expression now grave. "I wonder if you know how beautiful you are."

Octavia shivered, lost in the honeyed warmth of his voice, the luminous glow of his eyes. The press of his fingers on her skin seemed intrinsic to her flesh. She moved her hand to grasp his wrist, feeling his pulse beating strong and steady beneath her fingers.

"Cry peace, Octavia," he said softly.

She nodded. "Peace."

He smiled and bent to take her mouth with his own, and a dizzying flood of memory washed over her, her body awakening to recollected sensation. She inhaled the scent of his skin, tasted again the sweetness of his mouth, and her nipples rose hard and her loins burned. Her fingers tightened on his wrist, and she half rose from her chair in her instinctive need to press her body to his.

At this inopportune moment there was a knock at the door, and he drew back, releasing her face. "All in good time, sweeting." He moved casually away from her as Tabitha came in.

She offered Octavia a smile and a curtsy. "I'll be settin' the table now."

At least one person in this den of thieves treated her with civility. Octavia returned Tabitha's smile and sat back in her chair, trying to recapture her composure. She glanced at the clock, feeling like a small child eagerly waiting for some promised treat, unable to sit still, wanting to ask every few minutes, "Is it time yet?"

She kept her seat while dinner was set upon the table. Rupert, leaning against the mantelpiece, carried on an easy exchange with Bessie and Ben.

"There, now." Bessie surveyed the laden table with a nod of satisfaction. "An' I'll 'ave the fire started in yer bedchamber straightway. I daresay ye'll be wantin' to repair there shortly." She cast a dour glance at the still and silent Octavia.

Rupert made no response beyond a faint inclination of his head, and the two left the room.

"Come to the table, Miss Morgan." Rupert drew out her chair. "I venture to think that Bessie's dinner will surpass anything Mistress Forster could produce."

"Mistress Forster makes a very tasty steak-and-kidney pudding," Octavia said loftily, taking her seat. She smiled up at him, and he ran his palm over her head.

"I believe, if you don't object too strongly, that I shall unpin your hair."

Startled, she touched the heavy plait on her shoulder. "Now?"

"Yes," he said matter-of-factly, deftly extricating hairpins. "There, now, that's much better." He combed his fingers through the glowing red-brown mane, spreading it over her shoulders before taking his own seat opposite.

"Is there anything else?" Octavia inquired, taking shelter from renewed confusion in irony. "Perhaps you'd like me to unbutton my gown . . . or remove my stockings . . . or—"

"All of that shortly," he interrupted, leaning over to fill her wineglass. "As yet I haven't decided whether I wish you to do those things for yourself, or whether I wish to do them for you."

"Hell and the devil!" Octavia muttered, dropping a serving spoon into the dish of lampreys.

"Do you think it will snow again?" Lord Rupert inquired politely.

"I trust not," she replied, her voice quivering with laughter. "May I pass you the lampreys?"

"If you please." He helped himself, then said, "I had thought we would appear to solemnize our marriage on Saturday, unless you have some other more pressing engagement."

Octavia swallowed a lamprey whole. "Uh . . . uh, I don't believe so, my lord."

"Then we could take up residence as a married couple in Dover Street that evening."

"Yes," agreed Octavia. So soon! No time to prepare her father for this extraordinary change of circumstance. But she couldn't manage to worry about such a detail at the moment. She would have to settle accounts with Mistress Forster and redeem everything that Jebediah still held in pawn—but she couldn't worry about that at the moment, either.

"I'll advance you sufficient funds to settle all your outstanding debts in Shoreditch," Lord Rupert said calmly, slicing into the neat's tongue.

How did he always read her thoughts? Octavia dismissed the question as easily as she'd dismissed every other concern in the last half hour. Vaguely, she wondered how he was going to fund this enterprise and then nonchalantly dismissed that question as well. Rupert was navigating this ship, following his own charts. She had nothing to do but swing the helm at his direction.

"Do you care for the opera?" her companion inquired with polite interest.

"Except for Gluck," Octavia responded without missing a beat. "I detest Gluck."

"You perhaps find him a little heavy," her companion agreed solemnly, carving the venison. "But one must be seen at the opera. We should definitely hire a box for the season."

"Oh, most definitely. But I prefer the theatre. I once saw Garrick perform as Hamlet."

"His death last year was a great loss to the stage," Rupert said, laying a slice of venison on her platter.

Throughout dinner he maintained an easy flow of inconsequential small talk. At first Octavia thought he was simply playing a game, but then it occurred to her that he was testing her to see if she could hold her own in court circles.

"So have I passed?" Octavia inquired, after Tabitha had removed the dishes for the first course and placed a platter of cheesecakes with a bowl of apples on the table.

Rupert smiled, peeling an apple in one unbroken spiral. "Passed what?"

"You know perfectly well."

He leaned over to place the peeled apple on her plate. "Northumberland and Shoreditch are perhaps not the most obvious classrooms for training courtiers."

"Northumberland society has its refinements," she observed mildly, nibbling on an apple quarter.

"And I should imagine you rarely need to be told anything twice," he reflected. "Are you easy about moving in these circles?"

"Perfectly." She sipped her wine and met his gaze candidly.

He nodded and pushed back his chair. "Then shall we adjourn and move to the most serious lesson of the evening, Miss Morgan?"

A little chill ran down her spine. "Of course, you would teach me the tricks of seduction so that I may use them on your enemy."

"No," he corrected quietly. "No, I would rather teach you to take your own pleasure even as you give it."

He came round behind her and pulled her chair out.

Cupping her elbows, he lifted her to her feet and turned her to face him. His eyes had darkened, smoky with passion, his mouth a taut line, and she could feel the tension thrumming in his body held so close to hers.

"I want you, Octavia," he murmured. "Only you, and just for yourself."

Octavia touched her tongue to her dry lips. Her skin was hot as if she were in the grip of a fever. "Show me these things," she whispered. "This time I would know what's happening."

Something flickered across his eyes, a shadow remarkably like regret, and then it was gone as if it had never been. "Come."

He took her hand and led her out of the parlor, down the dark and drafty corridor and into the bedchamber.

He closed the door and dropped the heavy bar across it. Octavia stood in the middle of the room, feeling awkward and uncertain, as shy as any virgin on her wedding night. She was no virgin, but the dream loving had not prepared her for this sense of deliberation, for the intent she saw in his eyes as he came toward her with a springing, eager step.

He took her hands and chafed them. "Are you cold?"

She shrugged helplessly. "Cold . . . hot . . . both . . . I don't know." Suddenly, she withdrew her hands from his and said in a rush, "I feel shy and stupid because I don't know what to do. Shall I take off my clothes?"

He smiled. "I should like you to do that." Crossing to the fire, he propped his shoulders against the mantelpiece, watching her.

She felt Rupert's eyes on her, although she couldn't for the life of her look up at him. She sat down on the edge of the bed to pull off her boots, then stood up again. Swiftly she unhooked her gown and let it slip to her feet. Beneath, she had only a single cotton petticoat, shift, and woolen stockings. Corsets, panniers, and starched cambric petticoats were hardly necessary in Shoreditch. She stepped out of the petticoat, untied her garters, and pushed off her stockings, kicking them off her feet. She hesitated for a second, then with grim determination pulled the shift over her head and dropped it to the floor.

She turned to face him, keeping her hands at her sides, resisting the urge to shield the private parts of her body. "So?" She lifted her chin, meeting his gaze with an odd defiance.

"So," he said softly, pushing himself off the mantel-piece and coming toward her. "So, Miss Morgan." He placed his hands on her shoulders and ran his palms down her arms to her wrists. Her skin prickled as if little tongues of fire rippled in the wake of the caress.

"Would you like me to do for you what you've done for me?" he asked, smiling, still holding her wrists, his eyes roaming the length of her body, and those same tongues of fire licked every inch of her skin as his gaze moved over her.

"It might even things up a little," Octavia said, trying to respond with a light insouciance, but her voice didn't sound in the least like her own.

"Come to the fire." He drew her into the warmth, away from the needling drafts from the window.

Octavia was aware of the heat of the fire on her back, the corresponding coolness on her front. She could feel her nipples prickling as they hardened, whether with the chill, or her own nakedness, or what she was watching, she couldn't guess.

Rupert removed his clothes with an air of deliberation, and she remembered the other time when she'd watched in disbelief as he'd undressed in front of her as coolly as if she weren't there. But this time it was *for* her.

As he removed each article, he placed it carefully on a cedar chest at the foot of the bed. He turned away from her as he shrugged off his shirt, and she saw the muscles ripple across his shoulders and down the lean, powerful back. Her gaze clung to the shape of his hips and buttocks outlined in the kidskin britches, the muscular swell of his thighs as he bent to pull off his boots and stockings. Barely breathing, she listened to the clunk as he unfastened his belt. His hands moved at his waist, and then he pushed both britches and drawers off his hips, stepping out of both garments in one fluid movement.

Octavia examined his naked rear view . . . the way his broad back tapered into the slender waist and slim hips. She absorbed the neat muscularity of his bottom, the rock-hard thighs and calves. She had only an imperfect image of her own back view, but she was convinced it bore little resemblance to this pared-down masculine version.

He seemed to be giving her ample time for scrutiny, enough time to note the tiny mole in the small of his back, the dusting of dark hair along his spine, creeping into the narrow cleft of his buttocks, enough time for the examination to bring a flush to her cheeks and a quiver of excitement to her belly.

And then he turned to face her. He stood still, a half smile playing on his lips, as he offered himself for her gaze. Her eyes flew over the hard chest, the flat belly, and fixed upon his erect flesh. She had never looked upon such a thing, but her body remembered the aching joy as that shaft had penetrated her own flesh, moved within her, capturing some essence of her self that belonged only to the exquisite joining of bodies.

She took a tentative step toward him, but he moved quickly, taking them both closer to the fire's warmth. He held her close against him, so that their skins touched at every point and his erection pulsed hard against her belly. Her breasts were pressed against his chest, and she could feel his heart beating as she could feel her own like a crazed bird taking off on some mad flight.

He ran his hands down her back, stroking into the indentation of her waist, sliding round to cup her bottom. His smiling mouth kissed hers, a light, tantalizing brush that made her lips tingle.

"I would like to look at you," he said.

"I thought you just did." Her responding smile was tremulous as she placed her hands on his shoulders.

"Not as I would wish. You seemed uncomfortable."

"Well, it's not a situation I'm familiar with," she said candidly.

Smiling, he stepped back from her, taking her hands and holding them away from her body as his gaze swept in a long, leisurely caress down her length. His eyes burned into her as if they would brand her. He let her hands drop to her sides and placed his own on her breasts, cradling the soft mounds in his palms, fingertips flicking lightly at her nipples.

"This pleases you," he stated. He licked his forefinger and ran it damply down the deep cleft between her breasts. Octavia shuddered, the sharply defined edges of reality, of their surroundings, wavering as every part of her responded to what he was doing to her.

His finger dipped into her navel, then traced a path over her belly. The delicate probe slid between her thighs, and her breath came swift as her body jumped at the exquisite teasing touch. He cupped the mound of her sex in his warm palm, and his fingers danced over the sensitive bud until she could hear her moans in the quiet room as if coming from a great distance and having nothing to do with herself. A wave of sensation so intense she lost every grip on reality, crashed over her, engulfing her, and she would have slipped to her knees if he hadn't held her to him with a tight encircling arm.

"Lord of hell!" she muttered, hanging limply against him as her eyes focused again and the room came back. "What happened?"

Rupert chuckled richly. "You are exquisitely sensitive, sweeting. I barely touched you."

She looked up at him. "Could I do something like that for you?"

"Oh, yes."

Octavia straightened her still wobbly knees and looked down at his body. His arousal seemed to beg for her touch, and she held him gently, exploratively, curling her fingers, feeling the blood pulsing in the corded veins. "Like this?"

"Like that."

She allowed her fingers to roam, to reach further, to

stroke the hard globes. When she looked up at him, she saw that his eyes were closed, his head thrown back, his mouth curved with pleasure. He'd said he would show her how to give as well as receive the sensual joys of the bedchamber, and she found she was deriving the greatest satisfaction from feeling his pleasure in her fingertips, hearing his breathing quicken, feeling the dampness of his skin as she rested her cheek against his chest while the shaft of his flesh flickered against her caressing hand with a life of its own.

"Stop now!" His voice was a husky rasp of urgency, and he reached down to seize her hands, drawing them away from him. He carried her to the bed, where, holding her against one upraised knee, he pulled back the covers.

He dropped her gently onto the bed and came down with her, leaning on one elbow beside her as he stroked her body, a thoughtful look in his eye. "You have the most beautiful body. So rich and yet so delicate."

He bent to kiss the fast-beating pulse at her throat, and then his mouth fastened on her nipple, his tongue flicking upward, his lips tugging at the rosy crown, creating a responding tug in her belly and loins, setting loose a rampaging surge of inexpressible need. Urgently, she pulled him over her, stretching her body beneath him, her skin adhering to his, the ridged muscles of his thighs pressing into her own softer flesh.

"I shall be lost," he whispered in soft protest. "It's too soon."

"No . . . no," she reiterated firmly, lifting her hips, curling her legs around his waist. "No, it's not too soon. I want it *now!*"

He laughed, but his eyes were on fire, the contours of his face smudged with his own desperate desire. And then he was inside her, and it was both as it had been in her dream and quite different. This time her eyes were open in the candlelit room, her gaze fixed on the face above her, seeing the harsh planes of his face softening as his pleasure built, the tautness of his mouth as he struggled to hold back, the corded veins in his neck, arched with effort. Her hands ran up his arms, cupping the hard swell of the biceps supporting his weight.

This time when the waves of her own greedy hunger built in her loins, she felt the glorious urgency in every fiber, in every pulse of her brain. They gathered strength with each deeply penetrating thrust of his flesh until she seemed to burst asunder in a shower of sparks and she heard her cry ring through the room the instant before his mouth fastened on hers. Vaguely, she was aware that he'd left her body, but his length was measured along hers and she held him to her, linking her arms around his back in a fierce embrace as the sparks settled and her body re-formed.

Now she became aware of the mattress beneath her, her own sweat mingling with his, his weight crushing her breasts, hammering her into the deep feather bed. Glorious languor flooded her, turning her limbs to butter. Her arms fell away from him, the tension in her thighs and buttocks was abruptly released, and she sank deeper into her nest, her eyes closing as her heart slowed.

Rupert kissed her eyelids, the tip of her nose, the corner of her mouth; then with a groan he rolled sideways onto the bed.

She stretched a hand to pat his stomach in the only expression of recognition she could manage. After a minute she said with a great effort, "You withdrew from me at the last."

"You were so impatient, love, I didn't have time to don armor."

But of course, Octavia thought. Pregnancy would certainly ruin their plans . . . or at least her share in them.

It was a cold little niggle of grim reality that had no place in the warm, satiated languor of the present. She banished it easily, and as Rupert thrust an arm beneath her, she turned her head into his shoulder and slid into sleep.

Chapter 8

It was pitch-dark when Rupert awoke from a light doze and inched soundlessly from the bed, moving so carefully he barely disturbed the bedcovers. A slight glow from the fire's embers provided an inkling of illumination, and he padded to the armoire, listening to Octavia's deep even breathing from the uncurtained bed.

In ten minutes he was dressed. He threw a heavy black cloak around his shoulders, took up a dark tricorn hat and his gloves, and walked softly to the door. He lifted the heavy bar with the utmost caution, then eased up the latch. He opened the door just wide enough to slide sideways through the aperture and then drew it shut behind him.

Octavia sat up the minute she heard the faint click of the closing latch. What was going on here? What was he doing?

She leaped from bed, dragging the coverlet around her, and ran to the door, stubbing her toe on the leg of a stool as she weaved through the darkness. Cursing under her breath, she eased open the door and stepped into the corridor, where a tallow candle in a wall sconce threw a dim, shadowy light. She tiptoed down the corridor until she reached the head of the stairs.

Rupert was talking quietly in the hall below. Ben's voice answered him, but so low she couldn't make out the words. They spoke hastily and then moved out of the hall, into the kitchen.

Octavia raced back to the bedchamber and stood at the window, pressing her face to the glass, looking down into the stableyard. A lantern glimmered below, its light swinging across the cobbles, providing a small oasis in the surrounding blackness. The sky was thick with cloud, blocking out both stars and moonlight, but in the faint puddle of golden light she could discern Rupert and Ben, still deep in conversation. Then Ben moved away toward the stables, carrying the lantern, leaving Rupert in darkness.

Octavia stared stupidly down into the black yard, unable to make any sense of what she was seeing. Then Ben reappeared, leading a horse the color of starlight. He carried a saddle and bridle over one arm.

Octavia flew to the armoire. She fumbled through the garments, found a pair of worsted britches and a shirt, and ran to the window with them. Keeping her eyes fixed on the scene in the yard, she dragged on the britches, rolled up the legs until they cleared her ankles, shrugged into the shirt, tucking it into the waist of the britches, and then looked around for a belt. She found the one Rupert had discarded earlier . . . an eternity ago . . . and cinched it around her waist. The last buckle hole was too loose, but she tied the leather roughly together. It held up the britches but made a most inelegant muddle around her middle.

Below, Ben had finished saddling the silver horse. He stood back, holding up the lantern, as Rupert sprang into the saddle. In the lamplight, as she pulled on her boots, Octavia could just make out a brace of pistols in saddle holsters and a long whip curled around the pommel.

Rupert leaned down, took Ben's hand, and shook it briefly; then the horse sprang forward beneath him, disappearing into the darkness through the gate to the stables. Ben turned back into the inn with his lantern.

Octavia knew now what was happening. Lord Nick was taking to the road. She grabbed her cloak and gloves and left the chamber, closing the door behind her. At the head of the stairs she stopped, listening to see if she could hear Ben moving around below. A line of light showed beneath the closed door to the taproom.

He came out of the kitchen and went into the taproom. Voices swelled as the door opened, then faded as he closed it behind him.

Octavia ran down the stairs. In the deserted kitchen, lit only by the fire still burning in the great fireplace, she raised the latch on the back door and slipped out into the stable-yard. She flitted across to the stables, a dark shadow in the deep gloom. Rupert had ridden out on a horse she'd not seen before. It was reasonable to assume that Peter, the roan he'd ridden from London that first time, was also stabled at the Royal Oak.

She could see nothing inside the stable, although the shuffling of hooves in straw and the occasional whicker told of more than one horse bedded down there. A lantern hung from a hook just inside the door, flint and tinder beside it. It was a risk she had to take if she was to find Peter. Flint scraped on tinder, the oil-soaked wick caught, and the lantern threw long shadows on the wooden walls.

The beasts in the stalls moved restlessly as she walked down the length of the building, looking for Rupert's roan, her heart thudding in terror as she imagined Ben, or some-one even more terrifying, bursting in on her. She was there on sufferance, protected only by Rupert's interest, an inter-est that would extend even in his absence to his own apart-ments; but once she ventured out of that protected territory, she could well be seen as fair game.

Peter was in the last stall, a halter hanging from a hook in the wall beside him. She slipped it over his head and led him out of the stall, back through the building. She blew out the lantern before opening the door to the yard and then led Peter outside, his hooves sounding like a drumroll in the stillness.

Her heart thumped so loudly she could hear it in her ears, and her stomach was in her throat, but she managed to lead the horse to the mounting block and haul herself astride his broad bare back. Once mounted, her terror faded. The entire tribe gathered in the taproom could burst forth in pursuit, but no one on foot could stop her now.

She nudged Peter's flanks with her heels and directed him to the gate. Once in the street, her heart took an exultant leap. She knew which way Rupert would have gone. She pulled on the halter, guiding Peter up the hill to the heath. The horse was as well behaved as she'd guessed from her earlier ride and showed no inclination to take advantage of the slight restraint of the halter.

Riding astride, she could keep her seat with relative ease on the broad back, leaning low over Peter's neck, urging him into a canter as they reached the top of the hill and the black expanse of Putney Heath stretched to all sides. The thin ribbon of the road glimmered ahead of her, winding its way into the darkness. On all sides gnarled trunks and twisted branches bent to the wind, whistling in fierce gusts across the flat heath.

It was an eerie, inhospitable place, the sky so black it seemed to have swallowed all light. Only the road provided orientation, and Octavia drew Peter onto the gorse-strewn turf beside it, deadening the sound of his hooves.

She listened but could hear only the creaking of branches, the wail of the wind, the hoot of an owl. Lord Nick would not be far from the road. He would be waiting somewhere along that ribbon for his unsuspecting prey. Cautiously, she nudged Peter forward, and the horse obeyed almost reluctantly, sniffing the air as if scenting danger looming out of the darkness.

Suddenly the air was rent with a shriek of such pain and terror that Octavia's heart stopped dead, and Peter reared, his lips pulled back from his teeth. Octavia clung on to the halter and wound her fingers into the coarse mane, sweat beading her forehead despite the bitter cold. The shriek reached a crescendo and then died away. She began to breathe again, recognizing the sound as the death cry of some small animal fallen prey to a fox or an owl. But it did nothing to make the heath more reassuring.

Gingerly, Peter moved forward, keeping to the turf

beside the road. A stand of silver birch trees took shape ahead, their bark white in the darkness. Horse and rider drew level with the trees.

She didn't see the thing snaking out of the darkness behind her. She heard nothing until with a faint snap the whip curled around her body, wrapping twice around her, securing her in the heavy folds of her cloak. She felt no pain, but her mouth opened on a scream of shock that died in her throat as his voice spoke into her ear, "Not a sound!"

Octavia swallowed the scream and sat still, her arms imprisoned in her cloak, only her hands free, uselessly clutching the mane and the halter. Peter whinnied in recognition as the silver horse came up beside him.

Octavia turned her head. The silver's black-shrouded rider regarded her in silence. His eyes were gray slits behind a black silk mask, and he wore a black silk scarf knotted loosely around his neck. He flicked his wrist, the whip uncurled, snaked through the air to be caught and coiled in one deft movement. He looped it over the pommel again.

Suddenly, the silver raised his head and whickered softly. Peter shuffled on the turf. Lord Nick became very still, his head cocked. Octavia froze.

Then she heard it, the faint rumble of iron wheels coming out of the darkness around the curve in the road ahead.

"Move into the trees." His voice was as quiet as the grave, his eyes almost without expression as they rested on her face, but Octavia could no more have imagined disobeying the instruction than she could have stood up against an avalanche. She urged Peter backward into the stand of silver birch until they were out of sight of the road.

Lord Nick drew the silk scarf up over his mouth as he sat his horse beside the road. Then both horse and rider became totally still. Octavia strained eyes and ears into the darkness. She could just make out the shape of the highwayman; the rattle of wheels, the pounding of hooves, grew louder. The coach was coming at a fair clip. Now she could hear the crack of a whip, the voice of the coachman urging on his horses as they approached the bend and the stand of trees.

The coachman's frantic urgency seemed to indicate that he knew he was approaching some notorious point of ambush. The hair on her nape lifted, and a shiver of apprehension ran down her spine.

The coach lumbered around the corner, the coachman standing up on his box, cracking his whip, the six horses pounding the ill-made road, sending up a shower of gravel and larger stones.

Leisurely, the highwayman moved into the road. He raised a pistol and fired once over the team's head. The horses reared and plunged, the boxes on top of the coach swayed and thudded against the ropes holding them. The coachman cursed vilely, and within the vehicle a shrill scream ensued, followed by a confused babble of voices.

Lord Nick remained where he was in the middle of the road as the coachman fought to get control of his horses. The postilions hauled back on the reins of the leaders, and the equipage at last came to a steaming, clattering halt.

"I won't keep you long, gentlemen," Lord Nick said casually. His voice, despite the silk scarf over his mouth, carried on the still air, but to Octavia it didn't sound like the voice she knew. He was speaking with a faint but unmistakable foreign accent, and the timbre was higher, more musical. She listened and watched, fascinated despite the cold chill of naked terror.

"Would you throw down that blunderbuss, sir?" he requested the coachman politely. "And if you two gentlemen would throw down your pistols also."

The coachman cursed him, but the three weapons thudded to the ground.

"Thank you."

"Robert . . . Robert, do something!" shrilled a female voice from within the carriage. "You great lump, sitting there like a bowl of cold porridge! We're being held up! It's a highwayman!"

"Yes, my dear," returned a weary voice. "I know."

"Then do something! What are you? A man or a mouse? Protect my honor!"

"I doubt your honor is in danger, my dear." There was a muffled thump, a resigned sigh, and then slowly the carriage door swung open.

A thin gentleman in a bag wig stepped down, fumbling with the sword at his waist. He looked up rather helplessly at the highwayman sitting atop his silver horse.

"You . . . you blackguard. I'll see you hanging in chains before I give you a penny!" he declared with remarkable lack of conviction.

"My dear sir, I assure you I'm not in the least interested in your money," Lord Nick said calmly. "But I do beg you not to trouble with your sword, it will only lead to unpleasantness."

The man regarded him in frank bewilderment, his hand resting on the hilt of his half-drawn sword. "Not interested?"

"No, sir," the highwayman said pleasantly. "Not in anything of yours. Sheathe your sword, if you please."

"La, Robert! What're you doing out there? Have you run him through yet?" A florid face appeared in the window of the coach, a towering powdered headdress swaying perilously above. "Odd's bones, man, what good are you?" she declared in disgust, taking in the scene. "I could have been robbed and ravished by now. Run him through, I tell you. Do it this minute."

"Yes, my dear . . . but it's a little difficult, you see. . . ." The thin man, his hand still on his sword hilt, continued to gaze helplessly up at the highwayman. "He's on a horse, you see," he offered in desperate explanation.

"La, I can see that, you windbag!" The door crashed open, and a mountainous figure swathed in crimson velvet descended. "Give me that sword!" She grabbed for it. "I'll defend myself, you great lummox!"

"Forgive me, ma'am, but you have nothing to defend," Lord Nick said, his eyes now alight with laughter but his voice as steady as before. "Pray return to the coach."

"Don't you talk to me like that, you murdering thief!"

With a great wrench the lady managed to pull the sword out of the sheath with a jerk that sent the hilt crashing into the chin of the unfortunate gentleman, who fell back, tripped over a stone in the road, and sat down with a weary little sigh that sounded like air escaping from a feather pillow.

"Now, you dastard! Attack a defenseless woman, would you?" Her large frame lumbered toward him with a movement reminiscent of a dancing elephant. She flourished the sword wildly, and Lord Nick's horse shied.

The long whip snapped and curled around the hilt of the sword, effortlessly lifting it from her grasp. Then the blade fell to the road with a clatter.

Lord Nick leaned low over his saddle and scooped up the sword from the road, saying mildly, "I trust I didn't hurt you, madam. Now, perhaps you'd return to the coach." A touch of flint entered his voice at this point, and the woman stared at him, her jaw slack, her previously florid complexion now as white as whey.

Her husband scrambled to his feet, dusting off his coat. "Best do as he says, my dear." He touched her arm with a placating hand.

"Coward!" she spat at the poor unfortunate, jerking her arm away. With a swish of her skirts she climbed back into the coach.

"Sir?" The highwayman gestured in her wake. "I can see you might find it more peaceful out here, but I'm afraid I must insist."

The gentleman glanced over his shoulder at the coach, then, with a resigned shrug, followed his wife into the interior. The highwayman dismounted, still holding the sword, and leaned through the window. A small man in a dark-brown suit sat trembling in the corner, trying to make himself invisible.

The woman sat on the edge of the seat, for the moment mercifully silent, fanning herself with her gloves. When she saw the highwayman in the window, she hissed like a serpent, waving one pudgy hand, where a massive emerald winked among the folds of flesh.

"I'd give you my body sooner than let you have my rings . . . dastard!"

"Fortunately for us both, ma'am, I require neither," Lord Nick returned in a voice as dry as the Sahara.

"You . . . you . . . you blackguard!" she exclaimed. "Do something, Robert."

"Oh, do hold your tongue, Cornelia," begged the long-suffering Robert, finally pushed beyond caution.

"Bravo, sir," the highwayman applauded as the outraged Cornelia gobbled like a turkey. He leaned farther into the coach and politely addressed the man shrinking in the corner.

"Would you be good enough to pass me that leather satchel beneath your seat, sir?"

At this the little man sat up and stared at the highwayman as if he were looking upon a sorcerer. "How . . . how . . . ?"

"Never mind how, my dear sir," the highwayman said. "If you would just pass it across to me, then you may all be on your way again. It's an inhospitable night to be traveling, I can't think what you were thinking of."

"Oh, I said we should have stayed overnight in the Bell and Book." Cornelia recovered her tongue. "But you wouldn't listen!"

"But, my dear ma'am, you were adamant we must reach town tonight," her husband exclaimed. "I tried to point out the folly of crossing the heath late at night, but—"

"Oh, *you* hold your tongue!" Cornelia swiped at him with her reticule. "Don't you dare argue with me. . . . Your memory is like a sieve, and you have the gall to tell me that I am mistaken. . . ."

Lord Nick closed his ears as the tirade increased in volume. He took the leather satchel from the trembling passenger and withdrew his head from the window.

"To your left!" Octavia's yell cut through the night. He whirled, just in time to see one of the postilions grabbing up a pistol from the road.

Lord Nick sprang forward; the sword in his hand

flashed in the dark, and the postilion dropped the pistol with a cry of pain. He fell back against the coach, clutching his hand.

"Fool!" the highwayman declared bluntly, kicking all three weapons into the bushes beside the road. "You!" He beckoned the second postilion. "Bind your friend's hand and look sharp about it."

Lord Nick remounted while the lad slunk over to his wounded fellow and wound his kerchief around the bleeding hand. The highwayman waited until the postilions were back on their horses, the coachman on the box once more in charge of the reins. Then he moved his horse out of the roadway.

"Carry on, coachman." The man needed no second invitation. The whip cracked and the horses plunged forward. Raising his hat, Lord Nick bowed with a flourish as the coach passed him, and the face of Cornelia, scarlet with fury, filled the window aperture.

As the coach thundered out of earshot, Octavia emerged from the trees. She was convulsed with an almost hysterical laughter and wiped at her streaming eyes with the back of her hand.

"That poor man!" she gasped.

"Yes, one's heart bleeds," Rupert agreed dryly, pulling the silk scarf away from his mouth. Reaching behind him with one hand, he unfastened the mask and thrust it into the pocket of his caped cloak. Then he regarded Octavia steadily.

"Would you mind telling me just what exactly you think you're doing?"

"Ah," said Octavia. "Well, to be brutally honest, thinking didn't really come into it."

"No . . . ," he said musingly, stroking his chin. "No, I suppose it didn't, because if by some miracle you had given the matter an instant's reflection, you would not be here. Would you?"

"Well, I don't know about that," Octavia returned. "It seems to me that if I hadn't been, you might be lying with a bullet in your head at this point."

"Possibly. I'll take it into account, but I can't promise that my gratitude for your sharp eyes will weigh too heavily in the scale. I have little tolerance for interference in my affairs."

He turned his horse onto the heath away from the road before Octavia could respond. "Follow me closely. Peter will stick to Lucifer's tail without too much guidance." He dug his heels into the silver's sides, and the horse broke into a gallop, a pale shape fast disappearing into the darkness.

Peter, without instruction, galloped after him. Octavia concentrated on keeping her seat over the rough, frozen ground, which the horse negotiated with the sure-footed expertise of prior knowledge.

A sliver of moon appeared between scudding clouds, throwing a cold, pale light over the black figure of the highwayman, sparking off his mount's shimmering silver coat. All around, trees and scrawny bushes rattled in the wind, dark hunched shapes across the flat ground.

Octavia had no idea where they were going as they plunged farther into the heath, leaving the road to fires and warm beds and mugs of mulled sack far behind. She had no idea of the time, except that the moon, when it showed itself, was high. How many hours ago had she been locked in a lustful tangle of limbs with the man riding ahead of her? A man who now seemed a frightening stranger leading her through an alien landscape that only he understood. A man she had agreed to partner in a diabolical enterprise of fraud and thievery and seduction. An agreement that in this cold, dark hour of the night struck her as insane.

Lucifer wheeled to the right and galloped down a small hill. Peter followed, and at the bottom Octavia found herself on a narrow, rutted country lane. She heaved a sigh of relief at this return to some semblance of the ordinary world, but Lucifer's pace didn't slow and Peter galloped stolidly in his wake. They rode through a night-closed hamlet and approached a tiny stone cottage standing by itself some half a mile farther along the lane. A light glowed in the downstairs window.

Lucifer slowed and turned to the back of the cottage,

where he trotted without hesitation through the open door of a long, low outbuilding. Peter followed, and Octavia found herself in a dark stable, the frigid air heavy with the sweet scent of hay.

"All well, Nick?" Ben's voice spoke out of the darkness. Octavia jumped, totally disoriented. Where in the hell were they?

"Lord of 'ell!" Ben exclaimed softly, making out the second rider behind Lord Nick. " 'Ow d'she get 'ere?"

"Good question." Rupert swung off Lucifer. "And one I intend to have answered in short order." He lifted the leather satchel down from the saddle, and his teeth flashed white in the dark as he grinned. "Morris is worth his weight in gold, Ben."

"Fat pickin's, then?" Ben took Lucifer's bridle.

"Oh, yes, I believe so." Rupert slung the satchel over his shoulder and came over to Peter. "I'll leave you to bed down Peter, Miss Morgan. Ben has made preparations for only one horse, but Peter is no less deserving than Lucifer. You'll find a pitchfork and hay in the corner. Put him in the end stall and rub him down well, then throw a horse blanket over him before you leave. He mustn't get chilled." With that he strolled out of the stable, whistling between his teeth.

Octavia accepted her responsibility with a shrug. If the highwayman expected her to react with irritation to his orders, he would be disappointed. She swung herself down. "Can't we have a lantern in here, Ben?"

"No," was the uncompromising response.

Clearly not a man willing to engage in companionable discourse while they worked. Octavia peered around, her eyes gradually growing accustomed to the gloom. "Come on, Peter." She led the horse to the end stall, listening to Ben talking to Lucifer as he unsaddled him.

Peter went into the stall with his customary equability, dipping his head for her to remove the halter. She forked hay into his manger and looked for something to rub him down with.

"Is there a cloth or a currycomb, Ben?"

"Over yonder."

Yonder where? She looked around and found a torn strip of blanket hanging from a hook. She used it on Peter as he munched contentedly on his hay. He was a big horse and she had to stand on tiptoe to reach his back. Her arms were aching when she was finished, sweat beading her forehead despite the cold. Ben had finished with Lucifer long before and had banged out of the stable with the curt instruction that she should make sure the door was bolted behind her when she left. She'd controlled the urge to consign him and his incivility to the devil and concentrated on finishing her task.

She found a horse blanket thrown over the gate to the stall and tossed it over the horse, who whickered softly and nuzzled her shoulder. "At least you're friendly, old fellow," she murmured against his velvety nose. Then she braced herself to face what awaited her in the cottage.

A flicker of candlelight showed in the single window at the rear of the building. She pushed open the door and entered a square room that took up the entire ground floor. A narrow wooden staircase rose from the corner.

Rupert was sitting in a wooden rocker before a blazing fire, his booted feet resting on the fender. Ben sat in the rocker's twin beside him. Both men nursed pewter tankards, from which rose an aromatic steam. A copper pan simmered fragrantly on the hob.

Octavia stood uncertainly at the door.

"Close the door, Miss Morgan, it's not midsummer."

Her lips tightened and she kicked the door shut with her heel. She was now as chilled as she'd been heated with her stable exertions. The two chairs, a table, and two stools provided the only furniture in the room, and yet it seemed a haven of warmth and comfort with the golden glow of the oil lamp on the table and the red spurting fire in the hearth.

Resolutely, she walked over to the fire and bent to warm her hands. "Lord Nick and Lucifer," she commented casually. "Quite a combination, sir."

"Do you think so?" he said with a careless shrug.

"A devil's combination to tempt the fates," she said. "A highwayman who rides a white horse."

"One must spice one's life a little," he said, keeping his eyes on the fire. "You seem to understand the pleasures of courting danger, Miss Morgan."

"On the contrary, sir. I don't believe in taking fool-hardy risks with my neck."

"Ah." He looked across at her then, that little mocking smile playing over his lips. "And what do you think you've risked this evening, my dear Octavia?"

"Not my neck," she snapped back.

He leaned back in the chair, rocking himself gently with one foot on the fender. "No, your *neck's* in no danger from me."

Ben chuckled into his tankard, and Octavia regarded him with undisguised dislike. "Must we have this conversation in company?"

"Oh, Ben isn't company . . . *you* are," Rupert declared. "Ben is supposed to be here. You, on the other hand, are not."

"Ben didn't save you from a bullet tonight."

"There is that." He appeared to give this some judicious thought.

"Looks like she's bin' raidin' yer wardrobe, Nick," Ben observed. "I niver seen the like!" He chuckled again and buried his nose in his tankard.

"Good God!" For the first time Rupert took in Octavia's garb beneath her cloak. "Are those my britches you're wearing? If 'wearing' is the right word for whatever you've done to them."

"I could hardly ride astride in a gown," she retorted. "I would have asked if you hadn't sneaked out like a snake in the grass."

"I hardly consider going about my private business to be sneaking like a snake," he declared. "And compared with making free with my clothes and my horse, it seems positively saintly behavior."

Nonplussed, Octavia shifted the angle of the subject.

"You knew that satchel would be in the coach. What's in it?"

"Rent rolls," Rupert said readily, stretching his feet to the fire. "The Earl of Gifford's rent rolls. He's a stingy bastard, rich as Croesus. He won't notice the loss except in his mean-spirited soul."

"And that man who came to the Royal Oak earlier? Morris . . . he told you about it?"

"Precisely." Rupert smiled lazily. "Morris spends a lot of his time in the taprooms around the heath. He keeps his ear to the ground to good purpose and overheard the earl's steward trying to persuade his traveling companions to stay at the Bell and Book overnight, since he didn't wish to risk his precious cargo to the heath at midnight. Madam Cornelia, however, insisted on reaching town tonight." He shrugged. "So what could the poor fellow do? I'm convinced the dear lady was *very* persuasive."

Octavia was too intent on making sense of the night's work to smile. "But why didn't you take anything from that ghastly woman and her husband?"

Rupert shook his head. "It wasn't necessary. One mustn't be greedy. There's enough in that satchel to furnish you with a court wardrobe, my dear, even down to a pair of shoes with emerald-studded heels and diamond buckles."

"Eh . . . what's that?" Ben demanded, emerging from his own languid trance with a jerk. "She's in yer keepin' then, Nick?"

"No, I am not!" Octavia declared, her eyes flashing tawny fire. "We are embarked upon a joint enterprise. Isn't that so, my lord?"

Rupert laughed. "Yes, it is, my dear Octavia. There's no need to look daggers at me. Your integrity is in no way under challenge. But I'll give you one word of advice. Ben is the best friend a man could ever wish for, and in this joint enterprise you may need him as much as I. Best you remember that."

"In that case, best *he* understands the true situation," Octavia said tightly. "I am in no way beholden to you, Lord Rupert."

"Only as far as a pair of britches, a shirt, and a horse," he murmured. "Do you care for some milk punch?"

It was such an abrupt change of subject Octavia merely blinked, although her stomach lurched with anticipation at the thought.

Rupert gestured indolently to the simmering pan on the hob. "Help yourself. You'll find a tankard in the cupboard beside the mantel."

Octavia wasted no more time in pursuing contentious issues. If the highwayman was prepared to let bygones be bygones, then the least she could do was follow suit. She found the tankard and filled it with the creamy, fragrant contents of the pan. She hitched a stool over with her foot and sat down almost in the fireplace in her eagerness to get to the heat. The first sip made her knees weak. Someone knew how to make a milk punch to fell a grown man. The second sent her head spinning.

The two men behind her rocked placidly, sipping from their own tankards. The room began to lose its contours in the most delicious way, and the creeping languor started in her toes and inched upward, turning muscle and sinew to butter. She swayed on her stool, smiling into the fire, taking another sip from the tankard. She swayed and leaned backward, finding a pair of legs perfectly positioned as a back rest; a pair of knees perfectly positioned to receive her head. A hand moved through her hair in a languid stroking motion that blended with the warm, smudgy feeling in her belly as she drained the tankard.

"Such a busy night for a meddlesome little girl," the highwayman stated, a rich laugh in his voice. Vaguely, Octavia felt she should protest such a statement, but she could find neither words nor energy—any more than she could resist when she was pulled upward by her armpits and suddenly found herself dangling face down, sleepily gazing at the earthen floor.

The highwayman's shoulder moved beneath her belly as he mounted the narrow staircase. It was cold as they left the fire, and she murmured in faint protest, but then she was lying down, sinking into feathers and smothered in quilts, a great weight of them, and the cold air became a warm seal around her body. Hands were on her, deftly stripping her naked under the covers so the cold air didn't touch her exposed skin.

Vaguely she was aware of him sliding in beside her, his bare skin chilled by its brief exposure to the frigid air. She curled against him, sharing her own warmth as she fell asleep, her nose pressed to the now warm naked back, his scent invading her dreams.

Chapter 9

℘ "Striking woman that Lady Warwick." The Duke of Gosford came to stand beside his son-in-law. He took an overly generous pinch of snuff and sneezed copiously into his handkerchief. " 'Tis to be hoped the committee don't blackball her for such an appearance. Takes some nerve to appear in public like that."

"Almack's is not the court." His son-in-law didn't lower his eyeglass as he offered this curt comment. The duke had correctly guessed that Philip Wyndham was staring at the lady who'd just entered the ballroom at Almack's on the arm of her husband.

The three elegant salons at the assembly rooms were thronged with those fortunate members of the Upper Ten Thousand to be approved for membership by the fourteen-member committee of ladies whose draconian rules ensured that three quarters of London's nobility knocked in vain for admission. Among that powdered, painted, elaborately coiffured crowd at this subscription ball, Lady Warwick's appearance was remarkable.

She wore her hair unpowdered, her complexion was innocent of paint, her lips unrouged.

Octavia paused instinctively in the entrance to the ballroom, and Rupert, taking his cue from her, paused too. A whisper rustled through the company; then every eye turned toward the double doors.

Octavia's insistence on making her first serious public appearance in this unusual fashion had amused Rupert. He'd gone along with it because he couldn't see that it would do any harm, but when he'd watched her descend the staircase at Dover Street that night, he'd understood exactly what she was about. The men would flock like vultures. The women would hate her, of course. Such a perfect complexion, such wonderfully unusual coloring, displayed without artifice. Octavia had no need of beauty patches to draw attention away from smallpox scars, or rouge to brighten a complexion dulled by lack of sleep, overindulgence, the clogged grease of paint and thick-caked powder.

Her hair, piled high off her forehead and falling in soft curls to her shoulders, glowed in the candlelight in all its natural glory, setting off the pale translucence of her cheeks and the deep-set tawny gold of her eyes. Her gown was a dainty confection of white and pink muslin opened over a petticoat of apple-green silk, the sleeves of the gown banded in the same silk, delicate lace ruffs falling over her wrists. A white lace fichu tucked into the low neckline drew attention to the swell of her bosom while seeming discreetly to conceal it.

All in all, it was a masterly costume designed to complement the madonnalike innocence of her face, the delicate curves of her body, yet at the same time, with its bold rejection of convention, to hint at a certain recklessness of character, a touch of defiance and mystery.

She would have the men at her feet in minutes, or such had been his initial assessment. An underestimate, he now realized, as the Prince of Wales moved his substantial bulk across the ballroom, his face red and sweaty, a lascivious gleam in his eyes and an eager smile on his lips.

"Madam." He bowed low. "What a vision . . . a refreshingly unusual vision, indeed. Pray introduce me to your wife, Warwick."

Blandly, Rupert performed the introduction, and the prince seized Octavia's hand. "Where have you come from, my dear lady? To think of all the months we've been languishing here without a sight of you. How could you have kept yourself so far from our eyes? . . . Indeed, how could you have permitted this sly dog to steal you before anyone else had a chance?" He wagged a plump finger at Lord Rupert and laughed heartily.

"You are too kind, sir." Octavia curtsied, her eyes darting around the circle of men gathering behind the prince.

". . . Oh, no no no. Oh, no, I believe not," declared his highness. "Not too kind . . . not possible. Such a ravishing creature, Warwick. You're a dog . . . to steal a march on us like this. Where did you find her?"

For all the world as if she were a rare specimen of insect life discovered under some remote stone, Octavia thought.

"In the country, sir," Rupert responded as blandly as before. "In Northumberland, where I was recently visiting."

"Northumberland!" The prince turned his little eyes upon Lady Warwick in some astonishment. "Gad, I'd never have believed it possible. Very far north it is, isn't that so?" He glanced behind him for corroboration.

"Yes, sir," agreed a courtier. "I believe it's quite some distance from London."

"Gad," repeated the prince, examining Octavia through his quizzing glass. "If they keep such beauties as this up there, I must pay it a visit, meself . . . what?" He laughed heartily at this sally and extended his hand. "Come dance with me, you ravishing creature."

"But I've not yet been given permission by one of the patronesses," Octavia demurred, fluttering her fan. "I shouldn't wish to break the rules, Your Highness."

The prince roared with laughter. "As if you haven't already done so, ma'am. Dolly . . . Dolly, come over here and give this exquisite creature permission to dance with me." He beckoned vigorously to a lady in a gown of lilac tabby, her massive wig decorated with a score of tiny furry animals peeping from between what looked to Octavia to be tufts of grass.

The Duchess of Deerwater advanced, a stiff smile for the prince on her lips. She stared rudely at Octavia and curtsied infinitesimally. "Lady Warwick."

Octavia swept an elegant and deferential curtsy in response. "Ma'am."

"If you wish the name of a competent hairdresser, Lady Warwick, I should be happy to furnish you with one."

Octavia curtsied again. "You're too kind, ma'am."

"I am aware that people do things differently in the country," the duchess stated, her nose twitching, her mouth pursing. "But we don't bring country ways to London, madam. They don't suit."

"Oh, I believe there's always room for improvement, ma'am," Octavia said sweetly. "Even London should be open to modern ideas."

The duchess stared at her in disbelief, clearly wondering if she'd heard aright. Had this newcomer actually had the temerity to describe London fashions as outdated?

Rupert raised an eyebrow. Perhaps Octavia didn't understand the weight of this woman's influence. He was searching for something to smooth over the jagged silence when the Prince of Wales burst into a hearty peal of laughter.

"Quite right, Lady Warwick. We're shockingly stuck in our ways here. Too much convention and protocol and the lord knows what else. It's all the fault of the court, y'know. Devilish strict and old-fashioned it is. Just wait until it's my turn . . . then we'll all see some changes, you mark my words."

This shockingly unfilial statement that could only be interpreted as a desire to hasten his father's demise was received in a silence so deeply disgusted that Octavia's minor challenge sank without trace.

The prince seized her hand and whirled her away onto the floor, where a set was forming for a country dance. "His Highness is still only a boy . . . and somewhat headstrong," Rupert observed quietly, bowing to the duchess, offering her a smile that invited her participation in this mature reflection. "Youth tends to be."

"Yes, of course," the duchess agreed, dabbing her upper lip with a scented handkerchief. She examined the figure of Lord Rupert Warwick and seemed somewhat mollified by what she saw. His lordship was dressed in black silk, his hair conventionally powdered and tied at the nape. He wore a gold fob and a diamond pin sparked blue fire against the blinding white of his ruffled shirt front. His expression was attentive, his smile pleasantly complicit, as if his last statement were offered as much as excuse for his young wife as for the Prince of Wales.

"Youth must be guided by their elders, Lord Warwick," she said after a minute, her eyes going pointedly to the dance floor and the unconventional Lady Warwick. "Your wife appears to lack town bronze, sir."

"Oh, I don't believe that's the case." Lord Wyndham spoke suddenly from the attentive circle around them. "I suspect Lady Warwick merely dares to be out of the ordinary. What d'you say, Warwick?"

Rupert bowed in his twin's direction, his eyebrows lifting, a glint of humor in his eyes. "An accurate assessment, I believe, Wyndham."

The earl's full mouth twitched into a thin smile. His gaze returned to the puffing ballroom antics of the prince with an expression of frigid disgust, but as his eyes moved to the prince's partner, a spark of interest flickered below the cold gray surface.

How could Philip sense nothing? Rupert wondered. Every time they exchanged looks or words, his own body temperature seemed to rise, his blood to quicken in his veins as recognition and recollection hammered at the gates of his soul. Yet Philip showed not the slightest sign of unease or puzzlement in his brother's presence. Perhaps because he knew his twin to be dead, there was no room for even an inkling of some disturbing twitch of recognition.

"You met Lady Warwick in Northumberland?" Philip asked casually, turning away from the dance floor, offering Rupert his snuffbox.

Rupert waved the enameled box aside with a polite smile. "I don't care for scented snuffs, thank you. Yes, while I was visiting old family friends."

"This is her first visit to London, of course."

Rupert nodded. "We thought to postpone our honeymoon until after the birthday."

The king's birthday was in June and marked the end of the London season. Philip nodded again, his gaze returning to the dance floor. "But a honeymoon in London at the height of the season has its charms for the uninitiated, I would imagine." Philip bowed and strolled away, making his way around the outskirts of the room where the chaperons sat in groups, sipping negus and gossiping.

The Countess of Wyndham, sitting bodkin between two starched matrons, looked up as he approached her, a nervous smile on her lips. She patted at her coiffure, straightened the lace at her neck, her eyes filled with anxious appeal as she awaited some humiliating public criticism of her appearance. But her husband merely looked through her as if she were a garden slug and passed on, leaving her as mortified by his lack of acknowledgment as if he'd heaped scorn upon her.

The name of Lady Warwick was on every tongue. And it stayed there throughout the evening. The Prince of Wales refused to relinquish the lady, and Rupert watched from afar as she became the center of the prince's own sycophantic circle of young reprobates.

Octavia knew as well as did Rupert that for as long as she was favored by the prince, society might criticize, but it would never ostracize. For the plan to work, she must be identified with a circle that drank deep, played the tables to ruination, and threw conventional ethics to the four winds. The prince's intimates formed such a circle, and by the end of the evening she'd deflected a dozen oblique suggestions and turned down four outright proposals, one of which came from the prince himself.

"La, sir, but I'm a married woman," she protested as the prince held her hand tightly between both of his hot palms and beamed at her.

The prince guffawed but looked genuinely taken aback by this cavil. "I'd hardly suggest it, my dear ma'am, if you were not. A man can't enjoy himself with an unmarried gal. Now, don't tell me Lord Rupert is such a spoilsport as to be a jealous husband."

"Why, sir, I don't believe he's been a husband long enough as yet to know whether he is or not," she returned demurely. "I think it's a little soon to be contemplating a leap from the marriage bed. We've been wed but two weeks."

The prince chuckled and patted her cheek. "A forthright woman, that's what I like. No missish nonsense about you. Well, well, my dear, we shall see how long it takes for your husband to start wandering. And when he does, I dare swear you'll look upon the matter with new eyes."

"Perhaps so, sir."

Where exactly was Rupert? It was two o'clock in the morning, and Octavia glanced around the supper room, where the company had for the most part adjourned to nibble oyster patties and bread and butter and sip champagne.

She caught sight of Rupert in a window embrasure, deep in conversation with a highly painted lady in a gown of deep-red taffeta, a diamond collar glittering at her throat. Two heart-shaped beauty patches adorned the upper swell of her breasts, and when she moved an arm sideways to take a piece of bread and butter from the table, her right nipple popped out of her décolletage. She made no attempt to replace it, and as Octavia watched, Rupert delicately reinserted the nipple into her gown with a long, slender forefinger.

The lady laughed and tapped his cheek with her closed fan. Rupert's lazy half smile played over his lips as he leaned back against the wall, turning the stem of his champagne glass between finger and thumb.

"There, you see!" pronounced the prince, whose gaze had followed Octavia's. "Not a man to waste a minute is he? Warwick's known as a philanderer, dear lady. Can't expect a marriage vow to change a man's character."

Octavia offered a smile and a shrug of indifference.

The prince chuckled, wrapping an arm around her bare shoulders. His fingers played in the fichu at her neck. "Such a modest little thing," he murmured. "No chance of your revealing a little too much of anything, Lady Warwick. Not like Lady Drayton . . . eh?"

"Lady Drayton has the advantage of me, sir."

"Oh? How's that?" The prince's little eyes focused blearily. "A little more flesh there, is that it?" He patted Octavia's bosom with a grin.

"No, sir. She has the advantage of years," Octavia said smoothly, taking a step backward from the royal fingers.

"Oh, wicked! Such a little cat with her claws," the prince boomed, highly delighted with this sally. "But I tell you, madam." He wagged a finger at her. "Margaret Drayton would have your eyes out for that."

"Indeed, sir. I tremble." Octavia was at a loss to understand why there was an edge to her voice. Margaret Drayton was nothing to her. Rupert was simply playing his part, as she was playing hers. However, he'd certainly looked as if he was enjoying himself, dabbling in the lady's bosom. But, then, why shouldn't he? It was no business of Octavia's. So why this dismaying curl of indignation in her belly?

As she watched, Rupert bent his head, his mouth close to the lady's ear. Lady Drayton's laugh shrilled abruptly over the hubbub in the supper room.

"They seem to be amusing themselves." The dry voice spoke her thoughts. Philip Wyndham stood at her shoulder, his gaze fixed on the play across the room. A smile was on his lips, but it was a smile that sent a shiver down Octavia's spine.

She looked up, meeting his eye, and was startled by the strangest sense of discordance, as if the rather beautiful face was not what it seemed. As if behind the smooth, broad expanse of his forehead, the clear gray eyes, the almost delicate features, lurked something venomous.

"Yes," she said coolly, unfurling her fan. "They do. As does everyone else in the room. I do declare, sir, that this has been the most entertaining evening I've passed since we arrived in London."

"Oh, the best value in town, ma'am," the prince declared. "A ten-guinea subscription for a jolly weekly ball throughout the season . . . and such an elegant supper!" The group around him laughed dutifully at the heavy-handed sarcasm, and Octavia smiled.

"I am but new arrived, sir. My tastes are still unformed."

"Oh, but not for long, I'll wager," one young buck said with a leer. "I trust we may call upon you, Lady Warwick. Dover Street, isn't it?"

"I should be honored." Octavia curtsied to the prince. "I beg you to excuse me, sir. It grows late, and I should return to my husband's side."

"Allow me to escort you." Philip Wyndham offered his arm with a bow.

"Thank you, my lord." She placed her hand on his brocade sleeve, and they moved away from the still-chattering circle around the prince.

"You seem to have made a conquest of His Royal Highness. You're to be congratulated, ma'am."

"Is it matter for congratulation, sir?" Octavia looked up at him with a bland smile. "I would have thought it the opposite. His Highness does not appear to be particularly discriminating in his tastes."

Surprise flashed across the slate-gray eyes bent upon her countenance, and the bud of interest they held burst into full flower. He smiled, and this time it was a warm and appreciative smile that seemed to bathe her in approval. Octavia felt herself smiling in response, and it took a moment of effort to remind herself that this man was Rupert's enemy.

"It's good to see you're not blinded by consequence, ma'am," the earl said. "The prince is a fool, but he can be useful if he's played right."

"I had rather assumed that, sir."

The earl's chuckle was abruptly cut off as they approached the embrasure, where Rupert and Lady Drayton still stood, deep in conversation, their heads very close together.

"La, sir, but you've a wicked tongue," trilled Lady Drayton, tapping his wrist smartly with her fan. She turned to greet the new arrivals, her eyes very bright, her color higher than could be accounted for simply by rouge. "Why, Lord Wyndham, I didn't realize you were here this evening. Lord Rupert has been so monstrously entertaining, I've scarce had a moment to look around."

Philip bowed. "Then I'm certain there must be a great wailing and gnashing of teeth among your admirers, madam." His tone managed to imply that he was not of their number, and Lady Drayton's china-blue eyes flashed.

"I don't believe you're acquainted with my wife, ma'am." Rupert stepped into the breach with a lazy smile. "Octavia, pray allow me to make you known to Lady Drayton."

"An old acquaintance of yours, sir?" Octavia inquired with a sweet smile as she curtsied to Lady Drayton.

"Oh, no, a very recent one," Rupert corrected.

"I was sure you must have known each other since you were babes in arms," Octavia returned. "I was hoping Lady Drayton, out of friendship for you, would show me how to go on in society. She must have had so much more experience than I."

Rupert swallowed an appreciative grin as Margaret looked daggers at the smooth-complexioned young woman smiling at her with such deceptive innocence.

"Your husband, my dear Lady Warwick, has had quite sufficient experience to perform that service for you," Margaret said. "Indeed, it surprises me he hasn't explained society fashion to you. To allow one's wife to appear in such undress is . . . well, is quite cruel." She tittered and batted her eyelashes at Rupert.

"Oh, hardly cruel, ma'am," he murmured. "But I do believe one should learn through one's errors. What do you think, Wyndham?"

The question was startlingly sharp, belied by his air of languid amusement. Octavia waited for the earl's response, struggling with her resentment. For some reason she'd expected Rupert to defend her against that attack, instead of which he seemed to be agreeing with Margaret Drayton's mocking assessment.

"Oh, I believe Lady Warwick knows exactly what suits her," Philip said. "A woman who knows her own mind is always so refreshing. One is surrounded by so many sheep at court." He smiled at Lady Drayton, but his eyes were gray ice, and he hesitated a moment too long before adding, "Present company excepted, of course."

"Of course," Rupert said, turning to Octavia. "If you're ready to leave this scene of dissipation, my dear, I'm at your service."

"I'm quite ready." Octavia offered Lord Wyndham a curtsy. "You're very gallant, sir."

"I speak only the truth, madam." He bowed and took her hand, raising it to his lips. "I trust I may call upon you."

"I should be honored. . . . Lady Drayton." Another curtsy and she placed her hand on Rupert's proffered arm.

They moved sedately through the rooms, down the stairs to the hall. Rupert sent one servant scurrying for their cloaks and a second to call their carriage. They stood silent in the hall under the brilliant light of three chandeliers. The silence seemed awkward. Octavia tried to think of something to say to break it, but she felt strangely out of sorts, annoyed and resentful, though she could think of no good reason for it. Rupert appeared to be as relaxed as ever, one foot tapping on the marble floor in time to the strains of music drifting down from the ballroom, his gaze roaming lazily around the crowd of departing revelers.

"Oh, my dear Lady Warwick, leaving us so soon." The Prince of Wales tottered and swayed down the staircase. He grabbed hold of the banister as he reached the bottom step. "Come and play cards, ma'am. I can promise a good game at Lady Mount Edgecombe's tonight." He offered a skewed wink in Rupert's direction. "Your husband, I'll wager, isn't averse to a game of evens and odds. Eh, Warwick?"

"On any other evening, sir, I'd be overjoyed," Rupert responded. "But my wife is fatigued."

"Oh, yes . . . yes, of course." The prince nodded sagely, tapping the side of his nose. "And you're but new to the marriage bed. What . . . what?" he added in imitation of his father, laughing uproariously, his courtiers joining him.

"I trust we can persuade Your Highness to play in Dover Street on some evening," Rupert suggested once the paroxysms had faded somewhat.

"Oh . . . oh, what's this, then? Settin' up a faro house of your own, are you?" The prince's eyes sharpened as far as they were able to. "Is Lady Warwick going to join our Faro's Daughters, then?"

"I can promise an amusing evening, sir," Octavia said, smoothly picking up her cue. "I'll not presume to rival the salons of Lady Buckinghamshire or Lady Archer or Viscountess Mount Edgecombe, but I believe Your Highness might find some entertainment at our house."

"Oh, capital . . . capital," the prince declared, clapping his hands. "D'ye hear that, fellows? Lady Warwick is to join the ranks of Faro's Daughters." Leaning over, he kissed her heartily on the cheek. "Send a card, dear lady, when the tables are set up."

"Lord Rupert Warwick's coach!" a voice bellowed from the door. The servant ran up with their cloaks, and in the flurry the Prince of Wales and his cohorts moved noisily away. Rupert draped Octavia's cloak around her shoulders, took his own from the servant, and escorted her outside.

King Street was lined with coaches and sedan chairs, link boys running up and down, holding their oil lamps high to light emerging revelers to their vehicles. Two women appeared from the alley leading to King's Place, their gowns and hair artfully disarrayed. They lounged against a wall, watching the scene.

The Prince of Wales bumbled through the doorway behind Octavia and Rupert. With a whoop he charged across King Street to the two women. "I've a mind to visit a nunnery after all that respectable insipidity," he bellowed at the top of his voice. "Take me to your abbess, my dear delights." He swayed off down the alley, arm in arm with the two prostitutes, his cohorts following eagerly in his wake.

"What a poxy horrible creature," Octavia declared with feeling.

"He probably will be poxed if he goes with those whores," Rupert observed. "There are clean houses in King's Place and Covent Garden, but for some inexplicable reason our esteemed heir to the throne prefers to dabble in the sewers." He moved aside to hand Octavia into the coach.

As she put one foot on the step, a plump lady enveloped in a puce velvet cloak emerged from the assembly rooms. She caught her foot on a loose paving stone and pitched forward with a cry of dismay. Rupert dropped Octavia's hand and ran to help the woman to her feet.

"Are you hurt, ma'am?" He picked up her fallen reticule and handed it to her.

"No . . . no, I thank you, sir. So stupid . . . so clumsy of me."

"But you are ever thus, my dear," came a cold voice behind her. Philip Wyndham surveyed his wife with an air of utter contempt. "Stupid and clumsy as an ox. Aren't you, madam?"

Letitia looked down at the pavement and wished it would open to swallow her. There were people everywhere, eyes and ears open to catch her husband's icy contempt.

"Aren't you, madam?" he repeated with a deadly ferocity.

"Yes, Philip," she said softly. "Yes, I do beg your pardon." Tears filled her eyes and she kept her gaze lowered, staring wretchedly at the ground.

"Do you intend to stand here all night?" her husband inquired. "Allow me to point out that the chair awaits your pleasure, my dear." He gestured to the sedan chair with the Wyndham arms on the panel, and the two burly chairmen who were staring rigidly ahead down the busy street.

"I beg your pardon," Letitia apologized again, stepping toward the chair. She clambered awkwardly over the poles to enter through the front, the wide swinging skirts of her gown making her inherent clumsiness even more pronounced.

Rupert stood in the shadows, watching, waiting for his brother to offer a hand to assist his wife, but Philip remained where he was, his lip curled in disdain, until the door was closed on Letitia. The two chairmen hoisted their considerable burden onto their shoulders and trotted off down King Street, threading their way through the traffic.

Philip spun on his heel and walked away in the opposite direction. As he passed Rupert, he walked beneath an oil lamp, and the golden light illuminated his face. Rupert saw the Philip that only he had known in their childhood. The face that was no longer a beautiful mask but the true reflection of the twisted soul beneath. His eyes were narrowed, his mouth thinned with malice, his entire expression radiating the triumph and satisfaction of the sadist who has just inflicted pain.

Rupert turned back to the coach, where Octavia still stood poised, one foot on the step. She hadn't heard the exchange between Wyndham and his countess but had sensed its vicious nature. Now Rupert's face sent a cold dart through her belly. He looked haunted, pain etched in every line of his countenance, but it wasn't that that turned her blood to water—it was the fearsome anger that superseded the ghostly pain.

"What has he done to you?" she asked softly, involuntarily.

Rupert's eyes focused abruptly. "You don't need to know that." He took her hand and with his other palm in the small of her back urged her upward into the coach.

"There is an evil in him," Octavia declared with a fierce intensity, arranging her skirts on the leather squabs. "I sense it, and I know that you *know* it. And yet you would have me seduce this man without telling me anything of what you know. Is that fair, Rupert?"

Rupert sat opposite her. He regarded her in the darkness of the coach, frowning. "Fairness doesn't come into it," he said eventually. "Yes, Philip Wyndham is evil. But I won't permit any harm to come to you at his hands. If you fulfill your side of this bargain, you have no need to know what I know, and you need have no fear of him. He hurts only those in his power. And you will not be."

"How can you say that?" Octavia expostulated. "How can I not be in his power when I am in his bed? What power does a woman have in those circumstances?"

"Oh, you'd be surprised how much," Rupert said, his voice now light.

"I don't find it a subject for jest," Octavia said tightly. "You know perfectly well what I mean . . . how vulnerable I will be in such a situation. This is a man who preys on the vulnerable, you've just said so."

"My dear, you will not be vulnerable in the only way that appeals to Philip," Rupert said, leaning back, folding his arms. "He's interested in hurting souls, not bodies. And your soul will not be in his power. Besides, it may not be necessary for you to make the"—he paused as if considering his words, and then said wryly—"the ultimate sacrifice."

How could he make a joke of it? How could he be so derisively dismissive about something that touched her so nearly? Was it really a matter of indifference to him whether she prostituted herself with Philip Wyndham or not? But he probably didn't see it in those terms. No one in this depraved society would think twice about it. They all played these sordid little games.

Rupert had closed his eyes as if to indicate that the subject had ceased to be of interest. The coach slowed at a crossroads, and a link boy's lamp swayed in the window. Lamplight and shadow played over the planes of his closed face, throwing the harshness of his mouth, the clenched set of his jaw, into sharp relief.

His expression was utterly uncompromising, and Octavia was learning when it was pointless to push this man whose bed she shared, whose body she was growing to know almost as well as she knew her own. He could switch in the beat of a bird's wing from an amused and amusing companion to a chilly, distant, and dictatorial stranger. And she had not as yet learned how to resist those dictates. Any more than she'd learned to resist the magnetism of his personality, the way he could sweep her along his chosen path, making light of her objections when he didn't ignore them totally. Any more than she could imagine turning away from him when he reached for her with the hands of lust and the eyes of passion.

"We made a good start this evening, I believe," she said in level tones, drawing her cloak around her shoulders against the night frost.

Rupert's eyes opened and rested on her countenance. She saw a softness now in the gray depths and a glimmer of amusement. He began to count on his fingers as he spoke. "Yes, you've managed to arouse Wyndham's interest and the prince's unbridled lust; to establish yourself as a lady who enjoys pushing the bounds of convention; and to issue a general invitation for high stakes gaming in your salons."

He smiled lazily. "Against the law, of course. Justice Kenyon threatened Lady Buckinghamshire with the cart's arse if she came up before him for running a gaming house."

"He couldn't have meant it?" Octavia's eyes widened as she imagined the obese figure of Lady Buckinghamshire whipped at the cart's tail through the streets of London.

"No, I don't think even Kenyon would dare punish a member of the aristocracy in such fashion," Rupert agreed with a chuckle. "But the threat caused some alarm." He linked his hands in his lap, and the emerald on a slender forefinger glowed dully in the darkness.

"And while I was being so busy, what did you achieve this evening?" Octavia asked with a touch of acid, reminded of how that particular finger had tidied up Lady Drayton's escaping nipple. "Did you contrive to meet your prey?"

"I don't believe they were there," he said, making a steeple of his fingers. "I didn't see them, at all events."

"I see. And Lady Drayton? Was she useful to you in any way?"

Rupert looked sharply at her. "Why the acid-tipped tongue, Octavia?"

Octavia turned her head on the squabs behind her and gazed out at the darkness. "I just wondered why, while I was enduring the odious attentions of the prince, you were amusing yourself. I thought this was a joint enterprise."

"I was making it easy for you, my dear Octavia." He sounded amused, and she wanted to throw something at him. "Margaret Drayton is Philip Wyndham's mistress. I thought to prod him a little in your direction . . . to give him a reason to get back at me."

"I doubt he required a prod," Octavia retorted. "He seemed quite interested enough in me before you started dabbling in Lady Drayton's bosom."

Rupert laughed. "Such games are played, sweet innocent. A little dalliance means nothing . . . particularly with a known whore like Margaret Drayton."

"You don't care for her?"

"Oh, she can be quite amusing, particularly when she's annoyed. But she's a trifle overblown for me. I prefer my women a little fresher."

"Oh, you do, do you?" Octavia glared at the pale glimmer of his face across from her. "Like meat in the butcher's shop—best if we haven't been hanging too long."

Rupert's jaw dropped. "Now, just a minute, Octavia. Why are you so set on pulling caps with me? We've had a very successful evening. My quarry are not going anywhere —indeed, they'll be beating a path to Dover Street once the news of a high-stakes gaming table is spread around. And we can leave the spreading to the royal mouth," he added dryly.

When she made no response, merely continued to stare out of the window, he leaned over and took her gloved hands in his. "What's troubling you, sweeting?" His voice was dark and smooth as caramel, and she could never resist the endearment that belonged in glowing candlelight and soft damask sheets and accompanied leisurely caresses and the languor of fulfillment.

She couldn't admit the truth. Jealousy was a demeaning and petty emotion.

"I expect I'm fatigued," she said with a little laugh that

didn't sound particularly convincing to her ears. "Over-excitement, probably. Rubbing shoulders with royalty . . . sharpening swords with the likes of the Duchess of Deerwater."

Rupert was not convinced, but he didn't challenge her explanation. "Do you have the courage to continue ignoring the dictates of fashion?" he asked neutrally, releasing her hands and leaning back again.

"I don't believe it requires courage," Octavia said, accepting the change of subject with relief. "It might if I looked like a freak, but since I know I don't, then . . ." She shrugged.

Rupert relaxed. Her confidence pleased him. It was certainly not misplaced. She'd been the cynosure of every eye all evening. Not every eye had been admiring, of course, but one couldn't expect to stand out in a crowd without drawing resentment.

All in all, it had been a most satisfactory debut. It was only to be expected that Octavia would have a few flutters of apprehension and uncertainty, particularly in the aftermath of the evening. Such vulnerabilities would undoubtedly disappear as she became more accustomed to the part, and as the play took shape.

Chapter 10

The coach drew up outside a tall, narrow house on Dover Street. An oil lamp hung above the front door, and lights glowed in the downstairs windows.

"I wonder if Papa is still awake."

"If he is, perhaps we should pay him a good-night visit." Rupert opened the coach door and sprang down. "I don't know why it is, but I have the unshakable conviction that your father regards our marriage with a somewhat skeptical eye." He reached up his hand to help her alight. "Am I right?"

"Possibly," Octavia said, stepping down beside him. "One can never be sure what my father sees. In some things he's very shrewd."

The door opened as they walked up to it. "Good evening, Griffin. Has Mr. Morgan retired?"

"I don't believe so, my lady." The butler bowed her in. "He rang for fresh candles a short while ago."

"Then we'll go up and bid him good night," Rupert said, shrugging out of his cloak. "Lock up, Griffin." He strode to the stairs on Octavia's heels.

"You might wish to send Nell to bed," he murmured against Octavia's ear as they passed her bedchamber.

"There's nothing she can do for you tonight that I can't do as well."

Octavia looked over her shoulder at him, meeting the heat of a gaze that turned her limbs to honey. "Better, I would have said, my lord."

She turned aside to open her bedroom door. "You may go to bed, Nell."

The maid dozing in a chair beside the fire jumped sleepily to her feet. "Oh, ma'am, I'm quite awake," she protested with a guilty flush.

"Yes, I can see that. Nevertheless, I have no further need of you tonight." Octavia smiled at the girl, knowing how terrified she was that she would lose her position at the slightest dereliction. "Go to bed, Nell. And I'll see you in the morning."

"Yes, m'lady." The girl curtsied. "I'll trim the candles and make up the fire, though, shall I?"

"If you please." Octavia stepped back into the corridor, closing the door quietly behind her. Sometimes she felt as if they were all living within a stage set, the limits of their play set in a fixed time and place. Every member of their household was a member of the cast, although only she and Rupert knew it. And when the curtain came down, the supporting cast would be out of a job.

But not necessarily, she told herself briskly. If all went well, she and her father would be in a position to staff a household again. They weren't really playing with people's lives, just because they hadn't shared with the household the temporary nature of this employment. Besides, for as long as the play continued, these people were assured of food and warmth and a bed, and thus a great deal better off than the majority of London's population.

It occurred to Octavia that this uncomfortable social conscience that she'd developed had grown out of her own intimate acquaintance with poverty's grim and desperate face. Rupert knew that face too, but he seemed less troubled by it. Or perhaps he kept such reactions to himself . . . as he kept so much.

Now, however, was not the time for dwelling futilely

on the world's miseries and Rupert's apparent indifference to them. She hurried down the long corridor to the back of the house. She could hear Rupert's voice through the open door of her father's room.

"Good evening, Papa." Smiling cheerfully, she entered the bright, warm room. "You're up late."

"I could say the same of you," Oliver declared, regarding his daughter from a deep armchair beside a blazing fire. He looked well, his tawny eyes clear and sharp, his complexion smooth and pink, his thick mane of white hair luxuriant and glossy. He was wearing a fur-trimmed velvet dressing gown and fur-lined slippers, a rug across his knees. Books were heaped on the floor beside his chair, tumbled off the table at his side, lay open on the arm of his chair. He had a writing table across his lap, a quill in his hand, a sheet of parchment already covered in his spidery black writing.

"We had an evening of dissipation," Octavia said. "Rather different from work. How's it going?" She bent to kiss him.

"Very well, child. Warwick, do you remember that discussion we were having on Plato? About the influence of Pythagoras on his philosophy? Well, I have found the reference I was looking for . . . in Socrates . . . I have it here, somewhere." He began to rummage through the heap of books, from which bookmarks bristled like the spikes of a hedgehog.

Rupert took a seat beside the old man, and Octavia perched on the arm of a sofa across from them. Her father's cough had almost disappeared, and as she looked at him now, it was hard to imagine that the smooth course of his life had ever been disrupted. He behaved as if he had no recollection of their three-year sojourn in the East End alleys, of the days without sufficient food, the constant lack of warmth, the daily struggle to make and mend to keep adequate clothes on their backs. He had always behaved as if he had no idea how Octavia achieved her small miracles. He'd certainly shown no curiosity about the details of their past existence and had been singularly incurious about this change in their circumstances.

When Octavia had explained to her father that she and Lord Rupert Warwick had married without his consent because he had been too ill and feverish to be consulted, Oliver had offered no comment. Octavia had expected some reaction to this momentous fait accompli, and in the face of this calm acceptance of the new situation, she'd found herself expanding her explanation as if he were as skeptical and disapproving as she'd expected him to be. She'd rattled on about how he'd been so ill that she'd felt that his health was more important than convention and she'd agreed to a speedy and unceremonious marriage in order to hasten their move to somewhere warmer and more comfortable.

Her father had merely smiled, said he was sure she knew what she was doing. She'd always known what was best for herself and if she was happy, then so was he. And he had settled into his spacious apartments on Dover Street as if they had always been his.

Rupert had been surprisingly attentive to the old man, certainly above and beyond the call of duty in the circumstances, Octavia considered. And he'd evinced an astonishingly intimate knowledge of the classics that delighted Oliver Morgan. Not just knowledge, Octavia reflected, listening to the discussion. Enthusiasm. He seemed to find Oliver's forays into the more abstruse realms of classical philosophy as fascinating as her father did.

She, herself, had long exhausted her interest in Oliver's intellectual pursuits. He'd educated her rigorously in the classics, and she read and spoke Greek and Latin with an unusual fluency for a woman. Rupert, if he'd had the conventional education of a wellborn male, would have spoken Latin and Greek in preference to English throughout his school years. But somehow Octavia didn't think the young Lord Rupert Warwick, or whoever he truly was, had had a conventional upbringing. Nevertheless, he was perfectly at home in the ancient worlds of Greece and Rome.

How he'd acquired that education he wasn't saying.

"Now I'm making such progress with this article, I must write to my publishers and tell them how it's going.

Alderbury was most anxious I should keep them informed of my progress when we last corresponded," Oliver said happily, wiping off his quill.

A correspondence that had ceased three years earlier, Octavia reflected. But there was no virtue in pointing that out. It would only offend her father, and who was to say that Mr. Alderbury wasn't waiting with bated breath for the next progress report?

She stood up. "I think I'll go to bed, it's been a long evening. Do you have everything you need, Papa?"

"Yes, thank you, my dear." He smiled and kissed her as she bent over him. "I shall stay up a little while yet. Perhaps your husband would care to bear me company." He turned to Rupert, and there was no mistaking the mischief in his eyes. "But, then again, perhaps not."

"I beg you to forgive me, sir." Rupert hid his surprise at that mischievously shrewd look. "But I find myself a trifle fatigued."

"Of course, of course. Young people have no stamina these days." Oliver waved him away, his eyes bright with that same look. "Seek your bed, Warwick, and leave me to my philosophy."

"Good night, sir." Rupert bowed and turned to follow Octavia from the room.

The door closed behind them, and Oliver Morgan smiled to himself. Surely they didn't think he didn't know what was going on. Octavia couldn't really believe him to be such a dumb idiot as not to know this whole marriage tale was a gigantic fabrication. But fabrication or not, it had returned her to her rightful place in the world. And whatever lay behind this arrangement, it was one that clearly suited his daughter. He didn't care to speculate on what work she'd been doing when she'd leave him for long periods during their sojourn in Shoreditch. When she returned, his books were redeemed from the pawnbroker, they dined from the landlady's table, and there was fire in the hearth. But whatever she did to achieve those small miracles had taken a terrible toll.

Now the drawn look had left her face, her eyes glowed

again, and the frisson between her and Lord Rupert was as
apparent as a rainbow in a shower.

He let the book fall closed on his lap and leaned back in
his chair, closing his eyes. Perhaps he should be concerned
about his daughter's reputation, about her honor. But such
concepts had ceased to have any relevance after Harrowgate. And if he hadn't questioned her activities in
Shoreditch, he certainly didn't have the right to do so now.

The blackness filled his head as it always did when he
thought of his criminal idiocy, and he turned from the
knowledge. To confront it did no good and merely destroyed any chance for peace of mind.

Octavia was happy. That was all that mattered. Oliver
shook himself awake and returned to his books.

"You've never said exactly how you intend to accomplish my revenge," Octavia said, raising her arms to unpin
her hair. She was naked, and the movement lifted her
breasts, drew the skin of her back taut.

Rupert, shoeless but otherwise still fully dressed, lay
back on the bed, arms linked behind his head, watching
with leisurely pleasure as she disrobed. "The plan is not
fully formed as yet."

"But you do have a plan?" She took off the high pads
over which her hair had been piled and shook the cinnamon tresses free.

"Most certainly."

"And you're not going to tell me?" She picked up her
hairbrush and studied his reflection in the mirror.

Rupert laughed and swung off the bed. "Let me brush
your hair." He crossed the room, his stockinged feet sinking
into the Turkey carpet, and stood behind her.

The silk of his clothes brushed against the bare skin of
her back, a skin suddenly so sensitive that the silken caress
was almost abrasive. Octavia shivered, watching in the mirror as her nipples grew hard and erect.

He took the brush from her and began to draw it

through her hair, placing one hand on the top of her head as he pulled through the long, tangled curls.

"Are you going to tell me?"

"As yet there's nothing to tell. Now, don't distract me because I'm going to count to a hundred."

Octavia gave up for the present under the seductive strokes of the brush. Her eyes closed, her head drooped; she slipped into a sensuous trance, her body swaying gently as if she were a willow tree in the wind.

When he stopped brushing, her eyes fluttered open again, meeting his in the mirror. His expression was serious and attentive. Gravely, he placed the brush down on the dresser and lifted her hair off her shoulders, letting it fall forward over her breasts. Reaching over her shoulders, his long white fingers parted the strands of hair, revealing her nipples and the pale circles around them. All the while, he held her gaze in the mirror, his eyes now deep and dark as coal.

His hands slipped around her waist, cupping her breasts before sliding down over her ribs, his palms flattening on her belly.

Her body in the mirror was white as alabaster against the black silk at her back. Soft and vulnerable in its nakedness. Her heart beat faster as his thigh moved against her buttocks, his knee nudging her thighs apart. The silk of his britches rustled across the delicate skin of her inner thighs, his knee pressed upward, creating an exquisite friction that made her catch her lip between her teeth. She watched her eyes grow large and misty, her skin pinken, as her excitement grew. She watched herself grow closer to the peak, and she watched Rupert watching her.

He smiled, a long, slow smile of satisfaction, enjoying her excitement as the pleasure built in her belly in ever-tightening spirals, and at the instant before she could bear no more, he used his hands on her and the coil burst asunder. She fell back against him and he wrapped his arms around her, laughing softly into her hair.

"I do love playing with you, sweeting. You're so supremely responsive."

"Obedient to your every touch," Octavia mumbled with a weak chuckle. "I'm as clay in your hands, my lord."

"In matters of loving," he qualified with mock solemnity, tightening his arms around her waist, resting his chin on the top of her head. "I'm not so certain about other matters."

"And just what does that mean?" She tried to look and sound indignant but failed miserably at both.

"Oh, you know quite well." He swung her off her feet and over to the bed.

"If you mean I don't accept your mastery without question, yes, I do know what you mean." She lay on the bed where he'd dropped her, her hair a glowing fan around her.

"Well, perhaps I'll just settle for the areas in which I have undisputed mastery," Rupert declared cheerfully, throwing off his clothes with an unseemly haste. "At least for the moment."

Naked, he leaped onto the bed beside her and straddled her thighs. "Now, madam, you may await further dissolution and tremble!"

"Oh, I do," she said, running her tongue over lips, reaching to grasp the erect shaft as it brushed her belly. "Even my toes are trembling." The pad of her thumb danced over the moistening tip of his flesh as her fingers moved behind, stroking the hard globes.

"What did you mean, 'at least for the moment'?" she inquired, a gleam in her eye as she deepened her caress. His only response was a sigh of pleasure.

"Oh, never mind," she murmured, her thighs shifting beneath his weight. "I think I've lost interest in both the question and its answer . . . at least for the moment."

The clock on the mantel chimed four. The fire hissed and crackled. A gust of wind rattled the windowpane. From behind the bed curtains came low murmurs of delight as they moved in the darkness, their bodies blending in a fusion so complete, it denied the possibility of any dissonance.

"*F*our o'clock and all's well." The watchman's repetitive cry faded down the corner of King's Street as Margaret Drayton emerged from Almack's among the last of the evening's revelers. She was slightly tipsy, leaning on the arm of a stalwart young gentleman whose glazed eyes and somewhat rigid features indicated his own lack of sobriety.

"Where's my carriage, Lawton?" Margaret demanded, staring down the now rapidly emptying street. "I sent you to call for it."

"Oh, but I did, ma'am. I assure you I did." Her escort peered around intently, as if expecting the missing carriage to materialize from thin air.

"Then why is it not here?" her ladyship demanded peevishly, huddling into her cloak as the wind whistled around the alley leading to King's Place.

"My carriage is at your service, Margaret."

Margaret turned at the smoothly considerate tones of the Earl of Wyndham. "Oh, I thought you'd gone home hours ago, Philip."

"I've been playing at Mount Edgecombe's," he said, taking snuff. "But the party broke up a trifle suddenly when one of her ladyship's watchmen believed a troop of Runners was about to raid the house." He laughed, the sound clear and hard in the frosty air. "A false alarm, of course, but it did rather dampen enthusiasm."

"Yes, I can imagine. Lawton, you've proved yourself singularly inept. I suggest you take yourself home to bed." Margaret dismissed the hapless young man tartly.

"I did call your carriage . . . I do assure you," her erstwhile escort protested. "Can't think where it could have disappeared to."

"I daresay it turned into a pumpkin," the earl said. "Ma'am, my carriage awaits your pleasure." He offered his arm to Lady Drayton, and the two went off, leaving the Honorable Michael Lawton gazing disconsolately and in some bewilderment after them.

"You do know how to ensure a lady's comfort, Wyndham," Margaret observed appreciatively, as the footman spread a rug over her knees and adjusted the position of a hot brick beneath her feet. "In your company a woman would never find herself standing in the rain without an umbrella, or waiting for a chair in the wind, or finding herself seated at a bad table in the Piazza. Unlike that poor fool, Lawton."

"Setting up another flirtation, are you, Margaret?" the earl inquired casually. "I can't help feeling sorry for the infant. He clearly doesn't know you could eat him for supper."

Margaret laughed. "Oh, I was just amusing myself, Philip. There was a dearth of entertaining companions this evening . . . at least after the prince left. Indeed, I don't know why I persist in going to these insipid affairs." Delicately, she adjusted a beauty patch high on her cheekbone. "Of course, one must be seen."

"Of course," the earl agreed. "And were you amusing yourself similarly with Rupert Warwick?" The deceptively smooth, amused tone had vanished. He threw the question like a knife.

"La, Philip, what is it to you?" Margaret said with an artificial and uncertain laugh. "Warwick's a most entertaining gentleman."

"I like to know who else plays in the same garden," the earl said coldly. "I'm a trifle fastidious, my dear, in some areas. But I daresay that's quite a novel concept for you."

Lady Drayton whitened with anger beneath the rouge, taking on a garish almost clownlike appearance. "I don't believe I understand you, my lord."

"Oh, come now, Margaret, you're not such a fool," the earl said, leaning forward, catching her chin on his forefinger. "I thought I'd made it plain that I wish for exclusive rights to your body. Apart from whatever demands your husband might make, of course," he added with a careless gesture of his free hand. "I do accept that, as an obedient and loving wife, you must accommodate Drayton in whatever manner he wishes."

He smiled, an angelic smile of benign understanding, but his fingers now grasped her chin painfully.

Margaret gasped and tried to pull back. The carriage

jolted in a pothole, and she was thrown forward against the earl's knees. He caught her wrist with his free hand and held her in that position even as the carriage moved smoothly again. "I'm perfectly content to end our little arrangement, if you so wish. We understand each other, I'm sure." He released her abruptly and gave her a push that sent her back onto her seat. "I don't use whores."

Margaret stared in shock at the pale glimmer of his face. His possessive streak had become more pronounced of late, but she hadn't taken it very seriously. Her fawning courtiers were always too eager for her attentions to risk annoying her. She knew that Philip Wyndham was different, it was part of his attraction—that and his generosity. But she had always believed she could control him as she controlled the others. This was something new and frightening. She'd been frightened by men in her time in the King's Place nunnery, but there had always been a bell to ring and a muscular footman on call. Here, in this warm, swaying darkness, in Wyndham's carriage, driven by Wyndham's servants, there was no protection.

"Rupert Warwick means nothing to me," she whispered, her eyes darting to the window, looking for some familiar landmark in the darkness. The distance from Almack's to her house on Mount Street should have been accomplished in no more than fifteen minutes at this time of the morning, with no traffic. And yet they seemed to have been journeying for hours.

Her companion made no response to this assertion. He leaned back against the velvet squabs and regarded her, his eyes vacant, expressionless, like gray holes in the serene planes of his face.

Margaret began to shiver. It was as if she were in the presence of the devil. "Why are we not at Mount Street yet?" she managed to ask, shrinking into the corner.

"Oh, are you in a hurry to be home, my dear? I beg your pardon, I thought you might enjoy a little tête-à-tête." He smiled.

A suspicion popped into her head, became certainty. "What happened to my carriage?"

His smile broadened. "As I said, I thought you might enjoy a little tête-à-tête."

"You sent it away?" She felt like crying in bewilderment.

"An accurate deduction," the earl said dryly. "I'm surprised it took you so long to come to it." He reached up and knocked on the roof of the carriage. The coachman responded to the knock by swinging the vehicle to the right.

Margaret clutched the strap above the window. "Take me home."

"But of course," he said, raising an eyebrow as if surprised. "Where do you think I'm taking you? You should be at your door in about two minutes. By my estimation we should now be turning onto Audley Street."

Margaret huddled in her corner, nibbling a gloved fingertip. She was too frightened to speak, and when the carriage came to a halt and she recognized her own front door under the oil lamp, she flung open the door and tumbled to the street without waiting for the footman to lower the step.

The earl leaned out of the open door. "Forgive me if I don't walk you to your door, my dear."

"I don't ever wish to speak to you again," Margaret declared, her voice trembling but her courage returning with the safety of her own front door a mere three steps away.

The earl inclined his head in courteous acknowledgment. "You desolate me, ma'am." Then he withdrew into the carriage, pulling the door closed.

Margaret ran up the steps to her own front door and hammered on the knocker until the night porter sleepily stumbled to open it.

Philip smiled to himself as the coach took him home to St. James's Square. He'd been tiring of Margaret, although he hadn't realized it until he'd seen her flirting with Rupert Warwick. It was time for a new adventure. And who better to have it with than the young, fresh, and very spirited wife of a man he instinctively detested?

He jumped from the coach with a surge of energy more appropriate for the middle of the morning than the cold, dark hour before dawn. The front door opened before he could knock. The night porter in the Earl of Wyndham's house knew better than to sleep on duty and had been holding himself in readiness for the sound of the carriage throughout the night. He didn't lock the door behind the earl, however, since for the household the day's work had already begun.

A boot boy, fresh from his own night's rest on the chilly stone floor of the scullery, slunk into the hall from the kitchen regions, rubbing sleep from his eyes. The second footman, his immediate superior, resplendent in livery and powdered wig, strode behind the lad, a bundle of keys in his hand, preparing to open up the doors to the main salons for the maidservants to begin the day's cleaning.

The second footman saw the earl the instant before the earl saw him. He grabbed the collar of the boot boy's jacket and jerked him into the shadows of the staircase until the master was safely out of sight on the stairs. The Earl of Wyndham's gaze must not be offended by the sight of a seven-year-old boy with matted hair and filthy hands, his scrawny body enveloped in a grimy apron, roaming the public areas of the house—even at five o'clock in the morning.

Philip strode into his own apartments, where his valet stood waiting for him, an air of alert solicitude on his face despite his sleepless night.

"You passed a pleasant evening, my lord?"

"Yes, thank you." The earl flung himself into a chair and extended his feet. The valet bent and removed his lordship's shoes, then tenderly helped him out of his coat.

One glance at his employer's expression told the experienced valet that conversation would not be welcome, so he went about his duties silently and, once his lordship was arrayed in his velvet dressing gown, drew back the bed-curtains and turned down the coverlet. He stood expectantly beside the bed, while the earl, frowning, took a turn about the room.

"Oh, that'll be all, Fredericks." The earl waved him away. "I can put myself to bed."

"Very good, my lord." The valet bowed himself from the room and once outside straightened with a grimace. The earl was an erratic sleeper, and one could never be certain whether he'd sleep for two hours or six. He'd seemed restless this early morning, which probably meant he'd be ringing his bell again in a couple of hours, and Fredericks would be expected to attend him as fresh and alert as if he'd slept the night away. In the circumstances he daren't risk taking more than a catnap on his pallet in the attic before readying himself for his employer's next summons.

Philip paced his bedchamber for a minute. The encounter with Lady Warwick followed by his confrontation with Margaret had excited him, and his loins were heavy, his blood hot with a sexual appetite that needed gratification. He allowed his mind to dwell on the lissome figure of Rupert Warwick's wife, on the mischievous sparkle in her eyes that seemed to suggest collusion, on the curve of her mouth, the discreetly veiled swell of her breasts. There was a freshness about her that excited him most powerfully. And she'd seemed inclined to play a part other than that of the straitlaced ingenue bride.

How would Rupert Warwick take to wearing horns? The question amused Philip. His gaze flickered to the door connecting his apartments with his wife's. It was not a question he would ever have to ask of himself.

His blood grew hotter, so that a mist of perspiration coated his skin. His flesh rose beneath his gown, pulsating with the urgency of his need.

He had a wife. An unsatisfactory wife in all respects, but her body was there, available to assuage this need. He strode to the door, flung it open, and entered the dark chamber.

The curtains were drawn around the bed, and he threw them back.

Letitia had awakened as the door had banged on its hinges, and now she lay shivering under the covers. She knew what he'd come for and closed her eyes tightly as the bed curtains were opened and she felt his presence beside the bed. He always took her in this way, ever since she'd conceived Susannah. Always suddenly in the night, always waking her from sleep, so that many nights she lay awake until dawn in dread apprehension, straining her ears in the dark, waiting for the visitation.

He never spoke to her, except sometimes when he used coarse, vile language as he pushed hurtfully against the limits of her body, and the language seemed to excite him to greater fervency. There was never any pretense that she herself was important. He had a need, and it was her duty to supply that need.

The bed shivered as he dropped heavily onto the mattress. He raised her shift, then seized her hands, holding them over her head. He pushed into her, and tears squeezed behind her eyelids at the tight, unyielding pain.

When it was over, he left her—without a word, without even drawing the bed curtains again—so that now she could see the first pink streaks of dawn through the window, an offering of a new and bright day.

Letitia's tears flowed hot and strong as she lay in wide-eyed misery. This was her life, and there was nothing she could do about it. No one she could turn to. Her father would never listen to a complaint against her husband. Her husband was her lord and master in the eyes of the Church and the law, and how he chose to treat her was a matter for his own conscience. The Duke of Gosford would have nothing to say. The world would have nothing to say.

Chapter 11

ॐ♪ "No dinner engagement this evening, Octavia?"

"No, I thought I'd pamper myself with a little peace and quiet for once." Octavia turned her head against the rim of the bathtub, smiling through the fragrant steam at Rupert in the doorway. "Are you coming in, because there's a howling gale coming from behind you."

Rupert stepped into the room, closing the door at his back. "Nell, your mistress will ring when she needs you again."

Nell, who was smoothing the folds of a gown of dark-green silk, showed no surprise at this statement. One glance at Lord Rupert's coolly appraising gaze resting on the naked Lady Warwick in her bath had told her that her presence was about to be superfluous. She adjusted the gown on its hanger, curtsied, and slipped discreetly from the room.

Rupert hitched his foot behind the leg of a padded stool before the dresser and dragged it across to the tub, next to the fire. He'd become accustomed to Octavia's predilection for baths, although that was as unusual as her refusal to wear paint and powder.

"If you're intending to play, you're going to spoil your

coat," Octavia observed with a severe air. "Water and velvet are bad combinations, my lord."

"A problem easily resolved," he said, removing his coat of glossy black velvet and the black silk waistcoat beneath. He placed both carefully on the bed, then unfastened the tiny buttons hidden in the deep lace ruffles of his sleeves and twitched the fine lawn up to his elbows.

"But you might splash your britches," Octavia said in the same tone, idly flicking her fingertips across the surface of the water.

"I'll take the risk. What have you done with the soap?"

"Oh, I've already soaped myself," she said languidly.

"Then you'll have to be soaped twice," he declared, sitting on the stool beside the tub, bending to pick up the lavender-scented cake from the dish on the floor. "Now, where shall I start . . ."

Octavia chuckled and surrendered, her body malleable and obedient to instruction. Rupert always took the greatest delight in playing with her, and yielding herself in this way set her mind adrift from her body, bringing her a rich and pure sensual pleasure.

She knew that Rupert intended that this game would stay with her throughout the evening, her body, aroused and sensitive, waiting with eager impatience for the moment when the promise of these playful caresses would be fulfilled. She knew that throughout the evening Rupert would glance at her occasionally, brush against her, murmur something in her ear, and her body, already on the brink of passion, would be jolted by a current of hungry lust. Rupert would smile and move away, knowing exactly what he'd done, knowing that when they were at last alone, the mere brush of his fingers would send her plunging into the chasm.

"Where are you dining this evening?" Attempting to carry on an ordinary conversation was part of the game.

"Viscount Lawton has a small gathering," he replied in the same casual tone, his hands following their own busy path. "He's promised a degree of light entertainment."

"Women, in other words."

"Possibly," he agreed. "A party of Posture Molls, I believe. The Prince of Wales has made it clear that he relishes such spectator sports, and Malcolm assures me that the three ladies he's hired for the evening will provide a spectacle to satisfy the most prurient imagination."

He withdrew his hand from beneath the water and ran a fingertip over her lips. "One of them, I believe, specializes in flagellation, one of His Highness's most particular pleasures."

Octavia chuckled, licking the tip of his finger. "Does he prefer to administer or receive?"

"Oh, either or both, according to mood," Rupert said airily. "Unfortunately, he expects his companions to participate with the same enthusiasm, so I think I shall excuse myself before the entertainment really gets going." He reached for a large towel, draping it over his knee as he sat on the low stool. "Come."

"You'll be back here later for the gaming?" Octavia rose in a shower of drops, stepped delicately out of the tub, and deposited herself on Rupert's knee.

"Of course." He wrapped the towel around her and began to blot the water from her skin. "And followed by most of Lawton's guests, I trust. Once they tire of watching the sexual antics of a trio of whores."

"I thought Posture Molls considered themselves to be above whores." Octavia leaned forward obligingly so he could dry her back. "They don't actually sell their bodies, do they?"

"No, they merely perform in as lewd and depraved a manner as any slavering idiot could wish for. Stand up, so I can reach the rest of you."

Octavia did so, fighting hard now to keep the conversation going as the towel patted over her bottom and down the backs of the thighs. "Slavering, arrogant, and complacent idiots," she declared, her voice catching in her throat. "We're making fools of them all, and it would never occur to them that we might not be what we seem."

His hands on her hips turned her to face him, and it

dawned upon her that she was going to lose this particular battle.

Rupert laughed and leaned back, looking up her body with an amused and desirous eye. "Shall I have mercy, sweeting?"

"Would you take any notice of my wishes?" Her voice wouldn't come out right. Her body cried out now for the promised dissolution, and she wanted him to finish it, even though she knew that to do so would deny her the long hours of sensitized anticipation that brought their own exquisite delights.

"Oh, I might," he said consideringly. "But I think I'll leave matters as they stand."

Octavia's breath rushed between her lips, and she stepped away from his hands hastily . . . too hastily. The rim of the bath caught her behind the calves and she fell backward, arms and legs flailing, water slurping over the tub in a soapy gush.

"Clumsy," Rupert said, shaking his head reprovingly as she lay in an ungainly sprawl. "Now I'm going to have to start all over again."

"No, you're not!" She struggled to her feet again. "Go away, sir, and leave me to Nell."

He laughed, enjoying her indignation that was only half-feigned. He caught her chin and kissed her before replacing his waistcoat and coat. "I'll be back here by eleven at the latest. I don't imagine the serious business of the evening will begin before then, but you'll be able to amuse any early guests in your own inimitable fashion, my dear."

Octavia wrapped herself in the towel again. Two inducements were offered in the Warwicks' salon on Dover Street. The flirtatious and entertaining company of Lady Warwick, and the high-stakes gaming furnished by Lord Rupert. Between them they managed to entice to their house most of the younger members of the ton led by the Prince of Wales.

Enticed them and made fools of them, Octavia thought as the door closed on Rupert's departing back.

Gaming was against the law, but it remained the most

popular and ruinous activity in London. Octavia hadn't been surprised to discover that Rupert was an expert gamester. Expert and perfectly willing to take a fortune from any young blood eager and inexperienced enough to allow him to do so. It was one way to pay their household bills. Octavia, who had no skill and couldn't see the appeal in hazarding fortunes on the turn of a card or the fall of the dice, played the part of an easy, flirtatious hostess, offering a warm welcome and generous hospitality to all who came to play in her salon and pit their wits and nerve against her husband.

And it was an amusing business for all its deadly, serious purpose. The vain, posturing idiots deserved to be made mock of. The men with whom she flirted never showed the slightest reservation over her frequently outrageous flattery. The women who preened themselves under Rupert's suave attentions never evinced a hint of suspicion that he might not be in earnest. The greed, self-consequence, and vanity of George III's court defied belief, or at least to Octavia's blunt and clear-eyed way of thinking. She felt no scruples about using such failings against them and knew that Rupert had not a whisper of conscience about it.

It was an amusing game, but it was also an exhausting one. After a long evening's performance Octavia was drained and relished tonight's prospect of a few quiet hours before the curtain went up. She would dine with her father, who was so much his old self these days that he was once again the entertaining and informative companion of her childhood. And when Griffin announced the first guest, she'd be refreshed and ready for the fray.

ᗏ

Dirk Rigby and Hector Lacross were rather old to be part of the Prince of Wales's set, but they both affected a style more suited to men ten years younger than themselves, wearing brightly striped waistcoats, high powdered wigs, a plethora of fobs and pins and gold-frogged coats. They fawned upon the prince with all the slavering enthusiasm of a pair of anxious puppies.

Octavia found it hard to take her eyes off the men who had ruined her father. They were only two of the guests who had poured into Dover Street since the clock struck ten, but her eyes kept returning to them, her ears strained to catch their conversation, as she moved around the room, encouraging her guests to the tables where faro and evens and odds were being played.

"You're a trifle distracted, Octavia." Rupert's voice spoke in her ear, startling her. "The prince has been winking and beckoning you for the last four minutes, and you haven't once looked in his direction."

Octavia glanced guiltily across the room to where the prince sat at a faro table, waving a chicken-skin fan at her. She smiled and waved back, whispering distractedly, "I beg your pardon. It's just that it's the first time I've seen—"

"I know," he interrupted with a crisp edge to his voice. "But they're my pigeons, not yours. And if you keep staring at them in such a fashion, you'll draw attention to them and to yourself."

Chagrined, Octavia only nodded and moved away to obey the prince's summons. Rupert might say that her enemies were his pigeons, but he'd made no particular attempt to cultivate them this evening, or even to play with them. At first she'd assumed his plan was to win back her father's fortune at the gaming tables, but she realized now that that had been a naive assumption. There was too great an element of chance in such a plan to appeal to a man like Rupert, who plotted with such cold detachment. Lord Nick on his silver mount enjoyed taking risks, enjoyed courting danger. But Lord Rupert Warwick was a man of icy clarity, who planned to the last possible detail.

Rupert watched covertly as Octavia reached the prince and stood at his chair, laughing at some inevitably gross royal sally. His body stirred as he remembered their earlier game in the bathtub and what that game promised for later.

Tonight she was looking more striking than ever, in the gown of dark-green silk with ivory-ribbon knots, her hair clustered in loose, glowing ringlets on her creamy shoulders. The emerald eardrops and necklace were such a perfect facsimile that only the two of them could possibly know that they were paste.

She had taken to her part as if she'd been born to it, the daringly unconventional young bride who was always ready to welcome new guests and whose every gesture seemed to suggest that she was open to any suggestions for entertainment, however risqué they might be. Rupert played the indulgent husband, flirting with his wife as outrageously as other men did, and flirting pointedly with every woman who came his way.

They were the season's most attractive and sought-after couple, and to everyone's delight and no one's concern, the scandalmongers were having a field day.

And sometimes, when Rupert watched her laugh and flirt, when he saw the greedy eyes fixed on her bosom, the pawing hands reaching for her, he felt nauseated at the thought of that scented damask skin sullied by such attentions, at the thought of the lascivious fantasies behind every pat and hungry, covetous gaze. The rich glories of her body belonged to him, and he turned with disgust from the contemplation of other men's lust. And yet it was necessary.

His cold gaze sought and found Philip, standing beside the fireplace. The earl also watched Octavia over the lip of his wineglass. Philip Wyndham was not a serious gamester, but it didn't keep him away from Dover Street. And Octavia was playing him with all the skill of an accomplished fisherman.

Rupert closed his mind to the thought of his twin's hands moving in possession over Octavia's golden body. He thought instead of the Wyndham emeralds, of how, if he had his birthright, paste jewels would not lie against Octavia's skin. His hand slipped into his britches pocket. Fleetingly, his fingers brushed the silk pouch, the small round shape of his own Wyndham ring.

It was said that the tradition of the Wyndham rings went back to the times of the Crusaders, but its genesis was lost in the mists of generational memory. Every son born to the earl had his own ring, slipped onto his finger as the umbilical cord was cut. Convention dictated that the child

was thus bound to uphold the honor of his family above all
other commitments, and when his own son was born, the
ring and the commitment would be passed on. When it had
been suspected that Lady Wyndham was carrying twins,
their grandmother, a lady of whimsical temperamant, had
had fashioned two identical rings with a curious design
feature that she had fancifully intended would bind the boys
to each other as they were bound to the family. A fancy
doomed to disappointment from the first breath they'd
taken.

Gervase, as the eldest, had worn the earl's own ring,
and according to custom, because he had died childless, the
ring had been buried with him. Philip now carried the ring
that represented the Earl of Wyndham. Or thought he did.

Rupert's mouth curved in a grim smile. Octavia would
bring him Philip's ring. Only the twins knew the secret of
the rings' design. When Philip saw both in Rupert Warwick's possession, he would know his twin again. And the
knowledge would destroy him. Rupert wanted to see his
brother's face as he recognized his twin and understood all
that that twin's reappearance would mean. It would be a
moment of personal vengeance so sweet, it would compen-
sate for all the miseries of his boyhood.

Octavia would make that moment possible.

The conviction restored his cool equanimity, and he
turned his attention to Rigby and Lacross, new arrivals in
Dover Street. They were playing faro and drinking heavily.
Two youngsters were at the same table and Rupert was
convinced that Rigby, who held the bank, had marked
them both for fleecing.

Rupert had no objection to heavy winners. Indeed, for
his house to be a success, he needed them. He would offer
worldly advice and casual commiseration to the inexperienced youngsters who left his table with barely their shirts.
But he did object to cheating. He had no desire, though, to
provoke Dirk Rigby. Because the man's greed was the
weapon Rupert intended to turn against him, it needed to
be encouraged. But on this particular occasion it could be
foiled.

He strolled over to the table and stood between the two drink-flushed young men who were now scribbling IOUs with reckless abandon. "Gentlemen," he drawled, laying a hand on either shoulder, "I prefer not to take IOUs in my house. We play only for gold, I'm afraid."

The two looked up at him in startled dismay and met a level gaze that made them shift uncomfortably on their little gilt chairs.

"Oh, come now, Warwick, since when has a man not accepted IOUs?" demanded Lacross.

"I find them tedious," Rupert said mildly, taking snuff. "Such a nuisance having to chase around after one's debtors . . ." He glanced down at the two young men again, a lazy half smile playing over his lips. "If you have money, gentlemen, then you're more than welcome to remain at the table. If not . . ." He moved his hands apart in a gesture expressing reluctant resignation. "If not, I must ask you to leave."

"You . . . you would imply that I would not settle my debts," blustered one of the young men, his face flushing darkly. "I tell you, sir, you insult me. I demand satisfaction."

"Oh, don't be absurd, Markham," Rupert said. "No one's insulting you, lad. I am simply saying that you are playing under my roof, and I make the rules. I daresay you were not aware of those rules when you began to play. But now you are. So the choice is yours. If you can afford to play, then pray do so. If you cannot, then I'm afraid I must bid you good evening."

The two young men, scarlet with embarrassment, pushed back their chairs, bowed jerkily to the assembled company, and left.

"Harsh, Rupert," Peter Carson said, watching their discomfited departure.

"Young fools," Rupert said with a shrug. "They shouldn't be playing with grown-ups. They'll get over it. Loss of dignity is easier to bear in the long run than an extended stay in the Fleet."

He turned back to the clearly annoyed Lacross and

Rigby. "Shall we open at two hundred guineas, gentlemen? Pray refill your glasses." He gestured over his shoulder to a footman with a decanter of claret. "Let us begin anew and cut for bank. Lacross, do you play also? Peter, won't you join us?"

Rigby gathered up the IOUs that littered the table and stuffed them into his coat pocket. "You set rather eccentric rules at your tables, Warwick."

Rupert laughed easily and took his seat. "Eager young puppies will turn into real gamesters, Rigby, only if they're not ruined at the outset." He threw a handful of golden guineas onto the table, where they glittered in the lamp-light. A fortune tossed carelessly before the rapacious eyes of Rigby and Lacross.

Hector Lacross gave a shout of laughter, and in his enthusiasm knocked over his glass of claret. Red wine puddled on the table and dripped onto the waxed floor beneath. A footman moved swiftly to blot the mess, while another refilled the empty glass.

Rupert ignored the commotion, his expression as bland as milk pudding as he cut the pack of cards. "I must say, I favor a surer route to fat pockets than relying on the inexperience of babes and sucklings," he observed.

"Oh?" Lacross leaned over the table, his little blue eyes focusing with difficulty. "What's that, then, Warwick?"

Rupert smiled. "There are always schemes, I find. Shall we play, gentlemen?"

Octavia heard the immoderate laughter interspersed with Rupert's light tones. She tried not to show her curiosity as she devoted her attentions to the prince, aware of Philip Wyndham's still presence behind her. She could feel his eyes on her back as if they were burning probes, and there was something unnerving about his stillness, about his aura of focused determination. He was never suggestive, never flirtatious, but he was always in her vicinity. She wondered if he was waiting for her to make some move toward him, some acknowledgment of his interest. But instinct kept her from doing so. She sensed he would be drawn toward her more by an appearance of indifference than by the usual simpering affectation she saw on every side. And if perhaps she was a little frightened of Philip Wyndham, she didn't want to admit that even to herself.

"Lady Margaret Drayton," Griffin intoned from the doorway. Octavia turned sharply. Only women of hardy reputation patronized the Warwicks' gaming tables, but Margaret Drayton, whose reputation was of the hardiest, had not so far shown her face.

Rupert rose immediately from the table, crossing the room with hands outstretched. "My dear ma'am, ravishing as always," he declared, taking her hands between his and raising them to his lips. "You do our poor house too much honor."

"La, Sir Rupert, but you've a pretty tongue," Margaret said with a curtsy. "I've heard the fastest game of E and O in town can be found here."

"You won't be disappointed," he promised, drawing her forward. "Come and sit beside me at the faro table first, though. I've a game I must finish out."

Octavia glanced at Philip. His expression was carved in granite, his eyes gray pinpricks. His face was as smoothly beautiful as ever beneath the white wig, and yet Octavia was reminded of the face of a gargoyle, hideous and misshapen.

"Your husband seems to find La Drayton an entertaining companion," he observed as he caught her glance.

"He's not alone," Octavia said easily, with a graceful shrug.

"No, that's the truth, dear ma'am," chuckled the prince, leaning back in his chair and seizing Octavia's hand. "Margaret's the town Toast. But I'll say this"—he lowered his voice to an exaggerated whisper, his little eyes gleaming in the folds of his pudgy sweating face—"can't hold a candle to you, my dear lady. Not a candle!" So saying, he roared with laughter, mightily pleased with himself, and kissed her hand.

"You're too kind, sir," Octavia murmured, waiting patiently for his slobbering to be over and her hand to be given back to her.

She glanced again at Rupert and Margaret. Rupert was

whispering something in Margaret's ear, his hand resting on her bare shoulder. For a man who professed indifference to the lady, he was paying her remarkably close attention. Closer than he paid any other of his numerous flirts. He'd said he wanted to provoke Philip's interest in Octavia, but that was achieved now. So why continue this dabbling and fondling and secret whispering?

But, then again, why not? There was nothing to prevent his having a liaison with Margaret Drayton. No loyalty to a wife, or anything like that. He and Octavia were simply an instrumental partnership. Rupert was such a passionate man, with a great sensual appetite—perhaps one woman wasn't sufficient to satisfy him.

It was such a repellent thought that Octavia closed her mind to it.

"Your husband is certainly walking a well-trodden path," Philip said softly behind her. "But I find it's one that becomes wearisome soon enough."

"Indeed, sir." She couldn't help the touch of hauteur in her voice. For some reason Philip's apparent commiseration was deeply offensive, and she had to remind herself sharply of her part in the play before she could summon a careless smile.

"Do you not play, Lord Wyndham?" She linked her hand through his arm. "Let me be your luck, tonight. Do you wish to play faro or E and O?"

"I find little appeal in either, ma'am," he said. "But a game of piquet, perhaps?"

"You wouldn't consider backgammon instead?" Octavia peeped up at him from beneath her lashes with an almost guilty air of mischief. "It's shocking to confess, I know, but I'm an abysmal card player. Warwick has quite despaired of me. But I can play a passable game of backgammon."

Philip Wyndham laughed with genuine amusement, and it transformed his demeanor. Once or twice before Octavia had felt herself bathed in his warmth and approval and on each occasion had been drawn to him against her will and in the face of every instinct. At such moments he reminded her of something, or someone, and the memory brought only warmth and pleasure. But she couldn't identify the memory.

"Then let us play backgammon, ma'am. I haven't played since my nursery days, so I fear you'll have the edge."

"Oh, we won't play for serious stakes," Octavia said reassuringly, ushering him across to a small table in the window where a backgammon board was set up.

"But I think we should play for something worth losing," Philip said, seating himself before the board.

"Or for something worth winning, perhaps?" Octavia suggested, tossing the dice in her palms. "What would you wish to win, Lord Wyndham?"

"I believe you know that, ma'am," he said softly, his eyes fixed upon her mouth. "But shall we start with a kiss?"

So now it was in the open. The game had begun. Perhaps if she could get close enough to him in a simple embrace, she could discover where he kept the ring. Perhaps she could remove it without getting any closer.

Octavia glanced down at her fingers, wondering if they'd lost any of their nimble deftness since she'd last had occasion to use them for such a purpose. She should practice. It would be easy enough to work any of the crowded ballrooms and salons she frequented. She wouldn't keep her pickings, but it should be simple enough to drop them in strategic places where they would be found, and their owners would simply assume they'd somehow mislaid them.

She looked up at Lord Wyndham, an inviting smile on her lips. "An impudent wager, my lord. But one I daresay I could afford."

"And what would you wish to win, ma'am?" He aligned the draftsmen with an extended forefinger, his eyes still fixed upon her mouth.

"Why, sir, you may take me to the play," she said. "I hear Mr. Sheridan's *School for Scandal* is wondrous entertaining, but my husband has no time for such frivolities." She glanced over her shoulder at the faro table. "He seeks and finds other amusements, as we have remarked."

"It seems, ma'am, that whether I win or lose, I gain only pleasure," Philip said. "Shall we begin?"

At the faro table the atmosphere was more intense, the pile of gold at Rupert's elbow growing steadily. "What did you mean, Warwick, about schemes to improve one's circumstances?" Hector Lacross asked, draining his wineglass and leaning back as a footman refilled it.

"Oh, there are plans afoot in the City that could be turned to a pretty penny if a man can get in on the ground floor," Rupert said carelessly. "It requires a small investment initially, but I've seen some fine returns in the last few months."

"What kind of scheme?" This from Dirk Rigby, whose pale-brown eyes shifted away from Rupert's clear-eyed gaze.

"Houses," Rupert said. "Large houses being built on the south bank of the river. Prime land, perfect for the middle-class burghers. They're flocking to lay down their blunt for a stake in a piece of property that they believe will enhance their new-found status among the wealthy merchants."

He chuckled and laid three hundred guineas beside the knave of hearts. "Of course, the builder cuts a few corners here and there. Nothing that the buyers will notice. But it enables him—and, of course, his investors—to turn a handsome profit."

"How wicked of you, Lord Rupert!" exclaimed Margaret Drayton, fanning herself vigorously. "To take advantage of those poor people." Her voice dripped sarcasm.

"Oh, they lay themselves open to it, with their own greed and self-consequence," Rupert said, watching as the dealer turned over the knave of hearts. "Ah," he said, smiling, drawing the pile of coins toward him. "I seem to be having the luck of the devil tonight."

"I might be interested in investing a trifle myself," Lacross said. "What about you, Rigby?"

"Oh, yes, indeed," his friend said heartily. "Who's your contact, Warwick?"

Rupert leaned back in his chair, making a steeple of his

fingers. "That's a little difficult, gentlemen. The matter is a mite sensitive, as you can imagine. Things one wouldn't wish to become generally known . . ." He raised an eyebrow. "I don't feel I could reveal my friend's name without consulting him first. I'm sure he'd need some earnest of your intentions."

"Oh, quite, quite." The two sat forward eagerly. "No difficulty there. Perhaps we could talk more tomorrow."

Rupert inclined his head in a gesture of acknowledgment and pushed back his chair. "Ma'am, perhaps you'd care to try your luck with evens and odds."

Margaret Drayton took his hand as she rose to her feet. "I've lost so much at faro, sir, I daren't risk any more tonight."

"Then you must permit me to be your banker," Rupert said smoothly. He took her reticule from her, opened it, and dropped into it the pile of guineas he'd won so far.

Margaret laughed, but her eyes widened. "My lord, so generous."

"Oh, I insist on a half share of your winnings," he said, and escorted her to another table.

Octavia had heard none of the conversation over the general babble in the room, but she'd not missed the glint and chink of gold pouring into Margaret Drayton's reticule, and indignation warred with disbelief that Rupert would give away their precious funds to a whore. Was it payment for services rendered? Or an advance on services to come?

Somehow she kept her seething fury off her face as she continued her game with Philip, presenting a front of sophisticated indifference to her husband's conduct. However, when Rupert spoke laughingly over her shoulder, she couldn't conceal the daggers in her eyes when she looked up at him.

"Backgammon in *my* house! My dear, I must protest."

"A little tame for you, my lord?" she said sweetly. "Believe me, the stakes are far from tame. Are they, Lord Wyndham?"

"Far from it, ma'am." He bowed and took out his

snuffbox. "May I?" Reaching for her hand, he shook a pinch onto her upturned wrist, and carried it to his nose.

Octavia vividly remembered when Rupert had done the same, and she'd thought then that no lady would permit a gentleman such a familiarity. But they were not playing ladies and gentlemen here—at least, not the respectable version of that breed . . . the kind one might find in Northumberland.

Rupert cupped the nape of her neck in his warm palm. A casual gesture, yet one redolent of possession, and her skin leaped beneath the touch. Philip Wyndham's eyes narrowed as he closed his snuffbox and replaced it in his pocket. Of course, Octavia reflected, that gesture of possession was designed to prod the Earl of Wyndham's competitive spirit. Rupert had told her that the earl was a man who coveted the possessions of others and had little interest in acquiring anything that was available simply for the asking.

She resisted the inclination to arch her neck into the firm, warm grip and sat up straight, shaking her head. His hand dropped immediately, leaving a cold, lonely spot on her neck. On any other occasion the touch would have reminded her of what was to come, once this tedious evening had drawn to a close and they were alone. But she was now too angry to be stirred by that prospect.

Rupert strolled back to the gaming tables, concealing his own frown. The scorching anger in Octavia's eyes had taken him aback.

It was almost dawn when the last guest left. Octavia looked around the littered salon with an expression of distaste. Rupert poured cognac into two glasses.

"Here. You've earned it." He held one glass out to her as she stood in front of the fire, massaging the back of her neck.

"No, thank you." She shook her head. "I think I'll just go to bed."

"Sit down, Octavia." His voice was quiet and level.

She shot him a quick frown. "It's five o'clock in the morning, Rupert. I'm going to bed."

"Sit down, Octavia."

What was it about him . . . about that tone . . . that ensured her obedience? Annoyed with herself for doing so, Octavia perched on the arm of a sofa. "What is it?"

"You tell me. Something's troubling you about this evening. Is it Wyndham?" He rested one arm along the mantelpiece, his expression calm, although his eyes were warm and concerned.

"No."

Rupert sipped his cognac. "So why are you angry?"

"Well, why do you think?" Octavia demanded fiercely. "How am I supposed to feel when I see you pouring a small fortune into Margaret Drayton's reticule? What were you paying her for?"

The concern in his eyes vanished, exasperation in its place. He put down his glass with a snap. "You are being very foolish. If you don't understand something, then ask me before you jump to stupid conclusions."

"Don't talk to me like that." Octavia jumped to her feet, her face pale, golden fires ablaze in her eyes. "I didn't jump to conclusions. I *saw* you give the woman a mass of gold. Everyone saw you."

"Precisely," he said coldly. "*Everyone* saw me."

Octavia stared at him, then said slowly, "You mean . . . you mean people were supposed to see you?"

"Precisely," he repeated, folding his arms. He spoke with all the harshness of a man who didn't suffer fools gladly. "If you had paused to think for one minute before leaping to conclusions that would insult the intelligence of a baby, it might have occurred to you that the presence of Dirk Rigby and Hector Lacross could have influenced my actions this evening. It is necessary that they see me with money to burn."

Octavia began to feel very small. Jealousy, that most demeaning of emotions, had betrayed her into such a foolish attack. Did he guess that? She would infinitely prefer to be called stupid than to be accused of being jealous of Margaret Drayton. But then it struck her that she did have a defense, and one that would remove the attention from Lady Drayton.

"I fail to see how I could be expected to understand anything of the sort, since you've consistently refused to tell me anything about your plans," she retorted. "You tell me I should ask you if something puzzles me, but when I do, you refuse to answer."

Rupert picked up his neglected glass and stared into it for a minute. "I suppose you have a point," he conceded. "I tend to play my cards close to my chest."

"Then you can hardly blame me for drawing my own conclusions from what I see."

He looked up at that, and there was a glimmer of comprehending amusement in his eyes. "Oh, yes, I can, sweeting, when it comes to jumping to conclusions about my dealings with Margaret Drayton. That was foolish beyond permission."

Octavia pointed one toe and examined her satin slipper with a degree of interest such an ordinary article hardly warranted. "I don't see why. I assume she has a price. She seems to have been possessed by every male member of the court at some time or another."

"And you think I'm sufficiently undiscriminating to go panting into pastures so well grazed?" He raised a mocking eyebrow. "You insult me, Octavia. I really think . . . Yes, I'm afraid I really think that I'm entitled to demand penance." He took a sip of cognac, and in the silence the charged atmosphere in the salon crackled. But no longer with anger.

Octavia swallowed and tried to think of some light response, but her lips wouldn't form even the simplest words.

"The question is, just what kind of penance would be appropriate?" Rupert mused, gazing down into the fireplace where the dying embers glowed, throwing up an occasional spark. "Any ideas, Octavia?" He cast her a look of such sensual intensity she wondered if she would have the strength to walk out of the room on her own two legs.

"You would have me choose my own?" she managed to say, her voice thick with desire.

"I believe the lesson might have greater resonance if

you do," he observed judiciously. "I'm open to all suggestions, but I reserve the right to make the final decision."

Octavia touched her tongue to her lips. Her mind was a riot of lustful fantasy, passion's brilliant colors splashed across the gray canvas of fatigue and dismay, apprehension and resentment. It no longer mattered why they played this game, only that they did.

"Perhaps we should go upstairs, my lord," she suggested with a demure curtsy.

"By all means. I imagine you'll find it easier to apply yourself to the matter in your bedchamber."

"I believe so, sir." She curtsied again, holding the position for a long minute, gazing up at him over her unfurled fan, her eyes liquid with arousal, her lips slightly parted, promise in every line of her body.

Rupert gravely took her hand and raised her from her curtsy. "Come, madam."

Chapter 12

"The Earl of Wyndham, my lady. Are you at home?" Griffin's somewhat sententious accents intoned from the doorway to Oliver Morgan's sitting room.

"Yes, Griffin. Show him into the drawing room. I'll be down directly." Octavia put down the newspaper she'd been reading to her father. "You'll excuse me, Papa."

"Yes, of course, my dear," he said comfortably. "Go and do your duty. I must say the door knocker never ceases to fall these days. You seem to be a very popular couple, if I may say so."

"Yes, we do," Octavia agreed demurely, smoothing down the skirts of her pink muslin morning gown. "But I expect it's because we're new on the scene and society craves variety." She stood on tiptoe to examine her reflection in the mirror above the fireplace.

"Warwick maintains a lavish establishment, at all events," Oliver remarked. "I daresay his hospitality reflects it."

Octavia glanced at her father in the mirror as she combed her fingers through the cluster of ringlets on her shoulders. Was he probing? Surely not. It would be quite out of character.

"He's a wealthy man, Papa," she said, licking a finger and smoothing her eyebrows before turning back to the room. "Do you care to go for a drive this afternoon? It's a beautiful day."

"No, I think I'll take my usual promenade, thank you, child," Oliver said. "Your guest awaits. You'd better hurry."

She kissed him and hastened from the room, frowning slightly. Her father had always been somewhat vague about the everyday world, and that vagueness had become insensibility after the catastrophe, but he was beginning to recover some of the awareness he'd had before Harrowgate. It would not be at all convenient if he started showing an interest in the intricate ramifications of their domestic life. It was going to be difficult enough as it was to find a satisfactory explanation for the end of her marriage, the return of his fortune, and their reinstatement at Hartridge Folly. But she'd been relying on his customary willingness to accept her statements at face value. If he was becoming skeptical now, when everything looked perfectly ordinary, there was no knowing how the fantastic future would strike him.

But it was still very much in the future, Octavia reminded herself as she sped down the stairs. And the present required all her wits.

She paused on the bottom step, steadying her breathing. If Philip Wyndham was alone, and she assumed he was, this would be the first tête-à-tête they'd had.

The footman on duty in the hall sprang to open the double doors to the drawing room. Octavia composed her expression and sailed into the room.

"Lord Wyndham, what a delightful surprise." She curtsied in a delicate cloud of pale muslin.

Philip turned from his contemplation of the street outside the window. He raised his glass and subjected his hostess to a long assessment.

Unconsciously, Octavia put up her chin. There was something faintly insulting about such an appraisal in her own drawing room, without even a preliminary answer to her greeting.

The earl smiled and bowed. "Enchanting, ma'am. You have a flawless instinct with your dress."

"You count yourself something of an expert on female attire, sir?" She stepped toward him, a tinge of asperity to her tone.

"I know what I like," he said, taking her hands in a warm clasp. "Forgive me if my lack of formality has offended you. The sight of you drove all conventional conduct from my mind. I could only gaze."

"La, sir, I thought you above such outrageous sallies," Octavia chided playfully. "We both know what value to place on such compliments." She made a move to withdraw her hands from his, but his clasp tightened.

"I assure you that was no empty compliment, my lady," he said, his eyes fixed upon her face so that she found herself unable to look away from his gaze. Once again she had the uncanny sense of something familiar about him . . . familiar and yet completely wrong.

"Then I will accept it in the spirit it was intended, sir," she returned, once again trying to withdraw her hands. "May I ring for some refreshment? You'll take a glass of sherry with me?"

"By all means." He released her hands and she pulled the bellrope by the fire. "I've come to collect my wager, Octavia . . . if I may call you that?" A lifted eyebrow punctuated the question.

"Of course," Octavia said. "Griffin, bring sherry, please. Is his lordship in the house?"

"No, my lady. I believe he was visiting his tailor." The butler bowed and withdrew.

Had Lord Wyndham known that? "So," Octavia said. "Your wager, Lord Wyndham. I forget, did I lose the game?"

"Oh, yes, ma'am," he assured her, taking snuff, regarding her with his unreadable gray eyes. "You lost two games out of three."

"I have a shocking memory," she said. "Just leave it on

the table, Griffin. I'll pour for Lord Wyndham." She moved to the decanter as the door closed behind the butler and filled two glasses. "What shall we drink to, sir?"

"Wagers lost and won," he replied, raising his glass. "And to further games."

The man was not talking about backgammon. Octavia raised her glass with a little smile of mischievous suggestion and drank with him.

The earl placed his glass half-empty on a console table and turned back to her. "Will you renege on your wager, Lady Warwick?"

Octavia shook her head, putting her own glass down. Her fingers quivered, and she curled them into her palms. How did one kiss a man only with one's mouth, keeping one's mind and spirit on some other plane, unsullied by a loathsome contact?

She didn't know. She'd kissed only one man in her life, and her mind and soul were inextricably bound up with her body whenever she touched Rupert Warwick.

Philip placed his hands on her shoulders, drawing her close to him. Then he cupped her chin in the palm of one hand and brought his mouth to hers.

Octavia told herself to respond. She would achieve nothing standing like a dummy waiting for it to be over. Closing her mind as tightly as she'd closed her eyes, she parted her lips. His tongue immediately accepted the invitation, and she could taste wine as the muscular presence explored her mouth. His hand dropped from her chin, slipping around her body, holding her tightly against him, and the hard bulge of his erection in his tight silk britches pressed against her belly.

Touch him. Explore his body. Maybe she could feel what she sought somewhere on his person.

She moved her own hands inside his coat, stroking and kneading as if with an answering urgency, sliding her hands around to his back, over his buttocks, feeling for a pocket. He groaned and his teeth closed abruptly on her bottom lip. She tasted blood and instinctively tried to pull back. But he held her now with a powerful strength, crushing her against him so she could no longer insert her hands between their bodies. His fingers curled into the flesh of her hips with a bruising pressure, and she could sense the overpowering force of his arousal, hear it in the short moans against her mouth, feel it in the hot breath on her neck, the roughness of his hold, the ache in her compressed breasts.

She was suffocating in the heat of this passion, struggling like a bird in a trap. Faintly, she heard the door open. And then, after an infinitesimal pause, it closed again.

Octavia knew in her blood that Rupert had been there. Had returned from his errands. Had seen what was happening. Had quietly withdrawn because she was doing what she had agreed to do. She was seducing his enemy. Apparently it didn't matter to him that the mouth that opened with such willing warmth beneath his own kisses was being ravished by a man he detested.

It didn't matter to him. It couldn't matter to him or he couldn't tolerate it.

She struggled with a final desperation, and Philip Wyndham slowly drew back. "Why would you fight me? A minute ago you were as eager as I." His face was flushed, his eyes excited, and Octavia flinched from the predator, red in tooth and claw.

"You frightened me," she said with soft meekness, touching her swollen lip. "Such ardor, my lord. I confess . . . I'm not accustomed . . ." She turned away to hide the disgust she couldn't keep from her eyes.

"Oh, that husband of yours lacks passion, does he?" The earl laughed, a grating sound that mingled contempt and self-congratulation. "My dear, I'll show you what a man is capable of in these matters. You have passion in you, I could feel it. You need a man worthy of that passion. A man who can show you what desire is really like."

"And you are such a man?"

"I believe so." It was an assertion of such resounding complacence that Octavia, even through her disgust, wanted to laugh in astonishment. The vanity of the man. Did he really believe he could hold a candle to Rupert Warwick in *anything*?

"You must be gentle with me, my lord," she said, keeping her face averted. "I beg you will excuse me now. I must compose myself before my husband returns."

"Of course," he said readily, as if it went without saying that a woman who'd just had the earth-shattering experience of kissing Philip Wyndham would need time to compose herself before she could face anyone else, let alone her husband. "Until later, my dear." He brushed a hand down her back, allowed it to linger on her bottom. Then he was gone.

Shaking, Octavia turned back to the room. She examined herself in the glass. Her lips were swollen, her hair disarrayed. Her entire body felt sore, as if she'd been crushed by a python. Philip Wyndham's willowy frame was deceptive. He was a powerful man.

She spun round as the door opened. Rupert closed the door and stood for a moment leaning against it, his expression impassive. "So you have begun," he said.

"Apparently," she responded in the same tone, picking up her discarded sherry glass and taking a sip that became a gulp. The wine stung her bitten lip.

"That's good," he stated, moving from the door to pour a glass for himself.

"You came in earlier?" There was a slight tremor in her voice. Octavia took another gulp of wine, hoping that it would steady her, would smooth out this whirlpool of fear, bitter confusion, and resentment, bringing her once again into the calm waters of cold purpose, where Rupert Warwick swam with such single-minded deliberation.

"Yes," he agreed. "I thought it politic to withdraw." He kept his back to her as he sampled the sherry in his glass. He still had not mastered the wave of revulsion that had swept through him when he'd seen Octavia locked in his brother's arms, and now the sight of her bruised lip and disheveled hair filled him with such a violent anger, it required all the control learned so painfully over the years to keep it from his face. It would do Octavia no good to know how he felt.

"You have another assignation?" he asked casually, turning back to the room.

"Not precisely. But I don't imagine Wyndham will wait long before suggesting something." Octavia felt as if she was being examined by a tutor on some work in progress. "I tried to feel if he had something hidden on his person, but I couldn't find anything. It would help if I knew precisely what I was looking for," she said, refilling her glass.

Rupert withdrew from his pocket a small silk pouch. He opened it and shook the contents on the table. "This is what you're looking for."

Octavia came over to the table. A tiny, intricately worked silver ring lay winking in a ray of pale sun.

"It's so tiny," she said, picking it up between finger and thumb. "Wyndham's is identical?"

"Its pair." He held out his palm for it and she dropped it into his hand. "There's a mechanism that opens it . . . concealed in the eye of the bird . . . here it is." He indicated a minute speck representing the eye of a delicately carved eagle. "It's too small to be opened by human fingers; it requires a silver toothpick or the tip of a pair of compasses."

"Scissors, perhaps?" She rummaged through a basket of embroidery silks and produced a small pair of scissors.

Rupert took them, inserting the tip of one blade in the eye. The tiny circle sprang open. "The ring in Wyndham's possession locks into this one, forming a signet ring that would fit an adult's finger," he explained. "A slender finger," he added unnecessarily.

"But what's the significance?" Octavia gazed up at him in fascination, but his face, which had been open and receptive, closed at the question.

"You don't need to know that." He closed the ring and slipped it back into its pouch.

"Maybe not. But am I not entitled to?"

"How do you work that out?"

It was such a cold snub that she could think of nothing

to say. She wasn't entitled to anything, except what he'd promised her.

"Listen to me, Octavia." His voice changed, became soft and almost cajoling. He took her hand and drew her to the sofa, where he sat down, pulling her down beside him.

"I cannot tell you more than I have without confusing the issues for you. If you know what lies between me and Philip Wyndham, you may let something slip, and if he has the faintest hint of the truth—a truth so fantastic he will at first believe it impossible—everything will be over. You can know at this stage only what you *need* to know. You must trust me in this, Octavia. When it's all over, you will know everything. I promise you."

Octavia and the world would know everything.

He caught her face between his hands, smiling at her as if he could smile away her hurt and frustration, smiling as if a smile could smooth away the evidence of his twin's mouth on hers. He ran his fingers through the cluster of ringlets framing her face. "Trust me."

"I do," she said, wishing perversely that she didn't. "But it's very hard to work in the dark when *you* know everything there is to know about both of us. And why should you imagine I would let something slip, anyway? Why don't you trust me?"

Rupert sighed and his hands fell from her hair. "I wouldn't trust anyone but myself to keep this secret, Octavia. But if you wish to withdraw from our contract, then I will accept that."

"How could I do that?" she exclaimed in a fierce undertone. "You know that's not possible. We've gone too far to pull back now."

"I was hoping you would believe that," he agreed gravely. "But understand this, Octavia. I am not forcing you."

No, she thought bitterly. He wasn't forcing her. But if she didn't fulfill her side of the bargain, he wouldn't fulfill his. And how could she choose to take her father and return to the grim, mean streets of Shoreditch, the daily terror of haunting the crowds with stealthy fingers? It had hardly been endurable before. Now it was unthinkable.

She merely looked at him and his heart turned over at the despairing recognition of reality in the tawny eyes. He could release her. A word would do it. And he could still pursue her vengeance. Hector Lacross and Dirk Rigby were begging on bended knees to fall into his trap. It would cost him nothing; indeed, it would afford him considerable satisfaction to bring about the downfall of such a pair of vicious and greedy rogues.

But then he thought of the years wandering in the wilderness, the years of hand-to-mouth existence in the capitals of Europe with the man whose name he now bore. The real Rupert Warwick had been a rogue in his own right, a renegade and a rebel who'd taken advantage of men's greed and vanities—but never the frailties they couldn't help—to keep himself and his young companion in funds.

Rupert Warwick had saved the young Cullum Wyndham from a miserable death in a hovel in Calais. He'd saved him from despair and taught him everything he knew. And he'd died in a drunken brawl in a tavern in Madrid. And on his deathbed he'd told his young friend to go home. To take back what was his. Because the life that Rupert Warwick had led was no life.

So Cullum had taken his mentor's name and come home. And now he needed Octavia to enable him to be avenged . . . for Gervase, and for his own years in the wilderness.

He turned away from the mute appeal in her eyes. He knew she would do what she had to, because she always had. She was determined and courageous, and she would let neither of them down.

"Keep me informed of all your dealings with Wyndham," he said in his customary cool tones. "I wish to know when and where you'll be meeting with him."

"Why?"

"Because I'd like to keep an eye on you," he said.

"You think he might hurt me?" There was an edge to the question.

"No. If I thought that, we would be doing things differently," he returned patiently.

"But what if he catches me picking his pockets?"

Rupert frowned. "He must not do so. You've worked crowds throughout London and you've not been caught yet. Why should it happen now?"

Octavia shrugged. "There are always risks. And I'm out of practice."

"Then you must perfect your skills," he instructed briskly. "You must practice before you attempt anything."

"And just how do you suggest I do that?" she demanded, even though she'd already come to the same conclusion and decided exactly what she should do.

"You could do a little light-fingering among our guests," he suggested. "It would be simple enough to leave your pickings lying around afterward so it would look as if they'd been accidentally dropped or mislaid."

"Oh," Octavia said, nonplussed by this accurate rendering of her own plan.

"A good idea?" He raised an eyebrow.

How could she say it wasn't when it had been her own? "It'll serve, I suppose," she said grudgingly. "Although stealing from one's guests seems a bit much."

"Borrowing," he corrected gently. He took her face again and lightly brushed her mouth with his fingertip. "Go and wash your face and tidy your hair, sweeting. You'll feel more like yourself."

"Instead of like someone who's been crushed in an unwelcome embrace?" She couldn't help throwing it at him.

Rupert's eyes went blank. "No one is forcing you," he repeated. "You've had no difficulty with the idea before, why is it a problem now?"

It's a problem because it doesn't seem to matter to you what I have to do. It's a problem because I am not a whore. When I agreed to seduce Philip Wyndham in cold blood, I didn't know what it was to make love with you . . . when I am you and you are me. When we are one. That's why it's a problem.

But Octavia said none of this. She rose to her feet, smoothing down her skirt. "It isn't, of course. I suppose I'm a little shaken . . . now that it's begun."

Rupert concealed his relief. "The sooner it begins, the sooner it will be over," he said, getting up from the sofa with her. "I'll go and visit your father. I found a copy of Xenophon's *Memorabilia* in an old bookstore in Charing Cross. I think he might find it of interest."

"You're very considerate of my father."

"Should I not be?" He looked puzzled.

Octavia shrugged slightly. "It surprises me."

"You think me inconsiderate?" He frowned, looking both puzzled and dismayed.

"Single-minded." She dropped him a half curtsy and left the drawing room.

Rupert gazed at the door she'd left slightly ajar. The scent of the orange flower water she used to rinse her hair still delicately perfumed the air.

Octavia believed he didn't consider her feelings or her welfare. It was so far from the truth! She couldn't know how he was racked by the prospect of what she must do. She couldn't know, because he had gone to great pains to give the impression that it was a matter of indifference to him. Once it had been. But now that he knew Octavia, nothing to do with her could ever again be a matter of indifference to him.

Rupert paced the drawing room with long, angry strides, trying to convince himself that he wasn't manipulating Octavia. She knew what she was getting into. She knew what she'd agreed to do. And she'd agreed of her own free will.

Or had she?

What about the first time . . . what about the drug concealed in the cloves sprinkled on the brandy punch? He hadn't known her then. If he had, would he have done such a thing to her?

"Death and damnation!" he hissed through his teeth,

his hands gripping the mantelpiece until his knuckles whitened. He fought to regain the cold, detached clarity of his purpose. It was done. The stone was rolling and would gather momentum. No one was hurt. Octavia would not be hurt. He swore a silent oath on Rupert Warwick's grave that Octavia Morgan would never again be injured through his actions.

Calm once more, he left the drawing room and went to visit Oliver Morgan.

Chapter 13

℘ The soft scents of spring were in the air, and Octavia paused to break off a twig of golden forsythia from a blazing bush beside the steps leading up to the front door. She was in a strange mood, excitement mingling with apprehension, and her blood moved restlessly in her veins.

She felt as she always felt after spending time with the Earl of Wyndham. She passed those hours on a mental knife edge, matching her wits against his in continual verbal fencing, fighting to keep her emotions hidden.

She flirted with Philip. She kissed him with every appearance of passion. She promised more but continued to withhold it. He was beginning to grow frustrated, but so far he'd played her game. And so far she'd failed to discover anything remotely resembling that tiny silk pouch that Rupert had shown her. It was so small, she knew that it would be hard to detect with a cursory brush of her fingers, and the time was fast approaching when she would have to steel herself to take the next step.

Somehow, somewhere, Octavia believed that there was a way to avoid that final surrender, if only she could come up with it.

"Thank you, Griffin. Isn't it a beautiful afternoon?" she greeted the butler as he bowed her into the hall.

"Indeed, my lady."

"Ask one of the footmen to cut some of that forsythia and put it in the salon for this evening," she said, taking off her gloves. "It's so lovely, but it won't last for very long."

"Yes, my lady."

"In the copper jugs," she added, going to the stairs. "Is his lordship within?"

"No, my lady. Lord Rupert went out about an hour ago. He said he would not be here for dinner."

"Oh?" Octavia paused, one foot on the bottom step. Rupert had definitely been intending to dine at home; he'd asked the cook to prepare his favorite casserole of sweetbreads.

"Did he say where he was going, Griffin? Leave a message for me?"

"I don't believe so, my lady. He had a visitor and left soon after."

There was something in Griffin's voice that seemed to imply doubt or disapproval about the visitor.

"What kind of a visitor?" She glanced at the butler over her shoulder.

"I couldn't rightly say, my lady. Not a gentleman, I would have said. No, definitely not a gentleman."

"I see. Thank you, Griffin." Octavia continued up the stairs, a thoughtful frown creasing her brow. Ben. Perhaps it was Ben.

And what would bring Ben to Dover Street? Information that might be of interest to Lord Nick, of course. Rupert had mentioned a few days earlier that they were running low on funds. He hadn't mentioned how he intended to repair the situation, and Octavia had simply assumed he would increase his gaming. But perhaps Lord Nick was taking to the road again.

In her bedchamber she went to the window, frowning down into the street, tapping a fingernail against her front teeth. Restless, nervous excitement still coursed through her veins.

She didn't want to be sitting in Dover Street twiddling her thumbs while Rupert rode the highway across Putney Heath. He kept so much to himself, but this was something they could share. She enjoyed the fruits of the highway-man's activities, so she should surely share the dangers . . . and the thrills.

She grinned to herself, remembering the last occasion when he'd held up the coach that had contained the witch Cornelia and the Earl of Gifford's rent rolls. Presumably Ben had information about another richly loaded convey-ance crossing the heath.

Octavia gave the matter no further reflection. She ran to the armoire, pulled out her riding habit, boots, and cloak. Five minutes later, she was dressed. She pinned her hair out of the way in a knot on top of her head, slung her cloak around her shoulders, and drew the hood up over her head.

At the door she stopped. Highwaymen wore masks. With a chuckle of pure exhilaration, she took a black silk loo mask from a drawer and slipped it into the pocket of her cloak. Then she ran downstairs.

"Griffin, I shall not be here for dinner. Mr. Morgan is at the circulating library at the moment, but make my ex-cuses when he returns. Explain that Lord Rupert and I have an unexpected engagement."

"Yes, my lady." Griffin opened the front door, con-cealing his surprise. "May I summon a chair for you?"

"No, thank you." Without further explanation she jumped lightly down the steps and hastened to the mews. Her own dappled mare was fine for riding in the park, but not for a highwayman's work. She would take Peter again. Rupert, of course, would be riding Lucifer.

She waited while the groom put her saddle on the big roan. Rupert rode the distinctive silver stallion around town as often as he rode Peter. Octavia found it an extraordinary piece of recklessness for a man who planned with such care and foresight. She kept waiting to hear someone who'd fallen victim to Lord Nick on his silver mount exclaim in recognition of the singular horse.

Rupert laughed when she expressed these fears, and his eyes glittered with enjoyment at the defiant challenge he was throwing to the fates. One needed to take risks if one were not to fall asleep at life, he said. Octavia considered a highwayman's existence to be sufficiently risky without courting disaster, and yet she couldn't help responding to the boldness of his challenge. A challenge she was now taking up herself.

She mounted Peter with the aid of the mounting block and walked him out of the mews. She hadn't ridden him sidesaddle before, but the giant horse seemed no more perturbed by the unfamiliar weight and position of his rider than he had when she'd ridden him bareback with only a halter.

The five miles to the Royal Oak took less than an hour, and the April evening was drawing in as Octavia halted Peter at the corner of the street leading to the inn. The horse raised his head and sniffed the wind, then turned without guidance toward the inn and the familiar stable.

"No, wait a minute, Peter." Octavia pulled back on the reins. Peter stopped, patient puzzlement in every muscle. If she made herself known at the Royal Oak, there was no telling what reception she would get. If Rupert was there, he would be bound to insist she stay at the inn while he went about his business on the heath. And if he wasn't there, Ben or Bessie would be sure to make difficulties.

However, she didn't think Rupert would be at the Royal Oak. It was not yet dark, and there would still be traffic across the heath. Lord Nick would already be in position, waiting for his particular quarry.

Octavia tied the loo mask behind her head. It had the most astonishing effect. She felt as if she wasn't herself, as if she was a participant in some wild and dangerously exciting frolic. Which, of course, was only the truth.

"This way, Peter." She turned him toward the heath.

*R*upert, his own mask in place, sat Lucifer in the concealment of the stand of silver birch. A phaeton, a light post-chaise, and a heavy carter's dray had passed since he'd taken up his position. But he wasn't waiting for them. He was waiting for the delayed mail coach that, according to Morris, had thrown a wheel in Farnham and was going to be crossing the heath after the evening star appeared.

He sat patient and impassive, and Lucifer, knowing his business as well as his rider, was immobile beneath him. Then from the distance came the sound of the post-horn blowing the tantivy. Lucifer pricked up his ears. Rupert drew the silk scarf up over his mouth. He waited until the drumming of the team and the heavy pounding of the massive iron wheels were so close, the earth seemed to shake. He drew his pistols. Then he moved out onto the narrow ribbon of road that wound across the heath in the gathering shadows.

As he did so, the sound of galloping hooves came from behind him. He jerked his head, ready to pull off the road and be away into the trees before the inconvenient traveler took in anything about him. Then he recognized Peter.

Octavia reached him as the post-horn sounded again, an almost defiant clarion call to embolden the hearts of the coach passengers as they approached the notorious stand of trees.

"I've come to help," Octavia said, laughing with exhilaration, her eyes gleaming at him through the slits in her mask. "But I don't have any weapons. I can collect the booty while you keep them covered with your pistols."

"Get off the road!" he commanded, and again she could no more have disobeyed the order than swum against a tidal wave. She pulled Peter into the trees as the horn sounded again and the bright-yellow vehicle swayed and lumbered around the corner at its customary speed of five miles an hour.

Rupert closed his mind to Octavia. He fired over the team's heads, but the coachman was already hauling back on the reins at the sight of the dreaded figure on his silver horse.

The horses came to a stamping, steaming halt. There was a short silence—a silence that struck Rupert as unusual.

Someone always screamed or wailed or blustered. But the coachman sat on his box, the postilions on the leaders; the passengers, riding precariously on the roof with the baggage, huddled into their cloaks but made not a sound. It was as if they were waiting for something.

Then he saw what they were waiting for. Five men had dropped stealthily from the roof at the rear of the coach and now leaped onto the road, out of the shadows. Five Bow Street Runners, primed pistols in their hands.

Octavia didn't think. She came at them from behind with an echoing, fearsome war cry. They turned almost as one man, and she set Peter at them. The giant roan reared, his hooves flailing, the whites of his eyes rolling, lips drawn back from the bit. The Runners fell back. Rupert fired his second pistol, the bullet whistling through the crown of a hat.

It gave them a minute's breathing space. But that was enough. Lucifer leaped into the gorse beside the road and was gone, racing through the trees. Peter needed no encouragement from his own rider. His nose was against the silver's tail as they pounded across the turf. Confused shouts came from behind them; a volley of pistols discharged all at once. Octavia ducked her head instinctively, even though she knew they were out of range of the clumsy weapons.

Her heart was racing, keeping pace with Peter's thundering hooves. She kept her eyes on the silver shape ahead of her and allowed the horse to go as he would.

Then suddenly Lucifer vanished. One minute he was there, the next there was nothing but shadows and the bleak, gnarled specters of trees. Octavia's heart seemed to stop, and terror filled her. She was alone on the heath. Lord Nick and Lucifer had vanished into the earth—the devil into outer darkness.

But Peter was plowing ahead. He turned into a thick screen of greening bracken. A white rock face glimmered, and then the horse plunged forward into a dark crevice and Octavia found herself in a small black space. She could smell hot horseflesh, hear Peter's panting breaths matching those of Lucifer.

"Something of a surprise," Rupert said evenly out of the darkness.

"They were waiting for you," Octavia said. "They knew you would be there."

"Yes, I believe you're right. However, that wasn't the surprise I was referring to."

He sounded at his most sardonic. As cool and ironic as if they were sitting by the fire in Dover Street discussing the progress of an evening's gaming.

Octavia decided now was not the moment to enter into a possibly acrimonious discussion about her presence. "Where are we?"

"In a cave."

"A cave? On Putney Heath?"

" 'Cave' is rather a grand term for it," he said. "It's just a rocky outcrop in the middle of nowhere. With a hole in the middle."

"Oh." Octavia's eyes were beginning to grow accustomed to the darkness, and she could make out the pale shape of Lucifer and his dark rider, so close to her, the stallion's flanks brushed her legs. "How long will we stay here?"

"Until I say otherwise." It was a very flat statement.

"But they couldn't have pursued us on foot?"

"You consider yourself an expert on the methods of Bow Street Runners? Or are you perhaps prescient?"

Octavia winced.

"While we wait, perhaps you'd like to answer a few questions," Rupert said pleasantly. "Like, for instance, what doubtless brilliant if not inspired piece of reasoning brought you here."

"Don't you think that this is now as much—"

"Just a minute," he interrupted. "Perhaps you didn't hear me. *I* am asking the questions; *you,* Octavia, are answering them. I repeat: what, in the name of the good Christ, are you doing here?"

"I thought I could help," she said lamely, shivering. It was cold in the dark dampness of the cave, and the sweat was drying on her body now that the excitement of the chase was over.

"Wrong answer," he clipped. "Try again."

Octavia grimaced in the darkness. "But I *did* think that."

"No, you did not. Let's see if you can come up with the correct word for what you were doing."

Octavia tried to make out his expression in the darkness, but it was impossible. She could only deduce it from his tone, which was as cool and even as she'd ever heard it.

"I don't know what you mean," she said with another miserable shiver. "It seemed to me that since we're both playing this game together, then I should be involved in this aspect as well as all the others."

"Interference," he said. " 'Interference' is the word you're looking for, Octavia, and the word I'm waiting to hear. Now, tell me exactly what you are doing here, please. And get it right, this time."

"Lord of hell," Octavia muttered. "Very well, I am interfering. Satisfied?"

"I can't understand how I failed to make my feelings clear the last time it occurred," he mused. "I had thought I was quite lucid, but obviously not. It must take a sledge-hammer to get through to you."

Octavia didn't trouble to look for a response. He was far too intent on following his own train of thought to consider any defense she might come up with.

"Clearly, it was a fond hope to rely on the 'word to the wise' principle," he continued in the same musing tone. "I should have come up with some consequences to back the word."

Lucifer stirred and whickered softly. Lord Nick stroked his neck. "You think we've been here long enough, old boy?"

He turned the horse to the faint crack of gray light in the rock face, and Lucifer moved forward, his neck stretched, his nose twitching. Horse and rider slid out of the cave, leaving Peter and Octavia alone. To Octavia's surprise Peter didn't immediately follow his leader, and she didn't know whether to urge him forward. In view of the present atmosphere, she thought she'd remain where she was until instructed otherwise.

After a tense couple of minutes Rupert whispered tersely, "Come."

Peter needed no encouragement. He moved out of the cave into the pale starlight. The usual nighttime sounds of the heath filled the air: the rustles of small animals, the hoot of an owl, the soughing of the wind in the pale new leaf growth.

"Will they have given up?" Octavia whispered.

"I doubt it, but they'll not be beating this part of the heath for us." He nudged Lucifer's flanks, and the horse broke into a trot. Peter followed without prompting.

"Are we going to the Royal Oak?" Octavia broke the silence in a careful whisper.

"No. I don't lead rats to my friends' larder."

Stupid question. Octavia bit her lip. "What about the cottage?"

"No. We're going home, by a somewhat roundabout route. I daresay you've forgotten we're entertaining this evening."

"Lord of hell," she muttered again. "*You* didn't give it a moment's thought, either, when you dashed off without a word."

"On the contrary. I gave it considerable thought. But I was foolish enough to assume you would be there to hold the fort until I returned."

"Oh."

"Of course, impetuous interference doesn't allow for reflection."

This was growing tedious, Octavia decided. "Are you still going to be unpleasant when we get home?"

"Probably."

"*How* unpleasant?"

"Oh, I expect I shall strip you naked, flog you to within an inch of your life, and lock you in the attic for a week with a heel of stale bread and a jug of stagnant water for company."

"You don't think that's a little extreme?"

"No."

Octavia grinned in the darkness. She glanced at Rupert's impassive profile, and her grin broadened. "You don't think two against five to be rather better odds than one?"

There was no response.

"Peter and I did rather well, I thought," she observed. "We went straight at them without so much as an instant's hesitation. Of course, it would have been better if I'd had a pistol. Next time I must make sure I'm properly equipped."

Still no response.

"Of course, I don't know how to fire a pistol, but I daresay I could learn. . . . What do you think, Peter? Do you think I could learn? Do you think Lord Nick might be persuaded to teach me? . . . Yes, I'm so glad you agree. It makes much better sense to alert us to these excursions beforehand. Oh, you think it would be sensible to plan them together . . . to come up with a strategy so that we don't have to act impulsively, since impulsive doesn't seem to find favor? Yes, I quite agree. . . .

"Ah, do you think we've made him laugh, Peter? Is that the ghost of a smile . . . ?"

"Octavia, your father has a great deal to answer for," Rupert remarked. "I've always recognized that you were schooled with a very light hand, but I hadn't realized until now that you must have been allowed to run completely unbridled."

Octavia chuckled. "My father's views on child rearing are rather eccentric."

"Negligent, I would have said."

"Jesting apart . . ."

"Who is jesting?"

Octavia scratched her ear and tried again. "To change the subject slightly—do you think the Runners set a trap for you? They don't usually accompany mail coaches, do they?"

"Not as far as I know."

They were riding along the south bank of the Thames,

through narrow streets quite unfamiliar to Octavia. Ahead, she caught the glimmer of light on what must be Westminster Bridge. They'd approached it by a most unusual route.

"So they must have been expecting you?" she persisted.

"Or someone," he agreed. "Most surprisingly. Sir John Fielding's Runners don't usually show sufficient intelligence to set traps."

"Did Ben bring you the information about the delayed coach?"

They turned onto the bridge before Rupert answered her with a curt affirmative.

"But you don't think . . . ?"

"No, I do not."

"Well, who would have told Ben?"

"Morris, I imagine."

"Could he . . . ?"

"Possibly."

Octavia fell silent. If Rupert suspected Morris of betraying him to the Runners, there was no need to belabor the point. Rupert was again taking them through unfamiliar streets, approaching Dover Street by way of back alleys and unfrequented squares. It was most unlikely that the Watch would be on the lookout for them, but he was taking no chances.

"Are we very low on funds?" Octavia asked somewhat tentatively.

"Nothing that I can't put right at the gaming tables," he responded.

"But you won't take to the road again until you find out if there's a spy at the Royal Oak?" She couldn't keep the anxiety from her voice.

Rupert turned to look at her under the glow of an oil lamp. The slate-gray eyes glinted with amusement. "Believe me, Octavia, when I make that decision, you'll be the first to know."

"Ah," she said. "I seem to have made my point."

"But I doubt I've made mine," he commented dryly as they trotted into the Dover Street mews.

"Oh, I thought we were at peace," Octavia said, dismounting.

Rupert merely raised an eyebrow and swung off Lucifer, handing the reins to the groom. The house was brilliantly lit.

"It looks as if the party is going on without the benefit of a host and hostess," he observed, striding to the side door, Octavia on his heels.

Griffin was in the hall as they emerged from the side corridor. "My lord . . . Lady Warwick." He bowed. "Mr. Morgan is looking after the guests in the salon."

"My father?" Octavia looked at Rupert in horror. "But what if Rigby and Lacross are here?"

He took her arm, drawing her toward the stairs away from Griffin. "Go up and change," he ordered quietly. "You can't appear in riding dress."

"Yes, but what if they're—"

"Go and change," he repeated in the same tone.

Octavia hesitated for a second, then ran up the stairs. The sound of voices, laughter, the chink of glass came from the salon as she continued up the second flight to her bedchamber. If Dirk Rigby and Hector Lacross had met and recognized her father, then they'd know who she was. Surely they would then be suspicious of the hospitality they were offered? They wouldn't trust Rupert anymore.

And what of her father? How would he have reacted if he'd recognized them? And surely he would have recognized them, even after three years.

She pulled the bell for Nell and began to throw off her riding dress. What could have possessed her father to assume the role of host? He never showed the slightest desire to take part in the life of the household, apart from joining Rupert and Octavia for dinner when they dined alone. He'd always been reclusive, even at Hartridge Folly shunning the company of all but his few intimates. Octavia had gone into local society chaperoned by the squire's wife, whose eldest daughter was her own age.

"Nell, fetch me the lilac silk," she instructed as her maid bustled in bearing a jug of steaming water. Her stomach growled as she bent to splash hot water on her face, and she realized she'd had no dinner. But there was no time now. She had to get downstairs and see what damage had been done in her absence. If she hadn't gone after Rupert, none of this would have happened.

And if she hadn't gone after him, maybe he wouldn't have escaped from the Runners. Maybe he would even now be in Newgate.

Impatiently she stood still while Nell hooked the gown of lilac silk edged with dark-green velvet ribbons. "No, I won't dress my hair tonight," she said when the maid picked up the thick horsehair pads over which she would pile Octavia's hair in a fashionably high style. "I'll wear it loose, confined with the silver fillet."

It took only a few minutes to fasten the silver fillet around her brow and comb the glowing ringlets around her face and onto her bare shoulders. It gave her a rather medieval look that in any other circumstances would have pleased Octavia, but she was too anxious tonight to get downstairs to give more than a passing thought to her appearance.

"That'll do, thank you, Nell." She drew on her long silk gloves, picked up her fan, and hurried out of the room. The sounds of merriment still came from the salon, and she heard Rupert's light tones. Presumably, he hadn't troubled to change. But riding dress on a man in the evening wouldn't elicit too many raised eyebrows, particularly in his own home.

She entered the salon, her heart in her throat. One swift, all-encompassing glance revealed neither Hector Lacross nor Dirk Rigby. Relief flooded her, followed immediately by the thought that they might have been there earlier and already left.

Oliver Morgan was standing beside the window, deep in conversation with the Earl of Wyndham. Her father was dressed in a wine-red velvet coat, deep ruffles of Mechlin lace at throat and wrists. It was old-fashioned elegance, but it suited the patrician features, the thick mane of white hair.

"Ah, here's my daughter." He greeted her with an

expansive gesture. "The Earl of Wyndham, my dear Octavia, is almost as well versed in the theories of Pythagoras as your husband."

Octavia crossed the room, hoping her smile was not as strained as she felt. "Papa, it's not like you to grace the salon."

"Well, child, in the absence of the true hosts, I did what seemed best," he responded with a somewhat ironical smile. "It seemed my duty to take your place. Your husband has been regaling us with your adventures."

Octavia shot Rupert a startled glance. "Oh, yes?"

"Highwaymen, madam," Rupert said blandly. "I was describing how we were held up on Hampstead Heath when we went for a ride this afternoon."

"Oh, yes . . . Hampstead Heath," she said faintly. "Yes, it was quite terrifying. Fortunately, Rupert had his pistols and was able to drive them off. There were at least five of them, isn't that so, Warwick?"

"Five . . . oh, you exaggerate, my dear," he returned. "No more than three, I'm certain."

"You're to be congratulated on a narrow escape, ma'am," one of their guests said from the faro table. "Footpads and highwaymen are the bane of our lives. A man can't travel in peace anywhere after dark these days."

"How true," someone agreed, taking snuff with an overly liberal hand. "The roads won't be safe until we've strung 'em all up at Tyburn Tree," he stated through a series of violent sneezes. "Every man jack of 'em."

"Lady Warwick is to be commended on her fortitude," Philip observed quietly. "Most ladies would be prostrate upon their beds for a week after such an ordeal, and here you are, as radiant and glowing as ever."

"Oh, I'm made of sterner stuff than that, sir," Octavia said. "But I confess to being starving. I missed dinner in all the excitement."

She pulled the bell rope for Griffin. "Prepare supper in the dining room, Griffin. We won't wait until eleven tonight."

"Well, I think, if you'll excuse me, I shall leave you to

enjoy the rest of the evening." Oliver bowed to the company in general and made his way to the door. "I have some
reading to do."

Octavia accompanied him to the door. "Thank you,
Papa, for stepping into the breach."

"Not at all. If the truth be told, I rather enjoyed it," he
said with a chuckle. "Much to my surprise. But you and
Warwick should be a little careful, my dear, when you go
about your business."

Octavia looked at him sharply. Was he referring to
something other than footpads? Had he met Rigby and
Lacross? But his tawny eyes seemed perfectly candid, his
smile quite without artifice.

"Were there any other guests earlier, Papa?"

He shook his head. "I don't believe so, unless they
arrived before I came down and left in the absence of a
host."

She didn't think he would lie to her. "Good night,
Papa."

She kissed him and curtsied as he left the salon. Her
eyes darted to Rupert. Had he discovered whether or
not Rigby and Lacross had been there earlier? He shook
his head infinitesimally and turned back to his game of E
and O.

Octavia strolled over to Philip Wyndham. As she passed
Viscount Ledham, her hand brushed over his coat. The
viscount was too absorbed in making a wager on the
chances of a red spurt in the fire coming before a blue one
to be aware of anything more than his hostess, standing for a
moment very close to him, smiling and paying flattering
attention to his absurd wager.

She moved on, the viscount's fob watch tucked in the
palm of her hand. "Lord Wyndham, do you care to wager
on the fire's conduct?" She put her hand behind her on a
marble-topped pier table, then stepped closer to the earl.
The fob watch lay innocently on the table.

Wyndham shook his head. "Ledham will wager on the
speed of a raindrop on a windowpane."

"He's not alone. It's considered a poor-spirited man

who won't wager on every absurdity offered him." She smiled with a conspiratorial gleam in her eye. "I find it refreshing, my lord, that you at least don't slavishly follow where society leads in such foolishness."

Her hand brushed over his, and her head was very close to his shoulder, so he could inhale the fragrance of her hair and body. "It takes a wise and courageous man to stand alone."

Philip's head reeled at the contrast of Octavia's freshness with the prevailing scents of powder, pomade, and perfume, heavy and ripe, disguising the odors of none-too-clean linen and sweat-stiffened velvets and brocade.

She was a true original, he thought. Even the way she conducted this flirtation was different from anything he'd experienced before. She was light and fresh, nothing vulgar or overeager about her promises. Much to his surprise, he was willing to play the game at her pace. If any other woman had withheld herself for as long as Octavia Warwick, he would have taken her by force or abandoned the pursuit in disgust. But she weaved a spell around him, entangling him in the gossamer threads of her suggestive smiles and her kisses, where her natural passion lay barely hidden.

He glanced across the room at her husband. Rupert Warwick was deep in play, his expression unreadable. The man made Philip's skin crawl. He had a particular smile that filled him with a violent revulsion, almost as if the smile was poison. Just being in his presence disturbed Philip almost beyond endurance, and yet he had to endure it in order to pursue the lady.

But the thought of eventually enjoying the wife of a man he loathed with such a visceral hatred made the hours in Warwick's company bearable.

Octavia was smiling, her hand lightly caressing his flank. His skin prickled, his loins grew heavy. He looked down into that serenely beautiful oval, where the lambent eyes glowed like a tiger's in the dark.

"Supper," she said as Griffin appeared portentously in

the doorway. "I am famished, my lord. Will you accompany me?"

"With pleasure, ma'am." He bowed and offered his arm.

Philip Wyndham's silk-embroidered handkerchief fluttered to the floor as she accompanied him to the door. A golden sovereign clinked gently onto a table as she passed.

Chapter 14

℘ The warehouse just south of London Bridge on the south side of the Thames was a squat redbrick building with barred windows. The river lapped at the base of one wall, leaving a green slime against the brickwork.

The hackney carriage disgorged its two passengers before an iron-barred door at the rear of a narrow courtyard. The jarvey looked around from beneath lowering bushy brows. "Ye'll be wantin' me to wait, gents?"

Dirk Rigby wrinkled his nose at the prevailing stench of rotting weed, fish, and cesspit. He glanced at Hector, who was nervously touching the blinding white folds of his cravat. This run-down neighborhood seemed a most unlikely venue for a meeting of investors.

"Yes," Hector said brusquely. "Wait for us."

"I'll 'ave me fare this far, though, guv," the jarvey stated as his passengers turned toward the door. "Jest in case anythin' 'appens, like." He guffawed, wiping his eyes on a red-spotted kerchief.

"Don't be absurd, man," Dirk said. "We're here on business, and you'll remain here until that business is concluded." So saying, he rapped sharply on the door with the silver head of his cane.

The jarvey subsided on his bench, muttering. He knew the type. They expected a man to spend half his day waiting on them, losing fares by the minute, and then he'd be lucky to get an extra shilling out of them at journey's end.

The door bolts screeched in oilless protest and the great door swung open, revealing a dark cavernous area within. An elderly man stood in the doorway, holding a guttering tallow candle. His shoulders were hunched in a rusty black coat, grease shining on the lapels, and his hair was covered in a ratty bagwig.

"There y'are," he said in a creaky voice. "Late, y'are. Master was about to give up on ye." He peered around them at the hackney standing in the entrance to the court. "Best keep 'im. Don't get much traffic in these parts. Wouldn't want to walk these streets on yer own, neither. Not such fine gentlemen." He cackled and turned back into the interior of the warehouse.

Hector and Dirk followed him. The old man darted backward with a sudden spritely movement that belied his age and hunched impression of infirmity. The great iron door clanged shut as he kicked it. The candle flared and guttered, and they were suddenly in darkness.

"Odd's blood, man! What are you playing at?" bellowed Hector, hearing his own uncertainty beneath the bluster.

"Just the wind . . . just the wind," the old man muttered. " 'Ang on a minute." He shuffled around in the dark, flint scraped on tinder, and the candlelight flickered and steadied again.

They were in a vast, empty space, with a ceiling so high it disappeared into the darkness. In the meager yellow light, Dirk and Hector could make out against the walls shapeless piles that could have been anything. The air was thick with dust and wood shavings, cold and damp despite the balmy evening outside.

"Damn smoky, this," Hector muttered to his companion as their escort led them across the area toward a curving iron staircase against the riverside wall. "You sure this is the place Warwick meant?"

"The man seems to be expecting us," Dirk reminded him, but he was as uncertain as his friend. They were there to discuss a speculative venture that promised to bring substantial riches. These seedy, somewhat menacing, surroundings didn't lend themselves to confidence in any venture.

The iron staircase curved upward, and they followed the flickering candle, its light throwing their grotesque, wavery shadows ahead of them. The staircase stopped at a small wooden landing; the irregular planks creaked under their feet, treacherous spaces between them.

" 'Ere we are, gentlemen." Their escort scratched at a door at the rear of the landing. He put his ear to the oak and listened, then nodded as if satisfied and raised the latch.

"Those coves you was expectin', master. They're 'ere."

"Then show 'em in, you lazy rogue."

The response was reassuringly loud, if somewhat acerbic. Rigby and Lacross stepped past the old man with his candle and entered a square apartment, lit by an oil lamp and a small black-leaded stove, sputtering in the corner. Heavy shutters blocked the windows that would have looked out over the river to the north bank of the city.

A tall white-haired gentleman rose from a desk against the far wall and stood examining them through a quizzing glass.

"Well, come in, gentlemen, come in," he said, his voice rasping as if he had a sore throat. Indeed, he had a muffler wrapped several times around his neck and drawn up over his chin. His linen was grubby, his coat of brown wool spotted with the residue of several past dinners. He wore fingerless mittens, and his cuffs were frayed. A ragged black ribbon tied the queue at the nape of his neck.

He didn't look in the least like a gentleman who could guarantee a twenty-thousand-guinea profit on an investment of ten thousand.

"Ned, fetch wine," their host commanded. "We'll drink to our venture, gentlemen. Come you in, now. Come you in and feel the fire. It's cold as charity in here.

Always the same, rain or shine. The river damp gets into the walls."

He came toward them, hand outstretched in welcome. A jagged scar ran down the length of one cheek, pulling up his lip in a grotesque grimace that was exaggerated when he laughed, as he did now, reading their expressions.

"Not quite what you expected, eh, gentlemen? Well, I'll tell you, we don't want to draw attention to ourselves. We don't want to be easily found in our business, sirs." He shook both their hands with a vigor that surprised them both. "Come to the fire. Ned, where's that wine?"

He pushed them into two straight-backed chairs beside the stove. The leg of one of them cracked ominously under Hector's not inconsiderable weight.

"Here we are . . . here we are." Rubbing his hands with the muffled sound of rasping wool, their host poured three glasses of wine from a dusty bottle. He raised the bottle and sniffed at the neck. "Passable . . . passable, I think you'll find."

He handed them their glasses and then stood watching attentively as they sipped, his gray eyes eager for their opinion. "Good, yes . . . you find it good, sirs."

"Thank you," Dirk said. There was nothing the matter with the wine, but his glass was dusty and smudged with grease.

"So Lord Rupert said—"

"No names, gentlemen," their host interrupted with an expression of horror. "We keep the names of our associates close in this business. I honor the privacy of my investors, as I trust they honor mine."

"But we both know Lord Rupert Warwick," Dirk stated tartly. "There's no need to pretend otherwise."

"Maybe not . . . maybe not." Their host pulled a chair over and sat down beside them. His voice was suddenly brisk and authoritative. "Now, as I understand it, you'd be interested in making a small investment in this project we're developing in Clapham."

"If we're satisfied with the conditions," Rigby said.

"And what would satisfy you, sir?" Their host rocked

back in his chair, regarding Rigby with a quizzical air. "A hundred percent return on capital? Two hundred? Five hundred, perhaps?"

"You could guarantee that?" Hector breathed, his eyes lighting with an almost fanatical glitter.

"Perhaps . . . perhaps." Their host got up and went to an old cupboard in the far corner of the room. He rummaged for a minute, then came back with a parchment.

"Here, let me show you. You, sir, if you'd just take that corner . . . that's it." The sheet was spread out between them, revealing an architect's plans.

"These are the houses we're building. Three of them are already built, awaiting occupation. Their owners are very eager to move in." He chuckled. "These three, however, have still to be completed. They are open for investment at this stage." He indicated the three imposing-looking buildings at the right-hand side of the plan. "What do you think?"

· "I don't think anything," Hector said. "Where does the return on investment come in?"

"Ah . . . well, it comes in bricks and mortar, you see." Their host jabbed at the paper with a forefinger. "Bricks and mortar and fittings. People want only the best, when they're setting themselves up to be better than their neighbors."

He laughed, but there was an odd tinge of menace to the sound. "We promise only the best. On the surface they see only the best. Satisfies them, satisfies their neighbors. But beneath . . . ah, well, that's a different story." He folded up the plan.

"Oak floors are very expensive, gentlemen. Oak veneer on plain pine costs next to nothing. But when it's well waxed, who can tell? At least not for a few months."

"Are the houses safe?" Hector asked.

His host shrugged. "Safe as a house of cards, dear sir. Safe as a house of dreams."

Dirk sipped his wine. "And you can guarantee our profit?"

"Certainly. Safe as houses. Ah, that's an infelicitous

metaphor!" He laughed uproariously, rocking back on his chair again. "No, to be quite serious, gentlemen. I already have deposits for these three houses . . . buyers are falling over themselves for these and more. You invest in this stage of the project, and I can guarantee that within six months you'll have trebled your investment."

Hector's tongue darted over his lips with an asp's flicker. "How much would you expect for an initial investment?"

"Ten thousand guineas apiece, sirs."

"And what guarantees do we have?"

"We draw up all the documents, all right and tight," their host said, rising to his feet again. "I'll show you the kind of agreements, all signed and sealed by the lawyers. I've many investors, gentlemen. All very satisfied people."

He went back to the cupboard and drew out a folder. "Take a look through there."

The two men examined the sheaf of legal documents. "This is your name . . . Thaddeus Nielson?" Hector tapped the signature that occurred on the bottom of all the papers.

"That's me, sir." Thaddeus nodded, linking his hands across his ample belly beneath a shabby gray waistcoat. "Thaddeus Nielson, builder of elegant properties for the rising merchant. As elegant as anything you might find in Grosvenor Square or Mount Street."

"And you pay dividends every quarter?"

"Just as it says there, sirs. You'll see the committee members on our little project are gentlemen of considerable substance. Banker Moran, for instance. Lord Chief Justice Greenaway." He leaned over to indicate these signatures. "Board meetings once a month. You'd be welcome to attend, of course."

He drew a clay pipe from the pocket of his waistcoat and busied himself tamping down the tobacco before sticking a spill into the candle flame and lighting the pipe.

The smoke curled blue in the dank air. "Of course, most of our gentlemen prefer to keep themselves to themselves," he added, puffing reflectively. "But they make an exception for board meetings. And we prefer to keep the number of investors to a minimum. Greater profits that way."

"Quite so." Dirk stared down at his highly polished shoes; their silver buckles winked in the grimy dimness. Rupert Warwick had vouched for Thaddeus Nielson. Rupert Warwick lived very high on the hog. Only the other evening they'd all seen him tip a mound of guineas into Margaret Drayton's reticule just for the amusement of it. Ventures such as this one could only thrive under the table.

"I think we should see these houses you're building?" he said after a minute.

"But of course. You'll find them on Acre Lane. By all means take a look at them. You wouldn't want to buy a pig in a poke." He smiled, his scar twitching, and puffed serenely.

"We'll let you know if we're interested in investing after we've seen them." Dirk looked for somewhere to put his empty glass, found only the floor. He put it down and stood up.

"Oh, yes, take your time," Thaddeus said, still puffing, making no attempt to rise with them. "Ned, show these gentlemen out. And you'd best stay below, since I'm expecting some more visitors."

"More potential investors?" Hector asked sharply.

Thaddeus shrugged. "There's no shortage. I can take my pick. You worry about your business, my dear sirs, and I'll worry about mine." He didn't turn from his contemplation of the stove.

His visitors stood for a minute uncertain, weighing up his last words. Dirk looked as if he would say something further, but Hector touched his arm, nodding significantly toward the door. They left, accompanied by the shuffling Ned.

The man they'd left behind listened for the clanging of the outside door behind them; then he stood up with a lazy grin. He tapped the bowl of his pipe against the side of the stove, shaking out the glowing contents, then stretched before slipping a hand beneath his waistcoat and pulling out the small pad of wadded material that formed his belly.

"Eh, right pair of ninnyhammers," his companion announced, stomping back into the room. His back was suddenly straight, his eyes alert, the aged and infirm retainer transformed into a vigorous, powerful man of middle years.

"Greedy ninnyhammers, Ben. Bring me some hot water and a cloth." Rupert bent toward a spotted-looking glass and touched the livid scar. "It works rather well, don't you think?"

"Aye." Ben took a kettle from the stove and poured water into a small bowl. "You want me to do it for ye?"

"No, I can manage, thanks." He dipped the cloth into the water and scrubbed at the painted scar.

"Think they'll be back?" Ben picked up the discarded glasses from the floor.

"Oh, yes. In fact, I imagine they'll be back before the evening's half-done. I really alarmed them with the thought of a line of rival investors beating a path to this door. I'd like you to stay here and take a message when they return. Set up another meeting for Friday evening. Tell them it's a board meeting and they'll be able to meet the other members of the committee when we discuss how business is going."

"And who'll ye be gettin' fer this committee?" Ben raked through the embers in the stove, spreading them so that the fire would die more rapidly.

Rupert chuckled. "Old Fred Grimforth and Terence Shotley will be glad enough to play a part for a consideration."

Ben grinned. The Royal Oak had many customers adept at a variety of performances. "I'll stay 'ere fer a bit, then."

"Thanks." Rupert took off the tatty white wig and smoothed down his hair. He threw off his seedy garments and dressed again in his own britches and coat.

"I think that for the board meeting I shall don a frock coat and hedgehog wig. Show our potential investors that the man who's going to make their money for them can look as well-to-do as the next man in the right circumstances."

"Even if 'e does look a right villain," Ben commented, picking up the discarded clothes and shaking them out. "That scar's enough to make a grown man turn in 'is grave."

"Our friends expect a villain, Ben, so we must give them one. I'm sure they'd never believe in the authenticity of such a diabolical scheme if it was perpetrated by a man in court dress. Rogues and extortionists couldn't possibly look like themselves." His voice dripped sarcasm like honey off the comb.

"Aye," Ben agreed dourly. "If 'n ye says so. I wouldn't know."

Rupert made no reply. He took one last look at himself in the inadequate mirror before fetching his hat and a slender cane from the cupboard. He pressed a cunning little knob in the handle of the cane, and a wicked blade sprang forth.

"Expectin' trouble?" Ben inquired laconically.

"Around here it pays to be prepared." He pressed the knob again and the blade retracted. "I'm late and it's a court day. Octavia will be ready to slice off my ears and feed them to the crows if I'm not there to escort her."

"Doesn't sound like you, Nick, to let a woman rule the roost," Ben grunted, following him down the stairs.

Rupert smiled. "Oh, that's not how I would describe Octavia's methods for getting her own way, Ben. She doesn't force her own opinion exactly, she simply ignores the opposition if it's inconvenient."

"Meaning you, I suppose."

"Meaning me," he agreed. He turned at the bottom of the stairs to a small door built flush into the riverside wall. He pulled back on the heavy bolts, and the door swung open onto the river. A flight of weed-slick steps led down to the water, where a scull bobbed, fastened to a ring set in the wall.

"Not like you to work with someone else," Ben persisted, leaning sideways to unfasten the scull's painter. "Particularly a woman. Thought you didn't hold with women, 'ceptin' in bed or the kitchen."

"A man can change his views," Rupert pointed out. "Octavia doesn't fit usual categories." He stepped into the scull and fitted the oars into the rowlocks.

"You reckon she's reliable, then?" Ben dropped the painter into the boat. "Only Bessie was askin'."

"Was she, now?" Rupert raised his eyebrows and rested on the oars, peering up at Ben in the dusk. "Well, you tell Bessie to mind her own business, Ben. Much as I appreciate her concern, when it comes to Miss Morgan, I know my own business best."

"No offense meant."

"None taken. Send me a message to Dover Street when you've spoken with our friends again. And I'll see you here next Friday."

"Yes . . . oh, about that business on the 'eath the other day."

Rupert shipped his oars again. He'd very casually mentioned to Ben the unexpected appearance of Bow Street Runners with the mail coach, and Ben had made no comment.

"I'll be 'avin' a word with Morris, I reckon. Mebbe get a few folks to keep an eye on 'im. What d'ye think?"

"I think I don't want another such surprise," Rupert stated. "And most particularly not when Octavia's with me."

"She was on the road wi' ye, again?" Ben stared down at him in astonishment.

"Yes. One of those occasions when she chose to ignore the opposition," Rupert responded with a rueful sigh. "And since I imagine she'll continue to ignore it on such occasions, I want no more unwelcome surprises."

"Well, I never did." Ben scratched his head. "The road's no place for a woman."

"Don't I know it, Ben. Don't I know it." Rupert flashed him a smile of resigned self-mockery, then pulled strongly away from the stairs, turning the scull into the current as he rowed across the river to a flight of steps set into the opposite embankment.

His attempt to forbid Octavia ever again to follow him to the heath had failed miserably. She had simply refused to listen to him. He could see her now, sitting at the dresser, delicately paring her fingernails, listening with every appearance of docile submission to his forceful speech. But when he'd fallen silent, she'd said smilingly he wasn't to worry about anything. She knew exactly what she was doing, and since she'd been very useful on the two occasions she *had* followed him, he should be glad of her help in the future. It remained her contention that since they both enjoyed the fruits of the road, they should both take its risks.

There was something about her cheerful assurance and sunny obstinacy that had made him want to laugh. She partnered him beautifully in every other aspect of their deception, and she was no delicate flower to be gently introduced to a life of crime. Octavia had embraced such an existence long since. So he'd settled for a promise of absolute obedience when they were engaged in highway robbery, and yielded the issue. However, until he'd identified the spy at the Royal Oak, if there was one, he had no intention of risking either of their necks on the heath again.

The scull bumped gently against the steps, and a waterman peered over the top of the embankment. He came down the steps to take the painter as Rupert tossed it to him. "Growin' chilly on the water, guv."

"Aye. It'll be a week or two yet before the day's warmth lingers after sunset." Rupert sprang onto the step and handed the man a shilling. The sound of voices and tramping feet came from the embankment above. "What's that?"

"Oh, it's that there Protestant Association marchin' agin the papists, guv," the waterman said, securing the painter to a ring in the wall. "Full of ale and bluster they be, ready to follow that Lord George Gordon into 'ell's inferno."

He followed Rupert up the steps. "Not that I 'olds

with papists meself. An' I don't 'old with no Catholic Relief Act neither. But that Lord George talks a lot of nonsense too. I was jest sayin' to the missis—"

"Good night, waterman." Rupert cut off his loquacious companion in full flood and hurried down the street.

A small crowd of apprentices moved ahead of him, chanting "No popery," but without too much venom. They turned aside into the courtyard of a tavern, distracted by the smell of ale, and Rupert continued past, wondering if this growing anti-Catholic movement was going to prove a nuisance. For some reason Catholic emancipation seemed to touch a raw nerve with the populace, and Lord George Gordon's fanaticism was an effective bellows.

Of course, one always needed to believe there was someone worse off than oneself, and the worse one's own situation, the more one needed to, he reflected. And the worse one's own situation, the more one needed someone to blame. London's underclass was learning to blame Catholics for its every ill under the fiery persuasion of Lord George and his fellow rabble-rousers. They painted the prospect of Parliament's relieving a small part of the legal discrimination against Catholics as an edict straight from the devil's heretic mouth.

Rupert hastened up the steps to his own house as a nearby church clock struck seven. The royal family had come from Windsor Castle for the day to conduct a drawing-room reception at St. James's Palace. It was unthinkable for anyone who laid claim to the higher echelons of society not to put in an appearance. Octavia had grumbled mightily. Since one couldn't be seen in the queen's company with undressed hair, she had to submit to the attentions of a hairdresser in the powder closet.

Rupert, expecting the worst, strolled up the stairs, entering Octavia's bedchamber without ceremony. She was still swathed in a powder gown, examining herself in the cheval glass. "Oh, there you are," she said crossly. "Where have you been since dinner, while I've been enduring this torture?"

"Business," he said calmly, bending to kiss the exposed nape of her neck. "And don't exaggerate. Let me look at you."

"Don't, it's hideous." She pulled a face at her reflection. "I don't look in the least like myself."

"No, that you don't," he agreed, absorbing the towering white edifice that swayed above her small face. "But it's de rigueur, my dear." He strode to the door that connected his apartments with hers.

"What business?" Octavia stood up and followed him. She leaned against the doorjamb as he began to throw off his clothes. "Shall I ring for Jameson? Will you need him to dress your hair?"

"No, I shall wear a wig. It's a lot easier." He splashed water on his face from the basin on the washstand.

"It'll take all night to get this muck out of my hair." Octavia pulled disconsolately at a white ringlet on her shoulder, forgetting her earlier question. "But my own hair's too long to fit under a wig. Perhaps I should shave it all off."

"Don't you dare even jest about such a thing!"

"Who's jesting?" she taunted, cowering in mock terror as he glared ferociously.

"Lady Greerson has shaved her head . . . or so I've heard. And most of the ladies at court wear theirs shorn very close to their heads," she added mischievously. "It seems very sensible to me. Men shave their heads all the time. It helps the itching, as I understand it . . . nothing for the lice to nest in, I imagine."

Her eyes sparkled with amusement, her irritation forgotten as rapidly as it had arisen. Rupert's presence generally had that effect. When she was with him, she found it very hard to hold a grudge or maintain ill temper.

In fact, his presence was becoming absolutely vital to her. In fact, she couldn't imagine living life outside that presence.

She turned back abruptly to her own chamber, where Nell was waiting with her corset. There was no room in their present life to indulge in such maudlin fancies. Of course, she could—would—live life without Rupert Warwick . . . or whoever he really was. Just as he would live life without her. In fact, she would lay any odds that the prospect of not doing so had never entered his head.

She gave the maid her back, seizing the bedpost and breathing in grimly as Nell tugged on the laces.

"That's enough, Nell!" Rupert's voice spoke from the connecting door. "Hell and the devil, Octavia, what are you thinking of? You'll break your ribs."

Octavia realized that in her fierce reverie she'd completely forgotten to breathe. She let out her breath with a gasp and squeaked in pain. "Ow! Let them out, Nell!"

"I was waitin' for you to say something, madam," Nell said in hasty defense, releasing her death grip on the laces.

"I was thinking of something else," Octavia mumbled, massaging her aching ribs.

"Like what?" Rupert frowned at her.

You. "Oh, just about the evening," she said, stepping into the petticoat Nell held out for her. "How long do we have to stay at this drawing room?"

"Until Their Majesties retire. You know that."

He was still puzzled. Somewhere between her mischief in his bedchamber and now, something had disturbed her. He could see it in the little lines of tension around her eyes and the set of her mouth.

Octavia stood still as Nell fastened the three whalebone panniers at her waist; then she stepped into the straw-colored taffeta *robe à la polonaise.*

Nell hooked it up, then stood back admiringly. The ruched skirt was drawn up by cords beneath to fall in three draped swags over the panniers, revealing a flounced petticoat of bronze taffeta short enough to show the turn of an ankle and slender feet in straw-colored satin slippers. The décolletage was daringly low, and Nell dipped a hare's foot into a tub of powder and patted it across the swell of her mistress's breasts.

Rupert forgot his puzzlement in this new Octavia.

He'd never seen her dressed with this formality. He found the sight mesmerizing, and the thought of the simple beauty that lay beneath the frills and ruching was powerfully arousing.

To distract himself, he opened a small box of beauty patches and selected two black silk crescents.

"Allow me, my dear." Delicately, he placed them on her breasts, just above her barely concealed nipples. "That should draw the eye nicely."

He was presumably thinking particularly of Philip Wyndham, Octavia reflected, looking down at his fingers making a minute adjustment to the patch on her left breast. He was dressing her up to entrap and seduce his enemy. In her present costume she certainly rivaled Margaret Drayton for daring flamboyance. Everything she had to offer was on display.

Rupert was picking through the box of patches again and selected a small circular one. Taking her face between finger and thumb, he turned it this way and that, trying to decide where to place the piece of silk.

"I think the roguish." He placed a circular patch high on her cheekbone in the appropriate position.

"Anything else you wish to add?" Octavia asked. "Any further piece of artifice to enhance my attractions for those who must be attracted?"

There was a moment of silence in which she wished twenty times over that she hadn't spoken and most particularly not in that tone.

Rupert dropped his hand from her face. Anger and puzzlement flashed across his eyes at the sardonic bitterness in her voice.

"What are you talking about?" He glanced pointedly behind him to where Nell was busy at the armoire.

Octavia shrugged, tried to laugh it off. She picked up the hare's foot, dusting it across her cheeks, peering attentively at her image in the glass.

"Nothing really. I suppose I just feel uncomfortable because I look like every other woman at court. Like some peacock preening my feathers to attract a mate."

"It's the male peacock who does the preening," he pointed out, still frowning.

"Oh, you know what I mean." She licked a fingertip and smoothed her eyebrows, not meeting his eye in the mirror.

"I'm not sure that I do," he said quietly. "But I have a faint suspicion, and you'd better hope that it's incorrect, Octavia."

He leaned over her shoulders, placing his hands on the dresser, his face close beside hers, his eyes forcing her gaze in the mirror. "I am wrong, aren't I, Octavia? You couldn't possibly have been accusing me of preparing you for Wyndham's bed?"

Her mouth was suddenly dry, her skin hot. This was Rupert at his most intimidating.

"I don't know why you would think that," she said, clearing her throat. "And I don't know why you're glaring at me in that way. I don't like being dressed up in this fashion, it makes me feel like a whore. And it doesn't make any difference that every other woman will look just the same, because I don't like looking like other women."

To her relief he seemed to be convinced. He straightened slowly, his hands resting lightly on her shoulders. Then he nodded. "Believe me, Octavia, you don't look in the least like other women. You are unique."

He let his hands slip from her shoulders, and his eyes now smiled at her in the mirror. "I'll wager you'll have even the king at your feet—and you know what a prude he is."

With sudden briskness he moved back to the door to his own room. "I must finish my own peacock imitation. Don't disturb my handiwork," he added, seeing her fingers move restlessly to the patch on her cheek. "Trust me to know what suits you."

He probably did know. It seemed to be one of his areas of expertise, and she'd been stupid to react like that. It was just that increasingly these days she felt raw, as if she were missing several skins, and then she lost the ability to respond airily, to play the game with the buoyant enthusiasm that she knew he expected of her.

And Octavia knew precisely why she had lost the ability this evening.

She wandered restlessly over to the window. Her gown wasn't designed for sitting, although she could shift the back pannier sideways to perch on the edge of a stool if she wished. Not that she would be doing much sitting this evening. One didn't sit in Their Majesties' presence.

She knew exactly why she'd reacted with such sharp bitterness to Rupert's lighthearted ministrations. Tonight she was going to accede to any suggestion Philip Wyndham made.

The decision had made itself as she sat beneath the hands of the hairdresser and watched herself transformed into an artificial monstrosity. This creature could tangle in the bedsheets with the Earl of Wyndham and be completely untouched by the experience. There was no Octavia Morgan visible in this guise.

And when it was done, and she had the ring, then Rupert would complete his half of the bargain, and this suspenseful agony would be done. She wouldn't have to pretend to be carefree and buoyant and untouched by the grim realities of the game. She could crawl into a hole and be as bitterly miserable as she wished.

"Are you ready, Octavia?"

She jumped, closed her eyes for a second until she'd composed herself, then glanced casually over her shoulder.

She gasped at what she saw. Rupert, too, looked very different. He wore his favorite black silk, but with a gold-embroidered waistcoat and black stockings embroidered with gold clocks. A diamond gleamed in the black solitaire neck cloth he wore around his stock, and his powdered wig was as high as her own hair. A beauty patch in the corner of his mouth seemed to accentuate the cynical curve to his lips.

"Is that rouge you're wearing, my lord?" She stared in disbelief.

"A touch is customary." His smile was both sardonic

and complicit. "One must not fly in the face of custom all
the time, Octavia. Sometimes it's necessary to obey convention in order to achieve one's own ends."

He held out his arm. "Come, ma'am. Let us go and set
the court on its heels."

Chapter 15

♪♫ Queen Charlotte was disposed to notice Lady Rupert Warwick at the reception, although initially Octavia couldn't think why she should receive particular favor. The queen's equerry murmured in her ear that Her Majesty wished Lady Warwick to be presented, and Octavia found herself being ushered through the crowded drawing room, aware of the envious looks of the unfavored.

She caught sight of the Prince of Wales, standing close to his mother and her ladies. He nodded and winked pointedly and Octavia understood. Her Majesty wished to interview the woman in whose house her unruly son spent so much time.

She curtsied, low and Queen Charlotte returned the salute with a half curtsy. "Lady Warwick, I believe we haven't had the pleasure of your acquaintance," she said, unsmiling as her gaze drifted over Octavia's gown, skimmed over her décolletage. "Our son is a good friend of yours, I understand."

"I am honored to be called so, madam," Octavia said demurely. "But His Highness enjoys the tables, and I confess I am inept at cards and quite fail to see the appeal."

The queen's eyes sharpened and some of her hostility

faded. "Is that so, Lady Warwick? You must find yourself in the minority."

"Alas, yes, madam." Octavia smiled. "So my husband is always telling me. But in truth I cannot imagine why one would want to throw good money after bad on the strength of a card or the fall of the dice."

She was doing well. The queen looked almost benign, clearly reassessing her opinion of the woman she'd heard ran one of the most frequented gaming salons in the town.

"I wish you could persuade my son of your opinions, Lady Warwick," the queen said. "Indeed, I wish you would ban gaming tables from your salon."

Octavia curtsied again. "My husband plays, madam," she said gravely, a tentative smile suggesting that in common with all women, including Queen Charlotte, she had no influence over her husband's activities, and no choice but to obey his dictates.

"Ah, yes." The queen sighed and fanned herself. "Men seem to derive an inordinate pleasure from gaming." She bestowed a small smile of dismissal. "Are you acquainted with the Countess of Wyndham?"

She gestured to Letitia Wyndham, standing silently to one side, before turning her attention to another lady ushered forward by the equerry.

Octavia curtsied and retreated the requisite distance, careful not to turn her back even a fraction.

"I believe we've just been introduced, Lady Wyndham," she said, smiling at the sallow, dumpy lady in a gown of primrose yellow adorned with puce roses. Puce roses embellished a coiffure so tall, it dwarfed her short stature.

"Her Majesty considers it discourteous to turn from someone who's been brought to her attention," the countess said a little stiffly. "She always passes people on so they don't feel too abruptly dismissed."

"How thoughtful," Octavia said.

Lady Wyndham was very nervous, and Octavia felt jumpy just standing beside her. She cast a cursory glance over the countess's painted face. The powder was thickly applied, bright spots of rouge startling against her cheeks.

Octavia frowned. There was something the matter with the woman's right eye. The eyelid was swollen, and beneath the heavily caked powder could be seen a purple shadow.

"Forgive me, ma'am, but have you hurt yourself? Your eye?"

Color flooded Letitia's face, spreading beneath the white coating—color so hot, it looked as if it would melt paint and powder alike. She touched her eye with fluttering fingertips.

"I tripped . . . so stupid of me. On the corner of the rug, caught my toe in a loose fringe. So stupid and clumsy."

Octavia remembered when Letitia had tripped on the pavement outside Almack's. Philip had been there. She hadn't heard what was said between them, but she knew it hadn't been pleasant. Perhaps Letitia Wyndham was incurably clumsy. There were such people.

"We all have accidents," she said soothingly. "I once tripped all the way down a flight of stairs and ended up at the bottom with my petticoats over my head just as a party of guests arrived at the door."

Letitia's mouth flickered in a tentative movement that seemed to imply that she hadn't made up her mind whether or not to smile. She raised her other hand to pat nervously at her hair.

Octavia looked at the great purpling bruise on the countess's wrist. It didn't look like the kind of bruise one acquired by tripping over a carpet. Perhaps Letitia Wyndham was not incurably clumsy, after all. She glanced sideways to where the Earl of Wyndham stood in the circle around the king. Then she glanced back at the countess.

The other woman's gaze had followed Octavia's. When she spoke, her voice was very flat and low.

"You are acquainted with my husband, I believe, Lady Warwick."

"Yes," Octavia agreed.

"Quite well, I believe."

Was she probing? What did she want to hear? Or was the countess simply stating obliquely that she knew what was said about the Earl of Wyndham and Lady Warwick:

that if Lady Warwick was not her husband's mistress at this point, she soon would be.

"He frequents my husband's gaming tables, ma'am."

"But my husband doesn't enjoy gaming. There must be other inducements." Lady Wyndham now had the air of a woman about to jump off a cliff. Her color had died down and her face was a white mask again, but her eyes, dark green and brilliant, were fixed on Octavia's face with an almost fanatic intensity.

They were magnificent eyes, Octavia realized. Totally surprising on this insignificant, timid little dab of a woman.

"What are you saying, Lady Wyndham?" she asked directly.

The countess dabbed at her lips with her handkerchief. "I hear the rumors," she said in a low, rushed voice. "Please don't misunderstand me. I have no quarrel with you. Anything that keeps my husband from my side is welcome. And I am grateful for anything that distracts his attention from my daughter."

Octavia stared at her. It was an extraordinary conversation to be having in the middle of the king's drawing room at St. James's Palace. And yet, she thought, there was almost no risk of being overheard in the babble and general jostling for attention. Everyone was far too self-absorbed to give two chatting women a passing thought.

She glanced across the room again. And met Philip Wyndham's gray eyes. Her skin prickled, and her scalp crawled as if an entire nest of lice had taken up residence beneath the powder and pomade. Deliberately, she smiled at him, her eyes narrowing. Then she turned back to his wife.

Letitia was now looking wretched, as if deeply regretting her jump from the cliff. "Forgive me," she mumbled. "I don't know what I was thinking . . . to say such a thing."

"Tell me about your daughter," Octavia invited, knowing she could not respond adequately either to the confession or to this subsequent retraction.

Letitia's face lit up, and for a moment Octavia could see

beneath the plainness and the anxiety, to a radiance that was its own special kind of beauty. For a moment she saw the woman as she would have been if fate had not shackled her to Philip Wyndham.

"Susannah," she said. "She's only three months old, but she smiles all the time. Nurse says she's the sunniest baby she's ever had in charge. And I know she knows my footsteps. She coos like a pigeon when I—"

Letitia stopped abruptly, again flushing crimson to the roots of her hair. "Forgive me. I do rattle on so. I must return to the queen."

She turned to go, but Octavia laid a hand on her sleeve. "Your husband?" she said. "He doesn't care for the child?"

"He has no interest in daughters," Letitia said. Her eyes met Octavia's, and a message burned in the brilliant green depths. "My husband despises women, Lady Warwick."

Then she moved away with an urgent gesture of farewell that contained more than a touch of desperation.

Octavia stepped aside. Philip's wife had been warning her. But she hadn't told her anything she didn't already know. It was not possible to have any remotely intimate intercourse with Philip Wyndham without sensing his dark potential for violence.

"Pathetic little drab, isn't she?" A brittle laugh accompanied the soft, malicious voice. Margaret Drayton stood beside Octavia, fanning herself, the gilded plumes in her coiffure nodding in the gentle breeze. "It's no wonder her husband seeks pastures new."

"Don't most husbands?" Octavia asked dryly.

Margaret's scarlet-painted mouth moved in a smile. Her teeth were not good, Octavia noticed with satisfaction. In fact, she seemed to be missing rather a large number.

"Mine doesn't, my dear," Margaret said. "He barely knows what to do in his own pasture." She laughed coarsely. "Take my advice. Marry a man in his dotage. Pleasuring him is something of an ordeal." She shrugged her magnificent shoulders, and her nipples peeped above her neckline. "But it's a small price to pay for freedom. And it does mean one doesn't have to worry about whom he's been covering before he comes to one's own bed."

Octavia hid her disgust. It wasn't possible that Rupert could find this coarse creature appealing—although there was something horribly vibrant about her, something almost larger than life.

"It's a little late for me to take your advice, Lady Drayton."

"Ah, but you play your own games, don't you, Lady Warwick?" Margaret smiled over her fan, her eyes darting across the room to Philip Wyndham. "I don't know what you expect to gain from the Earl of Wyndham, but take my word for it, my dear, whatever your price, it won't be sufficient compensation." Her fan snapped shut and her face was suddenly ugly, stamped with a mixture of fear and loathing.

"The Earl of Wyndham despises women . . . or so I've been told," Octavia said evenly.

Margaret opened her fan again. "Whoever told you that knew what she was talking about." She smiled, her expression once more all sardonic malice. "I thought I'd drop a word in your ear. Those of us who play these games should look after each other, I believe." She offered an ironic curtsy. "I'd be grateful for any words of advice in my own game, if you think I might benefit from them."

Her gaze drifted pointedly to Lord Rupert Warwick and then back again to his wife. Her smile broadened. Then she moved away.

Octavia contemplated hurling her sharp-heeled slipper at that smooth white back. The woman had invited Octavia to give a few pointers on how to seduce *her* husband. Not that all the pointers in the world would do her any good. Rupert wasn't a man to be seduced. He preferred the active role in that play.

It was still annoying, however, to watch Margaret bobbing at Rupert's elbow, touching him, brushing his cheek with her fingers, tapping his wrist with her fan. And to hear his lazy laugh, and to see his mouth curve, his eyelids droop suggestively as he responded to her banter.

He must be enjoying himself, Octavia decided. However useful the flirtation, he clearly didn't find it unpleasant. And Margaret did have a raw kind of appeal—without subtlety, but magnetic in some way.

Octavia ground her teeth in an annoyance directed more at herself than at Margaret or Rupert. She was beginning to suspect that she had a very possessive nature. A most unfashionable trait, and in present circumstances, a most inconvenient one.

She became aware of Philip Wyndham's gaze on the back of her neck exerting an almost perceptible tug. She turned her head. There was a distinct command in the unsmiling gray eyes, and once again she had the strangest sense of distorted familiarity. Obeying the command, she moved across the room toward him.

"You were enjoying a conversation with my wife," the earl stated when she reached him. "I trust you found her a stimulating companion."

The vicious derision in his voice made her stomach curl, but she knew she had to respond in like manner.

She laughed—a brittle, mocking laugh. "La, my lord, I'm sure you know better than I the quality of Lady Wyndham's discourse."

Philip bowed, raising her hand to his lips. "Indeed I do, madam. Will you walk into the far salon?"

It was couched as a question, but it came as a directive. Octavia curtsied her agreement and tucked her hand into his arm. They walked through the crowded drawing room into an antechamber, where footmen and equerries stood about looking as if they had no useful purpose. A few courtiers were gathered in knots about the gilded chamber, taking a breather from the overheated air in the drawing room.

The Earl of Wyndham made his way to a long window in the far wall. Heavy velvet curtains were drawn tight, as if to keep out the faintest waft of the fresh night air. He drew aside one curtain, opened the French door, and ushered Octavia onto the terrace beyond.

"The air is pleasanter here, I believe."

"Yes," she agreed, unable to help a shiver as the breeze rippled across her bare shoulders, cooling her heated skin.

If Philip was aware of her momentary discomfort, he took no notice. Another man would have immediately offered to fetch her shawl, Octavia thought. Rupert would have draped his own coat around her shoulders.

"Let us walk a little way along the terrace." Her hand was still tucked in his arm, and he now covered it with his free hand. It could have been interpreted as a warm and friendly gesture, but to Octavia it felt as if he'd shackled her.

She said nothing, however, and allowed herself to be drawn away from the French door and the sounds and lights within. In the dark shadows of a group of box trees at the far end of the terrace, Philip suddenly pulled her against him in a rough movement that took her by surprise. His hands circled her neck, thumbs pushing up her chin, forcing her to look up at his face, where the gray eyes, deep-set in dark, shadowed holes, had a metallic glitter.

"I want you," he said. But there was no ardor in the statement of passion. It was a cold statement of fact. "I want you, and you want me."

His mouth came down on hers, crushing her lips against her teeth, then his tongue pushed into her mouth, drove to the back of her throat, making her gag and bringing tears to her eyes. But she was growing accustomed to these assaultive kisses and swiftly brought her hands around his body, slipping beneath his coat, stroking and patting across his torso.

And then she felt it. Her fingers stilled. Beneath the tight-fitting waistcoat there was something small and round and hard. But it was beneath the waistcoat. A pocket on the inside? A pocket in his shirt? Impossible to tell. And impossible to explore without removing the waistcoat.

Her hands dropped from his body and fell to her sides. Her head fell back beneath the pressure of his mouth. She held herself still and submissive as he ravaged her mouth and his fingers tightened for a second on her throat, then moved down to her breasts. Instinctively, Octavia knew that he liked her passive submission. That it excited him more than a vigorous response. And in many ways it was easier to do.

Her mind raced on its own course. How was she to extract that little pouch from beneath his waistcoat? Perhaps if she did throw herself onto him in an orgy of moaning ardor, scratching and scrabbling at his clothes in her eagerness to get at him, maybe she could reach it. But she couldn't do that here. Not on the terrace of St. James's Palace in the middle of a royal reception.

Philip raised his head, but his hands slipped back up to her throat, holding her just a little too tightly for perfect comfort.

"You will yield to me, Octavia," he said. "I've been patient . . . very patient. But the game is played out now. I can wait no longer."

"Neither can I, my lord," she whispered, feeling her throat moving against his thumbs.

He nodded, and his eyes flared with a satisfaction that turned her blood to ice. "I will send a carriage for you at two o'clock tomorrow afternoon. You will come to St. James's Square."

"To your house?" She couldn't help the shocked question.

"Where else?" he said.

"But . . . but your wife . . . your servants?"

"My servants are not paid to show interest in my business. And my wife knows better than to do so." Every word was invested with an icy contempt that Octavia knew touched her as well.

"Besides," he added with a laugh of pure derision, "your own reputation, my dear, will be much safer in such a situation. There will be no strangers involved. You will come and go in a closed carriage. Only my household will be aware of you. There will be no one to whisper, to set tongues awagging."

Octavia was silent. He still held her throat, and she met his predatory gaze as fearlessly as she could. She would agree because she had to. But surely there would be a way to avoid the ultimate surrender? Something would occur to her. At least she knew now that he *had* the ring. That she wouldn't be on a fool's errand.

"We should return inside, sir," she said after a minute, amazed at how calm her voice was. "If we're to be so careful of my reputation tomorrow, it seems a little pointless to risk it today."

He smiled and released his grip on her throat. "How true, ma'am. And perhaps by now your husband will have tired of Lady Drayton . . . or she of him."

Octavia contented herself with a shrug of indifference. But the earl continued smoothly, "I have the impression you find your husband's dalliance with the lady somewhat annoying."

"Whatever could have given you that idea, sir?" She laughed, hiding her shock. How could she possibly have given herself away?

"Oh, just a look you have when you glance in their direction. I assure you Margaret Drayton can't hold a candle to you. But, of course, husbands are notoriously unappreciative."

He stepped aside so she could precede him through the French door and back into the bright lights of the antechamber.

He lowered his head to her ear as she passed him. "Giving your husband a pair of horns will be some recompense for his lamentable lack of appreciation."

Octavia smiled and inclined her head. Through her revulsion glowed the bright light of her own knowledge that it was Philip Wyndham who was being played for the fool. Philip Wyndham who was falling into Rupert Warwick's trap.

ॐ

*R*upert had seen Octavia's departure with Philip and throughout their absence found himself on tenterhooks even as he flirted with Margaret Drayton and dallied amiably with several other ladies who showed willing.

What were they doing? The question wouldn't leave his mind. He thought of Octavia locked in his brother's embrace. Of her lips red and swollen beneath Philip's. Of her mouth invaded, sullied. Of her ivory damask skin pawed and pressed by his twin's long, strong fingers, so like his own. The images roiled in his brain, twisting and vile, and he could not endure them. There must be another way to do this.

"Ah, Warwick, we met your friend this afternoon." Dirk Rigby called out this greeting as he pushed through the throng, Hector beside him. "Rum fellow, that Thaddeus Nielson."

Rupert raised his quizzing glass and subjected the red-faced Dirk to a long stare.

"Your pardon, Rigby, but you talk in riddles," he drawled. "You met a friend of mine this afternoon?" His eyebrows crawled into his scalp, and his eyes were so cold and flat, it was as if they had no life.

Dirk, alas, was slow on the uptake. "Why, yes," he said, visibly puzzled. "That fellow you mentioned. You remember our little discussion . . . ?" He winked vigorously several times and twitched his nose.

Rupert's stare grew increasingly cold and distant. "Forgive me," he said. "But I have not the faintest idea what you're talking about."

"No, no, of course not!" Hector put in hastily, nudging his friend sharply in the ribs. "Dirk was confusing you with someone else . . . very forgetful, he is. Aren't you, dear fellow?"

The penny seemed to have dropped. Dirk's expression slowly cleared. "Oh, yes," he agreed fervently, wiping his perspiring forehead with his handkerchief. "Very forgetful. Can't think what I was thinkin' of, Warwick. Confusing you with someone else . . . yes, that's it. Sure you were someone else."

"Is there a remarkable likeness, then?" Rupert inquired with polite interest.

"Oh, yes . . . that's it." Dirk seized on this explanation with pathetic enthusiasm. "Yes, most amazing likeness. Could be twins. Don't you think, Lacross? Veritable twins. Most astonishing resemblance."

"Goodness me," Rupert said. "Do tell me who this double is. Do I know him?"

"Oh . . . oh . . . no, I don't believe so . . . um . . . what was his name, Hector?" Dirk appealed to his friend.

"No one you would know, Warwick," Lacross said calmly. "A man we met at the races the other afternoon. He had some business contacts who interested us." He took snuff. "His contact had a most interesting proposition."

Rupert bowed. "How gratifying for you. By 'interesting,' I assume you mean lucrative?"

"Possibly." Hector bowed and moved off, Dirk, after a minute's confusion, following.

It was astonishing, Rupert reflected, how someone as fearsomely intellectual as Oliver Morgan could have fallen victim to two such boobies. But, then, as Octavia had said, Oliver lived so much in his own world, he had only a tenuous grasp of the gritty realities other people lived.

Octavia and Philip had returned to the drawing room. They stood talking together just inside the door; then Octavia curtsied and walked away. Before she could reach Rupert, she was accosted by the Prince of Wales and borne off on his arm like a battle prize.

Rupert frowned. She was looking drawn and tired, as if the effort of holding her own throughout this tedious evening was getting to be too much. They couldn't leave before the royal party, however. Had something definitive occurred when she was outside with Philip? The question nagged at him like an aching tooth.

At last there was a rustle of movement around the king and queen, and the buzz of conversation died down. The royal couple progressed through the room, acknowledging the bows and curtsies with faint smiles. Then they passed through the doors, the Prince of Wales perforce accompanying them.

"Thank God for that!" Octavia breathed at Rupert's side. "I didn't think I could bear another minute. Will you take me home? Or should I go myself?"

The strain around her eyes was more pronounced. Rupert, aware of the people around them, resisted the urge to smooth the smudged shadows with his finger. "I'll take you home."

"Must you go on somewhere afterward?" She tried to sound bright, as if she were asking simply for information and not because her whole being ached and she didn't know whether she wanted to be cuddled and made to feel warm and safe, or lost in the turbulent whirlpool of shared passion that would chase away the specter of the morrow.

"No." He frowned down at her, hearing in her question everything she'd tried to conceal. He spoke in a gentle undertone. "You look in need of some nursery comforting, sweeting."

The caress in his voice was balm, and she felt the tension sliding away. "How did you guess?"

"I know you rather well." For a moment his eyes were soft; then he turned from her, saying cheerfully to the assembled company, "Well, ladies and gentlemen, I fear we must leave you to whatever further dissipation the evening might hold."

The sally was greeted with laughter, and Margaret Drayton reached up to brush a speck of dust off his shoulder. "The night is yet young, sir. I can think of many more exciting pursuits than can be found at one's own fireside."

"Ah, there you have me, ma'am." He bowed over her hand. "I confess I cannot."

It was such a direct snub, and yet for a minute Margaret didn't seem to have heard him aright. She began to smile as if in response to the compliment she'd been expecting; then her jaw went slack. Someone tittered.

Rupert turned to Octavia. "Shall we go, my dear?" He took her hand and tucked it firmly into his arm.

"What a set-down!" Octavia murmured as they stood in the antechamber waiting for their carriage. "How could you have said such a thing?"

"The woman grows tedious," he replied with an air of bored indifference.

"And perhaps no longer useful?" Octavia suggested.

Though she disliked Margaret Drayton, there was something chilling about Rupert's cold dismissal.

Someday she would no longer be useful to Rupert either.

He smiled lazily. "Perhaps not."

"Your plans are in place, then?"

"Oh, more than that, my dear. Up and running."

Octavia adjusted the folds of her satin cloak around her shoulders. She still had no idea what Rupert's plan was with Hector and Dirk.

"And what of yours?" he asked, his eyes sharpening, the languid tone vanished.

For some reason Octavia didn't immediately reply with her own news.

"Your coach, Lord Rupert." The footman spoke before her silence could seem marked.

"Thank you." Rupert nodded to the bowing footman and escorted Octavia outside to the light town chaise. He handed her in, then climbed up behind her.

"So what of your progress?" he asked again, folding his arms, leaning back, resting his head against the thick cushions. "Anything to tell me?"

"I believe I found the ring, in an inside pocket of his waistcoat." Was that all she was going to say? Her brain didn't seem to be functioning properly.

"Inside? Awkward." His expression betrayed no sign of a sudden surge of jubilation. He had been certain Philip would carry the ring at all times, but Octavia's failure to discover it so far had started to make him uneasy.

"Very. I'll have to induce him to take the waistcoat off."

"That shouldn't be too difficult at the appropriate moment," he observed, his voice as dry as the Sahara, even as the vile images again seethed and twisted beneath his calm exterior.

"No," Octavia agreed. She twined her hands in her lap. "He beats his wife."

"Many men do."

"I don't think it's a subject for flippancy," she flared.

"Curiously, I wasn't being flippant. It doesn't surprise

me in the least that Philip maltreats his wife. It would surprise me if he didn't." Octavia couldn't see his expression in the dark of the carriage but his voice rang with an acid contempt.

"You know him very well."

"Almost as well as I know myself."

She sensed an opportunity and pressed on. "How long have you known him?"

"As long as I've known myself."

She sat back in frowning puzzlement. He seemed to be talking in riddles. "But he doesn't know you."

"He doesn't think he does." He leaned sideways to look out of the window, moving aside the curtain. "He isn't a fool, Octavia. He won't treat you in the way he treats his wife."

"I'm reassured," she said ironically. "What makes you so sure?"

"Because he will have no reason to do so. And because you will be coming home to me. However loose he may consider the ties that bind you and me, he knows you're not unprotected. Philip never takes on a fight with an equal . . . let alone his superior in strength and courage."

This calm rationalization was as hurtful as it was infuriating. Abruptly, she decided not to tell him about tomorrow's assignation. He had no fears for her. He gave her no details of his own progress. Why should she report to him like a soldier to a commanding officer? As he saw it, it was simply the task of a whore.

When she'd performed this whore's task, she'd drop the ring into his hand without a word, and he'd never know what it had cost her to earn her price.

Chapter 16

℘ *The* chaise drew up in Dover Street. Octavia went into the house feeling flat and despondent and unutterably weary. "I'm going up to bed."

Rupert, handing his cloak to Griffin, said, "Dismiss Nell as soon as she's unlaced you."

"I'm very tired."

He smiled. "Nevertheless . . ."

For once she wanted to resist that smile, the caressing note in his voice, the promise in his eyes. Her fatigue was of the soul, not of the body, and much harder to overcome. She hesitated, one hand on the newel, then, with a tiny shrug, turned and went up the stairs. She couldn't persist in the hall with Griffin standing there. When Rupert came to her, she would send him away.

"Bring me a cognac, Griffin." Rupert went into the library. The butler followed him in a few minutes. "Will that be all, my lord?"

"Yes, thank you. You may lock up." He took the glass from the tray and sipped. It had been a long and strenuous evening for both of them. The cognac burned down his gullet to join the burning, seething turmoil in his belly.

Octavia must have submitted to Philip's embraces again

in order to discover the ring hidden so well against his body. Soon Philip would know Octavia's glorious body in all its rich intimacies. He would put his hands upon her and his flesh within her.

His glass crashed into the fireplace in a shower of brandy and shards of shattered crystal.

He couldn't bear to prostitute her in this way. And that *was* what he would be doing. He'd tricked Octavia out of her maidenhood so that he could prostitute her. There was no sense in pretending otherwise. It didn't matter that she'd agreed willingly and enthusiastically. She didn't really understand what she'd been agreeing to.

He couldn't let it happen.

A great calm swept through him at this final acceptance of something he'd tried to deny for several weeks. He would have to come up with an alternative plan. A highway robbery, perhaps?

The idea brought a wry smile to his lips, and yet it wasn't an impossible scheme. He didn't rely totally on Morris's information for potential quarry. He kept his own ear to the ground as he went about social London, and when he heard of a likely heathward excursion by some rich degenerate, he would be there on the heath to greet him. What was to prevent him from waylaying his twin in such fashion?

Instead of going to Philip's bed, Octavia would be the bait that would lead Philip to the heath. And on the heath, his twin would be waiting for him.

The idea bubbled, and he knew he would have to leave it to ferment and take its own shape. In the meantime Octavia was upstairs and waiting for him.

He left the library, his step light as he took the stairs two at a time. He arrived in Octavia's bedroom to find her in her nightgown, gazing in astounded repulsion at the bed.

"Look what Nell's put there," she said, gesturing at a hollowed-out wooden board on the pillow. "She assures me that if I put my head carefully on that to sleep, then my coiffure will be barely disturbed and the hairdresser won't have to come again for at least three weeks! Three weeks, with this filth in my hair!"

"But, my lady, in my last position my mistress always slept on a wooden pillow," Nell declared. "Her nightcap covered her coiffure, and it was barely disarranged in the morning." She sounded thoroughly put out that her foresight was so little appreciated.

Octavia regarded her in some exasperation. She knew that Nell had difficulties with her present mistress's generally unconventional appearance and considered that it reflected poorly upon herself, as the one responsible for sending Lady Warwick out into the world suitably attired and adorned. Nell's delight at the powdering ritual this evening had been exceeded only by Octavia's disgust.

"Nell, you should know by now that I have no intention of maintaining my hair in this fashion a moment longer than necessary. In the morning you shall wash it for me, but for now we will take out the pads and the pins, and you will brush it thoroughly to get the worst out."

Nell's mouth screwed into pursed disapproval, but she fetched the silver-backed hairbrush from the dresser.

"That's all right, Nell. You may leave this with me," Lord Rupert said, amusement dancing in his eyes. He took the hairbrush from her. "You may go to bed."

Nell bobbed a curtsy and left in a waft of injured sensibility.

"I had thought you were going to dismiss her as soon as you were unlaced," Rupert said, sitting in an armchair by the window, regarding Octavia through half-closed lids.

"I'm very tired," she said, unconsciously stroking her throat. Then the movement reminded her of Philip's hands around her neck and she stopped.

"Do you mind if we don't . . . I mean . . . I would like to go to sleep," she finished limply. Never had she turned Rupert from her bed and until this evening she could never have imagined wanting to do so.

"So you shall," he said evenly. "Bring the ottoman over here and sit down so I can brush your hair." He gestured to the carpet at his feet.

There was something about her that alarmed him—a dull, fatigued resistance, almost resentment, that he sensed came from deep within her.

A man who carved his way through life with the sheer force of his personality, Rupert could think of only one way to override this strange mood of Octavia's: with the power of his own will.

Octavia reluctantly pushed the ottoman across the floor with her foot and sat down.

There was silence in the room as Rupert's hands moved through her hair, tossing aside pins and pads, until the powdered and pomaded mass tumbled to her shoulders.

"How much did you pay the hairdresser this evening?" he asked casually, picking up her brush and drawing it through the sticky locks.

"Five guineas. Why?"

"It probably explains why most people try to keep his work intact for as long as possible," he observed with a chuckle.

"Are you excusing me of extravagance?" She tried to turn her head to look up at him over her shoulder.

He placed his palm firmly on the top of her head, turning her head forward again. "No, I'm not. I was merely making an observation."

The brush was coming more freely through her hair now, and despite herself, Octavia began to relax, white powder fluttering over her shoulders to the carpet. Rupert always enjoyed brushing her hair; he made of it a sensual ritual.

Her head bent beneath the rhythmic strokes, the brush stroked the back of her neck, and a wave of lethargy washed through her.

Rupert brushed until her hair fell in a gleaming canopy over her shoulders beneath the white nightgown. He dropped the brush to the floor, and his fingers dug deep and strong into the muscles of her shoulders and along her spine.

"I can't do this properly over your nightgown," he

said, his voice sounding unnaturally loud as it broke the languid silence. "Take it off and lie on the bed."

Octavia came out of her trance. She *still* wished to lie alone tonight. She didn't want to be seduced and stroked and persuaded. Not when all she could think of was tomorrow and that Rupert wanted her to sleep with another man.

"I'm very tired, Rupert," she managed to say, but it didn't sound as strong as she wanted it to.

"I know you are. Now, do as I say."

Rebellion stirred, flared, at the cool authority Octavia knew so well. She pushed herself away from his knees so that she was sitting bolt upright on the ottoman. "Rupert, I don't feel like making love tonight."

"Did I say anything about making love?" He put his hands beneath her armpits and hoisted her upward. "If you don't wish to make love, then neither do I, Octavia. It's not an activity I could enjoy without your pleasure, as I'd have expected you to know by now."

He was scolding her like an obtuse child even while he pulled her nightgown over her head in one swift movement. "I know you're tired, and I know you're wound as tight as a coiled spring. I intend to do something about the latter, so be a good girl and submit gracefully."

He laughed at her indignant expression. This was familiar territory.

"Go, Octavia." He turned her toward the bed with an admonitory pat, and when she glared at him over her shoulder, he swung her off the floor and onto the bed.

She bounced upright. "You're not listening to me. I want to be left alone."

"What kind of oils or unguents do you have?" he asked calmly, strolling to the dresser. "Something that will lubricate my hands?"

"Lud! What's the matter with your hands?" she exclaimed in disbelief. She seemed to be losing her rational mind as well as her ability to assert herself. "Are they chapped or something?"

"No, you silly widgeon. . . . Ah, this should do." He

picked up an alabaster jar of perfumed oil that Octavia used in her bath.

"What are you going to do?" She was still sitting upright on the bed, wearing nothing but her hair flowing over her shoulders, her tawny eyes no longer tired or dull.

"Boil you in oil, if you're not cooperative," Rupert said with a grin, putting the alabaster pot on the bedside table. As she continued to gaze at him in vexed confusion, he began without haste to take off his clothes, placing them neatly on the chaise longue. When he stepped over to the bed, Octavia saw with a shock of bewilderment that he was not in the least aroused.

"I have no desire to stain my clothes with perfumed oil," he explained cheerfully, taking up the alabaster pot. He made an imperative circular movement with his forefinger. "Lie on your belly."

"No. . . . I mean, why?"

"Because you want to go to sleep, so I'm going to help you to sleep," he explained with an air of exaggerated patience. "However, in the interests of harmony and tranquillity I suggest you don't oblige me to repeat myself."

"A plague on you, Rupert Warwick. You're a . . . a veritable Visigoth!" Octavia declared, flinging herself onto her stomach with a very poor grace.

"Oh, I wouldn't say that," he returned, swinging across her body and sitting firmly on her bottom. "I'm merely somewhat forcefully looking to your comfort. I wouldn't call that the act of a barbarian."

"Oh, I would," Octavia declared into the pillow, clenching her backside in an effort to heave him off.

He merely laughed, settling himself more securely as he poured oil into the palms of his hands. "We'll see if you think that in a few minutes."

His hands began to move over her shoulders, the soft perfumed oil smoothing into her skin as his fingers cleverly worked the tight muscles, pushed into her spine and along the column of her neck. Octavia sank into the feather bed, her eyes closing, resistance floating from her.

Rupert smiled to himself, feeling the change in her.

How often had he done this for his mentor during their ramshackle years together? A lifetime of abusing his body with drink and debauchery, of sleeping in damp attics and howling drafts, had reduced old Rupert Warwick in his last years to a mass of aches and pains, plagued with gout and arthritis. Rupert had learned how to give him relief, but working on this slender satin body was a very different experience. And he could see no reason, now that he thought about it, to stop at her neck and shoulders.

His fingers moved down her spine, pressed into the hollows in the small of her back. Octavia groaned, but he could sense no resistance. Inching back so that he sat astride her thighs, he caressed her buttocks, his palms rotating the firm, round cheeks.

He was careful to keep his attentions sensual but not sexual—to avoid the two entrancing dimples low down on the curve of her bottom—and the effort involved in the sacrifice set his blood afire.

He moved down her legs, massaging her thighs, again carefully circumventing the sweet secrets between them. Strong fingers kneaded her calves and the soles of her feet. He could tell she wasn't asleep by the little ripples running over her skin, although she was limp and formless under his hands.

Octavia was floating, lost in a blissful trance. When his hands turned her onto her back, she was as malleable as clay. She was vaguely aware of his thighs resting lightly now across her own, but his hands were on her face, delicately smoothing over her eyelids, over her cheekbones, her forehead. The smooth, circular movement of his palms caressed her breasts in turn, and then his hands were on her belly, delicate yet firm, sending deep currents of languid pleasure streaming through her veins.

He took her hands and pulled on her fingers; his thumbs pressed hard into her palms, stroked over her wrists, moved upward over the softness of her inner arms.

Vaguely, Octavia knew that she was smiling as she drifted way above her body on some delicious plane of purely self-absorbed pleasure. When he turned her onto her belly again, she burrowed into the mattress, then felt the length of him measured against her back.

"I have less control than I thought, sweeting," he whispered against her ear. "Do you mind?"

"No," she mumbled into the pillow. "Come." Her thighs parted to accommodate him, and he slipped his hands beneath her belly, lifting her onto the shelf of his palms as he slid within.

Octavia's smile of languid pleasure grew as his flesh massaged her inner body as skillfully as he'd handled the rest of her. And the warm wash of bliss that flooded her veins brought an overwhelming peace and gratitude that swept away the dull miseries of fear and resentment. There was no longer a lonely future to imagine—only this glorious physical present.

She was asleep almost before he left her body, and Rupert lay beside her, listening to her deep, even breathing in the silence of the house. His hand, heavy with his own relaxation, rested in the small of her back. He would find a way through this tangle. He would achieve his object, but he would not sacrifice Octavia to do it.

*P*unctually at two o'clock Philip Wyndham's carriage arrived before the door at Dover Street. Octavia had been watching from the window of the first-floor salon, and for all her mental preparation, her belly lurched as the vehicle drew up. The footman jumped from the ledge at the back, opening the door, letting down the footstep, before ascending the steps to the front door of the Warwicks' house.

She felt sick, her skin clammy. Rupert was out but expected to be back for dinner at four-thirty. How long did afternoon assignations take, as a rule? Was two and a half hours an adequate length of time? Philip had experience of these matters and he had set the time, so presumably he considered from two to four to be perfectly sufficient for the satisfaction of an afternoon lust. But how would she greet Rupert over the dinner table? Would she casually give him the ring and continue with her roast partridge as if nothing significant had occurred? Would he take it with a nod of thanks and drink his claret as if nothing significant had occurred?

Octavia drew on her gloves, smoothing the fine York tan leather over her fingers, and went downstairs. Griffin was waiting with her cloak. She responded automatically as he wished her a pleasant drive, and went out into the warm sunshine to be greeted by the Earl of Wyndham's impassive footman.

She entered Philip Wyndham's coach. The man put up the footstep and closed the door. The coachman's whip snapped, and the horses broke into a trot down Dover Street.

No, Octavia thought with a cold and miserable finality. Once this business with Philip Wyndham was done, then her relationship with Rupert Warwick was done too. There could be no repetition of such a loving as last night's once she had been in the bed of another man. Even when she'd yielded with the consent—nay, the encouragement—of her lover. *Even . . . ?* Or did she mean, *because*?

She let her head fall back onto the squabs and closed her eyes. It didn't matter which she meant. Once she had the ring, she would have fulfilled her side of the bargain. She would not be able to bear Rupert's touch again.

The coach drew to a halt and she waited, her heart thudding, a faint mist of perspiration on her skin, her hands wet in her gloves. The door opened, and the square of bright sunlight made her blink.

Octavia drew up the hood of her cloak. She alighted in St. James's Square before the imposing facade of Wyndham House. The front door opened as the footman escorted her up the short flight of scrubbed white steps. Her hand ran lightly over the wrought-iron balustrade, and she resisted the urge to cling to it, to curl her fingers around the slender railing and cling like a drowning man to a piece of drift-wood.

She stepped into a marble-paved hall. A butler bowed. A maid curtsied. No one said anything. It was almost as if she were a figment of the imagination, a ghost figure. The maid gestured to the double staircase that curved gracefully upward to meet on a circular landing at the head. Then the girl hurried ahead of Octavia up the stairs.

As she put her foot on the bottom step, Octavia caught the rustle of silk out of the corner of her eye. She turned her head sharply. Letitia Wyndham stood unmoving in the shadow of a doorway. Her luminous eyes were emeralds in a pale face.

Octavia turned away from those eyes and followed the maid. She felt now as if she inhabited a void—a cool, still vacuum in which she moved, making no impression on her surroundings. Her feet weren't really touching the stairs, her hand wasn't really running along the banister. Her steps weren't now really taking her along this carpeted corridor, weren't bringing her to these white and gilded double doors. Doors that opened at the maid's touch.

The girl stood aside with another curtsy, and Octavia moved past her into the room, her skirts brushing against the door frame.

It was a bedchamber. A large, elegant apartment. Philip Wyndham sat in a deep armchair beside the empty hearth, a book on his lap. He rose and bowed as Octavia entered.

"My dear, you are come." There was a huskiness to his voice she hadn't heard before.

Octavia curtsied. "As you see, sir." She drew off her gloves.

He came toward her, his step as light as a dancer's, his willowy frame moving gracefully. He pushed the hood from her head, then clasped her face with both hands and brought his mouth to hers in a rapacious assault that filled her anew with the terror and revulsion she thought she'd learned to overcome since the first time he had kissed her.

He released her head and unhooked her cloak, throwing it onto a chair, then stood back, regarding her unsmiling, his eyes harsh with hunger. His gaze ran over her, taking in her dress, the pale-blue silk caraco over the skirt of dark-blue figured cotton. His eyes lingered for a minute on the laced bodice; then he moved one hand in leisurely fashion, twitched at the lace with a deft twist of his wrist.

Octavia's breasts moved freely under the loosened bodice, and her heart beat hard and fast as she waited for him to make the next move.

His mouth curved in a tiny smile of satisfaction; then he turned from her and crossed to a pier table where stood a decanter and glasses. "Madeira."

It was a statement, not a question, and Octavia merely inclined her head in assent. She took the glass he gave her and sipped the mellow wine, hoping it would give her courage.

Philip was in dishabille: no coat or cravat, a loose dressing gown of brocaded satin over his waistcoat, shirt, and britches. Octavia's eyes were riveted to his waistcoat, almost as if she could see through the beige-striped silk to the pocket and the little pouch beneath.

She put her glass down on a small table and stepped up to him. Delicately, she slipped her hands beneath the dressing gown, pushing it off his shoulders.

He stood still, sipping his wine, his eyes narrowed. She ran her hands over his torso, and her fingers immediately detected what they sought. Her heart jumped. It was so easy to locate now that she knew where it was.

She began to unbutton his waistcoat, very slowly, button by button, praying that if he detected her anxiety, he would attribute it to passion.

Then he suddenly grasped her wrists. "No. I don't care for women to take the initiative in such fashion." His voice was oddly cold and his eyes were arctic gray.

Octavia let her hands fall to her sides. She felt like a whore who'd offended her client. "Your pardon, Philip, but I find myself most eager," she murmured, catching her lower lip between her teeth, looking up at him through her eyelashes.

He smiled, and a wild rage filled her so that she wanted to hurl something at him to wipe that complacent, triumphant smirk from his lips.

One-handed, still holding his glass, he began where she'd left off, unbuttoning his waistcoat, shrugging out of it with a graceful movement of his shoulders. The garment fell to the floor, and he kicked it aside with the toe of his shoe.

Somehow she had to be able to pick it up. Maybe a little domestic tidying. . . . If she smoothed it and folded it . . .

"Remove your gown." The rasped command shattered her frantic speculations. Her fingers trembled on the loosened laces of her bodice, the hooks of the skirt, the ties of the panniers beneath.

He pulled her to him, his hands hard as they explored her body beneath her chemise and petticoats. Octavia was numb. She took herself out of her head, concentrated only on the waistcoat on the floor, on the moment when she could casually pick it up, brush her fingers over the lining, palm the little pouch.

She became aware that he was pushing her backward. She felt the bed behind her thighs; then she was toppled over until she lay sprawled on the coverlet and he stood over her, his hands on the waist of his britches.

This was to be no dance of love, no leisurely preparation, no stoking of the flames.

She tried not to look as he pushed his britches to his feet and kicked them aside. He tugged at the buttons on his shirt, and for the first time she detected urgency in his movements. Shirtless, in only his woolen drawers, he knelt on the bed. He pushed up her petticoat, revealing her silk-clad thighs. His fingers were on her garters. Another inch, and she would be exposed to those cold gray eyes, her body bared and vulnerable for the assault of that hard, bulging flesh pushing against the wool of his undergarment. . . .

There was a sudden violent crash followed by a cascade of noise, a high-pitched scream, a long, drawn-out wail of pain and terror—and the room was engulfed in a cloud of thick black soot.

"By Christ!" The Earl of Wyndham was suddenly as limp as a drowned hen, his face a picture of astonishment and chagrin. Then he hurled himself off the bed and Octavia struggled up, choking as the thick, greasy black flakes rained down on the bed. A bubble of almost hysterical laughter rose in her throat, and her eyes watered with the effort to control it as she struggled to work out what had happened to shatter the earl's lust with such devastating effect.

The earl was standing over the fireplace, his face suffused with rage. Cowering on all fours at his feet was what appeared to be a small black animal, whimpering pitifully.

Octavia sprang to the floor, shaking down her petticoats, ignoring the scene at the fireplace. She had thought only for the waistcoat. She was bending to snatch it up when the violent impact of leather on flesh was followed by a heartrending shriek that was unmistakably human.

"No!" she exclaimed, whirling round to the fireplace. The earl, arm upraised, was about to bring down a riding crop for a second blow across the back of the shrieking scrap at his feet.

"No, it wasn't his fault!" She jumped across the room, grabbing the earl's arm. "He's just a child. He must have become lost in the chimneys."

The earl furiously shook off her hand and brought the crop down again. The child screamed, covering his head.

Octavia forgot why she was there. Forgot the waistcoat lying neglected on the floor. Forgot she was wearing only her chemise and petticoat. Forgot that the earl was only in his drawers. With every last fiber of strength, she wrenched the crop from his hands.

"No! I won't let you do this, Wyndham!"

Philip stared at her. Her face was smudged with soot, her eyes golden fire. She held his riding crop as if it were a weapon she would happily use on him. The undignified absurdity of the situation finally occurred to him. Together with the fact that for this afternoon his plans were at an end.

He turned with a vile oath and grabbed up his clothes. Octavia, with a dull thud of resignation, saw him put on the waistcoat again. Then she dismissed the disappointment and bent to examine the pathetic scrap of flotsam still weeping bitterly in the hearth.

He couldn't have been more than four or five, she reckoned, although he was so thin it was hard to be sure.

His vertebrae showed through the tears in his ragged, filthy shirt. Philip's riding crop had raised dark red welts across the already lacerated skin. His knees and elbows bled sluggishly through the caking black soot, and when she tried to lift him and set him on his feet, he cried out in pain. The soles of his feet were raw with burns and cuts.

"Poor baby!" she said softly. She'd seen climbing boys in Shoreditch, and she knew how their chimney-sweep masters lit fires in the hearth to drive the frequently terrified children up into the rat-infested darkness; how they sent older children up with sharp sticks and needles to poke at the soles of their feet to keep them moving. She'd known about these horrors, but she'd never really seen the results of them so closely before.

She looked up to find Philip, once more dressed, regarding her with an expression of acute distaste.

"Leave him alone," he said. "And get dressed. I can't summon his master with you in your petticoat."

The child's wails increased in volume at the mention of his master. " 'E'll kill me. 'E'll kill me 'cause I got lost agin," the mite sobbed. He knew that he'd committed the unforgivable sin of coming down in a room where he risked being seen by the inhabitants of the house. A risk that in this case had turned into hideous reality.

"He's not going to harm you," Octavia said firmly, fastening her panniers and stepping swiftly into her gown. "My lord, I'm going to take the child away with me. If his master complains, he may come to Dover Street, and I'll settle the affair with him there."

Philip Wyndham looked as he felt—for once in his life totally dumbfounded. He stared at Octavia, his jaw dropping. "Take him with you?" he managed to exclaim. "Gad, woman! You have windmills in your head. He's a sweep's urchin."

"Precisely," Octavia said, lacing up the bodice of her gown.

"And just where will you say you found him?" demanded Philip thinly, taking a step toward the child, who now sat in the hearth looking between the man and the woman, the whites of his eyes almost dazzling in his black, tear-rilled face.

"I don't see that matters," Octavia responded, lifting one foot to slip on her sandal.

"Of course it matters!" Philip seized the child's bone-thin arm and yanked him off the floor, holding him in the air by one arm. The child screamed again, and the earl dropped him with a shudder of disgust.

Octavia suddenly understood what was worrying Philip. An adulterous liaison was one thing in society, one not necessarily socially damaging to the participants, but to have one's passionate interlude interrupted by a climbing boy and a volcano of soot would have people weeping with laughter. The Earl of Wyndham would be the laughing-stock of London in ten minutes, and he'd never live it down.

That bubble of laughter rose to her lips again, and she dropped her eyes to the floor, slipping on her other sandal while she struggled for control.

"My lord, you need have no fear your name or this house will ever be mentioned. I'll say I found him in my own house."

"And when his master comes banging at your door demanding his property?" The earl dabbed at his lips with his handkerchief. "What then, madam?"

"I'll deal with his master," Octavia said confidently as renewed wails came from the hearth.

"And what of your husband?" Philip couldn't seem to believe what he was hearing. "How does he view such acts of philanthropy?" His voice was pure acid.

"I shan't tell him," Octavia said with a serene smile, flinging her cloak around her shoulders. "I run the house-hold, my lord. My husband has no interest in how I do so, only that it should run to his satisfaction. He won't know anything about it, I can assure you."

Philip looked around the ruined scene of seduction. While he didn't mind his staff knowing that he had a female visitor in his bedchamber, he couldn't bear the idea that they would come in while Octavia was still there and see this shambles and draw their own conclusions. If Octavia was out of the house before the scene became common knowledge among the staff, it would be as if she'd never been in the room. And if she was insane enough to take the hideous cause of the trouble with her, then it was no concern of his. And even if it were, he had no desire to continue this hideous scene another minute.

It was inconceivable that Octavia would tell the tale herself in society, since it made her as much of a jesting stock as himself. If he bought off the sweep himself, the incident would be as if it had never been.

"Hurry," he commanded curtly, going to the door.

Octavia picked up the child, heedless of the dirt immediately conveyed to her gown and cloak. "Lead on, my lord."

Philip was too intent on the need for haste and secrecy to notice the mockery in her voice. "You may leave through the side door. You won't mind taking a hackney, I trust. If I summon my own carriage, it will draw attention to you. Besides, I don't want that piece of gutter filth on my seats."

"A hackney will be no trouble, sir," Octavia said with the same serene smile that concealed the irony in her voice and the bitter contempt in her eyes. The child in her arms was still and quiet, and she thought he was probably too shocked to react to what was happening to him.

Philip hurried them down a side corridor, through a door, and down an internal staircase. Another door at the foot of the narrow stairs opened onto a small hallway that, judging by the faded flock wallpaper and worn carpet, belonged to the nether regions of the house. He opened the door onto a narrow alley running into York Street.

"You'll find a hackney on York Street, madam," he said stiffly.

"You're too kind, my lord." Octavia curtsied, while still holding the child, managing to invest the courtesy with a wealth of irony. But Philip was again too intent on getting rid of her—and closing this ghastly episode without further damage to his dignity—to notice anything untoward in the salutation.

Without so much as a half bow in response, he almost shoved them out into the alley and slammed the door behind them.

"Oh, what a gentleman!" Octavia murmured gleefully. "What an abject, cowardly gentleman! What wouldn't I give to spread that tale around town? But, alas, it can't be done."

She glanced down at the child. "Do you have a name?"

"Frank."

"Well, Frank, let's take you home. You weren't quite the prize I expected to bring away from this house this afternoon, but never mind. There's always tomorrow."

And she knew, as she tripped lightly over the cobbles, avoiding a steaming pile of manure and a dead cat, that her high spirits came purely and simply from the reprieve. It would perforce be only a short reprieve, but it was wonderful, nevertheless.

Chapter 17

ᗖ "Good God, Octavia! What on earth do you have there?" Rupert exclaimed in astonishment as Octavia entered the hall still carrying Frank.

"This is Frank," she said. Her eyes were dancing merrily, her mouth curved with amusement.

Rupert came closer. Raising his eyeglass, he examined her burden with an incredulous frown. "A climbing boy?"

"Precisely. Poor little mite, he's been most dreadfully mistreated." Octavia smoothed the jagged fringe of hair off the boy's forehead where bruises and dirt were so intermingled, it was hard to distinguish between them.

"Where did you get him?" Rupert moved a hand to touch the boy, and the child cowered against Octavia with a whimper.

"It's a long story, and *very* entertaining," Octavia said with a chuckle. "I'll tell you when I've seen to Frank and changed my dress. I must look as if I've been climbing chimneys myself."

There was something strange about her that transcended her amusement. Her eyes were too bright, the set of her jaw too tense.

"Griffin, will you take the boy to the kitchen, please?

He should be bathed, but be gentle, he's covered in sores and abrasions. See if you can find him some clean clothes, and feed him. Then bring him back to me."

She smiled radiantly at the butler, unpeeled Frank, who was clinging to her like a limpet, and deposited him firmly in the arms of the astounded Griffin.

The butler held the child at arm's length, his head turned away from the offending scrap. "As your ladyship pleases."

"Thank you." Octavia brushed at her skirt with a grimace. "And send Nell up to me, will you? This gown is probably ruined beyond salvation."

She hurried to the stairs, seemingly oblivious of the confusion and indignation she was leaving behind her.

Griffin turned and stalked off to the kitchen regions, still holding his burden as far from him as possible. Rupert stood frowning for a minute; then he followed Octavia upstairs and into her bedchamber.

"I don't believe Griffin has ever been so insulted in all his days," he observed, leaning against the doorjamb, arms folded, watching as Octavia began to unlace her bodice. "Where in the name of grace did you find the creature?"

"He fell out of a chimney." Laughter brimmed in her voice, but her fingers were all thumbs as they fumbled with the lacing. "He can't be more than five, and I'll wager he doesn't weigh much more than a starveling kitten."

"Which, or do I mean whose, chimney?" Rupert inquired, still casually, although he was convinced now that something was very wrong. There was a febrile glitter to her eyes, and an edge to her laughter that seemed closer to tears.

"Oh, it's a long story . . . ah, here's Nell." Octavia turned brightly to her maid. "See if you can reclaim this gown, Nell. It's one of my favorites. And I need lots of hot water. This soot is so greasy, I doubt it'll come off my skin with one washing. And I'm sure it's in my hair." She was unpinning her hair throughout this brittle racing speech.

Rupert's expression showed none of his unease. "I'll

leave you to Nell, my dear. Should I tell Griffin to put dinner back for half an hour?"

"Oh, no, that won't be necessary. I'm certain I shall be ready in plenty of time," she said with the same rushed breathlessness. "Aren't we to go to the opera after dinner?"

"It's not an irreversible arrangement," he said mildly.

"Isn't it *Iphigénie en Tauride*?" The question was muffled as Nell lifted her gown over her head.

"Your favorite Gluck," he agreed with a smile that didn't touch his eyes.

"Well, perhaps we could miss the first act." She sat down at the dresser and examined her soot-streaked face. "Lud, it's no wonder the jarvey looked askance. I dare swear he was about to refuse the fare."

"What were you doing jauntering around town in a hackney? I was under the impression we maintained both a carriage and a chair. Or am I imagining things?"

"Now, don't be sarcastic, my lord," she chided with a laugh, dabbing at her face with a washcloth. "I will tell you the whole story over dinner, if Papa doesn't join us. You'll find it monstrous amusing. But leave me to dress now, or it'll be midnight before we sit down to table."

"Of course, ma'am." He bowed and left her room, going downstairs to the library, a deep frown etched between his brows.

"My lord?"

"Yes, Griffin." He looked up as the butler entered the library, his impassive features still somehow managing to convey the deepest outrage.

"Lady Warwick's . . . uh . . . protégé, my lord."

"What about him, Griffin."

"My lord, he refuses to be bathed."

"Her ladyship assures me he's but five years old and weighs no more than a starveling kitten. I find it hard to believe that two footmen couldn't ensure his immersion in a tub of hot water."

"No, my lord. But he bites."

"Then muzzle him, Griffin."

"Her ladyship said we were to be gentle, my lord."

"Her ladyship will not know."

"No, my lord." The butler bowed himself out, every line of his body radiating umbrage.

Rupert poured himself a glass of sherry. A straightforward act of philanthropy on Octavia's part wasn't particularly surprising. He knew how sensitive her own experiences had made her to the miserable conditions under which most people struggled to survive. But there was more than philanthropy at work in this situation. She said the story was amusing, but her amusement didn't strike him as the genuine article. She said the boy had dropped out of a chimney—not an unusual occurrence, given the warren of chimneys threading their way through the houses of the gentry. But *which* chimney? Not one of her own. A friend's? But if so, why had she not said so at the outset? Why the secrecy? Why the excitement?

When Octavia entered the library ten minutes later, dressed for the opera in a caraco of tangerine silk over a wide hooped skirt of figured orange taffeta, he was ready with his questions.

Smiling, she tripped into the room on her dainty slippered feet, cinnamon ringlets clustering on her shoulders, a black velvet ribbon, sewn with perfectly copied diamonds and seed pearls, encircling the creamy slenderness of her throat.

"A glass of sherry, if you please, Rupert. I wonder how they're managing in the kitchen with Frank."

"With difficulty, as I understand it," he said dryly, pouring sherry. "He bites."

"I expect he's frightened," Octavia said as if it were the most natural thing in the world. She took the glass with a smile of thanks. "I wonder if it would be possible to civilize him sufficiently to make him a page."

"Where did you find him?"

"I think I'll hand him over to my father," she continued as if he hadn't spoken. "Papa dearly loves a project, and he might enjoy teaching Frank his letters. I wonder if he's coming down to dinner? He said he might if he'd finished his day's work."

She pulled the bellrope before Rupert could press his questions.

"Griffin, is Mr. Morgan joining us for dinner?"

"I believe so, my lady." Griffin still radiated grim disapproval, although his expression was completely neutral. "When would you wish to see the climbing boy, madam?"

"Is he presentable?"

"I would hardly say that, ma'am. He is, however, as clean as we can make him at present. We have no clothes small enough to fit him, so he's wrapped in a sheet."

"Has he been fed?"

"Copiously, my lady. He has the appetite of a boa constrictor. It's to be hoped he hasn't made himself sick with it."

"I think I had better see him after dinner," Octavia said as Oliver Morgan entered the library. "Papa, I have a surprise for you. A climbing boy."

Griffin departed, and Rupert could have sworn he heard the whisper of an outraged sniff.

"Good heavens, my dear. What am I to do with a climbing boy?" Oliver asked with mild curiosity as he took a glass of sherry from Rupert.

"I thought you might teach him his letters. He's so battered and bruised, poor mite, he can't possibly work, so I thought he might be company for you."

"Is he completely untutored?" Oliver's eyes sparked with interest.

"I'm certain he must be."

"Then I shall take him with pleasure. I've long wished to try a teaching experiment. A child with no learning at all is a clean slate on which one should be able to write anything one chooses. He has nothing to muddle his brain, and if he has any native intelligence at all, I expect to have him reading Latin and Greek before six months is out."

"Literacy in his own language might be more useful," Rupert observed, wondering whether he should pity the climbing boy who was about to be plunged from the hells of the chimneys to the rigors of scholarship.

"Pshaw, Warwick!" Oliver scoffed. "One is not inter-

ested in utility here but in the process by which language is
acquired."

He rubbed his hands gleefully. "I shall document the
experiment, and I'm certain some scientific journal will be
fascinated to publish the results."

Griffin reappeared in the doorway, looking no happier
than before. "Dinner is served, my lady."

"Thank you." Octavia took her father's arm. The ultimate fate of little Frank was yet to be decided, whatever her
father's plans, but nothing would be gained by disturbing
his contemplation of such a satisfying project. She herself
was inclined to think five rather young for classical scholarship, but Oliver would discover that for himself.

Throughout dinner Rupert maintained an easy flow of
small talk, but his eyes were watchful, his ears attuned to
every nuance in Octavia's conversation. She still appeared
to be in the greatest of good spirits, but her laugh was too
brittle, her color fluctuated wildly, her eyes darted everywhere and rested nowhere. And she paid more attention to
her wineglass than to her plate.

Her father's presence prohibited close questioning, so
he bided his time, but with some impatience.

"I'll leave you to your port," she said when the covers
were removed. "I'm eager to see my protégé."

Rupert and her father rose as the footman pulled back
her chair.

"I'll come to the kitchen, Griffin," Octavia said to the
hovering butler. "He's probably more at home there."

"I should think he's most at home with the devil,
madam," Griffin declared, a chip appearing for once in his
impassive facade. "He's pulled the cat's tail, spilt Cook's
sauce, and put boot blacking all over the damask tablecloth
that the parlor maid was ironing."

"In three hours!" Octavia exclaimed.

"Is it only three hours, my lady?"

A crack of laughter escaped from the head of the table
where Rupert sipped his port. "Octavia, my dear, I wonder
if you know what you've unleashed."

She grimaced. "I think I'd better find out."

In the kitchen she found one small boy wrapped in a sheet, an exasperated cook, a parlor maid armed with her flat irons, lamenting the state of the tablecloth, and a scullery maid scrubbing the great cooking pots with strong-smelling lye.

They all stared as the lady of the house hurried in for all the world as if she were completely at home in kitchens. But, then, they none of them knew how at home Octavia had been in Mistress Forster's kitchen in Shoreditch.

"Oh, dear, Frank. Whatever have you been doing?" Octavia, in a rich rustle of silk, her skirts swaying gracefully, came to the fire where the child sat on a stool. His pale, gnomelike face looked much older than his years, and his huge eyes stretched wide at the sight of this magnificent apparition.

"Nuffink." He shrank back warily as she bent over him. "Is ol' Bilbo comin' to get me?"

"Is that your master?"

The lad nodded and blinked. " 'E'll kill me when 'e comes," he said with a curious matter-of-factness. "Not supposed to git lost in them chimbleys, but I couldn't find me way out."

"Old Bilbo, or whatever he calls himself, isn't going to take you away," Octavia reassured, stroking his spiky hair.

He shrank suspiciously away from the caress. "Course 'e is." His eyes darted to the scrubbed deal table where the remnants of dinner waited to be dealt with. "Can I 'ave 'nother piece o' that apple pie?"

"For mercy's sake, my lady, he's had six slices already." Cook bustled over, wiping her hands on her apron. "He'll be sick if he has any more. His belly's as shrunken as a dried nut, poor little tyke."

" 'Afore ol' Bilbo comes fer me," the child pleaded, a knowing look in his eye as his gaze darted appealingly between the two women.

"He's not coming for you," Octavia said firmly. "And I think it's time you went to bed. In the morning we'll find you some clothes."

"I'll take 'im up to the attic with me, m'lady." The

scullery maid bobbed a curtsy, wiping her perspiring forehead with the back of her red, work-roughened hand. " 'E's about the same age as me little brother what always shares me bed at 'ome."

The scullery maid was little more than a child herself, and there was a note of homesick longing in her voice.

"If you think you can manage him," Octavia said doubtfully. Little Frank, clean and well fed, didn't seem nearly so docile and pathetic as he had tumbling in a volcano of soot into the Earl of Wyndham's bedchamber.

The recollection brought that rollicking wave of mirth again, and she hurried out of the kitchen before she yielded to it in front of the already startled kitchen staff. She felt so wonderfully lighthearted, as if she were walking on air. It didn't occur to her that having faced the worst and then having that fate so abruptly snatched from her was enough to unbalance the steadiest nature.

Rupert was alone in the dining room. Oliver, not a great port drinker, had retired to his own apartments to plan his new project.

Octavia was chuckling as she came in. "Has Papa gone up? Perhaps I'll join you in a glass of port."

She pulled out a chair close to Rupert's and pushed an empty glass toward him across the highly polished surface of the table. The candlelight was beginning to throw golden pools onto the table as the sun slowly sank below the horizon.

Rupert filled the glass from the decanter at his elbow, then leaned back in his chair, his forearm resting on the table, fingers curled lightly around the stem of his own glass.

"So am I to hear the story, Octavia? Something has been amusing you mightily all evening, and it seems hardly fair to keep the jest to yourself."

"No, I'll tell you. It was the funniest thing!" She went into a peal of laughter, sipped her port, and choked.

Rupert leaned over and thumped her back with a degree of vigor. "Let's start at the beginning, shall we?"

Octavia struggled to compose herself. She wiped a tear

from the corner of her eye with a fingertip. "We were in Wyndham's bedchamber and—"

"You were where?" All color drained from his face, and his eyes were featureless gray pools.

"In Wyndham's bedchamber for our assignation," she explained, taking another sip of her port. "And while we were in . . . in medias res . . . as it were, there's this great thump and bang and scream . . ."

Laughter overcame her again. "And all this soot pours from the chimney," she gasped. "It filled the air, fell down like filthy black rain all over the bed— "

"Stop it!" he shouted, slamming his fist on the table, setting the candle flames dipping, the silverware rattling.

Octavia stopped, staring at him. His face was deathly white, a rictus of rage. A quivering started in her belly.

"It was very funny," she said, not understanding this anger. "You should have seen Philip, in his drawers, totally bewildered . . . " She began to laugh again, but it was all mixed up with the quivering in her stomach and the lump in her throat.

Rupert's chair crashed to the floor. He leaned over and seized Octavia by the upper arms, half dragging her across the table as he shook her.

"Stop it!" he hissed with a low-voiced ferocity more frightening than the previous bellow. *"For God's sake! Stop laughing!"*

But she couldn't seem to stop. Tears poured down her cheeks, and the laughter welled in her throat and exploded in great gobbets of hilarity. He shook her until she was catching her breath on wrenching gasps and her body was limp in his hands.

He dropped her and she slid back into her chair, slumped against the back, her head drooping in defeat as her breath sobbed in her chest.

Rupert stood at the table, his white knuckles resting on the surface as he looked at her, waiting for the Octavia he knew to reenter her body. He was nauseated with rage and frustration, the image of his brother in medias res. God in heaven, how could she joke like that? Joke about his brother about to possess . . .

He pressed his hand to his mouth, for one dreadful minute thinking he was going to vomit.

"Why didn't you tell me?" he demanded when she seemed to be gaining control of her breathing. "I told you you were to tell me of every one of your dealings with Wyndham. You were to keep me apprised of your plans. You were to go nowhere with him without my knowledge."

Octavia raised her head slowly. Her eyes were blank, and when she spoke, her voice was dull, as if she were reciting by rote. As she spoke, he wondered if she'd heard him, for she made no attempt to answer his question or to respond to his own violent outburst.

"I nearly had the ring. It was in his waistcoat. He dropped it on the floor when he took it off—"

"Stop it!" He held up a hand, desperate to stop this re-creation, this spinning of images that he couldn't endure to picture.

But she continued as if she hadn't heard him. "I was waiting for the opportunity to pick it up, and when Frank dropped from the chimney, I thought I had my chance. But he started to beat the boy with a riding crop, and I had to stop him, so I dropped the waistcoat. I'm sorry."

She shrugged in rueful apology as if she were apologizing for losing his handkerchief. "Next time—"

Her voice died as he leaned over and seized her by the shoulders, his fingers curling like spines, his face very close to hers.

"Be quiet and listen to me. Why didn't you tell me what you were planning? You were instructed to do so. Why did you disobey me?"

Octavia blinked at him, his words penetrating the self-absorbed fog of her nightmare. "Why should I have told you? You don't tell me what you're planning."

"That has nothing to do with it," he said, shaking her again in furious punctuation. "It has been agreed from the outset that you follow my direction in *everything*. Now, why did you break that rule?"

Octavia winced as his fingers bit deep into the bare skin of her shoulders. But his anger didn't seem to touch her. It flowed off her like water on oiled leather. She felt none of his anguish, aware only of her own, of the violent surge of emotions flooding her now that her hysteria had been punctured and she could feel again, think clearly again of what she'd so nearly had to endure. And what had merely been postponed.

"What difference would it have made if I'd told you?" she asked, her voice low and bitter. "I was doing only what I'd contracted to do. You knew it was going to happen. Why should you need to know when? Did you want to sit here imagining it?" she threw at him with sudden vehemence. "Was that what you wanted? You'd bought a whore and she was doing a whore's work and you would get some twisted amusement out of imagining it?"

Where were these hideous words coming from? They tumbled from her lips, deadly as an asp's venom, and she didn't know how or why. She didn't know she'd ever thought like that. But some festering boil was lanced, and the poison gushed forth, unstoppable.

Rupert was gray, for a moment unable either to stop the tirade or to think of any response.

Octavia fell silent, as shocked by the words she'd spoken as he was by hearing them. Long shadows fell across the table with the last rays of the dying sun, and slowly Rupert's fingers opened on her shoulders and he stepped back.

"How could you say such a thing?" His voice was soft and puzzled, deep hurt in his eyes.

"You said yourself at the beginning that only my body would be involved in the transaction, that my mind and emotions would not be engaged. That is whoredom," she said flatly. "You engaged a whore. And why should you have thought otherwise? After the shameless way I came to your own bed?"

She turned her head away from the stabbing gray eyes, suddenly drained by the outpouring of emotion that she hadn't until this minute put into words even in the most secret places of her soul.

Rupert took a deep, shuddering breath. "There was nothing shameless about that first night, Octavia."

"Of course there was. I behaved like a wanton. We both know that if I hadn't, you would never have suggested that I seduce your enemy."

Rupert raked a hand through his hair, disturbing the dark-brown locks waving neatly off his forehead. He walked away from the table to the window, where he stood for a minute looking out into the fast-falling dusk.

Behind him Octavia still sat at the table, wondering now whether she had really meant every word she'd spoken. Although her behavior had been shameless that first night, she didn't regret it. But before she could put her thoughts into words, Rupert spoke suddenly into the quiet.

"You had nothing to do with what happened that night in the Royal Oak."

"How can you say that? Of course I had everything to do with it. You told me I invited you."

"So you did, but you weren't responsible for your actions," he said without expression, still staring sightlessly into the encroaching night.

"I don't know what you mean." Octavia was suddenly cold, her hands like ice. She had the feeling that something nasty was in the room, something nastier than her own outpourings.

"Do you remember having a tankard of punch?" He spoke still without expression.

"Yes." Apprehensively, she stroked her throat, frowning at his averted back.

"Perhaps you don't remember saying that it wanted ground cloves."

"Yes, I do." Apprehension grew now to fill the corners of the room with the evening shadows.

He turned from the window. His face was pale against the dark frame behind him, his eyes almost silvery.

"There was a substance in the cloves designed to relax

you, to remove your inhibitions . . . to stimulate your sexual responses."

Octavia stared at him. She remembered how she'd felt, the peculiar sense of excitement, of restlessness, of drifting in some wonderful, sensual world with no mental threshold, no emotional barriers. The dreamlike quality of that night of love.

"You drugged me?" She asked the question tentatively, as if she couldn't grasp the idea.

"Yes."

"You . . . you *violated* me."

He moved his hands in a gesture that could have been either denial or acceptance. "It could so be said."

"But why?" Her voice was a mere thread, yet filled with a desperate intensity.

Rupert came back to the table and sat down. The candlelight fell on his face, illuminating the harsh planes, the deep lines suddenly etched around his mouth and eyes.

"I needed your cooperation," he said simply. He could think of softer ways of putting it, but he'd deceived her enough. "I needed to bind you to me in some way. To show you another side of yourself."

"I see." Octavia took a sip of port. Maybe it would dissolve the lump in her throat, the constriction in her chest. "It worked, didn't it?"

He reached out to take her free hand lying limply on the table, but she snatched it away as if from a burning brand.

He withdrew his hand and said, "I ask you to believe that I haven't thought in those terms since we began this."

"I don't know what difference that makes," Octavia said dully. She wanted to weep and scream and throw things. She wanted to scratch his eyes out. Her icy-cold hands shook with the power of her need to hurt him.

She pushed back her chair with a violent scrape on the oak floor. "Excuse me, I think I'll go to bed. Since it's so important to you, I'll let you know when I have my next assignation with your enemy."

"Octavia—"

But she'd gone in a swish of silk, the door banging closed behind her.

Rupert swore every vile oath he knew. Then he filled his glass and drank in morose silence. The facts were damning and he didn't know how to soften them. If Octavia couldn't forgive, then there was nothing to be done. Except to release her from her obligation.

He rose from the table and left the dining room. At Octavia's door he raised his hand to knock, then decided not to risk a refusal. He lifted the latch and went in without ceremony.

Octavia was sitting on the window seat, still in her finery, and when she turned at the sound of the door, he saw her eyes were glistening, her cheeks wet with tears.

"Ah, sweeting," he said with soft remorse, crossing the room swiftly, hands outstretched to comfort her.

"Don't touch me!" she said, holding up her hands as if to fend him off.

His own hands dropped to his sides. He stood looking down at her, feeling as helpless as he had ever felt as a child in the face of his twin's malevolent machinations. And he couldn't rid himself of the ugly recognition that what *he* had done to Octavia was worthy of Philip.

"I'm not going to touch you," he said after a minute. "I came merely to say that I no longer hold you to your side of our bargain. I will fulfill my side but you have no further obligations. If you wish to leave here, then I will arrange for you to set up your own establishment with your father until I can return your fortune to you. If you wish to remain until my business with Rigby and Lacross is completed, then I will make no demands upon you."

Octavia shook her head. Once she would have given anything to hear those words, but that was when she believed they would have come voluntarily, out of respect and feeling for her. Now they were forced from him out of shame and remorse—if he was capable of feeling such things. And she wanted him to suffer that shame.

"No. I will not renege on my obligations. I will get that

ring from Philip Wyndham as I agreed to do. We have a business contract, but from now on that is all we have, sir."

Her face was set, her voice flat, her eyes cold. Her tears had dried, except those flowing from her heart in a wretched torrent of misery and betrayal. But those tears could not be seen.

"Very well," Rupert said quietly. He had injured her, and he'd lost all rights in this partnership. There was nothing more he could say on the subject of that first night in the Royal Oak.

He told himself that he had spent many years getting to this point and the time was close now when Philip Wyndham would know his twin again. If Octavia was still determined to play her part, then he would accept her help in the harsh spirit in which it was pressed upon him. He had already worked out how to achieve his object with her minimal involvement.

"But we will follow a different course," he said, and his voice was curt as he struggled for the detachment that would hide his own wounds. He had no right to inflict upon Octavia his own grief.

"I decided to change the plan a few days ago. There would have been no need for your assignation this afternoon, if you'd alerted me to it."

"Forgive me, but since I didn't know, I can hardly be blamed," she said with bitter sarcasm.

"On the contrary. If you'd followed your instructions, you would have known." He spoke with the same curt authority, his mouth set in a grim line.

"However"—he held up a hand as she opened her mouth to protest—"that's water under the bridge. Now you will lure Wyndham to Putney Heath, where I shall be waiting for him."

"You would rob him?"

"Just so."

"But he might recognize you."

"No, he won't."

"You will still be putting yourself at grave risk."

"No more than I am accustomed to. And you will not be at risk."

When she said nothing, he bowed and went to the door. "Good night, Octavia."

Octavia gazed down at her tightly clenched hands as the door closed behind him. Had he really decided before this debacle to change the plan to one that would not involve her sacrifice?

But even if he had, what did it matter? How could it possibly matter in the light of his confession? A man who could do such a despicable thing was capable of anything.

Chapter 18

℘ The hackney carriage slowed and came to a halt at the intersection of Gracechurch Street, Eastcheap, and Cannon Street. Within the carriage, Dirk Rigby and Hector Lacross simultaneously laid hands on their sword hilts as the raucous chant of the jostling throng in the streets swelled. Faces appeared in the windows on either side: bucolic faces, lean faces, faces suffused with liquor, faces drawn and twisted with anger, faces split in grins of holiday-making merriment.

"No popery . . . no popery." The chant was mouthed at the inhabitants of the hackney, rose on the sultry early-summer air in a great chorus. The carriage swayed as the crowd pressed ever closer.

"Gad, but this could be ugly," Hector muttered, half drawing his sword.

"No, don't draw upon them," Dirk pleaded urgently. "It'll only provoke them." He reached sideways and let down the window. "No popery, good citizens," he bellowed, waving his hand at the sea of faces. "No Catholic relief. No popery."

A roar of approval greeted this. "Let 'em pass," someone called.

The jarvey leaned down from his box and shouted, "No popery," at the top of his lungs. The throng roared its approval yet again and moved backward a fraction, pushing and shoving each other to create just enough of a path for the frightened horses to press forward toward London Bridge. The jarvey cracked his whip, the horses picked up speed, and they were out of the mob, although the rhythmic, vociferous chant pursued them across the bridge.

Hector sat back and wiped his forehead with a scented handkerchief. "Filthy scum. Who do they think they are, impeding the progress of their betters?"

Dirk pulled up the window again. The air in the hackney was close, but the stench of London under the midday sun was worse.

"They should call out the army . . . put Lord George in irons," he declared. "The man's mad . . . crazy as a bedlamite."

"But he knows how to rouse a rabble," Hector said. "Everywhere he goes, it's the same. People flock to hear him, and they come away from his meetings fired with antipapist zeal."

Dirk grimaced but made no other response. He leaned forward to peer out of the window. The redbrick warehouse loomed ahead beside the greasy water of the Thames, flowing sluggishly, gray beneath the suffused yellow light of a hazy sun. The hackney clattered off the bridge and turned into the courtyard, coming to a halt before the iron-barred door.

The two passengers alighted and looked around. It was as quiet this afternoon as it had been on their two previous visits. On the last occasion they'd attended a board meeting of Thaddeus Nielson's investors; this afternoon they'd been bidden to an emergency meeting to discuss urgent new developments in the building scheme on Acre Lane.

"Want me to wait fer ye, gents?" The jarvey leaned down from his box and sent a stream of tobacco-stained spittle into the kennel running down the center of the cobbled courtyard.

"We won't be above half an hour," Hector told him, stepping aside from the kennel, his lip curled in distaste.

"Right y'are, then." The jarvey settled back on his box and took out his pipe from the deep pocket in his caped greatcoat. "Let's 'ope that rabble's been an' gone by then." He lit the pungent tobacco. "There'll be trouble 'afore this is all over, you mark my words," he pronounced. "That Lord George Gordon's got a bee up 'is arse and it's buzzin' fit to bust." He grinned. "Beggin' yer pardon, gents, fer speakin' so free of the Quality."

Neither of his passengers deigned to respond, merely turned on their shining heels and picked their way through the debris-strewn cobbles to the door.

Ned opened the door on their knock, blinking into the sunlight, the cavernous dark stretching behind him.

"So y'are 'ere," he declared. He jerked his thumb over his shoulder. "Y'are the last. Master's waitin' on ye above stairs."

Rigby and Lacross obeyed the imperative gesture of the thumb and stepped past the elderly man into the now familiar interior. The great iron door closed with a reverberating slam. The air was as cold and damp as it had ever been, despite the late-May afternoon.

Ned preceded them up the curving iron staircase, lighting the way with the lamp held high. He muttered and grumbled under his breath the whole way, pausing every now and again to sneeze as clouds of dust rose with every step.

"Reckon ye knows yer way from 'ere." He stopped at the head of the stairs, sniffed liquidly, and wiped his nose with his sleeve.

Hector edged gingerly past him, Dirk on his heels, and by the wavering light of the oil lamp held up behind them, they trod to the door at the rear of the landing. Hector banged with his fist. The truculent knock gave him confidence, and he raised the latch and flung open the door with an assertive air.

"Ah, Mr. Lacross . . . is Mr. Digby with you . . . oh, yes, there he is, right behind you. So good of you both to come. Pray come in . . . come in . . . take a glass of wine. You remember your fellow investors, of course."

Thaddeus Nielson came toward them beaming, mittened hands outstretched in welcome. He was wearing a cutaway coat of threadbare gray velvet, with a greasy moleskin waistcoat and a spotted kerchief knotted in the neck of his collarless shirt. His beam widened, and the jagged scar lifted the corner of his mouth.

In honor of his guests he wore an unkempt wig perched askew, but despite his disreputable appearance, there was something about his presence that awed both of his visitors whenever they were in his company. A glitter in the gray eyes that seemed somehow too youthful and penetrating for the rest of the man; a power in the tall frame despite the slight hunch of his shoulders.

There were four gentlemen sitting around a pock-marked deal table in the middle of the room. An elderly group, they appeared for the most part to be half-asleep. As one body, they nodded and murmured acknowledgment of the new arrivals, who took the two vacant seats, Hector dusting his off with his handkerchief before sitting with a fastidious grimace.

"Wine, gentlemen." Their genial host filled two smudged glasses from a dust-encrusted bottle and passed them down the table before making the rounds, refilling the other glasses. "Now, to the order of the day."

"Just tell us where to sign, Thaddeus. We don't need any ramblin' explanations," growled the oldest of the crew into his long white beard.

"Aye, trust ye with my life, I would," put in another with a hearty slap of his open palm on the table. The glasses shivered, the table creaked.

Their host regarded him from beneath sleepy lids that concealed the sharp warning in his eyes from all but its recipient. The actor was being a little too fulsome for strict credibility.

"Why, Banker Moran, you do me too much honor," Thaddeus drawled, taking a sip of his wine. "But I'd not dream of taking your money without full disclosure."

"No, of course not," the pseudo-banker declared hastily. "Just what I was saying . . . just what I meant to say," he added, and retreated into his wineglass with a confused cough.

"So what's the urgency, Nielson?" demanded Hector with some asperity. "You need more money, is that it?"

Thaddeus stroked his chin with a thoughtful frown. "Well, as I was explaining before you arrived, it's a little complicated. There's been a small hitch with the Funds, where I invested your little nest eggs. They promised to pay seven percent but it seems as if they're only going to pay five percent this quarter."

He glanced around the table, seeming completely untroubled by this revelation. Indeed, all of his audience, with the exception of Hector and Dirk, appeared similarly sanguine.

"How should that be?" Dirk asked, frowning in the gloom, wondering why the man didn't open the shutters onto the river. At least it would let in some natural light. There was something very unpleasant, almost sinister, about sitting in this dark, dank cave on a warm, sunny day.

"Funds on the Exchange are always subject to market vagaries," Thaddeus said. "Isn't that so, Mr. Moran?"

"Quite so . . . quite so," corroborated the banker.

"Nothin' to worry about, though," put in a third member of the group with an indolent yawn. He was very splendidly dressed in crimson satin, with gold-frogged buttons and a hedgehog wig.

Hector regarded this gentleman respectfully. "You believe that, my Lord Justice Greenaway."

"Oh, without doubt, m'boy . . . without doubt," the justice said with another yawn. "What d'ye think, Bartram?" He nudged his so-far-silent neighbor.

"Well, I don't know about that," Mr. Bartram said solemnly, pulling at his angular chin. He was thin as a needle, with a pointed head and a shining bald pate revealed beneath a slipping wig. "Seems to me, if we're promised seven percent and we get five percent, it is a matter for concern. That means that Thaddeus here has less funds for his building . . . makes our investment less. See what I mean?" He looked around the table, blinking like a wise old owl.

"Yes, you're quite right, Bartram," Thaddeus said smoothly. "It does indeed mean that your investment is reduced, and I find myself a little strapped for cash to complete the project."

He reached behind him for another bottle of wine. The cork had already been drawn, and he pushed the bottle across the table to the chief justice. "Another glass, dear fellow."

"Capital . . . capital," the justice said with a rasping rub of his hands. He refilled his glass and passed the bottle along. "So what is it ye want from us, dear boy?"

"Another twenty thousand apiece," Thaddeus said coolly. "It will enable me to finish the houses on Acre Street and make a start on the next development. I have six customers for new houses, gentlemen. Tongues hanging out for a gentleman's residence befitting a substantial citizen with a hopeful family, to set up in a manner to encourage good connections." He smiled and the scar twitched. "The attractions of society are manifold for those who can't as yet aspire to it. But a grand mansion, good governesses, Eton and Harrow for the boys—and a dynasty is born." He gestured expansively. "Who are we to quibble at the vanities of the socially aspiring?"

"But what guarantee do we have that this twenty thousand won't go the same way as our other investments?" asked Dirk, refilling his smudged glass.

"Oh, have a little faith, sir," Justice Greenaway protested. "It's hardly Nielson's fault if the Exchange had a bad month. But we all know that what goes around comes around. Next month, it'll be paying ten percent or thereabouts."

"But unfortunately I cannot wait until next month to provide the materials to finish the houses already under construction," explained Thaddeus. "If we cannot finish them on schedule, then we lose our customers. If we lose our customers, we will be obliged to return to them their original deposits . . . and that, gentlemen, could be a little awkward at present time."

"For you," stated Dirk. "But not for us. It's nothing to do with us whether you have the money to repay them or not."

"Ah, well, I'm afraid it is," Thaddeus said, drawing a sheaf of papers toward him. "Surely you read the contracts before you signed them, gentlemen. It states here most clearly that you are members of a consortium that agrees both as a body and as individuals to fulfill the terms of all housing projects presently under contract."

He pushed the papers toward Hector and Dirk. "Pray refresh your memories, sirs."

The two peered in the gloom at the spidery writing. Hector drew the candle toward him with an impatient movement, spilling wax on his finger.

"Odd's blood!" He snatched the document from his friend's grasp and held it close to the flame. "So if you fail to fulfill your commitments, then *we* end up in the Fleet?" he exclaimed.

"Gentlemen . . . gentlemen," Thaddeus said softly. "Don't be so exercised. That's not going to happen. This is a very temporary setback. I need a further injection of funds just to bridge the gap until the houses are completed. Then the purchasers will pay the price of the houses, and we'll be sitting pretty."

"But this further twenty thousand. You'll not be putting that in the Funds?" Dirk asked uneasily.

"Oh, no, there's no time for that," Thaddeus explained. "The money must be used immediately to ensure we don't renege on our contracts with our customers. You need have no fear of losing a penny."

Dirk scratched his head. It sounded reasonable, and everyone else with the exception of Hector was nodding placidly. "What d'you think, Lacross?"

"I don't see that we have any choice," Hector said curtly. "But it had better not be good money after bad."

"My dear sir, you insult me." Thaddeus Nielson's voice was so low it was almost a whisper. There was an expression on his scarred countenance that caused Hector involuntarily to draw his head back as if away from the strike of a cobra.

"Surely you aren't questioning my probity, Mr. Lacross?"

"Of course he's not, Thaddeus," the banker said with a hearty slap on Hector's shoulder. "I daresay the man's not accustomed to dealing with Funds and the Exchange and such like. Daresay he knows nothing about percentages." He smiled kindly at Hector. "New to the business, aren't you, my dear sir?"

Hector was still trying to recover his equilibrium after that frightening glimpse of a very different side to Thaddeus Nielson.

"It's possible," he mumbled, shifting on his chair. "But I for one don't have another twenty thousand in cash. I'll have to put up a piece of property as security for it. Your bank will advance the money with that security, I imagine."

"My position, too," Dirk said.

"Oh, that's quite usual," Justice Greenaway said. "Do that all the time, don't we, friends?" He chuckled. "Have to take a few risks in this game, dear fellow. A form of gamblin', really."

"Yes, that's all it is," Dirk put in eagerly. "Like hazard or faro. Man makes a wager, lays down his blunt, and sees what comes of it."

Hector regarded him with an expression close to dislike. "Except that in this case we could both find ourselves languishing in debtors' prison."

"Could do that at the tables," Dirk said with an easy shrug. "Spent the night in the Fleet, m'self, once."

"Mr. Rigby, you have the spirit of the true investor." Thaddeus leaned over to refill his glass. "One must take risks to reap the greatest rewards. And I assure you, I've never lost yet. Neither have any of these gentlemen."

He looked for corroboration around the table and received fervent statements of agreement.

"So shall we drink to the next phase of our project?"

Thaddeus raised his glass, smiling benignly, and Hector found himself wondering if he really had seen that hooded cobra behind the disfigured facade.

The men around the table all raised their glasses, Hector following suit with the barest hesitation.

"Well, I'll write out my draft, Thaddeus," the banker declared. "If that man of yours can produce paper and a quill."

"Oh, I have that right here in the desk." Thaddeus pushed back his chair and went to the battered oak desk. He drew out paper, ink stand, and quill pen and placed them in front of Banker Moran. "At your leisure, my dear sirs."

Taking his seat again, he took up a long churchwarden pipe on the table beside him and busied himself with tamping and lighting his tobacco. Then he sat back, smoking peacefully while the writing materials circulated and banker's drafts were pushed toward him with various expressions of satisfaction.

Dirk and Hector wrote their own documents, each pledging his share of Hartridge Folly, the property they still jointly owned because neither one of them had found good reason to buy out the other.

Thaddeus took the pledges with a smile of thanks. He held the candle over the signatures and, when a blob of molten wax fell on each paper, passed them back to Rigby and Lacross with another of his benign smiles.

"If you'd just affix your seals, gentlemen . . . and we'll have Lord Justice Greenaway witness them for the record."

"No one else has done so," Hector pointed out.

"But they have given me banker's drafts," Thaddeus said silkily. "I must persuade my own bankers to advance me money based on your securities. A sealed and witnessed signature is necessary, as I'm sure you understand."

After a moment's hesitation Hector pressed his signet ring into the wax on his pledge. Dirk did the same. Thaddeus Nielson's expression remained smoothly affable. Justice Greenaway with much murmurings of pleasure, witnessed the signatures, and all the documents were once more in Thaddeus's possession.

"Thank you, sirs. I must say it's a pleasure to do business with you." He folded the papers carefully and placed them in his desk, turning a large brass key in the drawer and pocketing it.

"Another glass of wine to conclude such a pleasant occasion." He refilled glasses yet again.

Hector pushed back his chair, suddenly anxious to get out of this dark, dusty hole. The last thing he wanted was another dose of indifferent burgundy in a filthy glass, but just as he was about to make his farewells, the justice addressed a civil question to him on his experiences in Parliament, and he found himself drawn into conversation with a man whose stature and position in the world demanded the utmost respect.

Justice Greenaway was most flatteringly attentive as Hector waxed eloquent on the life and influence of a Whig member of Parliament for the pocket borough of Broughton. Dirk was drawn into conversation with the banker on the fascinating subject of horse racing and fox hunting and the rival merits of the Quorn and the Beaufort.

Thaddeus Nielson twirled the stem of his wineglass between finger and thumb and watched and listened, heavy lids drooping over penetrating gray eyes, as his quarry were soothed and smoothed with compliments, any possible qualms forgotten in the civilized company of eminent men.

Dirk glanced once toward his host and thought that his mouth had a rather sardonic quirk, but that, of course, was due to the scar. Poor man. It was such a ghastly disfigurement.

"Gentlemen, I must beg you to excuse me. But I have another urgent appointment," Thaddeus said eventually, when there was a brief pause in the discussions.

He pushed back his chair. "Ned will show you out." Going to the door, he opened it and bellowed for the old retainer.

"I'm acomin'. I'm acomin'. What's yer 'urry?" Ned's

creaky grumbles could be heard along the corridor as he shuffled to answer the summons.

"That jarvey out there says 'e won't wait more 'an three more minutes. An' he'd like his fare fer gettin' ye 'ere, if you gentlemen pleases."

Hector and Dirk rose to their feet. "Insolent dog," Hector stated.

"Aye, I don't know what the world's coming to," the justice agreed, nodding his head, smoothing down his crimson waistcoat. "And when Gordon holds his public meeting at St. George's Field, there's no knowing what will transpire."

"His acolytes are expecting a crowd of thousands, I hear," the banker said, moving to the door. "Turn that rabble loose on London, after listening to Lord George for an hour, and none of us will be safe in our beds."

"Paint a 'No Popery' sign on your door and you'll be safe enough," Thaddeus said with a poor attempt to conceal a yawn. "Good afternoon, sirs."

He bowed as his guests filed out in Ned's wake. The door closed behind them.

Rupert straightened and strode to the shuttered windows. He flung open the shutters and drew a deep breath of the warm, river-rank air, deciding that rotting weed and refuse made a relatively pleasant change after the fetid hothouse inside.

"Have they gone, Ben?" He turned back to the room as Ben came in with a crisp and spritely step.

"Aye, Nick. I told Will ye'd settle up with 'em all in the Royal Oak come Saturday."

Rupert grinned and removed his embonpoint. "Superb actors, they are. I wouldn't have believed it. Particularly Will and Thomas. Will makes an excellent Lord Justice."

He chuckled and dipped a cloth into the bowl of water Ben held for him. "And Fred and Terence make a perfect pair of sleepy old men, happy to let the world bob past them."

"Ye got what ye wanted?"

"Oh, yes." Rupert scrubbed at the scar. "I have exactly what I want. In a couple of weeks our friends will receive a demand for payment on their note of hand. They will look for Thaddeus Nielson. But Thaddeus Nielson will have disappeared off the face of the earth." His mouth twisted in a most unpleasant smile, and his eyes were as bleak and cold as the tundra.

"Sometimes I think y'are the devil hisself, Nick," Ben said equably. "What've them coves done to ye?"

"Not to me, Ben." He plucked the wig from his head, the kerchief from his neck, and threw off the ratty velvet coat and the moleskin waistcoat.

Ben handed him his own coat and waistcoat of dark-blue silk. He swallowed his curiosity and made no attempt to pursue the subject. Lord Nick had a look to his eyes and a curl to his lips that Ben knew meant he'd welcome no further questions.

"Have you been watching Morris?" Rupert asked evenly, fastening the buttons of his waistcoat.

"Seems clean as a whistle," Ben said. "Goes nowhere out of the ordinary, speaks to no one unusual. Leastways not that I can discover. Why? Are ye thinkin' of takin' to the road again?"

"Possibly," Rupert said, shrugging into his coat. "A personal matter."

"Ye'll take to the road on private business?" Ben's surprise and disapproval was manifest.

"Just this once," Rupert said, tying his stock. "I'll need the cottage afterward."

"Let me know when, then."

"Aye." Rupert took the large brass key from his britches pocket and went to the desk. He unlocked it and took out the two security pledges. Tomorrow Lacross and Digby would receive a request from his bankers for the deeds to the house to be lodged with the bank. It was a reasonable demand, and they would accede because they were in too deep to pull back.

He tucked the documents into his waistcoat pocket, then held the fake drafts from his confederates to the candle flame. The play was almost completed. And when Octavia had lured Philip to the ambush awaiting him on Putney Heath, then it would all be over.

The paper ash fell in a gray curl to the table, and he brushed it away. When he looked up, a shiver prickled Ben's spine. He'd seen Lord Nick at his most dangerous, but he'd never seen such bleakness on his friend's countenance.

"I'll leave you to lock up." Rupert strode to the door, but the look was still on his face, something very like despair in those clear gray eyes, and it was still there when he pulled away from the steps to row across the river, raising a hand in farewell to Ned.

He left the scull with the waterman at the Waterside steps and retrieved his horse from the Angel Tavern. There seemed more refuse than usual in the streets, mute witness to the earlier passing of the crowd, and a sense of suppressed excitement in the lanes as he rode past the narrow row houses, their inhabitants clustered on doorsteps, hanging out of windows.

But Rupert paid little or no attention to his surroundings. He could derive no lightening of his spirits either from the success of the afternoon's play, the crackle in his waistcoat of the papers that would return Oliver Morgan's family home to its rightful owner. He could think only of Octavia in Dover Street, of how she would greet him when he saw her.

Always polite, her smile unwavering, her golden eyes as distant and withdrawn as the eclipsed sun. If he attempted to touch her, even a casual, friendly gesture, she would move away from him, seeming to shrink within herself as if his touch repulsed her. So he no longer tried.

He no longer came to her bed, no longer expected to see that warm glow, the swift surge of passion in her eyes. If he could prod her into a sustained conversation, he counted himself fortunate. But she never laughed anymore. And his ears still rang with the sound of her dreadful laughter on that ghastly afternoon—laughter that had been harder to endure than a cry of anguish.

She was wounded. The Octavia he knew and loved was dug deep inside her shell, curled over her wound like an injured animal trying to heal itself. He knew all this, but he didn't know how to break through the carapace.

He'd thought he would be able to accept the situation. Accept that she would continue to play her part, fulfill her side of the bargain, and he would be glad simply of that. But it didn't work like that. He ached for her, and his own sense of self-disgust deepened every time he read the hurt and derision in her eyes.

He left Peter in the mews and walked round to the front of the house. When his employers were out, Griffin generally stationed a footman on the lookout for their return, but, unusually, the front door didn't open as Rupert mounted the steps. The answer to this neglect became clear as he entered the hall onto a scene of complete uproar.

A parlor maid was screaming at the foot of the stairs; the housekeeper, her apron thrown over her head, was providing an alto counterpoint to the parlor maid. It seemed to Rupert's incredulous eye that his entire household, from the lowliest bootboy to the austere Griffin, was making some kind of noise in his hall.

An enormous tabby cat raced between Rupert's feet, leaped off all fours directly into the air, seemed to reverse its position in midair, and was off again, its tail bushed, its ears pricked.

"Lord of hell!" Rupert slammed the door behind him. "Griffin, what the devil's going on here?"

"It's that *varmint,* my lord," the butler declared, his chest swelling with outrage. "Let loose a pack of snakes and mice all over the house."

"There's one . . . oh, over there, under the table!" A scullery maid pointed with a trembling finger, her voice rising to a pitch of hysteria. "It's a snake . . . it's a snake . . . "

"Silence!" thundered Lord Warwick. "Griffin, get these people back to work, unless they wish to have no work."

He stalked over to the console table where the cat was

standing at bay. A tiny and somewhat sleepy grass snake slithered backward into the shadows as his feet approached.

The cat flattened on its belly and reached into the shadow with one infinitely extending paw. The scullery maid screeched again, and a second round of pandemonium broke out.

Rupert lost interest in the cat and the snake and spun round in time to see a field mouse scamper across the parquet floor and disappear into the library just inches ahead of a second cat, this one a fearsome-looking black-and-white with only one eye.

"Where is Frank?" Rupert demanded in a tone no less ferocious for its low pitch.

"He's here." Octavia spoke from the landing. Her voice was trembling with what Rupert immediately recognized as laughter. His heart leaped in his chest at a sound he hadn't heard for days.

"Just you give him to me, my lady," Griffin declared. "I'll take him to the mews and teach him a lesson he'll never forget."

"I doubt you'd succeed, Griffin," Octavia said, coming down the stairs, Frank's collar grasped firmly between finger and thumb as she hauled him along with her. "He's had too many beatings in his short life for one more to make any difference."

"I didn't do nuffink, Miss Tavi!" Frank protested vociferously, struggling in Octavia's hold.

"Oh, yes, you did," she said, swinging him by his collar down the last step and into the hall. Her eyes were dancing, her mouth curved in amusement.

"He would have it, Rupert, that Papa told him to collect the snakes and mice for his lessons, and he was only doing what he was told."

"And did he?" It seemed entirely likely that Oliver would have set his pupil such an eccentric task.

"Not exactly," Octavia said carefully. "He was to draw a snake and a mouse from a picture book and give them their Latin names, but Frank thought it would be more realistic—or do I mean entertaining?—to draw them from life."

Rupert's lips twitched. Frank still jerked and wriggled in Octavia's hold. "And just how did they get loose?"

"Jumped outta the box, guv. Weren't my fault," Frank declared righteously.

"You lying little guttersnipe," Griffin exploded. "You deliberately put them on the kitchen floor where the cats could see them."

"I believe, Griffin, that it would please me if you would send my household back to work," Rupert said softly, one eyebrow lifting.

The butler's already suffused countenance turned a darker crimson. He bowed and waved a hand at the gawping assembled staff. In a very few minutes the hall was empty of all but Octavia, Rupert, and the now silent and watchful Frank.

The boy's gaze darted between them, the previous mischief in his eyes vanished to be replaced by the old man's wariness that had haunted them when he'd first arrived in Dover Street.

"What are we going to do with him?" Octavia inquired, leaping aside as the black-and-white cat raced out of the library.

"How many are there?"

"Mice or snakes?"

"Both."

"Well, according to Frank, there are three snakes and four mice. But how we are to find them, I can't imagine." Her voice cracked, and she doubled over on a surge of hilarity.

Rupert listened to the sound. It was a wonderful sound, banishing the memory of that other ghastly laughter that had been no laughter. A bubble of merriment grew in his chest and his shoulders began to shake.

Frank grinned as Rupert's laughter joined Octavia's. He couldn't really imagine why they found it so funny. He thought it was funny, but in his experience adults didn't share his sense of humor. These two, however, were not in the least like any adult he'd ever come across. Griffin and the housekeeper and Cook were all familiar types, but the guv and Miss Tavi were a different species altogether. And as for the old geezer upstairs . . . well, he was clearly off his rocker, but harmless enough.

"But what *are* we to do with him?" Octavia repeated as the spasms subsided.

"We'll decide that when he's retrieved the livestock," Rupert said, pulling a handkerchief out of his pocket. Without thinking he caught her chin and wiped her streaming eyes.

It was a gesture that came so naturally in the moment of warmth that neither of them reacted immediately, and then abruptly Octavia's smile faded, her eyes lost their glow. She turned her head away and his hand fell to his side.

He turned abruptly to the small boy, and his voice was stern, his gaze harsh. "Frank, you are to recapture every one of those creatures. I wish to see them back in their box before you have any supper." There was no more potent motivation for Frank than food.

Frank's expression became wary again. He ducked his head and hunched his shoulders and, when Octavia released her hold on his collar, slunk off, seeming to cling to the shadows of the wall as if to avoid further notice.

"He'll never find them in this house," Octavia said, no sign of her previous laughter on her countenance or in her voice. "They could be anywhere . . . in a hole in the wainscot, or under a carpet."

"Well, he'll have to try," Rupert said shortly, turning aside to the library.

"Knowing Frank, he'll simply go outside, find some more, and claim them as the originals."

Octavia followed Rupert, feeling dreary as the familiar chill set in between them. Even if she'd wished to offer a truce, she couldn't do it.

Her mind simply refused to let go of the image of the man drugging her with cold calculation, compelling a false

response from her that she had believed was essentially true
to herself.

He'd tricked her. Deceived her. Betrayed her. And she
couldn't bear the shame and the disappointment.

"I don't think I'll question his solutions too closely,"
Rupert said, trying to sound lightly amused again.
"Sherry?"

"Thank you." She took the glass he handed her, giving
him one of her polite, distant smiles. "I daresay we'll be
overrun with mice if they start breeding in the woodwork."

Her voice was so dull, her attempt to keep the conversation light so transparent, that Rupert abandoned the
topic. Their shared business was really the one thing they
had left now, and he took up the subject with a cool,
businesslike detachment.

"How close are you to persuading Philip to accept an
out-of-town assignation with you?"

"He's been rather wary since the debacle with Frank,"
she said in the same tone. "I think he wants to be sure I
haven't told the story and made a laughingstock of him. But
I've continued to pay him the right attentions, and he's
definitely still interested. You tell me when you wish it to
be, and I'll bring him." She turned aside, walking over to
the window.

Rupert regarded her averted back in silence for a minute, sipping his sherry. She no longer told him anything of
her dealings with his twin, and he no longer asked for a
progress report. He no longer had the right to direct this
operation.

"Let us say next Wednesday, then?" he suggested as if
they were planning a tea party. "I'll alert Ben."

"And what of the spy?" She didn't turn from the window, but her fingers tightened involuntarily around the
stem of her glass.

"I don't believe there is one."

"Morris?"

"Ben doesn't believe so."

"Then we'll make it next Wednesday."

"Very well." Rupert placed his glass on the table and left.

The door closed softly behind him. The fragile stem of the glass snapped between Octavia's fingers, and a bead of blood sprang up as a sliver of glass dug into her flesh.

Chapter 19

ᕭᕗ Philip Wyndham alighted from his phaeton outside Wyndham House and stood for a minute, frowning at the unfamiliar barouche drawn up before his front door. It was still relatively early in the morning and St. James's Square was devoid of activity, except for a footman walking a fat pug.

A lad was holding the horses of the barouche, but it didn't suit the Earl of Wyndham to inquire of a strange servant who was visiting Wyndham House at such an early hour. He strode up the stairs to his house, flicking at his boots with his driving whip.

"Who's here, Bennet?" he demanded as the butler bowed him into the hall.

"The physician, my lord. Lady Susannah has the croup," the butler explained. "I understand from nurse that she's been very sick throughout the night. Her ladyship is most anxious."

Philip's frown deepened; then he shrugged impatiently. "A fuss about nothing, as usual. Women always exaggerate these things. I won't have my house in an uproar over a sickly brat. Send the doctor on his way with all dispatch."

"Yes, my lord." Bennet's bow was wooden as his employer stalked toward the breakfast parlor at the rear of the house.

Philip, still with lowering brows, cast an eye over the *Morning Post* and attacked a veal chop and a plate of kidneys. The habitual serenity of his household was annoyingly fractured. He kept hearing footsteps hastening past his door, the sound of hurried voices, low-pitched but nevertheless urgent. Finally, he pushed back his chair and left the room just as the physician came ponderously down the stairs with his black bag, his hat beneath his arm. Behind him pattered Letitia, her eyes red, her face drawn with worry.

"Are you certain the hot compresses will help?" she asked. "The poor baby cries so when we administer them. I'm sure they must burn her skin."

"My dear Lady Wyndham, as I've explained, the child has a very severe case of the croup. It may well turn to a fever of the lungs." The doctor was both pompous and impatient, overriding Lady Wyndham's clear distress. "The compresses must be hot enough to raise a blister on her skin. If the fever reaches her lungs, then the matter will be very grave indeed. I cannot stress how grave it will be with such a small child."

"What's all this fuss?" Philip demanded of the doctor.

"Lady Susannah has a severe case of the croup, my lord." The physician bowed until his nose almost touched his knees.

"Oh, my lord, she is in such distress," Letitia said, her fingers knotting in her apron, tears springing to her eyes. "Nurse and I have been at our wits' end all night to know how to give her relief."

"Well, you have the doctor's advice now," her husband said dismissively. "Expensive advice, I'm sure," he added with a sardonic curl to his lip.

"Oh, but you wouldn't begrudge . . ." Letitia's voice faded. For one moment she'd lost her fear of her husband in her far greater fear for her daughter's safety, but it flooded back in full measure when he turned his cold gray eyes upon her.

"I do beg your pardon," she whispered. "If you will excuse me, I must go back to the nursery."

She turned to go, but her husband called her back sharply. "Wait," he commanded. "I have something to say to you."

He waved a dismissive hand at the doctor. "I give you good day, sir."

"My lord . . . my lady." The physician bowed again and strutted to the door, already being opened by the butler.

"And if your services are required again," the earl said indifferently, "you will find the servant's entrance more suited to your position. Bennet will show you the way."

The doctor blanched, and then crimson flooded his raddled cheeks. The butler stared impassively ahead as he held the door.

Letitia still stood on the stairs, her knuckles white as she gripped the bannister. Surely Philip wasn't going to castigate her for summoning the physician?

Her husband bent his cold stare upon her. "I do not care for my house to be thrown into chaos with nursery disturbances," he said in measured tones. "You will ensure that all matters to do with the child are confined to the nursery and the backstairs. As soon as she is well enough to travel, she's to be sent to Wyndham Manor. I daresay the country air will benefit her, and her absence will assuredly benefit me."

He bowed curtly and, without waiting for a response, turned and went into the library.

Letitia, after one startled moment, gasped and ran down the stairs, following him into the library. "You wish us to go to Wyndham Manor before the king's birthday, my lord?"

"The child, yes," he said. "I said nothing about you, madam."

Letitia's face was bloodless, her lips almost blue. "But . . . but she cannot go without me, my lord."

"Of course she can. She has a competent nurse." He

picked up a periodical from a table and began to leaf through it.

"But, Philip . . ." Letitia began.

He looked up with an air of bored indifference. "Well?"

Letitia swallowed. She twisted her fingers together, cracking the knuckles. The sound seemed to echo in the ghastly silence.

"You cannot send her away without me," she said. "She's my child. I'm her mother."

"Are you questioning my decision, ma'am?" His voice was the caress of a scorpion, and there was a flicker in his eyes that she recognized with terror. It was a flicker of anticipation that she was going to give him cause to punish her. Not that he needed cause, but it seemed to increase his savage satisfaction.

She stepped backward. "No, my lord."

The flicker turned into a flame. He dropped the periodical onto the table. "Are you sure, my dear? It sounded remarkably like it to me."

"No, my lord. No, indeed, I wasn't," she said desperately, taking another step backward toward the door.

"So you are of my mind that the child will do better in the country?" He tapped the back of one hand into the palm of his other. "Without her mother," he added gently.

"Yes," Letitia said, hating herself for her cowardice but knowing the hopelessness of making a stand. He would crush her like an ant beneath his heel. "If you will excuse me, sir, I must return to the nursery." She turned and fled before he could detain her.

Philip laughed derisively and picked up the periodical again. Letitia was hardly worth the trouble, really. As gutless as a worm. Unlike Octavia Warwick.

He allowed his mind to dwell on the smooth, pale oval of Lady Warwick's face, the tawny gold eyes so full of fire and light, the luxuriant cinnamon hair. She had such a surprisingly deep and rich voice, so suggestive and so amused.

And she had behaved with such impeccable discretion

over that debacle with the climbing boy. Not once had she mentioned it. Instead, she continued to treat him with flattering attention, offered him soft words and clandestine, brushing caresses as she passed him, her smile both mischievous and inviting.

His loins ached whenever he thought of her body as it had been the moment before the soot came down. He had been so close to baring her secrets, to possessing those secrets.

It was time to suggest another assignation.

He flung down the periodical and strode from the room. "Have my horse brought around immediately," he commanded as he took the stairs two at a time. It was the fashionable hour for riding or driving in Hyde Park, and on such a beautiful morning he would almost certainly come across Lady Warwick.

Half an hour later he descended the stairs in riding dress. There was a satisfactory hush to his house, he noted. No further intrusions from the nursery. He went out again into the bright morning, his step spritely, and mounted his elegant black gelding.

The town had come to life now, and the streets were busy as he turned to ride through Green Park. It was a bucolic scene, with milk maids tending their cows, ready to sell a cup of new-drawn milk to a thirsty passerby.

"Good day, Wyndham." A pleasant voice spoke from behind him. A pleasant voice but one that set his hackles on end.

He turned to see Rupert Warwick approaching on his distinctive silver mount. Lord Rupert smiled and doffed his hat, bowing courteously.

Philip returned the salute stiffly. "Warwick."

"Beautiful morning," Lord Rupert observed. "I'm almost tempted to take a cup of milk from one of those rosy-cheeked peasants. Such a pretty, rustic sight they make."

His companion made no response but continued on his way as if he had not been so irritatingly joined by a man he instinctively detested.

He glanced sideways after a minute and covertly examined Lord Rupert's calm profile. What was it about the man that disturbed him so? There was an air of menace about him, and yet it would be impossible to pinpoint its source. Philip had the sense in Lord Rupert's company that the man knew something he didn't . . . that he held a secret that amused him in some way. But it was not a pleasant amusement. It was as if he were anticipating some disagreeable surprise.

Philip shook his head with a muttered oath. He was indulging in foolish whimsy. The only man in for an unpleasant surprise was Rupert Warwick, who was about to be invested with a pair of horns. With a vicious kick he set his horse to the gallop, leaving his unwelcome companion behind him on the path without so much as a word of farewell.

Rupert smiled. His twin was beginning to sense something awry. Let him enjoy the sensation. He leaned down to pat Lucifer's neck. On Wednesday he'd leave the distinctive silver horse in the stable. He'd conduct his business on Putney Heath mounted on Peter. No point laying his cards upon the table prematurely.

Philip espied Octavia walking beside the tan in the company of three of the Prince of Wales's most obsequious acolytes. A footman trod discreetly in her wake, carrying a parasol and several books from the circulating library.

"Good morning, Lord Wyndham." Octavia greeted him with a radiant smile. "Isn't it a beautiful morning?"

"Beside your beauty, Lady Warwick, the morning pales," one of her escorts declared sententiously, doffing his plumed hat in an elaborate flourish.

"La, Mr. Cartwright, how you do flatter one," Octavia responded with a faint smile. "Will you dismount and walk with us, Lord Wyndham?"

"I fear if compliments are the payment for your company, madam, I have a meager purse," the earl said, swinging down to the path.

His voice was disdainful but his smile was complicit,

imparting his knowledge that he alone knew how Lady Warwick despised empty flattery.

"Lud, sir, I have no need of compliments from you," she said, taking his proffered arm. "I have more than enough from elsewhere."

She smiled at her courtiers. "Gentlemen, I have something most particular to say to Lord Wyndham, so I must beg you to excuse us."

"Oh, cruel damsel. I swear I am cut to the quick," exclaimed an effete, willowy gentlemen in a gold-striped waistcoat and hedgehog wig. "To be dismissed so harshly."

Octavia smiled and waggled her fingers at him in playful farewell. "I'll dance the quadrille with you at the next subscription ball by way of compensation, Lord Percival."

"And what of the rest of us?" demanded the remaining pair. "Are we to have no compensation?"

"Why, certainly," Octavia said sweetly. "I shall stand between you at the faro tables tonight and bring you luck."

With much protestation and lavish compliments, her escort dropped back, leaving her with Philip.

"Let us take a side path," she suggested. "Otherwise we shall be constantly having to acknowledge people. Basset, you may wait here and hold Lord Wyndham's horse. I shall return in ten minutes."

"Yes, my lady." The footman shifted his parcels into one hand and took the reins somewhat gingerly.

"You're not afraid people might whisper if you walk unchaperoned?" the earl inquired.

"La, Lord Wyndham, they cannot whisper more than they do already," she said, turning aside down a narrow path bordered by thick laurel hedges. "I was thinking it might be time to give them something to whisper about."

She said it so casually that for a moment he didn't react. Then he smiled. "We think alike, my dear."

He glanced up and down the narrow pathway. It was deserted. With a swift movement he pulled her into his arms.

Octavia endured the kiss as she always did. She was an automaton, responding by rote. Making the appropriate little noises of satisfaction as her lips parted beneath his mouth, moving her hands with appropriate eagerness, reaching against him with appropriate enthusiasm. It was easier now . . . now that she knew she would have to give him no more than this superficial submission. As always, though, her hands slipped inside his coat, fluttered over his waistcoat. And as always, they located the small hard circle against his heart.

Philip drew back, grasping her face between his hands, gazing down at her with a savage hunger in his eyes. "You will come to my house."

"No," she said quickly, shaking her head. "No, my dear. I believe it would be better to have our own place for this. Somewhere where we can be ourselves . . . enjoy ourselves . . ." Her tongue flickered over her lips. "Enjoy ourselves without fear of interruption."

His face darkened at this oblique reference to the mortification of the previous occasion, but she was continuing before he had a chance to articulate his annoyance.

"There is a place I know. The house of my old nurse. We will be quite private there. She will leave everything ready for us and then make herself scarce before we arrive."

She reached up to grasp his wrist as he continued to hold her face. "Will you permit me to arrange this? It will give me such pleasure."

"You have arranged such things before?" he asked with a touch of sullenness.

Octavia shook her head. "No, my lord. But I believe I know how to arrange this for both our pleasures."

She smiled and stroked his wrist with a fingertip. "When one desires something so powerfully, one derives much excitement from planning for the satisfaction of that desire."

She watched the vain complacence fill his eyes, his mouth curve in a self-satisfied smile, and her stomach turned over with repulsion and rage. How dare he imagine she could for one moment want him . . . imagine that he could begin to pleasure her? A woman accustomed to the delicate, skillful lovemaking of Rupert Warwick. A woman accustomed to the joyous laughter and the all-consuming ecstasy of Rupert Warwick's bed.

Rage swirled behind her eyes, but the smile remained on her mouth, and Philip Wyndham read only what he wanted and expected to read.

"Very well," he said, and his fingers tightened on her chin.

"Wednesday," Octavia said with another surreptitious flicker of her tongue, her finger again caressing the pulse at his wrist. "Will Wednesday afternoon suit you, my lord?"

"Perfectly."

"Then I shall come for you in a closed carriage. At two o'clock."

"At two o'clock."

Philip escorted her back to the waiting footman, who with clear relief relinquished his charge.

"Ah, if it isn't the fair Octavia!" The booming greeting heralded the Prince of Wales, buffeting down the tan toward them on a showy chestnut that looked barely up to his weight.

"Dear lady, you are balm for sore eyes." He reined in sharply, causing his mount to rear and wheel on the path in a flamboyant display of very poor horsemanship.

"I give you good day, Wyndham, and bid you take your leave," he declared with a loud laugh. "You've monopolized the lady long enough."

"As you command, sir." Philip bowed to his prince with ill-concealed mockery before raising Octavia's hand to his lips. "Farewell, ma'am. Until the next time."

"The next time," she agreed softly before making her curtsy to the prince as he dismounted heavily and with much puffing to the path.

Lord Wyndham took his leave without further ado, and Octavia resigned herself to a barrage of fulsome compliments and tasteless jests from her royal escort and his accompanying courtiers.

She returned to Dover Street at noon, her mouth aching with the artificial smile she'd had to maintain throughout the interminable promenade with the prince.

"Is Mr. Morgan in, Griffin?"

"I believe so, my lady."

The butler had the air of one struggling to restrain himself. Octavia drew off her gloves and invited with a sigh, "And Frank?"

Griffin exhaled, his chest almost visibly deflating as he unburdened himself. "I couldn't rightly say, madam. He failed to join Mr. Morgan for his lessons after breakfast. I caught him with his hands in the silver, my lady. But before I could remonstrate with him, he ran off. I haven't seen him since."

"He was stealing the silver?" Octavia looked incredulous and then immediately wondered why she should be surprised.

"He was putting two teaspoons in his pockets, my lady. I caught him redhanded. And things have been missing from the servants' quarters ever since he arrived."

"Oh, dear." Octavia frowned in dismay. "I'll discuss it with Lord Warwick, Griffin. If Frank returns, bring him to me."

She went upstairs to her father's apartments, still frowning. It was really inevitable that Frank would steal. He was an uncivilized little animal who knew only the imperatives of survival. The only difference in essence between Frank and herself and Rupert was that Frank had been born to a life of crime, whereas she and Rupert had chosen it as the most expeditious, and it was to be hoped temporary, means of survival.

"Good morning, Papa. Frank didn't come for his lessons today, Griffin tells me."

"No. He's not overly fond of the discipline of learning," Oliver remarked placidly, kissing his daughter as she bent over him. "He's too concerned about where the next meal is coming from to concentrate on sitting still and listening."

"But he knows he gets fed here." Octavia sat on a low stool beside her father's chair.

"Knowing and trusting are two very different things,"

Oliver said. "I doubt very much you'll make a model citizen of the lad."

"You sound like Griffin."

Her father merely smiled and stroked her head in a fleeting gesture. "Where's your husband these days? I find myself missing his company."

"Oh, he has business in the City," she said vaguely. "I haven't seen much of him myself."

Oliver nodded and cheerfully changed the subject. But when Octavia left him twenty minutes later, his liveliness vanished, and he slumped in his chair with a brooding expression on his patrician countenance. Something was amiss between Octavia and Rupert Warwick. Neither of them said anything, or even so much as hinted at difficulties, but they couldn't disguise the coldness and distance between them. Oliver could feel his daughter's unhappiness, but the urge to ask her what was troubling her was as always superseded by his innate reluctance to hear something he didn't want to hear. It would go away, if left alone. Once things were spoken aloud, they took on a shape and substance that became impossible to dissolve.

Restlessly, he rose from his chair and went to the window. Rupert was approaching the house from the mews, his caped riding cloak flowing from his shoulders, his riding whip tapping against his boots. Oliver couldn't discern his expression from two floors above, but there was a tension in the broad frame that shouted up from the street. Oliver watched as he mounted the steps to the front door and disappeared from view as he was let into the house.

Rupert was handing his cloak to Griffin when Octavia came down the stairs. "We have a problem with Frank," she said without preamble.

"Another one?" He raised his eyebrows wearily.

"He is a thief, my lord," Griffin declared with succinct satisfaction, smoothing his lordship's cloak as it hung over his arm.

Rupert grimaced at Octavia, who shrugged and preceded him into the library.

Rupert closed the door behind him. "So what's he stolen?"

"Things from the servants. And today he was in the process of making off with two teaspoons from the silver when Griffin caught him."

"It poses us with a somewhat interesting dilemma. Do we take the moral high ground, or the pragmatic low ground?"

"The latter," Octavia said without hesitation. "Always assuming he comes back. It wouldn't surprise me if we've seen the last of him."

"Probably," Rupert agreed. "I imagine he'll be too frightened to come back."

"I suppose it was foolish to hope that we could give him a different life," Octavia said. "The mud of the stews doesn't release its grip too easily."

Rupert heard her bitterness, but he could find no sugar with which to sweeten the pill. They had both lived the realities of the city's underbelly.

"Wednesday," Octavia announced with sudden briskness. "I will meet up with Wyndham at two o'clock in a hackney. We should reach the heath by three. It'll be broad daylight. Won't that be dangerous?"

"You'll instruct the coachman to take a different route across the heath. A less frequented road toward Wildcroft. We'll take our chance there."

"And after the robbery, where will you go?"

"To the cottage until the hue and cry has died down. You will play the hysterical victim of a highwayman for the benefit of the jarvey and Wyndham and return to town to lay evidence with the Bow Street Runners. You will, of course, be somewhat hazy in your details as a result of the shock."

"Of course."

And then what?

But Octavia knew the answer to that, so the question remained unposed. They would go their separate ways, and this sojourn in purgatory would be mercifully ended. She began to rearrange a vase of yellow roses.

"Octavia?"

"Yes?" She didn't look up from her task.

Can't you forgive me?

The words hovered on his lips, cried out to be spoken, but he couldn't say them. He didn't know how to ask for forgiveness. He'd been hardened over too many years of living a life dictated by the wrongs others had done him. He was a man to whom apologies were owed, not a man who owed his own. A man who had been hurt, and if he caused hurt to others, it was as a result of the hurt that had been done him. But he didn't know how to explain that, not in the face of Octavia's closed expression, the cool distance in the tawny eyes. And not in the face of his own haunting shame that he'd stooped to such a detestable deception . . . that he'd callously twisted such a courageous and candid spirit as indifferently as he would bend a pipe cleaner.

Octavia looked up from the roses, waiting for him to say what he had to say. He wanted to seize her in his arms, crush the anger and resentment from her body with the strength and warmth of his embrace. Press his lips to hers and take the bitterness from them with the sweetness of his kiss. He wanted to take her body with his own, plunge deep within her and exorcise the gall and wormwood of betrayal.

But she stood there behind an invisible wall that he didn't know how to scale or to tear down.

"Never mind," he said, shaking his head. "It wasn't important."

"Oh." She dropped her head, and he missed the flash of disappointment that crossed her eyes. "I have to meet with Cook to discuss the menu for tomorrow's dinner party," she said, going to the door. "You haven't forgotten that we're dining this afternoon with the Monforts."

"No, I haven't forgotten. But I have time to visit the Royal Oak first. I need to discuss arrangements for Wednesday with Ben." He moved to open the door for her.

As she passed him, he inhaled her delicate fragrance of orange flower water and lavender soap, and a wash of nostalgia swamped him. He allowed his hand to brush against her bare forearm, and for a second she paused. She glanced up at him, and the haunting unhappiness in her eyes tore at him.

"Ah, sweeting," he said softly, but the shutters immediately went up again. She drew herself aside as she slipped through the door, and he closed it quietly behind her.

Octavia stood for a minute in the hall, struggling for composure. How she yearned for him to take her in his arms, override her misery and her stubborn inability to forgive. She needed him to explain, to express his deep regret. She knew what she wanted, and yet it had to come from Rupert.

In the past he'd been so good at sweeping her along on the tide of his own plans and enthusiasms. So good at discounting her protests and her resentments. And now, when it mattered more than anything that he should do so, he simply stood back and accepted her withdrawal.

Desolately, she made her way to the stairs.

Rupert set off for Putney as soon as Octavia had left him. All he wanted now was for the business to be done. Then they could go their separate ways, and he would no longer be tormented by what might have been.

The front door of the Royal Oak stood open to the afternoon sun, and the taproom was busy as Rupert entered it. Bessie was behind the bar, drawing ale with her customary morose efficiency. Ben was sitting beside the empty hearth, engaged in idle chat with his cronies, blue pipe smoke circling above them.

Tabitha, carrying a laden tray of tankards to the bar, saw the new arrival first. " 'Ere's Lord Nick."

A chorus of greetings rose on the hazy air. "Eh, Nick, come and sit yerself down." Ben rose from the settle and pulled a chair over to the hearth.

"What'll ye drink, Nick?" Bessie took down a pewter tankard from a shelf behind the bar and polished it on her apron.

"A pint of ale if you please, Bessie." Rupert flicked

aside the skirts of his cloak as he took the chair, letting his riding crop rest across his knees.

He glanced around the crowded room and was pleased to see that there was no sign of Morris. For all Ben's confidence in the man, Rupert was not entirely convinced of Morris's reliability. He knew how easily the informer could be bought.

"Ye've not brought miss with you this time," Tab observed, dropping a curtsy as she handed him a foaming tankard.

"Not this time," Rupert agreed placidly. He took a deep draft of ale and wiped the foam from his upper lip with the back of his hand. "That's good. I've a thirst on me powerful enough to drain an ocean."

"Aye, it's 'ot out there," one of the smokers said comfortably. "I 'eard that Lord George 'as called a meetin' fer next week. St. George's Field or some such place."

"An' then a march on Parliament," one of his fellows declared knowledgeably. "You goin' along?"

"I might," the other said as comfortably as before. "Then agin, I might not."

Ben raised an eyebrow at Lord Nick and gestured with his head to the door. Rupert nodded and drained his tankard.

The two got up and left the taproom as the arguments for and against Lord George Gordon's rabble-rousing activities grew heated.

They made their way by mute consent into the stable-yard.

"You've a new stable lad," Rupert commented, leaning his shoulders against the warm red brick of the wall and closing his eyes for a second as the sun beat down on his eyelids.

"Aye. Freddy's pa needed 'is 'elp in the fields fer the summer. So young Bobbie there is takin' 'is place."

Rupert opened his eyes and languidly regarded the lad grooming a shire horse in the shade. Then he pushed himself off the wall. "Let's walk a bit."

Ben followed him out of the yard and into the lane beyond. They strolled slowly in the shadow of the wall.

"Y'are plannin' to take to the road fer this personal business?"

"Wednesday," Rupert said. "But on the Wildcroft road. It's less populated."

Ben nodded, bending to pluck a grass stem from the roadside. He sucked reflectively.

"There's a goodly stretch of that road that runs through trees. That'd be as good as anywhere."

"I know where you mean. I'll need more time than usual, since this operation requires stripping my quarry to his small clothes." Rupert's lazy smile was far from pleasant.

"Ye'll need someone to watch yer back," Ben declared. "I'd best come along . . . watch the road while y'are doin' your business."

"No, Ben. I'll not involve you more than usual. Have the cottage ready. That's all that's necessary." The drawl had vanished from Rupert's voice.

"What 'arm would an extra lookout do?" Ben was reluctant to yield.

"No, Ben. I work alone."

Ben glowered. "An' what of miss? Ye work with 'er."

Rupert was silent for a minute. Then he said, "Be that as it may, old friend, I'll not risk your safety. You've too many people dependent upon you. What would happen to the Royal Oak if you found yourself swinging from Tyburn Tree?"

Ben grunted and didn't look any happier but he shrugged his acceptance. "What time Wednesday?"

"Midafternoon, or thereabouts. I'll stop in here first."

"Right y'are. I'll 'ave yer pistols primed. Ye want Lucifer?"

"No, I'll take Peter for this."

"That's something, I suppose," Ben said grudgingly.

Rupert merely smiled and punched him lightly on the shoulder before they turned to walk back along the lane beneath the wall, reentering the stable yard where the new lad was whistling between his teeth as he lovingly combed the shire's thick mane.

"Ye'll come in fer a bit of dinner?" Ben invited. "Bessie'll be expectin' ye."

"No, I have to get back, thanks. Tell Bessie I'll be up Wednesday night, once the coast is clear. She can feed me to her heart's content then."

Ben smiled a little grimly and called to the stable lad. "Bobbie, fetch the gentleman's 'orse?"

Bobbie left the shire and went into the stable, returning in a few minutes with Lucifer. " 'Ere y'are sir."

"Thanks, lad." Rupert tossed him a sixpence as he mounted. Than he leaned down to clasp Ben's hand in a firm grip. "Until later, old friend."

"Aye. And 'ave a care." Ben waited until Lord Nick and Lucifer had trotted out of the yard then he turned and went back to the inn.

The lad stood for a minute, tapping the sixpence against his teeth. Then he ran back to the shire horse, hurriedly returned him to the stable, and five minutes later was weaving his way through the somnolent streets of Putney. It was clear from his expression and his speed that his errand was an important one.

Chapter 20

"You are quite clear in your mind what you have to do?" Rupert was standing at the window in Octavia's bedchamber, his hands resting on the sill behind him. His expression was impassive, his eyes veiled so that Octavia could read nothing in them.

"Yes, I'm quite clear." She hitched herself farther up against her pillows and took a sip of her hot chocolate. Rupert hadn't been in her bedchamber for two weeks and she felt uncomfortable, almost embarrassed, to be sitting up in bed in her nightgown while he stood there, immaculately clad in a suit of bronze silk, his hair unpowdered and tied back with a matching silk ribbon.

"Are you going to the king's levee?"

"I shall put in an appearance," he replied. "Let it be known that I'm going out of town for a day or two."

"Will you be at the Royal Oak?" she asked tentatively, lifting the small silver pot and pouring another dark, fragrant stream of chocolate into her cup. She didn't really want a refill, but it gave her something to do with her hands.

"No. Once I have the ring, there will be other arrangements to make. People I must see."

Like the family lawyers and old Doctor Hargreaves, who'd brought him and Philip into the world. When Cullum Wyndham announced himself to his twin, he intended to leave nothing to chance. Philip would have no room to maneuver. No choice but to accept the fait accompli.

"You won't need me here, then? Once you have the ring, I mean. There will be nothing further for me to do?" Her cup clinked in the saucer, and chocolate slurped over the delicate gold rim onto the pristine-white tray cloth beneath.

"If you wish to leave after this afternoon, of course that's for you to decide," he said with a completely credible dispassion. "But you must let me know how to get in touch with you. I will have things to return to you . . . things that belong to you."

"Yes," she agreed in a wooden little voice. "I suppose you've nearly completed your side of the contract."

"A couple of weeks more and I will have done." He pushed himself away from the window. "Where will you go when you leave here?"

"I don't know." Octavia picked at a hangnail on her index finger. "I haven't decided as yet."

"How will you explain things to your father?"

She shrugged, her creamy rounded shoulders lifting beneath the delicate fabric of her nightgown. His eyes sought and found the dark crown of her nipples veiled in gossamer. Her hair fell forward, shielding her face from his view.

Deliberately, he stepped to the bedside. Leaning over, he caught her face and lifted it, brushing aside her hair with his free hand. She looked startled and dreadfully vulnerable as she met his gaze. But she said nothing. Made no move either to free herself or to respond to his touch.

"Good-bye, Octavia." He lowered his head and kissed her mouth. The heady scent of her filled his nostrils, the taste of her lips, her skin, flooded his memory, stimulated his nerve endings, sending a rush of blood to his head that made him dizzy. But still she made no move, her lips lifeless and unresponsive beneath his.

He drew back, straightening slowly. "Good-bye, Octavia."

His hand fell from her face and he turned away from the golden eyes, the pale, beautiful countenance of his madonna.

"God go with you," she said, but so quietly he didn't hear as he opened the door and left the room.

Tears splashed onto the tray on her knees, fell into the shallow cup, salting the chocolate, and Octavia simply sat there, allowing the tears to flow.

Finally, she pushed the tray aside, flung off the covers, and stood up. It was over and done with. She had one last part to play, and she would play it to the hilt. Rupert would be taking all the danger, but he wouldn't find his partner lacking in support.

*A*t two o'clock a hackney drew up outside Wyndham House. The Earl of Wyndham came down the steps immediately. He climbed into the carriage, slamming the door behind him. The heavy leather curtains were pulled down across the window apertures, and to any casual observer he had stepped into an empty vehicle.

"Good afternoon, my lord." Octavia spoke softly from a shadowy corner.

Philip didn't speak, merely seized her hands and pulled her across the narrow space, crushing her against him, his mouth battening on hers, pressing her lips hurtfully against her teeth.

"So eager, sir," Octavia gasped with a little laugh when he finally released her.

"You drive me to madness, woman," he rasped, leaning back against the squabs, regarding her through narrowed eyes. "For two pins I'd take you here and now." The gray slits glittered at her in the dimness, and his mouth was a thin curve that reminded Octavia of a hawk.

"That might invite interruption, my lord," she said lightly, moistening her swollen lips. "For all that we're shielded from prying eyes."

Philip smiled and folded his arms. "I'll restrain myself, madam, for the moment. But I promise that you will learn this afternoon what it is to be truly possessed."

Octavia controlled her shudder and the spurt of contemptuous rage, hoping that the dimness would conceal the involuntary curl of her lip. "I hope you will be pleased with the arrangements I've made, my lord."

"Where is this house?"

"A small village called Wildcroft on the edge of Putney Heath."

Philip frowned. "That seems a long way to go for an afternoon."

"That depends on the afternoon, I would have said." She smiled suggestively. "I venture to think, sir, that you will find this one worth the journey."

He laughed. "And you, my lady. And you."

"That goes without saying, sir."

Somehow she managed to keep up this anticipatory banter as the hackney took them across Westminster Bridge and through the small villages on the south bank. At one point she drew aside the leather curtain and looked out. They were passing through Wandsworth. Putney was the next village. She let the curtain fall again. Would it be better to be unaware and in darkness when the attack came? Or ready and waiting for it?

The dim light at least allowed her to conceal her expression. And she was sure she couldn't keep her countenance completely clear of the dread and excitement that now surged through her veins, making her feel sick. Perspiration trickled down her rib cage and gathered between her breasts.

Suddenly, Philip leaned forward and raised the curtain, fastening it to the hook on the ceiling. "It's airless in here. We're in no danger from prying eyes in this godforsaken wilderness." He mopped his own damp brow with a handkerchief.

So much for the shadows. Octavia dabbed at her breasts with the lace edge of her fichu and turned her face to the window, hoping thus to conceal her expression even as she took the benefit of the light breeze.

The horses were pulling up the hill toward Putney Heath. The coachman suddenly leaned down from his box, shouting toward the window. "The Wildcroft road, is it, lady?"

"That's right." Octavia stuck her head out of the window. "I'll direct you to the house when we reach the village."

The coachman muttered something inaudible and cracked his whip. The horses reached the top of the hill and broke into a canter. Octavia sat back, licking her dry lips. How far along the road would Rupert make his move?

The coach swung sideways, and she glanced out of the window again. They were rattling along a dirt road much narrower than the main highway across the heath. She could see trees up ahead, lining the track. Would it be there?

She sat back again, searching for a neutral topic of conversation that would distract them both. But nothing would come to mind, and her companion seemed content to watch her with that glittering, predatory gaze that she knew was stripping her naked.

She closed her eyes, tried to relax, to allow the swaying motion of the carriage to insinuate its rhythm into the flow of the blood in her veins. She told herself she had nothing to worry about. All she had to do was scream, swoon, have hysterics. Any or all of them, while Rupert dealt with Philip.

Rupert would have only the jarvey to worry about, and Octavia was convinced the man carried no weapon beyond a sturdy blackthorn. Rupert should be able to deal with him very easily. Philip, of course, had a sword at his waist. But he wouldn't have pistols, not on a romantic assignation.

The thoughts circled wildly in her head, and yet the pistol shot made her jump, made her heart leap into her throat, her gut turn to water.

The jarvey swore and hauled back on the reins. The horses reared and came to a stamping halt.

"Odd's blood! It's a damned highwayman!" Philip declared, hissing through his teeth as he unsheathed his sword. He cast a cursory glance at Octavia, who had shrunk cowering into a corner, her eyes wide with fright, her hand pressed to her mouth; then he wrenched open the door just as Lord Nick turned from disarming the coachman.

For a second two pairs of slate-gray eyes met. Philip paused, stunned by the cold power emanating from behind the highwayman's black silk mask. Then he leaped to the ground, flourishing his sword.

"Cowardly blackguard! I'll see you hang for this!"

Lord Nick swung off his horse, and his sword was in his hand in almost the same movement.

"I'd be delighted to fight for my spoils," he remarked lightly, in that slightly husky accented voice Octavia had heard before. "On guard, sir."

Philip hesitated as the highwayman easily took up his stance. The gray eyes in the slits of the mask seemed to be amused now, but the humor did nothing to disguise the danger they held.

Philip raised his sword point. And then it happened.

There was a great crashing in the trees, and four men on foot erupted onto the path. They were burly ruffians, dressed in buff coats and leather britches, flourishing pistols and staves, and before Lord Nick could take a step, they had him surrounded.

"We got 'im," one of them declared. "We was a bit late. But better late than never, eh?"

One of his companions guffawed. "Got 'im redhanded. Lord Nick hisself, unless I'm much mistaken."

He walked all around the highwayman, who stood still in the path, saying nothing as he assessed his chances of escape.

Philip Wyndham put up his sword. "I'm glad to see the Runners aren't quite as useless as their reputation would have us believe," he observed dryly. "What brought you here?"

"Oh, we 'ad a tipoff, sir," one of them informed him as he took a length of rope from his belt. "An' beggin' yer pardon, sir, but we does our best wi' little enough 'elp from the public."

"That may be." Philip waved a dismissive hand. "Shouldn't you unmask the ruffian first?"

He stepped close to the highwayman, and Lord Nick suddenly lunged forward with his sword, pinking one of the Runners on the shoulder. A stave swung, and the highwayman went down to the path, blood pouring from a gash in his head, black spots dancing before his eyes. But in the melee, Philip had been distracted from his intention, and Rupert knew that a broken head was a small price to pay to keep his anonymity. Not only for himself, but for Octavia.

Octavia had begun to scream, a distracting, high-pitched keening that couldn't be ignored. Philip turned back to the carriage as the Runners were binding their quarry's wrists behind him.

"For God's sake, woman, stop that caterwauling," Philip snapped. "You're not hurt. No one's hurt—with the exception of that ruffian. And if I had ten minutes with him, he'd be begging for the hangman on the spot," he added savagely. "We can be on our way again immediately."

Rupert, still on his knees, retching miserably as the nausea caused by the blow to his head became invincible, heard these words with a dull desperation. His own fate was immaterial at this point. But he was going to be forced to abandon Octavia to Philip . . . Philip, whose physical appetites would only be sharpened by the afternoon's excitement and his part in bringing a felon to execution.

"We'll be needin' some details, sir, afore ye go," the leader of the group said. "Ye'll be a material witness, sir, in the crown court when they brings our friend 'ere from Newgate to trial at the Old Bailey. If ye'd be so good as to write yer name and direction fer me."

With an air of great self-importance, he pulled a sheet of grubby paper out of his waistcoat and handed it to the earl.

"I've a lead pencil in 'ere, somewhere. Never goes

anywhere wi'out 'em. Useful for material witnesses and tipoffs, you see, sir."

Philip tapped his foot impatiently on the road. He snatched the writing materials from the man and scrawled his name. "There."

"Oh, thank'ee, my lord. Thank'ee, your lordship." The Runner looked at the scrawl and then gazed respectfully at his lordship.

Octavia's distraught face appeared in the carriage window. She was still weeping hysterically, but her eyes were sharp and assessing as they went to Rupert, who was being dragged roughly to his feet by two of the Runners. The blood still poured from his forehead, soaking his mask and blinding him, but she could do nothing for him.

If she tried to wipe away the blood herself, she would jeopardize her own role as a woman out of her head with shock. If she suggested they wipe it themselves, they would remove his mask to do so. Either course would give one of them away, and once Rupert's true identity was known, then everything would be irreparably lost.

So she continued with her low keening, although her heart filled with rage as she saw how savagely they hauled him onto his horse, fastening his bound hands to the saddle behind him, tying his feet into the stirrups.

Rupert swayed in the saddle, still dazed by the blow to his head. He tried to shake the blood from his eyes and focus on Octavia's face, feeling her eyes on him, but she was lost in a hazy fog.

And through his hopeless dread ran the thought of his own arrogance in refusing Ben's assistance. If Ben had been watching, this might have been averted. Now he would be hurled into the void of Newgate jail, and he was abandoning Octavia here. Leaving her to Philip. Because Philip now would expect her to make good her promises.

One of his captors pulled Peter around on the path, and the big horse snorted and tossed his head at the rough hand on his bridle. His master's weight was not properly distributed in the saddle, and the horse was confused by the sense of being riderless even though he wasn't. He skittered and

Rupert lost his precarious balance, slipping sideways. He managed to curl his fingers over the saddle behind him and pull himself up again. But the effort increased his nausea.

It was going to be a long ride back to London.

They moved off, his captors walking briskly beside the horse. And Octavia watched them go.

Her brain was working furiously now. If she allowed herself to think of Rupert's plight, she would be paralyzed. If she allowed herself to think of his physical miseries at this point, she would be engulfed in futile compassion, feeling those hurts herself. Now she had to get away from Philip. And when she'd done that, she could think about the next step.

"Carry on, jarvey." Philip snapped his fingers at the coachman, who'd remained on his box the entire time, staring open-mouthed at the scene unfolding on the path below. "Wildcroft village."

He jumped back into the carriage, then stared. "Hell and damnation!"

Octavia lay on the floor, unconscious, her skirts billowing around her, her eyes closed.

"What the devil is this?" He knelt beside her just as the coach lurched forward. Unbalanced, he fell heavily sideways and knocked his elbow painfully on the edge of the seat.

"Odd's blood!" Swearing, he bent over her again. "What's the matter with you?" He slapped her cheek, and when it had no effect, slapped her harder.

Octavia's eyes fluttered open. "Oh, my lord. I must have swooned. It does happen sometimes in these circumstances, and I don't believe I have my smelling salts. I wasn't expecting it, you see. Oh, sir, I feel so ill."

Astounded, Philip continued to stare at her. "What the devil do you mean, in these circumstances?" he demanded. "And of course you weren't expecting it. How the hell many times have you been held up?"

Octavia closed her eyes again. "No, I didn't mean that, my lord. Of course such a dreadful thing has never happened to me before. It's . . . oh, dear, I don't how to explain."

"Sit up." He put his hands under her arms and heaved her up. "By God, you're no light weight," he muttered, hauling and shoving at her until he had her on the seat, where she slumped in the corner. "Now, what are you talking about?"

"The shock . . . it must have brought it on . . . ," she whispered. "I don't know how to say it . . . I'm so embarrassed, my lord. It's a woman's thing. . . ."

"What?" He stared at her. "What the devil is this nonsense?"

Her eyelashes fluttered on her cheeks. "The flowers, my lord," she whispered. "The shock must have brought them on. It's early . . . but sometimes . . ."

"Dear God in heaven!" he exclaimed, flinging himself back onto the seat. "Are you telling me you're unclean?"

Octavia whimpered. "I am in such pain, my lord. My belly aches most dreadfully. Please take me home."

Philip's glare of rage and disgust would have seared a piece of meat. He banged on the roof of the carriage with his sword hilt.

"Yes, guv?" The coachman's upside-down head appeared in the window.

"Turn around. We're returning to London."

"Lady's a bit upset, I daresay," the coachman observed considerately.

"Turn this damn hackney around!" was all he got for his pains.

He withdrew with a phlegmatic shrug and turned the vehicle on the narrow path. They rattled down the narrow track, the iron wheels clanging on pebbles, the horses as anxious as their driver to get back onto the main and more populated thoroughfare.

Within, Philip sat back in his corner, morosely nibbling a fingernail, glaring in the darkness at the hunched and still whimpering figure of the woman he'd expected to make his mistress. Some devil was abroad in this matter.

But he would have her.

His fingers curled. Part of him wanted to be done with her and her feeble female complaints. But stronger than that part was the determination not to give up when he'd set his mind to this. He still wanted her, even now, when the strong and spirited woman who had originally attracted him had proved as weak and spineless and susceptible as the rest of her breed.

He would have her. He would make a cuckold of Rupert Warwick.

As they crossed Westminster Bridge, he banged on the roof. "Take me to St. James's Square first," he instructed. "You won't mind, my dear, returning alone to your house?" he inquired with mocking solicitude.

"Not at all, Philip," she said.

To his relief she seemed to have recovered some of her composure. Her countenance strangely bore few signs of her earlier distraction and the violent storm of weeping. In fact, it was more beautiful than ever, so pale in the shadows, her eyes golden pools, liquescent with the faint residue of tears.

"I beg your pardon," she said humbly as the carriage drew to a halt before Wyndham House. "I don't know how to apologize enough. But in all the upset . . ."

"Oh, never mind," he said impatiently. "I'm not really interested in the intimate workings of the female body. The next time *I* will make the arrangements, and there will be no mischance and no put-off, madam."

He jumped from the carriage as if he couldn't wait to get out of her contaminated presence.

Octavia breathed a sigh of relief. It had been a desperate ruse, but all she could think of on the spur of the moment. She'd suspected that her shock at the holdup wouldn't have been sufficient excuse for Philip. He might have compelled her in some way to go through with the assignation. Which could have been very awkward, not least because there was no convenient little love nest awaiting them in Wildcroft village.

But now she was free of him. And the first thing she had to do was go to Ben.

Ben would know how one visited prisoners in Newgate. He would know what Rupert would need to make his imprisonment more comfortable. She had a vague notion that one could buy all sorts of things—like easement of shackles, and medicines. And his head wound would need tending.

For a dreadful moment she saw the gibbet at Tyburn Tree as it had been on the day she had met Rupert Warwick. Two bodies, black stick figures in the dawn, swung from the scaffold. She blinked the images away. She mustn't think of them. She mustn't think of anything but first improving the conditions of his imprisonment, and then effecting his escape.

There had to be a way. The knowledge that no one ever escaped from Newgate was another unhelpful reflection. Maybe she could buy his freedom. The jailers were all corrupt. It was common knowledge. And they had money.

Buoyed up by these plans, she sprang down when the carriage drew up at Dover Street. Philip hadn't paid the jarvey, of course, even though it would have been the gentlemanly thing to do. She handed the man a sovereign and ran into the house.

"Have my horse brought round, Griffin. And I'll not be dining at home today."

Griffin had already been informed that Lord Warwick was going out of town for several days, so she had no need to explain Rupert's absence to the staff, or indeed to anyone. Not unless it became prolonged.

No, don't think like that!

Ten minutes later she was riding back toward Westminster Bridge. She pressed her mare to increase her speed, wishing that she were riding Peter on this errand. What would they do with Peter in Newgate? Would she and Ben be able to take him away? It was an issue irrelevant to Rupert's safety, but her mind fixed upon it until she could think of nothing else.

The mare did her gallant best, but she couldn't match Peter's pace, and it was almost six when Octavia reached the Royal Oak.

The gangly Freddy didn't appear as she rode up, so she

flung herself from her horse, looped the bridle over the railing, and entered the inn. "Ben? Bessie?"

Rupert had said these two had stood his friends and would stand hers if she ever needed them, so when Bessie appeared from the kitchen, with a scowl on her face and a dripping ladle in her hand, Octavia said simply, "Nick is taken. Where's Ben?"

Bessie's angular features twisted, and Octavia thought the woman was going to cry.

Then Bessie said brusquely, "He's at the cottage, waiting for Nick. Come you in and tell me what's 'appened. I'll send Tab to fetch 'im."

"No, I'll go, if you tell me the way. My horse is outside."

"Where've they taken Nick?"

"To Newgate. Bow Street Runners. Tell me how to find Ben."

Bessie responded to the urgency in her voice with a curt nod. She walked out into the street.

"Take the road to the end. Take the footpath across the fields. Cross the stream and keep to the right. Ye'll break through the hedge onto the lane after a quarter mile. Turn right on the lane. Cottage'll be ahead of ye."

"I'll recognize it," Octavia said. "Even though it was dark when I was last there." She remounted the mare.

"Bring Ben back 'ere afore 'e goes off wi' ye. 'E'll need a steadyin' hand," Bessie said. "You, too, I shouldn't wonder."

It sounded grudging, but Octavia was beginning to learn to ignore the woman's tone and listen to what lay beneath.

She followed the directions in the gathering dusk and reached the cottage just as the evening star popped into the sky. The building looked deserted, windows and doors closed tight. The stable was a low hunched shape in the small yard behind.

The mare's hooves clattered on the cobbles. The kitchen door flew open.

"Where's Nick?" Ben ran into the yard.

"Newgate," Octavia said.

"I knew it!" he muttered. "I knew 'e couldn't be this long fer no reason."

"Bessie wants us to go back to the Royal Oak." Octavia leaned down, holding out her hand. "Can you ride pillion?"

"Aye." He took her hand and clambered in an ungainly fashion onto the saddle behind her. "Tell me what 'appened. I knew 'e shouldn't be doin' personal business on the road."

He was doing it because of me. Because I couldn't go through with the original contract.

But Octavia didn't say this. Instead, as calmly as she could, she explained what had happened. "They were waiting for him, Ben. The Runners said they'd had a tipoff."

Ben cursed under his breath. "God 'elp me, but I told 'im I thought there was nothin' to that spy thing. I'll 'ang Morris up by 'is fingernails until I get the truth outta him."

"Later," Octavia said. "We've other concerns first."

"Aye," Ben agreed. "Nick'll be needin' funds for easement an' such like. Then we'd best look fer a lawyer."

"A lawyer?" Octavia exclaimed. "A lawyer isn't going to save him from the hangman, Ben. He was caught in the act. We have to get him out of there."

"Aye," Ben said again, but his voice was low and dispirited.

"Don't tell me it can't be done," Octavia said fiercely. "Don't tell me that, Ben."

His hand touched her back in a fleeting gesture of comfort. "We'll see what we can do, miss."

Chapter 21

⏺ *R*upert shuffled across the slimy earthen floor, the shackles at his ankles clanking with each arduous step. His eyes were not yet accustomed to the darkness, but he could hear groans, chinks, and scraping sounds as irons shifted with the movements of his fellow inhabitants of this dungeon deep beneath the streets of London.

It was bitterly cold, and when he managed to locate a wall, his hands encountered a thick coating of viscous filth running down the stone. He changed his mind about leaning against the wall, although he ached in every limb and an entire percussion orchestra played merrily in his head. His captors had been far from gentle with him, and several booted feet had found their way into his ribs and kidneys before two jailers had hurled him into this foul oubliette.

He yearned to sit down, but he knew he wouldn't be able to get up again in his present weakened condition, loaded as he was with the double set of eight-pound irons. Already his ankles were rubbed raw, and when he lifted his chained hands to try to scrape some of the caked blood from over his eye, the effort brought sweat to his brow and left him gasping for breath.

Someone coughed, a painfully dry, hacking sound, and

a whole chorus started up. Rupert's eyes were growing used to the dark now, and he could make out huddled shapes on the ground. Bundles of rag-covered sticks, they looked to him, and all completely mute, apart from the coughing.

Jail fever, he thought. With every breath, he was drawing in the contagious, infected air of this putrid dungeon, reeking with the stench of excrement. But maybe jail fever was an easier death than the scaffold.

His knees shook with the effort of keeping himself upright, and the chains at his wrists weighed down his arms like cannonballs. But he didn't think they'd keep him in this hole too long.

It was standard procedure to throw a new prisoner loaded with chains into the worst dungeons, to let him languish for a while so that he'd be all the more eager to pay whatever extortion was demanded by his jailers if it would lighten his fetters and bring him more comfortable quarters.

But how long would they leave him to meditate in this horror? He was thirsty but could make out no water container in the darkness. Yielding at last, he leaned back against the foul wall, bending his knees and pressing his shoulders and the small of his back into the stone so his legs carried slightly less weight. Someone whimpered on the floor at his feet, and he shuffled sideways to avoid touching him with his boots.

He tried not to think of Octavia, but he couldn't keep from his mind the tormenting images of her enforced submission to Philip. He saw her as she had been that morning, sitting up in bed, her glowing hair tumbling over her shoulders, the dark peaks of her breasts outlined beneath her nightgown, her eyes so filled with hurt and betrayal.

Surely he could have done something to lessen her hurt, to repair the breach. He hadn't permitted obstacles to stand in the way of his goals since he'd run from Wyndham Manor as a despairing child. And yet, when Octavia had thrown up the wall against him, he'd bowed his head and accepted her judgment. He'd accepted it because he'd told himself it didn't matter. He'd told himself he didn't need

Octavia beyond the part she had to play in their joint venture. He'd told himself that, but his aching heart gave him the lie, and he knew that he had accepted her withdrawal because what he'd done to her was indefensible.

The narrow grating in the door scraped back, the sound loud as cymbals in the fetid darkness. Then it banged shut again. A key turned in the lock, and there was a crash as the heavy bar across the door was flung upward.

Rupert's heart jumped and he pushed himself upright. When they came for him, they'd not find him enfeebled and begging. But they hadn't come for him. The door opened a crack and something was flung into the dungeon. It rolled over the stones, and the heaps of rags at Rupert's feet seemed to come to life. They crawled, snatched, growled, tore at the loaf of bread, like so many starving dogs.

Rupert closed his eyes to the sight. God help him if he ever got to that stage. But it wouldn't happen. His law-enforcing captors had robbed him of every last sou, including his watch, but Ben would come with money. Octavia would surely tell Ben of the disaster. Once she was able to get away from Philip . . .

A groan escaped him, the despairing sound so like the ones he'd been listening to that he began to feel more akin to his fellow prisoners, still scrabbling and feebly fighting over the scraps of bread. His head drooped onto his chest, and his arms hung loose in front of him, the weights dragging at his shoulders. He was going to have to sit on the floor. And yet stubborn pride still kept him on his feet.

The only sounds in the dungeon were the animal whimpers broken with violent spasms of coughing, and he found the lack of a human voice as disorienting as the darkness . . . and much more terrifying. His companions were so far lost in their subhuman misery that they couldn't even acknowledge a fellow human being.

His hands and feet were numb with the cold, and his shoulders screamed with agony as the shackles pulled at them. He tried to stand very still because even the slightest movement of his feet caused the irons at his ankles to dig deep into his abraded skin.

He had drifted into a nightmare trance of physical pain and excruciating fatigue, but he was still on his feet, though sagging against the wall, when the grill in the door scraped open again. It was followed by the rasping of the key and the thump of the bar.

This time the door opened fully, and Rupert blinked painfully in the sudden light from a lantern that the jailer held high, illuminating the filthy prison for the first time.

And then he saw the figure behind the jailer. A slender figure clad in black from head to toe, her face concealed behind a thick black veil.

"God in heaven!" Octavia said in a voice of horror, pushing the jailer aside as she stepped into the vileness.

Terror flooded Rupert. "Get out! You dolt, get her out of here!" he bellowed at the jailer, panic in his voice. "There's infection in this foul air. Get her out!"

"Eh, 'old yer 'orses," the jailer said. "Yer lady friend 'ere wanted to see 'ow you was doin'. Thought I was doin' ye a favor." He leered at the prisoner in the light of the lamp, one eye squinting up to the dripping ceiling.

Rupert lunged forward with a supreme effort, dragging his chains, ignoring the shrieks of his outraged muscles and galled skin. "Octavia, *leave!*"

But she ignored him, taking a stumbling step toward him. "Oh, my dear, what have they done to you?" She grabbed his hands, helplessly chafing his numbed fingers.

"All right, out ye come, then," the jailer said to Rupert with another leer. "Yer friends 'ave bought ye some ease-ment. Lucky fer you, Lord Nick."

Rupert shuffled toward the light of the oil lamp. He felt like a very old man who'd been dwelling in a subterra-nean cave, far from the light. And yet he guessed he hadn't been imprisoned in this hell hole for more than a few hours. How long would it have taken to break him? Less time than he would once have believed possible. It was a humbling recognition of his own frailty.

Octavia was still clutching his hand, pulling him desperately toward the door, as if afraid that if she didn't get him out, he'd be condemned to this oubliette forever.

"You had no right to come here," he said furiously, all his weakness miraculously vanished under his fear for her. "Of all the chuckle-headed things to do. Why didn't you tell Ben, instead of coming yourself?"

"I did. He's negotiating with the jailers for Peter," Octavia said, tears springing to her eyes, not so much at the harshness of his tone as at her shock at his condition. How could a few short hours wreak such devastation on a man?

"Jailer, take these shackles off!" she demanded, grabbing the man's arm as he walked ahead of them down the corridor. "How can he walk in these? There's miles of this passage. His ankles are scraped to the bone."

Tears clogged her voice but did nothing to lessen the fury of her determination. She knew they were both entirely dependent on the goodwill and avarice of the jailer, who could throw Rupert back into the dungeon if he chose, regardless of how much money she offered him, but her voice was still imperious as she fought to overpower the man's potential malice with her own will.

"Do it, man! Do it now!"

"Can't," he said. "They'll 'ave to be struck off in the lodge. When we gets upstairs, it'll be done."

"Dear God," Octavia said in distress. "Let me hold them up for you." Bending, she tried to lift the chains, but they were too heavy for her, and she dropped them with a cry of distress.

"It's all right, Octavia," Rupert said, wincing as her efforts to help caused more harm than good. "I walked here, I can walk back."

"But it's barbaric!"

"Yes," he agreed dryly. Suddenly he wanted to laugh as the sweetest relief seeped through his veins. This was the Octavia he'd been missing during the last bleak weeks. Once again she was the appealing, courageous, candidly responsive partner whom he'd insensibly grown to love and need.

And beneath that recognition flowed the knowledge

that she could not have fetched Ben and come to his aid so speedily if she'd been forced to keep her assignation with Philip.

"You're a veritable angel of mercy, my dear, but I wish you hadn't come." But he knew he was lying through his teeth. Just as he knew he had to ignore his own wishes and ensure that Octavia didn't jeopardize her health or her identity a second time.

"You didn't expect me not to, did you?" She sounded indignant, but he could see nothing of her face beneath the thick veil.

"I expected you to have more sense." He paused, breathing heavily, trying to ignore the pain of his ankles. How much farther was it before they reached the light and air?

He began to speak softly but with conviction as the jailer, seemingly unaware that they'd stopped, plodded on ahead.

"If you stay away from me, there's not the slightest need for you to be compromised. No one knows my true identity, and it probably won't come out until the trial. By that time you and your father will be long gone, back to Northumberland. The news of a highwayman's trial and execution won't travel that far, and if it does, it won't cause any particular interest."

"Don't talk like that," she said in a fierce undertone. "And, anyway, I'm not compromised. No one knows who I am under this veil, and they won't. Prisoners have visitors all the time."

"Eh, you there! You comin', or did ye like yer 'ousin' so much, ye've a mind to stay below," the jailer called, holding his lantern high.

"Vile brute," Octavia muttered. "Lean on me, Rup—I mean, Nick. Put your hand on my shoulder."

He smiled slightly but didn't avail himself of the offer, instead distracted his thoughts with what he was going to say to Ben when he saw him. The man must have been insane to have brought Octavia to Newgate. And not just brought her, but allowed her to venture alone into the poisonous bowels of the dungeons.

At long last a spiral staircase appeared at the end of the freezing, dank passageway.

"How will you climb?" Octavia asked distressfully.

"I've climbed down them once," Rupert said with a grimace. In fact, he hadn't really climbed down them, his escort had essentially shoved him from top to bottom.

The climb was worse than he could have imagined, however, and he was pouring sweat when he finally managed to haul himself to the top of the staircase.

But at the top there was light and air of a kind. The air was still fetid, still stinking of excrement, but it moved a little in the faint breeze from the tiny windows set high up in the walls of the passage. Faces pressed to the barred gates of the crowded wards as they progressed down the corridor.

Octavia kept her eyes on the ground ahead, thankful for the veil that hid her face from the leering spectators, who called out to them as they passed, jeering oaths for the most part, with an occasional sympathetic remark for Rupert's plight.

The jailer opened a door at the end of the passage, and they passed out into the press-yard. It was deserted, the prisoners all locked up for the night, and Rupert drew a deep breath of the warm night air. A blackbird burst into song, imitating a nightingale, and he was filled with an overpowering sense of the precious fragility of life.

"This way." The jailer led the way into the narrow street between the two wings of the prison. It led to the jail gate, where a small building stood at the threshold of the prison.

Rupert recognized it from his admission—the lodge where they'd hammered the fetters to his ankles and wrists.

Inside, a brazier glowed red and a burly, bald-headed man looked up from his bellows as they entered.

"Strike 'em off, Joe," the jailer said, spitting into the dust.

The man showed no reaction. With a grunt he indicated a block in the middle of the room, and Rupert heaved his right foot up. The man swung his hammer twice and the links flew apart. Rupert put his left foot on the block, and the bald-headed man attacked the links with red-hot pincers.

Octavia stood in the doorway, her heart in her throat as she waited for the pincers to slip against Rupert's leg. But the links glowed and fell apart and the highwayman stood free. His wrist manacles were dealt with in the same way, and he flexed his shoulders with a groan of relief.

" 'Ave to put 'em on again when ye goes to the Old Bailey," the jailer remarked. "But so long as ye pays yer garnish proper like, ye can move free about the state side . . . until they moves ye to the condemned cell, a'course."

This last was said with a blunt matter-of-factness that Rupert blocked from his mind.

So they were moving him to the state side, the part of the prison reserved for those rich enough to pay for the comforts and privacy of a gentleman's residence. The fee for admission was three guineas. Rupert had paid it himself for Gerald Abercorn and Derek Greenthorne, together with the ten shillings and sixpence a week rent for a single bed apiece. Presumably, Octavia and Ben had seen to the necessary payments.

He and Octavia followed the jailer to an internal gate and up a flight of stairs. Spacious, airy rooms opened off a passageway at the top. The air was clean and fresh, and the sound of voices and the chink of glasses came from behind the doors, locked for the night.

At the end the jailer flung open a door. " 'Ere y'are, Lord Nick. Thanks to yer friends, ye've a whole room all to yerself."

He gestured expansively, then with another leering grin said, "Well, I'll leave you with yer lady friend. When miss is ready to leave, I'll be at the gate below."

"Twenty-eight shillings a week," Octavia said gravely as the jailer stomped back down the stairs. "But you wouldn't want to share with anyone."

She threw back her veil and regarded him anxiously; her eyes were enormous in the deathly pale oval of her face.

"No," he agreed, looking around the accommodations. It was a room that would normally house four men, which explained the exorbitant fee.

"And there's a laundress who will clean and look after you," Octavia continued with the same anxious gravity. "And your meals will come from the Keeper's own kitchens. Do you think you'll be comfortable?"

Rupert's smile was wry. "As comfortable as it's possible to be in prison," he said. "Now, Octavia, you are not to come here again."

"Don't be absurd," she said. "Sit down and let me wash the blood from your head. There's hot water in the jug, and Ben is fetching you wine and dinner from the tavern outside."

She pushed him down into a chair and delicately brushed the matted, blood-soaked hair away from the gash in his head.

"That bastard," she said, pouring hot water into the ewer. "He had no reason to hit you like that."

"How did you get away from Philip?" He gave up the attempt to remonstrate with her. His head ached too badly for coherent thought, and her touch was cool and soothing.

"Oh, that," Octavia said, catching her lower lip between her teeth, a frown of concentration drawing her brows together. "Well, I told him I had my monthly terms . . . that the shock of being held up had brought them on unexpectedly."

"Octavia!" he exclaimed with a shout of laughter that made him wince immediately as shooting pains darted through his head.

"It seemed rather apt," she said with a grin, gently disentangling the matted strands of hair.

For the moment the grim circumstances faded into the background under the wonderful sense of being together again, without the hideous constraint of the last weeks. What had once assumed such vital importance now seemed trivial, and she couldn't imagine how she'd allowed it to separate them. But, then, all things were relative, and beside the ghastly realities of the present, very little could assume much importance.

"Eh, Nick. I'm right glad ye've found somethin' to laugh about." Ben spoke from the doorway, his voice both somber and puzzled.

He came into the room and placed the basket he was carrying on the table.

Rupert turned with a swift smile. "My friend, it's either laughter or tears at this stage." He held out his hand, and Ben took it between both of his in a firm warm grip.

"What's to do?" he said helplessly. "I'll get the best lawyer . . ."

"Don't waste money on a lawyer," Rupert said. "You know as well as I do it won't do any good."

"That's what I said," Octavia said, still bathing the ugly wound. "We have to get you out of here."

Rupert and Ben exchanged looks over her head, but they said nothing.

"Did you bring enough supper for all of us, Ben?" she went on as if she hadn't noticed their silence, although she had. "I own I'm famished, and I'd love a glass of wine."

"Aye, there's a veal and 'am pie, a smoked eel, a goodly round of cheese, and a couple bottles of burgundy." Ben began to unpack the basket. "Plenty for three of us."

"There, does that feel better?" Octavia examined her handiwork with a frown. "It's very deep. I'm sure you should have the physician to sew it up."

"No, there's no need for that."

"But you'll have a massive scar."

Rupert shrugged. One scar more or less on a dead man was neither here nor there. He didn't say it but he didn't need to, and Octavia turned away abruptly, her lips compressed.

"Are there any cups for the wine, Ben?"

"Aye, I brought some from the tavern." Ben poured wine into three pewter cups. "I never expected to drink wi' ye in 'ere, Nick. And I blames meself."

"There's no need." Rupert drank deeply.

"Someone tipped off the Runners. An' who could it 'ave been? Someone in the Royal Oak, stands to reason."

Ben frowned into his cup. "Morris weren't there that afternoon, when we talked of this. But the new stable lad was. Workin' by the wall where we was talkin' on t'other side, now I think about it."

"What do you know of him?"

"Little enough. But I'll know more right quickly," Ben said grimly.

"Locking the stable door after the horse has bolted," Octavia remarked.

The determination to ensure Rupert's comfort had buoyed her up so far, but now that she'd achieved what little she could achieve, a cold apprehension was creeping over her skin. This was still Newgate. The bars and walls were as thick, even in this spacious apartment. And she couldn't begin to think how to effect his escape.

"If I brought woman's clothes," she said slowly, "you could disguise yourself and slip out of the prison with all the other visitors."

"My dear, they'll be watching me every minute of the day," Rupert said gently. "And they'll check everything you bring in. Lord Nick the highwayman is too precious a prize to be neglected. If I'm discovered trying to escape, I'll find myself ironed again and back in the dungeon."

"But you can't just give up!" she exclaimed, shaking her head impatiently as Ben offered her the veal and ham pie. She'd suddenly lost all appetite. "They'll *hang* you if they find you guilty."

Rupert sighed. "Let's not talk about this now. Finish your wine and Ben will take you home." Lines of fatigue were etched around his mouth, and his eyes were heavy with strain and the pain of his crushing headache and battered body.

Octavia stood up immediately. "I'll come in the morning."

"I'd rather you didn't," he said quietly. "Ben will look to my needs."

"Better than I could?" The golden eyes were hurt, her mouth soft with distress.

"Not in everything," he said with a tiny complicit smile.

Ben coughed. "I've stabled Peter at the tavern. Mr. Akerman, the Keeper, gave 'im up wi'out too much trouble."

"Good." Rupert stood up a little unsteadily as a wave of dizziness washed over him. "See Octavia safe home, Ben."

"Aye, that I will. Come along, miss."

Octavia stood irresolute. "Why don't I stay here tonight? Your wound will need tending and—"

"No," Rupert interrupted firmly. "Go now."

Reaching for her, he drew her against him and lightly kissed her brow. "Do as I ask, Octavia, and stay away. I don't want to risk compromising you."

"I can't do as you ask," she said. "I'm sorry." She stood on tiptoe to brush his mouth with her own. "And I'll not be compromised. Wait till you see me tomorrow. You won't recognize me."

She was smiling, but she couldn't disguise the effort it cost her. "Rest now, and I'll bring you some laudanum tomorrow. I should have thought of it today, but there was so much . . ." She opened her palms in a gesture of frustration, then turned to go.

Rupert listened to their footsteps recede on the stone staircase; then he flung himself down onto one of the beds, linking his arms behind his head.

How long before they brought him to trial? A lawyer could spin the process out, of course. It would be the only advantage. But did he want to spin it out? Did he want to spend his days and nights in this room, knowing that there was no future? That when he left this place, it would be on the cart that would take him to Tyburn?

Surely it would be better to have done with it quickly. But he knew, too, that even after sentence of death was pronounced, a man could languish for many months awaiting his execution. And he would languish through those months in the condemned cell.

He must stop Octavia's visits. They would hurt both of them too much. How ironical it was to have achieved harmony again only because he now faced his death.

But before he met that death, he must conclude the business with Rigby and Lacross. He must write the official demands for payment. Ben would deliver them at the correct intervals, and Ben would summon the bailiffs. At the very last the bank would foreclose on the mortgage of Hartridge Folly.

Another four weeks would see the business finally completed. And he could play his part from within Newgate's walls, always assuming he had four weeks. But the law, even without the help of defense lawyers, was notoriously slow moving.

He closed his eyes, trying to quiet the hammer behind his temples. Philip's face drifted into his internal vision. He'd been so close to bringing an end to the business begun that day at Beachy Head. So close to exposing his twin, to avenging Gervase. So close, but it might just as well have been a million miles.

The usurping Earl of Wyndham would shortly hold his title safe from any challenge.

Chapter 22

℘ *R*upert awoke stiff in every joint. The pounding in his head had lessened, however. Swearing vigorously, he struggled off the bed and stumbled to the window that looked down into the press-yard.

The yard was full of people—men, women, and children milling around, stall holders and barrow boys pushing through the throng, doing a lively business in the necessities of life in prison.

"Ye want some breakfast, sir?"

He turned at the sound of a female voice in the doorway. A young girl stood there, smiling tentatively, wiping her hands on a grubby apron.

"Who are you?"

"Amy. Your laundress, sir." She bobbed a curtsy, her eyes wide as she gazed at the notorious highwayman. His clothes were torn and stained, but their original quality was still visible. And there was no concealing the physical presence of the man, despite his battered face and tangled hair.

"I could bring ye a nice mutton chop and some eggs, if ye'd like."

Rupert debated this fare. Decided he needed all the strength he could muster and said, "Thank you, Amy."

The girl curtsied again and vanished. Rupert gingerly stretched, his muscles complaining vociferously. He felt as if he was one enormous bruise from head to toe.

A cracked glass stood on a makeshift dresser in the corner of the room, and he examined his countenance with a grimace. Unshaven, hollow-eyed, bruised. He was a sight to frighten children. He touched the gash on his forehead. It was no longer bleeding, and Octavia's ministrations had cleared away the caked blood, but it was an ugly-looking cut. It probably did need a surgeon. But what was the point of stitching up a dead man?

He had to stop thinking like that. It would neither alter the reality nor make it easier for him to accept.

" 'Ere we are, Lord Nick." The girl came back with a laden tray. "An' there's a pint of ale."

She placed the tray on the table. "Cooked in the Keeper's own kitchen, sir. Just as yer friends arranged."

Rupert nodded and sat down, realizing just how hungry he was as the aroma set his saliva running. The girl bustled around the room as he ate, straightening the sheets on the bed.

"D'ye 'ave any clothes for the wash, sir?"

"At this point I have only what's on my back," he said wryly, draining his tankard before pushing back his chair from the now empty platters.

"I'll be bringin' yer dinner at four o'clock, sir." Amy took up the tray, offering another bobbed curtsy. "If ye needs me afore then, jest let Timson, the jailer, know. 'E'll send fer me."

"You could bring me some hot water," he said. "And soap and a razor."

The girl nodded and went to the door. As she reached it, a voice sang up the stairs. "Bring that bath carefully now, ye great lummox! Good money I paid fer that, and yer spillin' it all over the stairs."

"All right, all right, girl. You watch yer tongue around 'ere."

"Pah," came the scornful response. "Never mind my

tongue. So long as me money's good, that's all ye've got to worry about."

Rupert listened incredulously. The voice was unmistakably Octavia's, for all that she was speaking in the vigorous accents of the street. Labored breathing, muttered curses, and heavy footsteps accompanied her continued stream of encouragement and castigation as whoever it was struggled up the stairs with some weighty burden.

"That's right, then. Put it down over there. Look lively now, don't go spillin' any more of it."

Octavia appeared in the doorway, pointing imperiously to the middle of the room. "An' ye can fetch me up two more jugs of 'ot water."

Reaching into the pocket of a coarse apron, she pulled out a handful of coins, saying loftily. " 'Ere, that's fer yer trouble. An' I thank ye kindly. Look sharp about them other jugs, now."

The two men, who had nobly borne the weight of a filled tub of hot water up the long flight of stairs, took the coins with a morose grunt and left with a nod toward the highwayman, who was staring in astonishment at his visitor.

Octavia wore a bright-orange dress that had clearly seen better days. Her breasts jounced above the low neckline edged with torn and grubby lace. Her skirt was kilted up above her ankles to show a dirty petticoat and a pair of rough wooden pattens. She had a scarlet kerchief on her head, tied beneath her chin, and what he could see of her hair hung over one shoulder in a long plait.

A smudge of dirt adorned her nose and her cheek. And her nails were encrusted with grime.

She put down a basket and a cloth-wrapped bundle and grinned at him. Putting her hands on her hips she twirled in a swirl of orange skirts and dirty petticoat. "Don't I make an excellent tavern wench?"

"Hell and the devil, Octavia!" he exclaimed. "What is this?"

"I thought you should have two different female visitors," she explained. "One will be the mysterious veiled lady, and the other will be the tavern wench. That should confuse them nicely, don't you think?"

He shook his head in disbelief, but before he could say anything, Amy reappeared with the razor, soap, and a jug of hot water. She too stared at Lord Nick's visitor. But with an air of unfriendly suspicion.

"Who're you?"

"A friend of Lord Nick's," Octavia said haughtily. "If it's any business of yours, girl."

" 'E's my gennelman," Amy said, her mouth pursing. "An' 'e don't need the likes of ye lookin' after 'im. This is my area, an' I'll thank'ee to keep out of it."

"I've every right to visit the prisoner," Octavia declared, twitching her nose as if at a bad smell. "You're 'is servant, an' I'm his friend. So I'll thank *you* to remember that. Put them things down by the bath an' be on yer way. We'll call if we needs anythin' else."

Amy puffed out her chest and tossed her head, obviously preparing to launch into a stream of invective. However, Rupert, struggling with laughter, interposed himself between the two of them.

"Thank you, Amy," he said warmly. "I'm most grateful for your help. I know I'll be relying on you a great deal from now on."

Amy bridled and cast the highwayman's visitor a glowering look of triumph. "I'll be 'ere whenever ye needs me, sir," she said. "Not like visitors what 'ave to go away."

"Just so," he said, ushering her to the door.

With a final toss of her head in Octavia's direction, Amy left. Rupert closed the door behind her and stood leaning against it, regarding Octavia with eyes brimming with laughter.

"I suppose it's ridiculous to be surprised at what an actress you are."

"Of course," she said matter-of-factly. "You know what an actress I am. Haven't we been on stage ever since we met?"

"I suppose we have. But the play's over, Octavia."

She shook her head. "Nonsense. Now, come and have

this bath. I've brought you clean clothes, laudanum, arnica, all your toilet articles. So you may be quite comfortable until we can find a way to get you out of here."

Her mouth had a stubborn line, and there was something in her voice that told Rupert it would be pointless to argue with her. If it helped her to believe that something could be done, then who was he to disabuse her? She would face the reality soon enough.

"You seem to have thought of everything," he said neutrally.

"Yes, I believe I have." She smiled and came over to him. "Now, you don't have to do anything. Let me look after you."

She gently eased his torn coat off his shoulders. Deftly, she removed his waistcoat and unbuttoned his shirt. As she opened his shirt, a little cry of dismay broke from her at the purpling bruise across his ribs.

"What did they do to you?"

"Oh, they amused themselves a trifle," he said. "But I'm not made of glass, sweeting."

"No," she agreed, pushing the shirt off his shoulders. "But if I could get my hands on them, I'd cut out their cowardly hearts!" She glared fiercely up at him, her hands spanning his narrow waist. "Chicken-hearted bullies!"

"Very true," he agreed, smiling at her fierceness, feeling his depression lifting under her vital presence.

Her hands were busy at his waist, unbuckling his belt, unfastening his britches. She pushed them down his hips together with his woolen drawers, then gave him a little push backward onto the bed. "Sit down."

"This is not the most seductive disrobing I've been subjected to," he grumbled, sitting on the edge of the bed as she bent to pull off his boots. "You're behaving more like a nurse than a lover."

Octavia looked up from her task and smiled, her tawny eyes clearly showing her relief that he was entering the spirit of her visit. "Wait," she promised. "That'll come all in good time."

"Oh, good," he said with a mock sigh of satisfaction,

stretching out his legs so that she could pull his britches and drawers clear of his feet.

"Now, get in the tub," Octavia said. "Ah, here are those men with the other jugs."

She went to the door and greeted the arrival of her two laborers with a cheerful vulgarity that sent Rupert's eyebrows into his scalp. Octavia had clearly not wasted her time in Shoreditch.

He lowered himself into the steaming water and groaned with a mixture of pleasure and pain as the heat stung his scratched and abraded skin. Resting his head against the rim, he let his feet dangle over the far edge of the tub.

Octavia closed the door firmly on the departure of the water carriers and came over to him, struggling with two heavy cans.

"I can wash your hair now," she said briskly, kneeling beside the tub, hefting one of the cans. "Sit forward and put your head back."

Rupert complied, closing his eyes as the warm water washed over him. He felt as if he were back in the nursery, being attended to by his nursemaid, and the idea both amused him and relaxed him.

Octavia's hands were gentle on his scalp, but they were clever as they massaged and stroked. He found himself remembering how he'd once attended to her in the same way, soothing her tension. His fingers twitched, remembering in their nerve endings the suppleness of her skin, the lithe, slender body rippling beneath his hands.

"You seem to be enjoying this," Octavia commented casually, her hands sliding down his body to the jutting evidence of his enjoyment.

He groaned with soft pleasure, his flesh pulsing between her caressing hands. "I'd enjoy it more if you'd take your clothes off," he murmured plaintively.

Octavia smiled and leaned over the bath to kiss him, her lips brushing over his mouth, her tongue darting across his cheeks, over his eyelids, her eyelashes fluttering against his forehead.

Sitting back on her heels, she unlaced her bodice and pushed it off her shoulders. The straps of the grimy petticoat followed; then, bared to the waist, she knelt and reached for the soap. She lathered it between her hands as she leaned over him. Her rounded breasts hung like peaches above his mouth, and he captured a nipple between his lips, stroking with his tongue, grazing delicately with his teeth while she soaped his neck with long, seductive strokes.

His hands slipped down her rib cage to the bunched material at her waist. "Take the rest off," he directed, drawing his tongue up through the deep cleft of her breasts in a hot, languid sweep.

Octavia smiled, fumbled with a hook and wriggled out of the gown and petticoat. "Better?" She knelt upright so he could see her body, naked down to midthigh and the top of her gartered cheap cotton stockings.

"Much!" Taking a firmer grip of her waist, he yanked her over the edge of the tub, sending water slurping over the oak boards as she landed on her knees astride him in the narrow bath.

"Oh, now you've soaked my stockings!" she exclaimed in feigned annoyance.

"You should have taken them off," he responded coolly, encircling her neck with his hands, his thumbs stroking the fast-beating pulse at her throat. His eyes narrowed abruptly, the amusement dying out of them.

"I've missed you, Octavia. More than I can describe."

"And I you," she said, caressing his face with her fingertips. "I so much wanted you to sweep my miseries aside. To compel me to forgive you. And yet I knew I wasn't giving you the slightest opening. But I couldn't help myself."

"It was a loathsome thing to do," he said. "My only excuse lies in the past."

"And you still won't tell me?"

He shook his head, but his eyes darkened with that pain and anger she now recognized.

"It's a tale I must carry to my grave, Octavia. There's

no way to redress the wrong now. And nothing to be gained by passing it on."

Her own eyes flashed. "You are wrong," she stated flatly. "You have never been more wrong, Rupert Warwick."

Before he could say anything, her mouth fastened on his in a kiss of such desperate hunger that he was engulfed in the power and passion of her conviction. His own certainty of the hopelessness of the present and the future dissolved under the sweeping wave of her need and the force of her will.

Her hands were hard on his shoulders as her tongue drove into his mouth, drinking his sweetness, devouring, possessing with all the fervor of a vampire in agonized need of his life's blood. Her lower body moved sinuously over his loins, her thighs parting as she captured his erect flesh in the throbbing cleft of her body. She lowered herself onto him without releasing his mouth, and he pressed deep within her as she rose and fell against him, her nails scribbling against his skin, her teeth nipping his lip.

He had no active part to play in this. Octavia was loving him with all the possessive, driving need of a long-deprived lover, and he lay still beneath her orchestration, his body thrumming with pleasure as her own was on fire, her wet skin searing his, her hungry words of earthy sensuality rustling against his ear.

She raised her head and he looked up into her face, transfigured by desire and its growing fulfillment. Her skin glowed translucent, her eyes were huge with wonder, her lips hungrily parted. She ran her tongue over her lips, then bent and licked the salt sweat that beaded his forehead.

"I want you," she whispered. "God, how I want you."

She surged above him, her hips moving rapidly with each thrust that drove him deeper and deeper inside her. And when he touched her womb and her eyes widened as the explosion of glory grew ever closer, she said fiercely, "I will not let you die, Rupert."

And then her body convulsed around him and he was devoured in her fires, swept into dissolution on the tidal wave of her passion, and her words flew away like torn scraps of paper in a tornado.

Until the tide receded and the fires went out. And then he heard them again, whispered against his ear. He had no answer for her, and Octavia didn't ask for one.

She lay beached upon him in the rapidly cooling water, her heart slowing, matching the rhythm of his, beating against her breast. Then she pushed herself up onto her knees and laughed down at him, her expression so light and easy, her eyes so full of amusement and the glow of fulfillment that he wondered if he'd imagined the intensity of those whispered words.

"There, now. Isn't that a wonderful cure for bruises?"

"None better," he agreed, grasping her hips firmly. "And perfectly appropriate behavior for a tavern wench." His hands slipped behind to pat her bottom. "But not, I fear, for the veiled lady."

"Oh, I daresay she'll be making very few visits," Octavia said airily, moving her backside seductively against his palms. "Only enough to create a degree of mystery."

"Hop out," Rupert said, releasing her with a final pat. "Before young Amy comes in and starts fussing."

"Jealous child, isn't she?" Octavia observed, clambering dripping from the tub. "Now, where did I put the towels? . . . Oh, here they are, still in the basket."

She drew out a thick white towel and wrapped it efficiently around herself before holding up a second. "Come, my lord. Allow me to dry you and anoint your bruises."

Smiling, he stepped out in a shower of drops and stood obediently as Octavia rubbed him dry, walking all around him with a little frown of concentration as she blotted the water from his skin and then smoothed arnica on the livid bruising.

"How about here?" she murmured mischievously, her hands sliding down over his belly. "I'm sure a little here would be beneficial."

Rupert grasped her wrists and held them away from him. "Mercy, Octavia! I need some recovery time."

"Pshaw!" she said scornfully. "Since when?"

"Since I was worked over by a trio of hefty barbarian bullies," he declared.

Octavia was instantly contrite. "Oh, poor sweet, how thoughtless of me."

She hurried over to the bundle she'd brought with her. "See, I have here clean linen and your riding clothes. I thought you'd be more comfortable in buckskins, rather than anything more formal."

"I'm not expecting an invitation to St. James's Palace, certainly," he agreed wryly, taking the bundle from her.

Octavia looked as if she was about to say something; then she closed her lips firmly and bent to pick up her own discarded garments. There was silence for a minute as she peeled off her soaked stockings.

Rupert buttoned his shirt and tucked it into the waistband of his britches with a sigh of relief. Clean clothes had a most amazingly revivifying effect, he reflected. Although, of course, he probably should put his present sense of well-being down to rather more than a new wardrobe.

He glanced at Octavia, who was slipping her bare feet into the wooden clogs. She looked up quickly, feeling his eyes on her, and smiled.

"You look much more yourself."

"I feel much more myself," he agreed, passing a hand over his chin. "And once I've shaved, I shall be completely restored."

"Ben said he'd come to see you. He said Bessie would be bound to load him with victuals and other goodies for you."

She perched on the broad windowsill, idly swinging her legs, enjoying the warmth of the sun on her back, as he lathered his face and applied the razor.

"He's taking it very hard," she added.

Rupert made no reply. He knew how Ben would be feeling. The tavern keeper had lost two of his closest friends to the hangman in February. Gerald Abercorn had been almost a brother to him. To face the loss of another dear friend would be dreadful to endure.

Octavia looked over her shoulder, down into the press-yard. The scene had an anarchic air to it, and it was almost impossible to tell those prisoners without irons from their friends, families, or the various shopkeepers who moved among them with their wares. Surely, it ought to be possible to smuggle one man out in the melee?

She glanced back at Rupert, his broad back bent over the mirror. Lord Nick would be hard to disguise, but there had to be a way.

Looking back again, she saw Ben shouldering his way through the throng. He carried two panniers slung over his shoulders.

"Here's Ben."

"Ah, good." Rupert wiped the lather from his face with a towel and examined himself in the cracked glass. "I feel a new man. You're a miracle worker, sweeting." He turned and opened his arms to her.

"Just a minor miracle," she said, coming into his arms, resting her head against his breast. "I'm sure I can work a bigger one."

He stroked her hair, ran a tracing finger over the line of her jaw, but said nothing.

"Ah, there y'are, Nick. I see miss 'as brought ye some fresh raiment." Breathing heavily from the steep climb with his burdens, Ben came into the room. His voice was cheerful, but it was belied by his haunted eyes and drawn countenance.

"Bessie's sent me with enough victuals to feed an army." He dumped the panniers onto the table.

"Young Amy's nose really will be out of joint," Octavia said, jumping off the sill. "She's Nick's laundress, Ben, and most possessive. Practically tried to throw me out."

Ben regarded her in some astonishment. "Beggin' yer pardon, miss, but I'm not surprised. Right little trollop ye looks."

Octavia offered him a merry twirl. "I doubt my identity will be compromised in this guise."

"No, reckon not," Ben said.

"Well, I'll leave you two together," Octavia said. "I have some errands to run."

"Not dressed like that, I trust." Rupert raised his eyebrows.

"No, dressed as Lady Warwick," she said. "It wouldn't do for both of us to disappear from society at this point. People believe you're out of town for a few days, and they must continue to believe that. When you reappear, we don't wish for any awkward questions."

The two men exchanged a look; then Rupert said, "No sign of Frank, I suppose."

"Not so far." She came over to kiss him. "I'll come back this afternoon . . . as the veiled lady. Is there anything you want me to bring?"

"A chess set and books. Ask your father's advice. Something that will occupy my mind . . . some Roman history, perhaps."

Octavia nibbled her bottom lip. "He thinks you're away on business. How can I explain such a request?"

"You'll think of something," he said, kissing her brow. "You'll find money in the strong box in my book room, if you need it. The key is in the top drawer of the desk. You'll also find the deeds to Hartridge Folly in the box."

"Already? You have the house from those swine?"

"Almost. There are a couple of formalities to go through first. But Ben knows what to do."

"Aye, that I do," Ben said, nodding. "Don't fret yerself on that score, missie."

"I wasn't," she said truthfully. How to explain now what a hollow triumph it seemed?

"Until later, then?" She managed a smile and left them.

Rupert went to the window, watching as she reappeared beneath. She looked up and waved. He waved back and stood looking as she threaded her way through the crowd to the dark, narrow passage leading to the great gate. He watched her say something to the gate keeper at the entrance to the passage, her head in its bright kerchief nodding briskly; then she passed on and disappeared onto Holborn, into the freedom of the outside world.

He turned back to Ben. "Well, old friend. Let's not be melancholy. I've some instructions for you."

"Aye." Ben sat down at the table and pulled one of the panniers to him. "Let's take a glass of port while we're about it."

వ⌐

Octavia hurried along Holborn. Rupert had given up. He'd given up before they'd even begun. How could he do such a thing? Maybe no one *had* ever escaped from Newgate, although she found that hard to believe; but even so, there had to be a first time. She would not give up. And she would not give up her part in their joint venture, either. Maybe if she got the ring back, Rupert would see that there was still a future, if he'd fight for it.

And even if he couldn't see that—even if he continued to believe there was no future—at least he'd have the satisfaction of knowing that he had redressed whatever dread injury Philip Wyndham had done him. He might say that there was no longer anything to be gained by it. He might say that he would carry the secret to his grave. But she would prove him wrong.

How to do it, though?

She ducked into an alley as a crowd of chanting, banner-waving apprentices surged up the street toward her.

"No popery . . . no popery." The familiar chant filled the sultry air. Their faces glistened with sweat and enthusiasm as they passed. One of them bent and picked up a stone. It crashed into a pastry cook's stall.

"Eh, you!" The pastry cook bobbed up from behind the stall, red-faced with outrage. "You there! What d'ye think you're doin'?"

"No popery!" the lad jeered. "You write that on yer stall, mate, and you won't get no more stones." Someone laughed, and a chorus of agreement swelled in the ranks of the group. Another stone flew to crash harmlessly against a door post across the street.

Octavia drew back into the shadows. Something ugly was in the air.

She waited until they had passed and then went on her way, reflecting how strange it was that a few short hours ago

Rupert's deceit and trickery had assumed such ghastly proportions in her mind—so ghastly that she couldn't imagine ever being able to forgive, and certainly never to forget. And now it seemed the merest nothing. A misunderstanding that had happened between two people before they had known each other. Rupert had had a desperate plan that had required desperate measures, and he had simply used what measures were at his disposal.

At his disposal. She stopped abruptly in the middle of the road. Bessie had presumably supplied the drug. If there were drugs that could release such responses, surely there could be drugs that would do the opposite.

She stood still as the idea blossomed. It was perfect. All she needed was Bessie's cooperation. And for Nick, Bessie would do anything.

Chapter 23

Letitia stood in the empty nursery, her arms crossed over her breast. She felt as if she'd lost a limb, or as if the blood had ceased to flow to a part of herself, deep inside. Susannah's crib, hung with filmy pink gauze, still stood beside the window, but the delicate baby smell, that enticing melange of new-drawn milk and vanilla, no longer invested the air.

Letitia moved around the room, her fingers trailing over the chest, the low armless chair where she'd rocked her child. She picked up a knitted lamb with a pink ribbon around its neck. Susannah had loved it and somehow it had been forgotten in the flurry of departure. Was she crying for it?

The nursery at Wyndham Manor was a low-ceilinged room high under the eaves. The furniture was heavy and old-fashioned, the walls crossed with oak beams, the floor sloping and creaky. Unlike this bright, airy room overlooking the London square. A room where Susannah's cooing still echoed in the corners and Letitia could still see her toothless smile from the crib.

She replaced the knitted lamb on the mantelpiece and went to the door, her step slow and reluctant. It was already the beginning of June. It wouldn't be long now before society made its exodus from town and dispersed to the country or to the fashionable spas like Bath.

Philip had not yet told her what his plans would be for the summer, but she couldn't believe they wouldn't include some time at Wyndham Manor. However, she didn't want to ask him in case her anxiety was too apparent. If he sensed it, he would exploit it, and maybe deprive her of a visit to Sussex altogether.

As she descended the staircase, she heard the butler greeting a visitor in the hall below. Letitia turned to go back upstairs. She was expecting no visitors of her own and had no wish to meet any of Philip's.

Then she paused, listening, as a woman's voice said, "If you'd be so good as to ask Lord Wyndham if I could have a word with him on urgent business."

"I'll tell his lordship that you're here, ma'am," the butler replied. "If you'd like to wait in the salon."

Letitia nibbled a fingernail. The voice was Lady Warwick's. Did she have another assignation with Philip? Somehow Letitia had gleaned the impression that all was not smooth sailing in that ocean, but whether that was because the lady was playing hard to get, or Philip was losing interest, she couldn't guess.

She remained where she was as her husband crossed the hall, his booted feet clicking on the marble tiles. He opened the door to the salon, and his voice, cool and ironic, rose upward.

"Lady Warwick. This is an unexpected pleasure. To what do I—" The door closed on the rest of his sentence.

Letitia thoughtfully made her way to her own apartments. If matters were awry between her husband and his mistress, she devoutly hoped that they were about to be put right. Philip's mood was even more vicious and volatile these days, and he was paying his wife far more attention than she could stoically endure.

In the salon Octavia smiled warmly at the earl, drawing off her gloves as she stepped toward him.

"Philip, my dear, I had to come and apologize for that

stupid business the other day. I am so embarrassed and discomfited." She clapped her palms to her cheeks as if to cool their heated flush, and her eyes fixed him with a pleading, self-deprecating gaze.

"I'm to assume you're no longer indisposed," he remarked, unsmiling. He turned to the decanter on the table and poured two glasses of wine, taking a sip of his own before carrying the second glass to her.

"Thank you," she said almost timidly. "I know you have every right to be put-out, Philip. It was a damnably inconvenient thing to happen. But so was being held up by that dreadful man."

She shuddered and took a large sip. "Thank heavens they have him fast in Newgate. Shall you go to see him hanged?"

Philip laughed. "How bloodthirsty you sound, my dear. But yes, most certainly I shall."

He regarded her over the lip of his glass, thinking how desirable she was with those enormous liquescent eyes and the pink flush on her cheekbones against the ivory tints of her complexion. His eye drifted to her bosom, swelling gently above the lace edging to her gown of pale-green cambric over a white muslin petticoat. A sash of dark-green velvet accentuated her waist and the curve of her hips.

He licked his lips unconsciously as a greedy rush of desire filled his loins, brought a mist of perspiration to his brow. She was there because she wanted him, too. No other reason would have brought her, after that humiliation, to issue such a mortifying apology.

He placed his glass on the table. "Come here."

She came to him with gratifying obedience, her step quick, her smile tentative yet eager. He pulled her against him, catching her face between his hands, bending her head back on her neck with the pressure of his mouth as he assaulted her lips and the delicate softness of her mouth.

She moaned and moved sinuously against him, pressing her loins to the fullness of his, her hands sliding over his body, under his coat, around to his buttocks to grip and knead with busy fingers.

"Goddammit, Octavia," he said savagely, as he raised his head just as she was afraid her neck would snap. "Goddammit, but you drive me to madness, woman! I *will* have you!"

"Yes . . . yes," she whispered. "Soon . . . when . . . it must be soon."

She looked up into his intent face, his eyes slate-gray slits. Such a beautiful face, Octavia thought. But something was wrong with it. Again she was haunted by that strange, disorienting sense of something familiar gone awry.

She closed her eyes on a sigh of immoderate passion, concealing whatever expression he might otherwise have read in her gaze, and moved against him with a little moan of need.

"Where's your husband?"

The rasping question shocked her, although she'd been prepared for it. A little quiver ran through her as she said, "He had to go to the country, to see to estate business. He won't be back for a se'ennight."

"Then I will come to you," he declared, pinching her chin between finger and thumb. "I want no more jauntering over hills and dales, madam. I will come to Dover Street tonight."

"Very well," she said. "I am going to the play with some friends, and supper in the Piazza afterward. If you come after midnight, I will be waiting for you. And there will be no prying eyes upon the street."

"Until then," he said, releasing her chin, his fingers leaving bloodless indentations. "The butler will see you out." Without another word he left her standing in the middle of the salon.

Octavia rubbed the bruising fingermarks on her chin, then briskly drained her glass and stalked to the door just as the butler appeared.

"This way, madam."

He escorted her to the front door rather as if she were a doubtful guest who might have pocketed the silver. Her sedan chair was waiting in the street, and she stepped in, unaware of the eyes on her from an upstairs window, where

Letitia stood, wondering what could bring a woman voluntarily to seek out Philip Wyndham.

The sky was heavy with thunder clouds, and large drops of rain began to fall as the chairmen trotted through the streets. When they reached the house on Dover Street, they carried the chair up the steps and into the hall so that their passenger was spared the necessity of getting her coiffure wet or putting a foot to the damp ground.

"Pay the men, Griffin," Octavia instructed as she stepped out of the chair. "I suppose there's been no sign of Frank?"

"I have a suspicion, my lady, that the little devil's hanging around the back." The butler paid off the chairmen from a leather wallet he carried in his pocket and nodded to the footman to see them out.

"Cook thinks so too. He won't show himself properly, but we keep catching a glimpse of his shadow, like. And Cook put a plate of iced buns on the step this morning, and they were gone in a jiffy."

"Sounds like Frank's tastes," Octavia said. "Maybe he'll show himself properly if we continue to leave food for him. At least it'll show him that we're not angry with him. He's probably afraid we're going to give him up to the constables."

"If you ask me, my lady, that's the best thing to do," the butler stated. "Can't go around encouraging the thieving little beggars . . . begging your pardon for speaking so freely, ma'am."

Octavia shook her head ruefully. "Feel free to speak your mind, Griffin. But I have no intention of giving the child up to the law. And neither has Lord Warwick."

"No, my lady." The butler bowed. "We should expect his lordship's return at the beginning of next week, I understand."

"Yes," Octavia said, her voice slightly muffled as she turned to the stairs. "Unless there's a put-off." She hurried up the stairs, refusing to think beyond the expected week of Rupert's absence. He *would* come back.

And in the meantime she had her mission to complete with Philip Wyndham. A scene of seduction to set.

She looked around her bedchamber where Nell was going through her wardrobe, checking for garments that needed pressing or mending. It was a pleasant room, and it was utterly redolent of Rupert. Everywhere she looked there was a physical memory. They had played in this room throughout the hours of many a long night. She would not entertain Philip Wyndham in here.

"Nell, would you have flowers put in the small salon?" She wandered over to the armoire, wondering what to wear.

"And tell Griffin I would like supper to be laid out in there for when I return from the theatre. I'm expecting a guest and I won't wish to be disturbed. So . . . something we can serve ourselves. Oysters, perhaps. Crab patties. Smoked goose. And champagne, of course."

"Yes, m'lady." Nell bobbed a curtsy. "What gown will you wear to the theatre?"

"I'm trying to decide." Octavia riffled through the rich materials crowding the armoire. "The gold taffeta, I think."

It was an extravagant gown, richly embroidered in silver thread, fitting tightly at the bosom and waist, but flowing from her shoulders at the back in a billowing saque.

It was one of Rupert's favorites.

Tears blinded her, clogged her throat. She swallowed vigorously. She must think of nothing but the present. Live each moment as it happened. Anticipate no future. Expect nothing. Tonight she was going to get the ring from Philip. That was all she needed to think about.

But it was an interminable evening. Her stomach was alive with spiders, her palms damp with apprehension. Somehow she managed to respond to her companions, to give the Prince of Wales what he wanted and expected when he came to their box in the interval. She flirted, teased, joked, and no one would have guessed the agony of her soul as she fought to keep from her mind the thought of Rupert in Newgate. The thought of Rupert in the cart on the way to Tyburn.

Her eyes had a febrile glitter, her cheeks a somewhat hectic flush, but if anyone gave it a thought, it was simply ascribed to champagne and the pleasures of the evening.

At supper she picked at a portion of green goose and sipped burned champagne. Her head was beginning to ache with the noise, the glitter of myriad candles in the supper room, and the effort of keeping up her end of the conversation. She could hear her voice rasping a little, her sentences sometimes not coming out properly. But her companions were so merry, and so awash with champagne that her own lack of coherence went unnoticed.

She kept expecting to see the Earl of Wyndham, but he didn't appear.

It was soon after midnight when her carriage returned her to Dover Street.

"Everything is as you wished in the small salon, my lady." Griffin bowed her in, his voice expressionless. Whatever he thought about Lady Warwick's entertaining tête-à-tête in her husband's absence was not to be revealed.

"Thank you. When my guest arrives, you may show him up, then you may go to bed. The night porter will lock up when his lordship leaves."

Octavia didn't look at Griffin to see the effect of her words as she handed him her cloak. She went swiftly up the stairs to the small salon at the back of the house, drawing off her long silk gloves. The curtains were drawn, the room softly lit with two branched candelabra, the air perfumed with bowls of roses.

She examined the dishes laid on a round table beside the window. Pearly oysters glistening in their craggy gray shells; an asparagus tart; a covered dish of scalloped potatoes keeping warm on a chafing dish; a platter of macaroons and a bowl of strawberries. Two bottles of champagne.

Octavia nodded her satisfaction. She was perfectly calm, her hands completely steady as she placed her gloves and fan on the sideboard. Completely steady, as she opened a drawer in a console table and took out a little screw of paper, slipping it into her bosom.

A chaise longue upholstered in straw-colored taffeta

stood before the Chinese screen in the empty hearth. Octavia plumped up the cushions, smoothed the taffeta. It was an inviting piece of furniture, easy to recline upon, no inconvenient arms to get in the way.

Then she stood and waited for the footsteps in the corridor outside.

Too keyed up to sit down, she waited and listened, and yet the footfall outside still took her by surprise. Griffin knocked and at her invitation opened the door and stepped aside.

The Earl of Wyndham walked in, slapping his gloves against the palm of one hand, eyes assessing the room and its furnishings.

"Thank you, Griffin."

"Good night, my lady." The door closed behind the departing butler.

"You came," she said, smiling.

"Did you doubt it?" He threw his gloves onto a chair and massaged his fingers. His knuckles cracked.

"I trusted," she responded, coming toward him. "I have been in such suspense all evening. I hoped so much to see you at the theatre, but I was doomed to disappointment." Her shoulders lifted expressively. "And now you're here."

His mouth curved in a smile of such complacence that Octavia was hard pressed to keep down the surge of repulsion. She wanted to stick a knife between his ribs and twist it slowly. Instead she took his hands and drew him toward the chaise longue.

"Will you sit, my lord, and allow me to bring you a glass of champagne?"

"Bring the bottle to me and I'll open it." He sat down, lounging against the scrolled back.

"No, sir. You have no tasks to perform this evening except for one." Her eyebrows lifted, and her mouth curved in a wickedly suggestive smile that reminded him of the spirited woman he'd first been drawn to. It pleased him to see this resurrection after their last couple of meetings, and his eyes snapped with satisfaction.

He turned his head lazily against a cushion, watching her back as she busied herself with the champagne bottle. The cork emerged with a discreet pop, and he listened to the fizz as she poured the pale wine.

"So, my lord. A toast." Smiling radiantly, she came back to him with two glasses. "I propose a toast to satisfaction, Philip."

He laughed and took the glass. "I've always admired your spirit, my dear. Does your husband appreciate it, I wonder?"

Her eyes were lowered for a second. "Hardly at all, my lord. It's wasted on him, I fear." She touched his glass with her own. "First my toast, and then it's for you to make one."

He drank and her eyes held his. Then he frowned.

"Is something the matter?"

"No. I'm trying to think of a suitable toast."

Octavia sipped her champagne and waited.

"Ah, I have it. To the comfort of lovers and the discomfort of husbands." His harsh laughter rasped in the quiet room, accompanied by Octavia's tiny little chuckle. But again she lowered her eyes, and he saw only her smiling mouth.

"I would see you naked," he said abruptly, his laughter dying, his narrowed eyes taking on the predatory glitter that sent a shudder of apprehension and loathing along her spine.

But Octavia smiled and sat down beside him. "Why, sir, let us dally a little over the champagne. I will take off one garment, and then you will remove one."

Philip sipped his wine. "So you would direct this play, madam?"

"I wish only to enhance the pleasure," she said humbly.

Why wouldn't he finish the wine? Bessie had said it would take half an hour for the effects to be felt. She didn't want to gallop along the road to seduction.

"You will enhance my pleasure by your obedience," he

said with a touch of ice to his voice. He took another sip. "Bring the bottle here. And then disrobe."

Octavia rose and fetched the bottle. She would just have to do as he ordered very slowly. Strangely, she was not unduly concerned about revealing her body to Philip Wyndham. If it proved necessary, then it was a very minor sacrifice to make. But she did need to get *his* clothes off. Or at least beyond his waistcoat.

Bending over him, she refilled his glass, thankfully noting that it was almost empty. She allowed her breasts to brush against his chest as she bent farther to kiss his neck.

Philip's fingers found her breasts, curling over the delicate swell, sliding into her decolletage to find her nipples. Octavia grimly closed her mind and devoted all her attention to the business of getting his waistcoat off.

It took fifteen minutes of nibbling, nuzzling, moaning. But her heart surged with triumph when she slid the garment from his shoulders and tossed it with apparent indifference to the floor, before with greedy, fumbling fingers unbuttoning his shirt.

Philip lay back, exulting in her passionate need to touch his body. She now wore only her lace-trimmed shift as she moved over him, and with a savage movement he tore the material from neck to hem.

Octavia gasped and fought the urge to fling herself away from him. When he rolled her beneath him, she closed her eyes tight. There could be no put-off now unless he instigated it.

And then suddenly his rough, excited movements ceased. He stared down at her, a flash of puzzlement in his eyes.

She reached up and touched his cheek, smiling seductively. "Shall I feed you some oysters before we proceed, my lord?"

He moved off her. "Yes. Fetch them . . . and bring the other bottle." As she slipped off the chaise, he grabbed the collar at the back of her torn shift and dragged it away from her.

Naked, Octavia stood up. But now she was completely

indifferent to her nakedness, all her attention focused on the waistcoat. Now was her chance.

As she moved across the room to the table, she casually kicked the garment with her foot. As casually, she bent and picked it up, shook it out, carefully laid it across the arm of a chair. The garment was in her hands for no more than a second; then she had reached the table. Her fingers lightly brushed over the petals of a deep-pink rose before she picked up the platter of oysters and came back to the couch.

Perching on the edge of the couch, she held a craggy shell to the earl's lips. Philip opened his mouth, and the succulent morsel slid down his throat. Steadily, she fed him the better part of a dozen, smiling to herself at the thought that he was swallowing them with such eagerness because they were a known aphrodisiac, and for some extraordinary reason Philip found himself in sore need of an aphrodisiac.

Never before had he experienced this confusing, mortifying powerlessness. Nothing he tried, nothing that he made her try, had any effect. Her smile became doubtful, hesitant, and then anxious. A deep loathing filled him as he stared down into that smooth, beautiful face, the golden eyes wide with astonishment at this extraordinary failure from a man who'd promised to possess her as she had never been possessed before. She was a witch, he thought with a surge of savagery. Three times, through some kind of demonic workings, she'd foiled him. She smiled and touched and offered soft words of encouragement and sympathy, but beneath that madonnalike facade he saw now the twisted cunning of a sorceress.

He left her an hour later. He left, cursing her in vile words as if she were a whore who'd failed to please him. He left her with deep finger bruises on her arms and breasts. But he left her essentially untouched.

Octavia listened to his feet on the stairs. She listened for the opening and closing of the front door by the night porter. Then she ran to the bowl of roses on the table. The tiny pouch was tucked into a curling leaf, snug against a thorny stem.

Her fingers trembled for the first time that evening as

she lifted the pouch from its resting place. She opened it and shook the tiny ring onto the palm of her hand. It exactly matched the one Rupert had shown her. She pressed the eye of the bird with the tine of a dessert fork on the table. The mechanism sprang open, and she pictured it fitted to that other ring to form a signet ring.

Her hand closed fiercely over her dearly won prize.

She had it.

And now that she had it, what next?

She went to the window and flung back the curtains. Gray streaked the eastern sky. She opened her palm and looked at the circular imprint of the ring where it had dug into her skin.

Was Rupert's life worth this ring? Was any vengeance worth risking the hangman? What kind of injury could cause such a man as Rupert to risk his life to avenge it?

Octavia shivered, aware for the first time of her nakedness. The crimson glow of triumph faded, leaving her feeling cold and gray and bleak.

Turning back to the room, she gathered up her clothes, dressing herself as decently as she could to make the quick dash to her own apartments.

How long would it take Philip to discover the loss of the ring? Somehow she didn't think he would go straight home. He would visit the stews, find some whore on whom he could wreak his rage and humiliation. But daylight would presumably bring him banging on the front door. It wouldn't occur to him in a month of mad Sundays that Octavia might have purloined his ring, so presumably he'd make excuses for searching the parlor. Always assuming he could bring himself to face again the scene of such mortification. He wouldn't want to see her, of that Octavia was convinced.

But before he came, both she and the ring would be safely out of the house. The gates of Newgate opened in two hours, at seven, and Lord Nick would receive the veiled lady as soon as visitors were permitted.

She tugged on the bellpull to summon Nell and began to throw off her evening dress.

"Y'are up betimes, my lady." The maid hurried in fifteen minutes later, blinking sleepily. She set a tray of hot chocolate and sweet biscuits on a table and tried to stifle a yawn.

"Yes, I'm sorry to wake you so early, but I have an errand to run," Octavia said. "Lay out my riding habit." She poured a cup of chocolate and dipped a biscuit into the steaming drink. A sleepless night had made her hungry. Or at least she assumed hunger and fatigue were responsible for her queasiness and the uncontrollable shivers that ran through her.

She certainly felt stronger after the chocolate and biscuits, and her face, after the application of hot water, looked a little less drawn.

"Should I tell Mr. Griffin to summon the carriage, my lady?" Nell pinned up the cinnamon hair in a knot at the nape of Octavia's neck.

"No, I shall walk," Octavia said. "Pass me the black hat with the veil."

Nell obliged, hiding her curiosity as her mistress adjusted the hat and dropped the veil over her face. "The black cloak, my lady?"

"Thank you." Swathed in anonymity, Octavia hastened from the house.

Griffin, summoned early from his own bed by his mistress's unusually early call for her maid, closed the door behind her as she hurried down the street in the fresh morning air. He was frowning as he went to his breakfast. Entertaining a gentleman late into the night in the absence of her husband and then leaving at crack of dawn, on foot and unescorted, dressed as if for a funeral, was not the usual behavior of a fashionable lady. Or at least, he amended, the early-morning jaunt in that strange garb wasn't.

Octavia hailed a hackney on the corner of Piccadilly, gave the jarvey directions to Holborn, and sat on the very edge of the seat as the vehicle swayed over the cobbles and the cries of the street sellers rose on the morning air.

The ring was in the palm of her hand inside her glove, and her fingers were closed tightly over it. With her other hand she hung convulsively on to the strap above the window as she perched precariously on the edge of the seat, unable to relax sufficiently to sit back.

Her eyes were on the window aperture, monitoring their progress, and she realized she was murmuring encouragement to the driver under her breath, urging him to increase his speed; and once, when he took a turn that she thought was out of the way, she had to restrain herself from banging on the ceiling to put him right.

But eventually he drew up outside the prison. "This what you want, lady?"

He sounded doubtful, leaning down from the box as Octavia stepped out of the carriage.

She made no reply, merely handed him his fare, before hurrying to the gate. The gate keeper peered at her veiled countenance. "Who you come fer?"

"The highwayman, Lord Nick," she said in a low muffled voice.

"Does all right fer visitors, that gennelman does," the gate keeper said jovially, unlocking the postern gate. "Quite a party 'e 'ad last even. Sent out fer 'alf a dozen bottles of sherry an' the makin's fer a punch bowl. Very jolly they was. Very merry."

Octavia again refrained from comment, assuming Ben and Rupert's other cronies from the Royal Oak had made up the party. And who was she to object if his friends came to cheer him up? If only she could persuade them to help her come up with a way to effect his escape.

She crossed the press-yard, already thronged with prisoners and their families, and went through the internal gate leading to the spacious chambers on the state side. She ran up the stairs, glancing occasionally into the rooms she passed where doors stood ajar. They were all comfortably furnished with what seemed in some cases to be their occupant's personal possessions.

She had brought Rupert's books and the chess set, but she could arrange for more comforts to be brought in. A decent bed, chair, washstand.

His door was closed and she raised her hand to knock, then changed her mind and lifted the latch. The door swung open and she stepped inside.

"Amy? Bring me some tea, there's a good girl." Rupert's sleepy voice came from a mound of bedclothes on the narrow cot. "I've a head on me to fell a prizefighter!"

"Serves you right!" Octavia declared, throwing off her veil. She bounded across the room and jumped on him, sitting heavily astride him. "I hear you had a great party last night, with punch and immoderate quantities of sherry."

"Oh, you weigh a ton!" Rupert moaned, heaving himself onto his back in an effort to dislodge her. "Get off me, woman!"

"No!" Leaning over, she pulled the covers off his face and kissed him. "How could you amuse yourself without me?"

"I doubt you'd have enjoyed it, sweeting," he said with another groan. "We played cards all night and I lost a fortune."

"Well, I brought you some more money," she said, settling herself firmly on his belly. "And books and a chess set . . . and something else."

Rupert squinted up at her. He could feel her suppressed excitement, the currents of tension running through her. She looked happy, almost convincingly so, as if the cheerful exterior was not simply masking her dread and despair.

"What else?"

She drew off her gloves with an air of great mystery and slowly uncurled her palm. Delicately she extracted the ring from the little silk pouch and dropped it onto his chest.

"What the hell . . . ?" His hand closed over it but he stared at her, and his eyes were abruptly filled with a dark and savage fury. "What did you do for this?"

Octavia's stomach began to churn. She hadn't known what to expect, but she hadn't expected to see this terrifying rage. "Nothing, really," she said, shaking her head.

"Get off me!"

His voice was low, but the command was so ferocious, she had scrambled to the floor without realizing it.

Rupert flung aside the bedclothes and stood up. "Damn you, Octavia! I told you it was over. I told you I would not have you involving yourself with that sewer rat! Now, what did you do? Tell me. Every damn thing!"

"Nothing. I . . ."

"Tell me!" His eyes were great holes in a face that had the gray-white tinge of a corpse.

Octavia pressed her fingers to her lips, struggling to gather her senses. Her voice as leaden as a winter sky, she told him how she'd sought Bessie's help. She described the encounter with Philip as flatly and objectively as she could, hoping with her cold, clear words to distance the reality, to banish the ghastly degrading images she could see flying through his mind. But his face grew grayer, his eyes emptier, and finally she lost her composure.

Her voice cracked as she stepped toward him, one hand outstretched in appeal. "Oh, God, Rupert. *Please* don't be so angry. I did it for you. I wanted to show you that you mustn't give up. That things can be done . . . that . . ."

"Quiet!" he thundered, thrusting her hand away. "You talk arrant, self-deceiving nonsense. This place is not an illusion. Grow up, woman, and face the truth."

"No." She shook her head. "No, I won't face your truth. It's not the truth. There is a way."

"Go home, Octavia," he said with abrupt weariness. "It doesn't help me to listen to your fairy tales."

"But—"

"Go home, I say!"

"You be wantin' yer breakfast now, Lord Nick?" Amy's pert voice came from the doorway. "Now that yer visitor's leavin'."

She glanced at Octavia with smoldering triumph. Clearly she'd been listening to the last exchange.

"Yes, and bring me tea and hot water," Rupert said.

He turned from Octavia and strode to the window where he stood looking out into the yard. He opened his hand and Philip's ring fell to the floor. It rolled across the boards and came to rest against the skirting, a bright circle in the dust.

Octavia dropped the veil over her face. The sound of her running feet stumbling down the stairs echoed in his head.

Chapter 24

꩜ It was a long time before Rupert moved from the window. Amy brought in his tea and breakfast, but he didn't turn as she set it down with a clatter of crockery and cutlery.

"This'll get cold, sir, if 'n ye don't eats it soon."

"Leave it, Amy."

"Well, will there be anythin' else? Should I jest tidy up while—"

"Leave, girl!"

Amy backed to the door and scuttled away without another word.

Rupert bent and picked up Philip's ring. He let it lie in his palm before taking out his own from his shirt pocket and slowly marrying the two. He slipped the signet ring onto his right hand and held it up to the light. The eyes of the bird seemed to gleam knowingly at him from an exquisitely engraved tree branch.

He had it. And when Philip saw the whole ring on Rupert Warwick's finger, he would know his twin again. Watching that knowledge dawn on his twin's face would be Rupert's moment of vengeance. All that would follow from it would be simply restitution. Philip might try to fight publicly Rupert's claim to be the missing Cullum Wyndham, but once he saw the ring, he would know in his blood that he couldn't succeed. And he would know that the harder he fought, the more fool he would look.

The ring would serve as Cullum Wyndham's introduction to the family lawyers and the family doctor, those who would find concrete proof of the returned heir's identity when they examined and interrogated him. His body bore scars and marks that the doctor would know, and the claimant possessed details of domestic history that only a member of the family could know.

The ring would bring Philip's house of cards tumbling to the dust.

And the ring bound Cullum to uphold the honor of the Wyndhams, preventing him from forcing his brother to face his own ruin and his own past. Revealing his identity now would drag the name of Wyndham through the mud. It would broadcast to the world that the true Earl of Wyndham was a common highwayman on his way to the hangman. And he couldn't do that. He could not dishonor Gervase's memory.

Hell and damnation! Rupert poured himself a mug of tea and gulped it down, scalding his tongue and the back of his throat. But the burning liquid cleared his head.

He refilled the mug, then began to pace his prison, unable to lose the images of Octavia tangling with his twin.

It didn't matter that she'd outwitted Philip . . . that she'd subjected him to the most telling mortification a man could endure. She had still exposed herself to the hands and mouth of a vicious cur, and she'd done it without Rupert's knowledge and at a time when he could do nothing to help her. She was quite without protection and he was stuck in this place, helpless. Powerless to alter his own situation or to have a role in Octavia's.

Didn't she understand how that made him feel? How his frustration and his self-contempt were a sour well bubbling deep inside him. And instead of understanding, sympathizing, lending him gentle sweetness and comfort, she had put herself in danger. She had acted, while he could only sit and twiddle his thumbs and contemplate his execution. And what she'd done was futile. Pointless. His secret must go to his grave. And the possession of the ring now only highlighted the powerlessness of his position. The futility of his vengeance.

"Don't ye want yer breakfast, sir?"

Amy's voice piping hesitantly from the door brought his head up from morose contemplation of the ring. "No, take it away."

"I could bring ye summat else, mebbe. A slice of rare beef, per'aps." She looked at him with hopeful eyes.

Rupert struggled for patience. "If I want anything, I'll call you, Amy."

Disconsolately, the girl took out the laden tray, and Rupert resumed his pacing.

He could find patience with Amy, but not with Octavia, he reflected with a surge of remorse, seeing again the deep hurt and shock in her tawny eyes, the tremulous line of her mouth, hearing again the desperate appeal in that rich voice.

Maybe she wouldn't come back. He could hardly blame her. But, dear God in heaven, how could he endure this captivity, this hideous impotence, another minute?

Ben's unmistakable tread on the stone stairs outside helped him to break the spiraling panic. There were two sets of footsteps.

"See who I've brought ye, Nick." Ben marched in, very smartly dressed in his Sunday clothes and a powdered wig. His companion was dressed most elegantly in gray silk, with a black silk ribbon around the queue of his white wig.

The stranger's occupation was clear to Rupert before Ben finished the introduction with a grand flourish. " 'Is Honor Mr. St. John Moreton, barrister-at-law."

"Mr. Moreton." Rupert bowed.

"Sir." The barrister returned the bow and looked around. "I see your friends have ensured your comfort."

"For the moment," Rupert agreed.

"They have also retained me to represent you. I am, of

course, doing all I can to put off the trial," the barrister added as if it were self-evident.

"Because to hasten it would hasten my execution?" Rupert inquired dryly.

"My dear sir, we don't talk like that!" the barrister exclaimed. "No such thing . . . no such thing."

"No, that's right," Ben put in stoutly. "An' miss is right, y'know, Nick. She said we've given up afore we've even started."

Rupert sighed. "The facts speak for themselves, Ben."

The barrister coughed. "If I might ask for some details of the facts, Lord Nick. Perhaps you have another name?" He raised his eyebrows. "A name less . . . well, less notorious, shall we say? One a little less likely to raise the judge's hackles."

"No," Rupert said coolly. "I'm sorry to have to disappoint you, Mr. Moreton, but Lord Nick is how I will be known at my trial."

The barrister looked disappointed. "As you please, of course. But it's strongly against my advice."

"Duly noted." Rupert ran a hand through his disordered locks. "Much as I appreciate your interest, I really don't feel we have anything useful to discuss at this stage. And I would rather like to make my morning ablutions. . . ." He stroked his unshaven jaw in an explanatory gesture.

The barrister looked most put out and Ben extremely displeased. But if the highwayman wasn't prepared to cooperate in his defense, then there was little anyone could do.

The lawyer left and Ben followed him to the door. There he paused. "You want company, Nick?"

Rupert shook his head. "I'm the devil's own company today, Ben. But don't think I'm not grateful. However, instruct Mr. Moreton to stop his delaying tactics. I want this over with."

Ben shook his head. "What's the point of 'urrying it, Nick?"

"I can't stand the suspense," Rupert responded with a cool smile.

Ben glared at him, clearly not pleased with this attempt to make light of the dire situation. Then he shrugged and stomped off in the barrister's wake.

Rupert flung himself onto the bed and lay staring up at the plaster ceiling. At this rate he was going to drive off all his friends. But why couldn't they understand that there was no comfort to be gained with false hopes? His only possible comfort lay in coming to an acceptance of the inevitable—an acceptance that would enable him to face his death with calm and grace. An acceptance that would enable him to face the loss of Octavia and a love that sang so deeply in his veins, it was intrinsic to his whole.

Perhaps, if he had come to recognize and accept that love earlier, it would have been enough. He would have been able to let go his vengeance and settle for a joy that he was certain came to very few men. Instead, he'd ignored the recognition and focused only on the obsession that had lived with him through every waking moment since Cullum Wyndham had run away from Wyndham Manor. And the obsession had brought him to the foot of Tyburn Tree.

Octavia walked blindly away from Holborn, turning toward the Embankment. Tears ran down her cheeks beneath her veil. She was stunned by the mistake she'd made. Instead of convincing Rupert of the possibility of action, she'd merely underlined for him the powerlessness of his situation. She knew how much he needed to be in control of events. How much he needed to know that every strand was in his hands. And by acting as she'd done, succeeding where he had not, she'd rubbed his nose in his own failure.

By doing something where he could do nothing, she'd made him more vulnerable, not less.

And yet, try as she would, Octavia could not imagine acting other than she had done.

She turned away from the river, back toward the Strand. Her head down, lost in her own misery, she didn't notice anything at first. Then she was pushed against a wall, a blast of foul breath swamped her nostrils, and the sound of running feet and yelling voices penetrated her blind self-absorption. She could see little through the thick veil and pushed it up as she cowered against the wall.

The street was full of people, hurrying, intent, and for the moment silent. They carried staves and bricks, and their faces were contorted into an expression of almost transfixed hatred.

They surged past Octavia, and a yell went up from the end of the street. "To Westminster . . . to Westminster."

They were streaming across Westminster Bridge from St. George's Fields on their way to petition Parliament for the repeal of the Catholic Relief Act. Lord George Gordon had spoken to the masses that morning, and judging from their faces, every word had struck home.

Octavia edged backward into a narrow alley. She didn't want to get caught up in the tide—and what a tide it was. The mass of humanity flowed on and on, and on every face was the same look. The same fanatical glitter, the same twisted features. And every voice now roared their battle cry: "No popery . . . no popery."

A carriage forced its way through the middle of the throng as she cowered in her alley. But no horses drew this vehicle: it was pulled by sweating, exuberant men, and the crowd chanted and cheered, pressing back to allow the carriage passage.

A young man, smiling and waving, appeared in the window, and the crowd roared again and banged on the panels and cheered on the laboring men.

"Lord George . . . Lord George," they yelled. "Make way for Lord George."

Octavia stared, fascinated, at this man who could so inspire such a massive mob. The youngest son of the Duke of Gordon was an unremarkable-looking figure. Bright-eyed and lively, certainly, but not the stuff of which heroes were made. And yet he was the hero of this mad, wild-eyed mob.

There were thousands of them, and she began to wonder if they would ever pass and she could be on her way.

But at last the tide had passed and there were only a few

stragglers in the street. The roar of the crowd could still be heard, however, and it was a sound that sent a shiver down Octavia's spine.

She hurried home along Piccadilly, where she noticed that the merchants were boarding up their shops and people were gathered on corners, whispering and looking anxiously around. Several people were painting "No popery" slogans on their doors and shutters—a talisman against the mob if it should turn violent.

And after what she'd seen, Octavia had little doubt that it would take almost nothing for that to happen. If Parliament refused their petition, if one man stood against them, they would turn into a pack of ravening wolves.

She turned into Dover Street, breathless, her tears dried, superseded by trepidation at being on the streets in this volatile atmosphere.

As she ran up the steps to the front door, a small voice piped from the basement steps beneath. "Ye've got to write 'no popery' on yer door, Miss Tavi."

"Frank!" She leaned over the rail, peering down at the small figure huddling on a step. "Where have you been? We've been so worried about you."

Frank stood up, but he was ready to run, a small animal sniffing the wind, his eyes sharp, frightened, watching her every move. "You goin' to 'and me over to the beak?"

"No," she said. "Come on up here. No one's going to hurt you, I promise."

Frank, however, remained where he was. "I jest comes to tell you to write that thing on yer door. I 'eard 'em talkin'. They're goin' to burn any 'ouse that doesn't 'ave it."

"Who did you hear?"

"Men in the tavern. I was 'idin' under the table . . . catchin' scraps. I 'eard what they said. So you do it, Miss Tavi."

Before she could say anything else, he'd gone in one swift, darting movement, up the area steps and off along the street as if all the devils in hell were after him.

"Is that Frank, my lady?" Griffin, who had just opened the door, stared up the street at the flying figure.

"Yes." Octavia stepped into the hall, frowning. "There's mischief afoot, Griffin. Frank says we should paint 'No Popery' on the door if we're not to be burned in our beds. He came to warn us. Interesting, don't you think?"

"Maybe so, ma'am. But why did he run off, in that case?"

"He's still afraid. It takes a long time to gentle such a wounded little creature," she said. "But I think we should take his advice, Griffin."

"Aye, ma'am. There's tales abroad . . . rumors . . . scare-mongering probably, but it's best not to take chances."

"No, I agree." She went to the stairs.

"Oh, by the way, my lady. Lord Wyndham was here earlier. He seemed convinced he'd lost something in the small salon last night." Griffin spoke without expression, his eyes fixed on a copper plate bearing visiting cards.

"Oh? What was it he lost?" Octavia inquired with an air of indifference.

"He wouldn't say, my lady. But he had two footmen and the parlor maid turning the room upside down."

"Did he find it?"

"I don't believe so, ma'am. He was not best pleased when he departed."

"How strange," Octavia said carelessly. "But I daresay, whatever it is will turn up when the room is cleaned."

She continued on her way upstairs. It was to be hoped that Philip would not confront her with his loss. He had no possible reason for suspecting she might have purloined the ring and every reason for avoiding her.

"Octavia, dear child, I'm feeling in need of a little company." Oliver's voice greeted her as she passed his apartments. "I find myself sadly dull today."

"Then I will come and keep you company, Papa," she said.

"Why in the world are you dressed in widow's weeds?"

her father exclaimed, taking in her appearance. "Has something happened to Warwick?"

His voice was sharp, and Octavia was glad of her veil, reflecting as she'd often done that it was almost impossible to be sure what Oliver saw and what he didn't. What he guessed and what he chose to ignore.

"Of course not, Papa. But something's amiss in the streets. Lord George Gordon has held his meeting, and the people are marching on Westminster."

"Oh, are they, indeed!" His eyes lit up and he was immediately diverted. "Then come and tell me all about it."

"I'll just take off my cloak."

She went into her own apartments, deciding that devoting her attention to her father for the rest of the day would be a welcome and peaceful diversion. She would tell Griffin to deny her to all callers and retreat into the hermitage of her childhood.

But there were no callers that day, only news from the streets brought by terrified servants and messengers. The mob, some twenty thousand strong, had presented their petition at St. Stephen's at Westminster. Parliament by a vote of 192 to 6 refused to receive the petition and turned away Lord George and his petitioners.

Throughout the evening and into the night, the city resounded to the sounds of the mob as they raced in large troops on an orgy of destruction. Fires burned against the midnight sky as they torched the houses of ministers and ambassadors and anyone they considered a friend of Catholics.

Twice a mob surged down Dover Street, and Octavia and her father watched from the roof as they waved their burning brands and hurled stones and staves at the windows across the street. Their own house had the talisman upon its door, and the mob passed them by.

At dawn the sound of a pitched battle came from over the roofs from the direction of the Strand. The shrieking of the mob was joined to the roar of soldiers as the military charged with bayonets and horses. The mob came streaming back down Dover Street chasing the soldiers, who fought step by step as they dragged a handful of prisoners they'd arrested to the Old Bailey and Newgate.

"May heaven preserve us," Oliver muttered. "What people do to each other in the name of the living God!"

He turned back to the trap door leading down from the roof into the attic. "I'm for my bed, child. For a few hours, at least."

"I'll stay awhile." She huddled into her cloak, aware of the group of servants behind her, like herself awed and horrified witnesses of the mayhem below.

But a hush seemed to fall over the city as dawn broke and the night's madness and blood-letting gave way to exhaustion. The air was still pungent with smoke, a thick haze hanging over the roofs, when Octavia followed her father's example and went to bed. Her last waking thought was of Rupert.

Did they know in Newgate what was happening in the city? There would be no regular visitors through the little wicket gate. But they would hear the noise. And they would see the arrested rioters brought in. They must surely know, and he would know why she hadn't come to him again. He would know that she hadn't abandoned him just because of this morning.

It started again as evening fell. The hideous screams and shouts, the crash of broken glass, the bright flames, the drink-suffused, maddened faces storming through the streets.

"Where are the soldiers?" Octavia asked, almost in a whisper.

After that early display there was no sign of any opposition to the rioters. Unimpeded, they went about their orgy of destruction, firing the houses of suspected papists and their supporters, dragging priceless books, furniture, draperies, linen, into the streets and making bonfires, dancing black-faced in the eerie light of the flames, broaching at every stop the casks of wine and kegs of beer they raided from the taverns as they went.

"Probably can't find the right person with the authority to order them out," Oliver said with a kind of grim satisfaction. Anarchy pleased him. It had historical precedents that had always fascinated him, and seeing such scenes enacted before his eyes was an empirical treat for the scholar.

Extraordinarily, his explanation seemed to be the only possibility. The mob continued its orgy for four days without let or hindrance, while sensible citizens painted the talisman on their doors and stayed inside and trembled.

Chapter 25

It was on the evening of the eighth of June when Griffin entered the salon. "There's a man come to the kitchen, my lady. He said he must see you immediately." His face was stiff, his voice outraged.

"Eh, get out of my road, man." Ben's voice came from behind the butler, his hands pushing him ungently aside. "Miss, a word wi' you."

Griffin's chagrined expression told Octavia exactly what had happened in the kitchen. The butler had tried and failed to stop this unseemly visitor, and he didn't dare to try again.

"It's all right, Griffin. This man is known to Lord Warwick," she said soothingly, although her heart fluttered wildly and she could feel the pulse in her temple pounding.

Griffin bowed himself out but left the door ajar. Ben closed it. He came over to Octavia, his eyes shining. His face was blackened with soot, his clothes torn.

"The mob's all set to fire Newgate," he said. "Set free them folk the military arrested that first day. There's a group of us reckon we'll see who else we can set free."

Octavia was on her feet in one bound. "You think they can do it? Fire the jail? It's all iron and brick."

"If you'd seen what I've seen these last days, miss, you'd not question the power of fire," Ben said somberly. "But I jest wanted to tell ye what we're about. Thought it might cheer ye a mite."

"Oh, Ben!" To his astonishment and distinct unease, Octavia flung her arms around him and kissed his sooty cheek with heartfelt fervor. "Wait here just a minute, and I'll be ready to come with you."

"Eh, no, miss. This business isn't fer the likes of you!" Ben exclaimed in alarm.

"Pshaw!" Octavia scoffed. "Neither is taking to the king's highway, Ben, and I've done that. And a deal of other things too that make this business very fit for me. Wait here. I'll be no more than five minutes."

She'd whisked herself out of the room before he could think of anything else to say, leaving him to pace the salon, pulling at his chin and wondering how Nick would react to his mistress's involvement.

In less than five minutes she was back, dressed in the bright-orange tavern-wench's costume, the scarlet kerchief around her head, the rough wooden pattens on her feet.

"Come on. I'm probably not dirty enough, but I'll find something to smear on my face and hands as we go."

"Lord love us," Ben muttered. "What'll Bessie say when she sees ye like that?"

"Bessie's here?"

"Aye, a'course. We all are."

"Yes, you would be," Octavia replied, leading the way to a side door. "And what of the new stable boy and Morris?"

There was an edge to her voice as she unlocked the door, and Ben flushed darkly. "Ye've no need to worry about them, miss. They'll not be troublin' anyone again."

There was a finality to his voice that made Octavia's scalp crawl, even though she thought she would cheerfully have driven a sword through both of the men who had betrayed Rupert.

Out in the street all was quiet. But then she saw the shadows in the corners. Shadows that materialized into the familiar faces of the Royal Oak. Lord Nick's friends had come for him. Bessie separated herself from the rest.

"You comin'?" But she sounded approving rather than otherwise and, when Octavia merely nodded, nodded herself and turned back to the group. "Let's be on wi' it."

The streets felt quite different from a few days ago, when Octavia had hurried back from Holborn, frightened of falling foul of the crowd. Or perhaps, she thought, it was because *she* was different. Dressed as she was, surrounded by the folk from the Royal Oak, she blended into the street scene, became a part of the mob instead of an outsider and potential victim. And from down below, as a part of it, the scene looked different, less frightening than when she'd watched from the roof, a distant spectator. And yet she knew the mood of the crowd was both frightening and very dangerous.

All around her were faces suffused with drink, wild-eyed with the heady lunacy of riotous anarchy. They burned and destroyed everything that came into their path, no longer needing the excuse of manifest Catholic sympathy in the owners and occupants of the properties they razed. Octavia was swept along, trying to keep herself in the middle of the group of familiar faces.

At Charing Cross a massive crowd of several hundred came sweeping into the intersection to join with Octavia's own mob.

"To Newgate . . . to Newgate" was on every tongue. They carried sledge hammers, staves, flagons of turpentine, and rags soaked in rosin as they roared toward Holborn.

Octavia, to her horror and astonishment, found herself infected with the crowd's wildness. She heard her own voice yelling in unison, her arm pumping emphatically in the air as the mass of humanity pounded over the cobbles and paving stones, making the ground shake, a behemoth set on destruction. And nowhere did they encounter an obstacle to their progress. It was as if the authorities had abandoned the city to its rioting populace.

The crowd came to a stop outside the great barred gate

of Newgate and the stone facade of the Old Bailey. They stood rows deep, packed shoulder to shoulder, faces glistening in the light of torches held aloft.

Octavia pushed and wriggled her way to the front, no longer needing the protection of familiar faces, her mind as one with the mob's: to get into the prison; to break down that massive, iron-bound gate.

All around her were the contorted, savage faces of the city's underclass, people for whom Newgate was the loathed symbol of their wretched existence, the most dreaded lodging, and the start of the final journey to Tyburn.

The Keeper of the jail appeared on the roof of his house as the mob roared for him.

Octavia fell silent, thinking how slight and insubstantial Mr. Akerman looked up on the roof, flanked by his staff. What could he possibly hope to do to stop such an unstoppable mob?

Defying the odds, Akerman refused to accede to the crowd's bellowed demand that he open the gates and surrender the jail. Octavia shivered as a cold breath of reality pierced the mad euphoria of the march. The Keeper was the representative of the city magistrates. He embodied the authority of the king. Surely, now, the government would summon the militia?

But Akerman and his cohorts disappeared from the roof. The crowd roared, surged toward the gate. Someone attacked the great gate with a sledge hammer, and then the frenzy began.

They flew at the massive stone walls of the prison, swinging crow bars in a paroxysm of energy. They broke into the Keeper's house, and as Octavia watched mesmerized, horrified—yet fascinated—they stripped the house of everything that would burn. Furniture, books, pieces of paneling, floorboards, linens. They made a massive bonfire before the gates and hurled turpentine over the pile. Rosin-soaked rags were ignited and thrust into the bonfire.

The flames crackled, leaped into the air, took hold, became a raging blaze as the crowd fanned the flames, constantly feeding the fire with anything that would burn. Snatching burning brands from the bonfire, they flung them over the walls, onto the roofs of the wards, and into the yards behind.

The crowd was so densely packed around the fire at the gates that Octavia couldn't have fought her way free, even if she'd wished to. She gazed in the same fascinated paralysis as the flames licked at the iron bands, the massive bolts and bars of the door. The faces around her glowed red in the crimson light from hell. Bloodshot eyes stared without any sense of human awareness at the fire's progress, and when the wood finally caught, the roar of triumph could be heard clear across London.

Within the jail Rupert heard the roar rising above the general level of cacophony that had startled him an hour before. The smell of smoke was heavy in the air, and he could see in the press-yard below his window a flaming brand that had been tossed over the wall. Tongues of fire licked across the cobbles toward a wooden platform in the center of the yard.

Amy had been full of stories of the riots during the last few days when the prison had been locked up tight; the prisoners, both those who were untried and those already convicted and sentenced, were kept confined in their wards and cells, the internal gates barred to the yards. But nothing the little laundress had described had prepared Rupert for this assault.

He leaned his elbows on the broad windowsill and stared toward the narrow passage leading to the gate. He could see nothing clearly, and as the fire in the yard below caught the base of the wooden platform, he began to wonder if he was about to be burned to death.

Clearly, some of his fellow inmates had the same fear. Shouts and banging now came from other parts of the prison as prisoners shook the barred gates of the wards, bellowing for information. A woman was screaming from somewhere in the wing to Rupert's left.

Rupert moved back from the window. He was barefoot, wearing only his britches and shirt, and swiftly he pulled on his stockings and boots. He fastened his belt at his waist and thrust his arms into his riding coat. If opportunity was about to knock on his prison door, it would not find him unprepared. Then he returned to the window.

He still could see nothing of the gate itself, but the roaring of the crowd had become even wilder, with a frenzied edge of excitement.

Rupert couldn't see what was happening, but outside, Octavia, her cheeks scorching with the power of the blaze, watched as the gate slipped from one of its top hinges and hung sideways, revealing a narrow gap at the top.

As the crowd continued to pile more fuel onto the fire, the gate began to slip slowly, dragged down by its own weight. For one breathless second there was utter silence as it settled into the pile of ash and glowing embers at its base, before it very, very slowly toppled.

Octavia shielded her face from the heat with her hands as she was thrust forward with the mad, bellowing throng, almost ploughing through the fire itself, scrambling over the burning, broken spars of the gate into the dark, narrow passage beyond that led directly to the press-yard.

Octavia was practically air-borne as the tide of humanity swept her through the passage and out into the yard. She was yelling with them, waving her arms, screaming her jubilation, and as the crowd eddied in the yard, unsure which way to take first, she found her feet and darted across to the building that housed Rupert.

Standing below, she cupped her hands and bellowed; then she saw him at the window and she began to dance, a wild tarantella with her orange skirts flying and her loosened hair whipping around her face, flinging her arms wide in an all-encompassing embrace.

"Come on, sweeting. Enough dancing . . . the gate," Rupert murmured, his heart in his mouth as he waited for this extraordinary scene to be wiped away with a wizard's wand. Any minute would surely bring the soldiers to avenge this violation of one of authority's most sacred institutions.

But even as he murmured to himself in an agony of

suspense, Octavia darted to the gate of the state side, disappearing from his line of sight.

She grabbed a stone and began to hammer on the locked gate and was immediately joined by a group of men with crow bars and sledge hammers, following her lead with no clear purpose except that locked gates must be destroyed.

The wood splintered. Octavia tore at it with her bare hands, but one of the men shouldered her aside.

" 'Old 'ard, missie." He raised his crow bar and brought it down with a massive swing, rending the door from top to bottom.

"My thanks," Octavia gasped, leaping through the gap. "Please help me with the door to the prison room upstairs. It's bound to be locked."

With great good humor they followed her up the stairs, and Rupert stood listening as his door shook beneath repeated blows. Then the lock shivered, cracked, and the door flew open.

"Oh, thank God. Rupert . . . Rupert . . . Rupert!" Half-crying, half-laughing, Octavia exploded into the room, leaping into his arms. The men at the door stared for a minute, then one of them guffawed and clapped his hands, and the others joined in with a ringing burst of laughter and applause.

Rupert glanced over Octavia's head at his saviors. "My thanks," he said.

"Eh, y'are good an' welcome, mate," the leader said, winking. "Wouldn't do to keep a man from 'is lass." Then they turned and clattered down the stairs, pausing at each landing to attack locked doors with their crow bars.

"Come quickly." Octavia pulled Rupert to the door. "I'm so afraid this will turn into a dream and I'll wake up in bed and everything will still be horrible."

"Eh, Nick. Nick . . . come quick, now." Bessie appeared panting in the doorway. "Miss got to ye first, I see. But there's no time to waste."

"Aye, now they'll bring out the troops in no time,"

Ben said, crowding with the others into the doorway behind Bessie.

"Let's get out of here." Rupert caught Octavia's hand and strode to the door. "I'll express my thanks, good friends, at a more suitable moment."

They thrust him out ahead of them, desperately pushing him down the stairs as if at any moment the tide would turn and they'd all be swept back again.

But Newgate jail was open that night to all who chose to come and go. The Keeper's house was burning merrily, its occupants long since fled across the rooftops. The wards and cells of the prison stood open; prisoners, many wearing the shackles of the convicted, were being dragged by their uproarious saviors from their cells, even up from the subterranean darkness of the condemned cells. Their rescuers muffled their irons in handkerchiefs as they hustled them out into freedom, and Rupert was fleetingly grateful that his own flight was not similarly hindered.

In the street they stopped. Octavia gripped Rupert's hand and smiled up at him, her face smudged with soot, her cheeks flushed with the heat of the flames. "We did it."

"Aye, that we did," Ben said behind her. "But the best place for Lord Nick right now is in Lord Warwick's 'ouse, seems to me."

"Aye, my thinking too, Ben." Rupert held out his hand. "When things have settled down, I'll come to the Oak."

He shook hands with them all, smiling into their weary yet exuberant faces. "I owe you more than I can ever repay."

"No one wants repayment, Nick," Bessie said gruffly. "We're all in debt to you one way and t'other. Be off and be safe now."

They went off toward the Embankment, and Rupert and Octavia turned their steps along Holborn toward the Strand.

Octavia tucked her hand firmly into Rupert's. "You'd best look as if you're with me if we meet any rioters," she said gravely. "You look too much the gentleman to please them."

"You certainly look like the jail bait," he returned with a grin, pulling her into a side street. "It's quicker this way."

The sounds of the riot pursued them all the way to Dover Street. They met stray groups of ruffians, who responded to Octavia's cheery ribaldry with bawdy, drunken comments and hearty laughter and paid no particular attention to the tall, well-dressed figure beside her.

"I left the side door unlocked," Octavia said as they reached their house. "I hope we don't bump into Griffin. He's never seen me dressed like this."

"I doubt he'd recover from the shock," Rupert observed solemnly.

They were both behaving as if they inhabited a dream, making conversation that had nothing to do with the tumultuous emotions of the last week—let alone the events of the evening. Much still lay between them, but he felt as if he were stepping onto new-sown ground, where the fragile shoots were peeping above the earth, still in danger of an early frost or a heavy foot or a hungry squirrel. There must be no more mistakes . . . no more trampling on the delicate growth of love.

Octavia's hand trembled slightly as she turned the handle on the door. Behind that door lay safety. No one would seek for Lord Nick the highwayman in the house of Lord Rupert Warwick, frequenter of the court of St. James's, habitué of the most exclusive establishments in the land.

"I told Miss Tavi ye'd be safe, if'n ye put the sign on yer door, guv," a little voice whispered from the shadows.

"Frank?" Octavia whirled around.

The child crept out of the darkness and surveyed them warily, clearly ready to run at the slightest hint of danger. "Ye goin' to 'and me over to the beak?"

"No, I've already said not," Octavia reassured briskly. "Are you going to come inside?"

"Is that Mr. Griffin goin' to beat me?"

"No," Rupert said. "No one is. But if you don't come inside now, then we'll leave you outside, because we've had enough of the streets for one night and are going in right now."

There was something about the impatience in his voice that seemed to reassure Frank much more than cajoling would have done.

"Awright." He dived for the door as Octavia opened it and ducked sideways into the passage leading to the kitchen.

Octavia shot the bolts across the door. "He's probably off to raid the pantry."

"I don't think this is a good place for him," Rupert said. "Once the city's quiet again, we'll take him to the Royal Oak. Bessie will know what to do with him."

"Poor Frank," Octavia said with a weary grin. "Does he really deserve such a fate?" Then she leaned back against the door, her legs suddenly weak.

"Come," Rupert said softly. "You're exhausted, sweeting."

"No, jubilant," she corrected, but she offered no resistance when he swung her into his arms and carried her up the stairs through the quiet house to her own apartments.

There he set her down.

They stood looking at each other in silence for long moments, as if they would drink in this miraculous reality; as if they would absorb and finally come to accept that the nightmare was over.

Hesitantly, Octavia took his hands, her own cold fingers closing over his warm ones. She lifted his right hand, where the Wyndham ring glinted in the candlelight.

"You have it," she said softly.

"Yes, I have it." He took his hands from hers and ran them up her bare arms.

"How could you have done what you did with Philip, Octavia? After everything that had gone before? You knew how I felt about it."

"It seemed the right thing to do," she said simply. "It gave me a purpose, otherwise I would have given up. I'm sorry if it upset you, but I had to do it for myself. Not you, if that makes you feel any better."

The truculence in her voice was feigned, and the fire in her eyes had no relationship with anger.

"I'd still like to wring your grubby little neck," Rupert said, cupping the back of the slender column in his palm.

"Could it wait?" She arched her neck into his hand.

He nodded judiciously. "For an hour or so."

They stood poised in the charged silence, then with a low, "God in heaven!" he hooked her closer, tipped up her chin with his free hand, and brought his mouth down on hers.

Her hands scrabbled with his belt as he released her chin and fumbled with the lacing of her bodice, freeing her breasts. His fingers teased her nipples as she pushed his britches and drawers off his hips. They stopped at his boots and tangled around his ankles, but he ignored it, pulling her dress from her body, pushing her shift up to her waist, his fingers stroking over her belly before delving into the heated furrow between her thighs. He gripped the soft mound of her sex with one hand, while his other fastened on her bottom, pulling her body into his as if he would dissolve all physical boundaries between them.

Octavia moaned and bit his lip, her legs twining around his as she pressed her belly against his, rubbed her loins against his aroused flesh. She went down to the floor as he fell to his knees, pulling her with him. As she fell onto her back, he rose above her, his hands gripping her wrists, drawing them high over her head.

"Will you wed the Earl of Wyndham, madam?"

Shock sprang into the golden eyes gazing up at him. Her lips parted on a little gasp, and then he drove deep within her, and Octavia was lost to everything but the glories of this fusion. He could have told her he was the abominable snowman at that point, and she would have thought it perfectly reasonable.

Cullum Wyndham smiled down at the woman he would make his countess and laughed with pleasure as he felt her body convulse around him. Her eyes opened with the surprised wonder that always delighted him.

He watched her face, transformed and glowing with

joy as the glory tore through her, as powerful a force as the fire that had brought down Newgate jail. A force powerful enough to bring down and trample in the dust the walls of treachery and deceit; to bring down and trample in the dust the barriers of old hurts and mistrust.

And when his own joy exploded in a shower of sparks, he rolled sideways, bringing her with him, holding her tight against his body, shield and buttress against anything that might do harm to his love.

Chapter 26

The terrace at Windsor Castle was thronged with courtiers. Among them strolled the royal family and their entourage, the little princesses skipping merrily in the wake of their parents under the benign eyes of their governesses and ladies.

The Prince of Wales, sweating in the afternoon heat, made no attempt to hide his disgruntlement as he stalked along, two paces behind his parents. He nodded morosely when someone he favored caught his eye but mostly kept his gaze on the ground, dabbing at his forehead with his handkerchief, now and again running a finger between his flushed neck and the now limp folds of his cravat.

His expression brightened, however, when he saw Lady Warwick on the arm of her husband. Her ladyship was attired in a caraco of pale-blue taffeta over a skirt of midnight blue. A turquoise pendant nestled in the deep cleft of her breasts, swelling enticingly above the lace-edged bodice of her caraco. Her hair, powdered and dressed high on her head, was ornamented with dark-blue velvet ribbon knots sown with pearls. She wore a small round patch on the outermost corner of her right eye that gave her smile a mischievously sensual quality that made His Highness beam fatuously.

As the royal party approached the couple, standing by themselves a little to one side of the general throng, Lady Warwick curtsied low to the king and queen. Lord Warwick, resplendent in a suit of charcoal gray edged with silver lace, bowed.

"Ah, my lady . . . Warwick . . . good day to ye both," the king said with his genial smile, raising Octavia from her curtsy. "Missed all the excitement, Warwick . . . what . . . what? Thank God the militia have the City under control again."

"It is indeed a relief, sir," Rupert agreed.

"Well, glad to see you back in circulation again, Warwick."

"You're too kind, sir." Rupert smiled, and his wife once again tucked her hand in his arm. "I'm not such a coxcomb as to believe I was missed for such a short time."

"Oh, believe it, dear fellow, believe it, what . . . what . . ." the king said, clapping him lightly on the shoulder. "Your dear lady was pining sadly. Isn't that so, my lady?" His little eyes sparkled with good humor, and he reached for his wife's hand.

" 'Sadly' is a vast understatement, sir," Octavia said demurely. "When my lord is not at my side, I find myself quite distracted."

The queen was pleased to smile at this and offered an affable comment on the beauty of the afternoon before passing on.

Letitia Wyndham, in the group of attendants upon the queen, glanced quickly, almost guiltily, at Octavia; then her eyes darted to Octavia's husband.

He smiled at her, and there was a look in his eyes that made Letitia feel strangely comforted. Strengthened, almost. As if for some reason he was offering her reassurance. A responding smile flickered tentatively on her lips; then she hurried on.

The Prince of Wales hung back for a moment, raising

Octavia's hands to his lips and planting a distinctly sloppy kiss on her palm.

"Ravishing, as always, my dear. Y'are a lucky dog, Warwick."

"Don't I know it, sir."

The prince seemed dispose to linger, but the royal procession was moving rapidly and inexorably ahead like a ship on a full tide, so he was obliged to hurry back to his place on board.

Octavia chuckled. "There is something so delicious about the thought that this time four days ago you were a common felon, languishing in Newgate, and here you are making small talk with the king and no one could possibly guess."

"They might not have to guess if you continue to shout it from the rooftops," Rupert rebuked, but without force. His eyes moved over the gaily dressed throng, searching for his brother. Unconsciously, he curled his finger with the signet ring into his palm.

"Do you think he'll come?"

"Yes," he said. "And you're not behaving like an experienced conspirator, Octavia. Anyone looking at you would guess immediately that you had some secret."

"Oh, I can't help it," she said. "I *am* excited. After all these years of suffering because of . . ." Her voice died as her eyes followed Rupert's.

The man known as the Earl of Wyndham strolled onto the terrace. He stood for a minute surveying the crowd through his glass as if deciding whom to grace with his greeting; then he let the glass fall and sauntered over to a group of ladies standing at the edge of the terrace.

He was dressed in emerald-green silk and wore two beauty patches, one on each cheekbone. The angelic golden curls were hidden beneath his wig, but his face was as beautiful, his features as regular as ever, hardly marred by the slight downturn of his mouth and the icy expression in the narrowed slate-gray eyes as his gaze fell upon Octavia.

Deliberately, she curtsied to him, and as deliberately he turned away.

"Me thinks the gentleman still nurses his wounded pride," she murmured.

"Keep out of his way, Octavia. One doesn't humiliate Philip Wyndham with impunity." Rupert's voice was crisp, and Octavia knew she'd been given a most direct command. It was not one she had any inclination to disobey. The thought of another tête-à-tête with Rupert's brother made her skin crawl.

"When will you speak to him?"

"No time like the present," he drawled with a cool smile. "Go and talk to Letitia."

"Yes, my lord." Octavia offered a mock curtsy. "Your word is my command."

"When hell freezes over," he commented, and walked away from her, crossing the terrace, pausing to exchange greetings but always moving purposefully toward his twin.

Octavia watched. She knew she was staring, but she couldn't help herself. She knew she was supposed to stay with Letitia, to warn her of what was about to happen, so that when the story broke, Letitia would not be taken unawares and would have some support. It was hardly the fault of Philip's wife that she was about to be dispossessed of a title and estate.

Rupert had reached his brother. The two men were exchanging bows. Octavia could hear nothing, and could divine nothing from their expressions.

She searched Philip's face for a twin's resemblance to Rupert . . . or Cullum, as she must learn to call him. It was in the eyes, in the shape of the mouth, and now she understood what had disturbed her about Philip—that sense of familiarity gone awry.

The two men had grown together in the same womb, had fought their way into the world within a few minutes of each other. The same blood ran in their veins, and yet they were as unlike as two men could possibly be.

With an effort she dragged herself away from the drama about to be enacted and went to play her part with Letitia.

Philip regarded Rupert Warwick with a chilly stare. "You've returned to town, I see."

Rupert nodded, smiling. He moved his right hand to the froth of lace at his neck and deliberately adjusted the position of a diamond pin. The delicate signet ring sparkled in the sunlight.

Philip's eyes snapped into focus, and for a second naked shock and fear stood out on his face as the blood drained slowly from his cheeks. His hand fluttered to his waistcoat and then fell to his side.

His ring, joined with that other. It could mean only one thing, and now everything fell into place.

"You?" he whispered. *"Cullum!"*

It could mean only one thing, and yet his voice was disbelieving as he looked at the brother he'd believed dead these last eighteen years. But as he looked at him, he knew in his blood that Cullum stood before him now.

"Yes, Philip," Rupert said quietly. The moment was everything he had known it would be. With the grim satisfaction of a man who's waited long for his vengeance, he watched his brother's face, watched the struggle for control played out in the slate-gray eyes, watched the moment when cold calculation took over from shock and desperation. He watched his brother's eyes narrow and sharpen as they had done that long-ago afternoon at Beachy Head, the instant before he'd put out his foot and tripped Gervase.

"This is hardly the place for a joyous reunion," Philip said with an ironic smile. "Shall we adjourn to the garden?"

"By all means." Rupert turned and walked to the far end of the terrace, where three shallow stone steps led down into a shrubbery. His back prickled as his brother followed him, and it was only with a great effort that he managed not to look over his shoulder.

"That whore you call wife did her work well," Philip said. "Where did you find her? She's a little more delicate than one usually finds in the stews."

Rupert spun on his heel, and Philip took an involuntary step back at the power of the contemptuous rage in the icy gray eyes.

"You refer to Octavia in such terms again, brother, and

I will cut out your tongue." His voice was cold and deadly as venom.

Philip touched his lips and there was fear on his face. The fear Rupert recognized from their boyhood, when, goaded beyond endurance, beyond fear of punishment, young Cullum had finally attacked his twin with his own greater physical strength.

Rupert waited for a minute, allowing his words to settle in the hot, stagnant air. There was no other sound, not even the buzz of a bee or the faintest chirp of bird song.

Then he said, "If you choose to contest my claim—"

"Choose to?" Philip spat. "Who do you think you are? Of course I'll contest it. I'll challenge you in every court in the land. If you think I'll give up everything for you, Cullum, you are moon mad. You think you can leap into my life and simply walk off with the title, with the manor, with Wyndham House. By God, man, you're even more stupid than I thought you."

Rupert raised his hand and slapped his brother with his open palm. "No more insults, Philip," he said gently. "I'd had a lifetime's worth from you before I was twelve. There'll be no more."

Philip stepped back, his hand touching the raised mark on his face, his eyes wide with shock. "You dare to strike me!" he whispered.

"Now I do," his twin said with a casual shrug. "But only in response to unendurable provocation, my dear brother. You have nothing to fear from me if you put a bridle on your tongue."

Philip hissed through his teeth, and something small and silver appeared in his hand. He lunged, his face a rictus of fear and loathing.

The knife cut upward in a movement that would have ripped Rupert's guts from his belly had he not leaped sideways, deflecting the point on one of the silver buttons of his coat. The knife slashed through his shirt and grazed his ribs as he spun again on the balls of his feet. His hand went to the hilt of his sword, but Philip was on him again, his mouth contorted, his eyes frenzied with the madness of one who faced the unfaceable.

Too late, Rupert remembered how his brother had loved playing with knives. How, lighter on his feet than his sturdier twin, he had danced rings around Cullum, playing . . . always playing . . . but there'd been a dangerous edge of reality to the game, and Cullum had always in the end retired from the fray, mortified by his own inability to match his twin in this vicious, deadly ballet.

But now this was no game. The blade tore through Rupert's sleeve. He grabbed for his brother's wrist, but Philip danced backward with the graceful agility that had been his mark throughout his life. Rupert had his sword half out of the sheath when he dodged the plunging knife yet again.

And his foot caught in a root.

He fell to one knee, shielding his face with his arm, as the mask that was his brother's face blazed above him, the point of the knife glittered, pointed at his throat. He flung his arm sideways against Philip's wrist, but the angle was wrong, and he had not sufficient force to throw the weapon off course.

Philip was beyond reason. His hatred and purpose were all-consuming. He had no thought for consequences, only for the fact that out of the blue his world was in jeopardy. And no one and nothing could be permitted to destroy the edifice he had so painstakingly constructed.

Rupert looked into his twin's eyes and he looked into his own death. For what seemed an eternity, he gazed mesmerized into the dark pools reflecting a twisted soul.

The twisted side of his own soul?

And then his mind tore itself free, and he flung himself sideways the instant before Philip, with a strange sighing sound, fell forward, pinning his brother's turned shoulder. The knife slipped from his grasp.

"Dear God in heaven." Octavia's voice broke the astonishing quiet. "Letitia!"

Philip's wife stood above her husband, her fine emerald

eyes filled with loathing. She stared wordlessly at the large stone in her hand.

Rupert eased his brother off him and got to his feet. He bowed to Letitia. "You have my undying gratitude, ma'am."

Letitia looked down at her husband. "When your wife told me what was happening . . . I . . . I knew he would try to kill you. I know him, you see."

"I thought *I* did," Rupert said ruefully. "I didn't believe he would lose control. It was never his way. He always chose his own time and place to make trouble and would never risk being implicated himself. I believed I could outthink his every move this time."

Philip groaned, stirred. Slowly, he pushed himself onto his knees, shaking his head like a hurt and bewildered animal. He struggled to his feet and looked at his wife, at the stone in her hand. Gingerly, he touched the swelling on the back of his head and stared at her in utter incredulity.

"I'm leaving you," she said in a flat voice devoid of all expression. "I'm going to Wyndham Manor to collect Susannah, and then I'm going back to my father. And if he won't take me, then I'll find some way of managing on my own."

"You tried to kill me," Philip said, the same bewildered disbelief in his eyes. "Pathetic little worm, you tried to kill me."

"Worms turn," Letitia said in the same flat voice. "I don't care what you do, Philip. I don't care what you tell people. You can divorce me, in fact I wish you would. But you'll not keep my child from me."

She opened her hand and the stone fell to the ground. Then she turned and walked away, her back straight, her head up, and for the first time, the dumpy little figure with the ostrich plumes in her overlarge coiffure had an air of quiet dignity.

Octavia bent and picked up the knife. Its blade of tempered steel was thin enough to slide between a man's ribs leaving barely a puncture mark. It was an assassin's weapon.

"I have it in mind to make my announcement on the

terrace," Rupert said evenly, smoothing down his coat, adjusting the disordered lace at his neck. "Do you care to accompany me, Philip, and lend your congratulations to the rest? Or do you prefer to challenge my claim? The latter course will provide society with a much better story. I dare swear they'll find such a course of events infinitely more entertaining than the joyful reunion of long-lost brothers."

"You'll not win," Philip spat at him, but there was uncertainty in his eyes.

"Oh, yes, I will. The lawyers have already acknowledged me. Old Doctor Mayberry has welcomed me like the prodigal son. He has an intimate knowledge of the body of Cullum Wyndham." Rupert's smile was serene. "Oh, yes, Philip. I can prove my identity beyond question, and if you contest it, you'll look a fool. And we know you're not that." The mockery in his smile taunted his brother. "Gervase's murderer, certainly, but no fool," he added softly.

"Damn you, Cullum. I should have drowned you myself." Philip turned on his heel and pushed his way through the bushes, away from the terrace.

Octavia shivered. "If Letitia hadn't . . . I was two minutes behind her, I would have been too late . . ." She gazed up at him, the full horror of what might have been only now sinking in.

"I would never have believed she was capable—" She shook her head in astonishment.

"There's always the last straw," Rupert said.

"We must look after her . . . and the child."

"Of course."

He reached for her, and she came into his arms with another convulsive little shiver. "Is it really over, my love?"

"Bar the shouting," he said, stroking the back of her neck. "And a loose end or two with Digby and Lacross . . . and, more important, a visit to the bishop with a special license."

"What'll we tell Papa?"

"The truth?" He raised a quizzical eyebrow.

"Yes, perhaps that would be simplest. He'll find it no stranger than anything else these last months."

She leaned into him. "I feel very peculiar, as if I've been swimming against a tidal wave and suddenly I've been dropped into a mill pond."

"Do you think you could settle for the quiet life, sweeting?" He smiled down at her.

She shook her head. "No. Could you?"

"No."

He stroked her cheek with a slender finger. "We'll just have to create another earthquake to produce a tidal wave."

"There's one way we could be certain to make the earth move," she suggested mischievously. "On that bench over there."

Rupert glanced over his shoulder at the stone bench. "Discreetly?" he queried.

"You like taking risks," she reminded him with a grin. "And besides, my skirts are so voluminous, they could conceal a multitude of sins."

She took his hand. "Shall we try it? Before you go and drop your bombshell on the terrace?"

"Start as we mean to go on?"

"Or continue as we've already started, my lord Wyndham."

He laughed softly, sitting on the bench, drawing her down astride his lap, one hand deftly unfastening his britches. She raised her skirts and settled them in a rich taffeta puff around them. The sound of voices came from the terrace, the strains of a violin from the musicians entertaining Their Majesties' guests.

"Shall we make a baby?" Octavia whispered as he slid deep within her.

"I think I might enjoy that." Rupert smiled, letting his head fall back with a sigh of pleasure. A ray of sunshine touched his face, and the warmth of happiness seeped slowly into his blood. Octavia's face hung over his, her lambent eyes aglow, her face transfigured with her own happiness.

Finally, he unloosed the long chain of hurts and anger and bitterness and watched it float away from him.

"I don't know," he murmured languidly, reaching up

to touch her face, "but I think there's something to be said for the mill pond, after all."

Octavia smiled and turned her mouth to kiss the palm of his hand. "There's a time and a place for everything, my lord."

ℰpilogue

ℬℑ Philip Wyndham walked through the queen's drawing room, and for all the notice anyone took of him, he could have been invisible. As he passed Margaret Drayton, she drew back with an ostentatious movement, twitching her turquoise skirts to one side. A rustle of whispers followed him, a burst of laughter, hastily moderated, and he heard someone say, "A climbing boy, would you believe. No . . . no, I had it on the best authority . . . soot everywhere." The laughter rose to a gale, and the hairs on his nape prickled as his rage burned deep and futile.

He glanced across the room to where Octavia, the Countess of Wyndham, stood talking to the Prince of Wales. Her eyes met his and she dropped a half curtsy, a mocking smile curving her mouth.

The story of the climbing boy's inconvenient appearance had hit the town a week before, and it was still the joke of the season. Only Octavia could have told the tale, but it seemed that no one knew the identity of the lady in question, although it was a subject for constant speculation. But on no one's lips had Philip heard the Countess of Wyndham's name mentioned.

Philip forced himself to continue his progress through

the room. The Duke of Gosford offered a chilly bow when his son-in-law greeted him with a punctilious courtesy that the duke was unaccustomed to meeting from that quarter. Letitia and Susannah remained safely ensconced at Wyndham Manor, the permanent guests of the Earl and Countess of Wyndham. And speculation as to the reason why she should have sought the protection of her brother-in-law rivaled that of the identity of the woman in the climbing-boy debacle.

Philip Wyndham was providing society with more delicious entertainment than it had enjoyed in years.

His gaze sought his brother. The Earl of Wyndham, in black silk and silver lace, was engaged in an animated conversation in the circle surrounding the king. He stood in the sunlight, and for the first time in his life, his twin skulked in the shadows.

From his earliest memories Philip had striven to push his brother into the darkness. He had basked in the golden glow of parental love and approval, and in adulthood had gathered into his hands the reins of a far-reaching power and influence. His vanity had fed greedily on the supplications of other men, the eager submission of their women, the flattering attentions of the most influential courtiers. And now it was all gone—replaced in this fickle society with a mockery and contempt that seared his gut like acid.

And Cullum was responsible. Cullum had won in the end. Philip had always feared his twin. Even when he believed him dead, the fear had lurked in the dark reaches of his mind. He had always known that Cullum was the stronger and that his only chance to defeat him was to exploit his one fatal weakness. Cullum, like Gervase, was incapable of malice or deceit. In the hands of their younger brother, they were clay. And Philip had removed them both and enjoyed the sun alone.

But now Cullum stood in the sun.

The earl's slate-gray eyes met his twin's. The earl was smiling but his eyes burned with contempt. And Philip knew he could expect no mercy from his brother. Cullum would continue to hound him with innuendo and mockery, would continue to use the power and influence he now held to reduce his brother to a nonentity. He would continue until he'd driven him away. Just as he, Philip, had hounded Cullum eighteen years ago.

Unable to bear his brother's steady stare, Philip turned on his heel and pushed his way out of the reception.

Cullum watched him go; then he looked down at the signet ring he still wore. Philip had forfeited his ring when he had betrayed the trust and commitment it embodied. He had betrayed the honor of the Wyndhams with every action he'd taken since childhood. If the child Octavia carried should be a son, he would bear the name of his dead uncle and he would wear his father's ring. Then Cullum would destroy the ring Philip had dishonored.

The earl moved discreetly out of the royal circle and crossed the room to his wife's side. As discreetly, she edged her way out of the prince's vicinity.

"It shouldn't be long before Their Majesties take their leave," he said in a low voice, resting his hand on her bare shoulder.

"Thank God," Octavia murmured. "This is such a poxy tedious way to spend an evening."

"It'll be the last for some months," he said. "In a couple of weeks you'll be enjoying a peaceful summer with your father in the Northumberland countryside."

"I can't wait to show you Hartridge Folly." Octavia inched backward toward a curtained window embrasure. "I want to share all my childhood memories with you. Show you all my special places."

"I thought I knew them all," her husband said with a grin.

"Far from it," Octavia replied loftily. "You should know, husband, that I have enough mysteries to keep you guessing for a lifetime."

"Oh, I do know that," he responded, his gaze now running in a leisurely caress from the top of her powdered coiffure to the toes of her satin slippers. "Enough for this lifetime and the next, my love. But you will unfold them all for me, won't you?"

"Oh, yes," she whispered. The buzzing room around them disappeared into the mist, and she quivered under the familiar hot and surging wave of lust. "Piece by piece, layer by layer, until it's all laid out before you."

Cullum twitched the heavy crimson curtain aside and stepped back into the narrow embrasure, drawing Octavia with him. The curtain fell again over the archway, enclosing them in their own velvet darkness.

ABOUT THE AUTHOR

Jane Feather is the nationally bestselling, award-winning author of *Violet, Valentine, Velvet,* and many more historical romances. She was born in Cairo, Egypt, and grew up in the New Forest, in the south of England. She began her writing career after she and her family moved to Washington, D.C., in 1981. She now has over a million books in print.

Jane Feather continues her spectacular
rise to stardom with her
intoxicatingly passionate romance novel

Vice

on sale in the summer of 1996
Here is a tantalizing glimpse . . .

Juliana was suffocating. Her husband was making no attempt to protect her from the full force of his weight as he huffed and puffed, red-faced and bleary-eyed with wedding drink. She was perfectly resigned to this consummation and indeed was quite well disposed toward Sir John, for all his advanced years and physical bulk, but it occurred to her that if she didn't alert him to her predicament in some way, she was going to expire beneath him.

Her nose was squashed against his mountainous chest and her throat was closing. She couldn't think clearly enough to work out what was happening to the rest of her body, but judging by John's oaths and efforts, matters were not proceeding properly. Black spots began to dance before her eyes and her chest heaved in a desperate struggle to draw air into her lungs. Panicked now, she flailed her arms on either side of her imprisoned body, and then her left hand closed over the smooth brass handle of the bed warmer.

With an instinctive desperation, she raised the object and brought it down on her husband's shoulders. It was not a hard blow and was intended simply to bring him back to his senses, but it seemed to have the opposite effect.

Sir John's glazed eyes widened as he stared at the wall behind her head, his panting mouth fell open, and with a curious sigh like the air escaping from a deflated balloon, he collapsed upon her.

If she'd thought he was heavy before, he was now a dead weight and Juliana shoved and pushed, calling his name repeatedly, trying to wake him up.

If she'd been panicked before, she was now terrified. She tried to call out but her voice was muffled by his body and lost in the thickly embroidered brocade bed curtains.

There was no way anyone could hear her behind the firmly latched oak door. The household was asleep, and George had passed out after his third bottle of port on the couch in the library. Not that she could have endured being found in this mortifying exposure by her loathsome stepson.

Juliana wriggled like an eel, her body slick with the sweat of effort; then finally she managed to draw up her knees and obtain sufficient leverage to free her legs. Digging her heels into the mattress, she heaved with her arms and shoulders and John rolled sideways, just enough for her to squiggle out before he flopped back again.

Slowly, she stood up and gazed down at him, her hand over her mouth, her eyes wide with shock. She bent over him.

"John?" Tentatively, she touched his shoulder, shook him lightly. "John?"

There was no sound and his face was buried in the pillows. She turned his head. His sightless eyes stared up at her.

"Sweet Jesus, have mercy!" Juliana whispered, stepping back from the corpse. *She had killed her husband.*

Dazed and incredulous, she stood by the bed, listening to the nighttime sounds of the house: the ticking clocks, the creaking floorboards, the wind rattling open casements. No sounds of human life.

Dear God, it was her cursed clumsiness again! Why, oh why, did everything she ever did always come out wrong?

She had to waken someone. But what would they say? The round mark of the bed warmer stood out on the dead man's back. She must have hit him harder than she'd intended. But of course that was inevitable given her blunder-headed, accident-prone nature.

Sick with horror, she touched the bed warmer and found it still very hot. She'd struck and killed her husband with a burning object.

George would waste no time. He would listen to no reasonable explanations. He would accuse her publicly as he'd done privately that morning of gold-digging. Of marrying a man old enough to be her grandfather just for his money. He'd accuse her of manipulating his father's besotted affections and then arranging his death so she'd be free and clear with all that had been allotted to her in the marriage settlements. Property that George believed was his and his alone.

It was petty treason for a woman to kill her husband. Just as it was for a servant to kill his master. If she was convicted, they would burn her at the stake.

Juliana backed farther away from the bed, pushing aside the bed curtains and rushing to the window, where she stood drawing deep gulps of the warm night air, enlivened by a faint sea breeze from the Solent. *They would burn her at the stake.*

She'd seen it happen once, outside Winchester jail. Mistress Goadsby had been convicted of killing her husband when he'd fallen down the stairs. She'd said he'd been drunk and had been beating her and had tripped and fallen. She'd stood in the dock with the bruises still on her face. But they'd tied her to the stake, hanged her, and set fire to her.

Juliana had been little more than a child at the time, but the image had haunted her over the years . . . the smell of burning flesh embedded in her nostrils. Nausea swamped her and she ran back to the bed, dragging the chamber pot from beneath, vomiting violently.

Perhaps the magistrates would believe that John had died of natural causes in the midst of his exertions . . . but there was that mark on his back. He couldn't have put it there himself.

And George would see it. A stepmother convicted of murdering her husband couldn't inherit. The marriage settlements would be nullified and George would have what he wanted.

Juliana didn't know how long she sat on the floor, hunched over the chamber pot, but gradually the sweat dried on her forehead and her mind cleared.

She had to leave. There was no one here to speak for her . . . to speak against the facts before their eyes. Her guardian had negotiated the marriage settlements and thankfully washed his hands of her. There was no one else remotely interested in her.

She stood up, thrust the chamber pot back beneath the bed with her foot, and took stock. The stagecoach for London stopped at the Rose and Crown in Winchester at four o'clock in the morning. She could walk the ten miles to Winchester across the fields and be there in plenty of time. By the time the household awoke, or George emerged from his stupor, she would be far away.

They would pursue her, but she could lose herself easily in London. She just had to ensure that she wouldn't draw attention to herself at the Rose and Crown.

Averting her eyes from the bed, Juliana went to the armoire, newly filled with her trousseau. But tucked at the back, she'd secreted a pair of holland britches and a linen shirt. In this costume she'd escaped Forsett Towers on the frequent occasions life had become more than usually unpleasant under the rule of her guardian's wife. No one had ever discovered the disguise, or the various places where she'd roamed. Of course, she'd paid the price on her return, but Lady Forsett's hazel switch had seemed but a small price to pay for those precious hours of freedom.

She dressed rapidly, pulling on stockings and boots, twisting her flame-red hair into a knot on top of her head, tucking telltale strands under a woolen cap pulled down low over her ears.

She needed money. Enough for her coach fare and a few nights' lodging until she could find work. But she wouldn't take anything that would be missed. Nothing that would brand her as a thief as well as a murderess.

Why she should concern herself about such a hairsplitting issue Juliana couldn't imagine, but her mind seemed to be working on its own, making decisions, discarding possibilities with all the efficiency of an automaton.

She took four sovereigns from the cache in the dresser drawer. She had watched John empty his pockets—hours ago, it seemed. After the revelers had finally left the bedroom door and taken their jovial obscenities out of the house, leaving the newlyweds to themselves.

John had been almost too drunk to stand upright. She could see him now, swaying as he poured the contents of his pocket into the drawer. His bloodshot blue eyes gleaming with excitement, his habitually red face now a deep crimson.

Tears suddenly clogged her throat as she slipped the still unfamiliar wedding ring from her finger. John had always been kind to her in an avuncular way. She'd been more than willing to accept marriage to him as a way of escaping her guardian's house. More than willing, until she realized she'd have to contend with George . . . malicious, jealous George. But it had been too late to back away then. She dropped the ring into the drawer with the remaining sovereigns. The gold circlet winked at her, its glow diffused through her tears.

Resolutely, Juliana closed the drawer and turned back to the cheval glass to check her reflection. Her disguise had never been intended to fool people close to, and as she examined herself, she realized that the linen shirt did nothing to disguise the rich swell of her bosom, that the curve of her hips was emphasized by the britches.

She took a heavy winter cloak from the armoire and swathed herself. It hid the bumps and the curves but it was still far from satisfactory. However, the light would be bad at that hour of the morning and with luck there'd be other passengers on the waybill, so she could make herself inconspicuous.

She tiptoed to the bedroom door, glancing at the closed bed curtains. She felt as if she should make some acknowledgment of the dead man. It felt wrong to be running from his deathbed. And yet she could think of nothing else to do. For a minute she thought hard about the man whom she'd known for a bare three months. She remembered his kindnesses. And then she put him from her. John Ridge had been sixty-five years old. He'd had three wives. And he'd died quickly, painlessly . . . a death for which she had been responsible.

Juliana closed her mind to the thought. She let herself out of the bedchamber and crept along the pitch-dark corridor, her fingers brushing the walls to give her a sense of direction. At the head of the stairs she paused. The hall below was dark, but not as black as the corridor behind her.

Faint moonlight filtered through the diamond panes of the mullioned windows.

Her eyes darted to the library door. It was firmly closed. She sped down the stairs, tiptoed to the door and placed her ear against the oak. Her heart hammered in her chest and she wondered why she was lingering, listening to the rumbling drunken snores from within. But hearing them made her feel safer.

She turned to leave and her foot caught in the fringe of the worn Elizabethan carpet. She went flying, grabbed at a table leg to save herself and fell to her knees: a copper jug of hollyhocks overbalanced as the table rocked, and crashed to the stone-flagged floor.

She remained where she was on her knees, listening to the echo resound to the beamed ceiling and then slowly fade into the night. It had been a sound to wake the dead.

But nothing happened. No shouts, no running feet . . . and most miraculously of all, no change in the stertorous breathing from the library.

Juliana picked herself up, swearing under her breath. It was her feet again. They were the bane of her life, too big and with a mind of their own.

She crept with exaggerated care toward the back regions of the house and let herself out of the kitchen door. Outside, all was quiet. The house behind her slept. The house that should have been her home. Her refuge from the erratic twists and turns of a life that had brought her little happiness thus far.

Juliana shrugged. Like a stray cat who had long ago learned to walk alone, she faced the haphazard future with uncomplaining resignation. As she crossed the kitchen yard, making for the orchard and the fields beyond, the church clock struck midnight.

Her seventeenth birthday was over. A day she'd begun as a bride and ended as a widow and a murderess.

"I give you good day, cousin," a voice slurred from the depths of an armchair as the Duke of Redmayne entered the library of his house on Albemarle Street.

"To what do I owe this pleasure, Lucien?" the duke inquired in bland tones, although a flicker of disgust crossed his face. "Escaping your creditors? Or are you simply paying me a courtesy visit?"

"Lud, such sarcasm, cousin." Lucien Courtney rose to his feet and surveyed with a mocking insouciance the two men who'd just entered.

"Well, well, and if it isn't our dear Reverend Courtney as well. What an embarrassment of relatives. How d'ye do, dear boy."

"Well enough," the other man responded easily. He was soberly dressed in gray, with a plain white neckcloth, in startling contrast to the duke's peacock-blue satin coat, with its gold frogged buttons and deep, embroidered cuffs. But the physical resemblance was startling: the same aquiline nose and deep-set gray eyes, the same thin, well-shaped mouth, the same cleft chin. However, there the resemblance ended. Whereas Quentin Courtney regarded the world and its vagaries with the gentle and genuine sympathy of a devout man of the cloth, his half-brother saw his fellowman through the sharp and disillusioned eyes of a cynic.

"May I offer you some refreshment, Lucien?" Tarquin inquired, going to the decanters on the sideboard. "Oh, but I see you've already taken care of yourself," he added, seeing the brandy goblet in the younger man's hand. "You don't think it's a little early in the morning for cognac?"

"Dear boy, I haven't been to bed yet," Lucien said with a yawn. "Far as I'm concerned, this is a nightcap." He put down the glass and strolled to the door, somewhat unsteadily. "You don't object to putting me up for a few nights?"

"How should I?" returned Tarquin with a sardonically raised eyebrow.

"Fact is, my own house is under siege," Lucien declared, leaning against the door and fumbling in his pocket for his snuffbox. "Damned creditors and bailiffs bangin' at the door at all hours of the day and night. Man can't get a decent night's rest."

"And what are you going to sell to satisfy them this

time?" the duke asked, pouring madeira for himself and his brother.

"Have to be Edgecombe," Lucien said, taking a pinch of snuff. He sighed with exaggerated heaviness. "Terrible thing. But I can't see what else to do . . . unless, of course, you could see your way to helpin' a relative out."

His pale brown eyes, burning in their deep sockets like the last embers of a dying fire, suddenly sharpened, and he regarded his cousin with sly knowledge. He smiled when he saw the telltale muscle twitch in Tarquin's jaw as he fought to control his anger.

"Well," he said carelessly. "We'll discuss it later . . . when I've had some sleep. Dinner, perhaps?"

"Get out of here," Tarquin said, turning his back.

Lucien's chuckle hung in the air as the door closed behind him.

"There's going to be little enough left of Edgecombe for poor Godfrey to inherit," Quentin said, sipping his wine. "Since Lucien gained his majority a mere six months ago, he's run through a fortune that would keep most men in luxury for a lifetime."

"I'll not stand by and see him sell Edgecombe," Tarquin stated almost without expression. "And neither will I stand by and see what remnants are left pass into the hands of poor Godfrey."

"I fail to see how you can stop the latter," Quentin said in some surprise. "I know poor Godfrey has no more wits than an infant, but he's still Lucien's legitimate heir."

"He would be if Lucien left no heir of his own," the duke pointed out, casually riffling through pages of the *Gazette*.

"Well, we all know that's an impossibility," Quentin declared, stating what he had always believed to be an immutable fact. "And Lucien's free of your control now; there's little you can do to influence his behavior."

"Aye, and he never ceases to taunt me with it," Tarquin responded. "But it'll be a rainy day in hell, my friend, when Lucien Courtney gets the better of me." He looked up and met his half-brother's gaze.

Quentin felt a little shiver prickle his spine at this soft-spoken declaration. He knew Tarquin as no one else did. And unlike Lucien, he knew not to underestimate him.

"What are you going to do?"

Tarquin drained his glass. He smiled, but it was not a humorous smile. "It's time our little cousin took himself a wife and set up his nursery," he said. "That should settle the matter of an heir to Edgecombe."

Quentin stared at him as if he'd taken leave of his senses. "No one's going to marry Lucien, even if he was prepared to marry. He's riddled with the pox and the only women who figure on his agenda of pleasure are whores from the stews, prepared to play the lad."

"True. But how long do you think he has to live?" Tarquin inquired almost casually. "You only have to look at him. He's burned out with debauchery and the clap. I'd give him maybe six months . . . a year at the outside."

Quentin said nothing, but his gaze remained unwaveringly on his brother's countenance.

"He knows it, too," Tarquin continued. "He's living each day as if it's his last. He doesn't give a damn what happens to Edgecombe or the Courtney fortune. Why should he? But I intend to ensure that Edgecombe, at the very least, passes intact into competent hands."

Quentin looked horrified. "In the name of pity, Tarquin! You couldn't condemn a woman to share his bed, even if he'd take her into it. It would be a death sentence."

"Listen well, dear brother. It's perfectly simple."